WEDDING NIGHT

Carefully, head bent and his eyes fixed on his self-appointed task, Robert untied the blue silk ribbon that bound Alyce's hair, then slowly began to unweave the heavy tresses. Inch by inch, he undid the intricate braid until he could spread the shining mass of red-gold hair out on the blankets like a length of rare silk, bright against the dull brown covers. Just as slowly, he dragged his hand down the length of hair, pressing lightly over her breast and belly and hip as he smoothed out the crinkles the braid had left.

Despite the thick covers that divided him from her, Alyce moaned and arched into his touch, helpless to prevent the wanton, revealing motion or suppress the heat that was consuming her.

Once more he traced the fall of her hair, then again, and again, and again. At the moment when Alyce thought she could bear it no longer, he dragged the covers away, swept her hair to the side, and let his mouth and tongue trace the same tormenting path over her breast and down her side and back again.

And where he touched her, bright fire bloomed.

BARTERED BRIDE

ANNE AVERY

BANTAM BOOKS

New York Toronto London
Sydney Auckland

BARTERED BRIDE

A Bantam Fanfare Book / March 1999

FANFARE and the portrayal of a boxed "ff" are trademarks of
Bantam Books, a division of Random House, Inc.

ISBN 0-553-57933-9

Published simultaneously in the United States and Canada

Bantam Books are published by Bantam Books, a division of Random House, Inc. Its trademark, consisting of the words "Bantam
Books" and the portrayal of a rooster, is Registered in U.S. Patent
and Trademark Office and in other countries. Marca Registrada.
Bantam Books, 1540 Broadway, New York, New York 10036.

PRINTED IN THE UNITED STATES OF AMERICA

OPM   10   9   8   7   6   5   4   3   2   1

BARTERED BRIDE

THE DIE
IS CAST

T
HE GUARDS AT the gate and the servants who took his horse and led his men away out of the rain were courteous enough. The twelve-year-old page who guided him through the ill-lit corridors was surly, no doubt irritated that a mere merchant should disturb the Lord Edward—or himself—at so unseemly an hour and on such a night.

⌒ Windsor, December 1263

Robert Wardell glanced at the scowling face as the boy threw open a door and stood aside. Usually, he ignored the pretensions of those who had been raised to think themselves superior to anyone not of their breeding, but tonight he was cold and tired and hungry, the meal he'd taken at midday long since a lamented memory. He had no patience left for fools, especially not young, well-bred ones.

"Bring me wine," he said curtly over his shoulder as he strode to the fire. "And send someone to the kitchens for food, bread, and some meat."

He turned and threw back his cloak, then slowly drew off the fine leather gloves that had managed to keep out the sleeting rain through which he'd ridden for the past three hours. The firelight must have revealed something of the richness of his clothes and the jewels in his sword hilt. Or perhaps it was merely his arrogant dismissal of a nobleman's son that made the boy hesitate in the open doorway, his eyes wide.

"Hot food, preferably," Robert added sharply, letting his own eyes narrow.

The boy wilted under the cold-eyed stare that Robert had used to good effect against far more formidable adversaries. He bowed, only a little, but more than was due a merchant from the Lord Edward's personal page.

"I'll inform milord of your arrival," the boy said, then withdrew, carefully shutting the door behind him.

It wasn't a guarantee of either food or wine, but it was something. Robert tossed the rain-dampened gloves on the table, spread his heavy cloak over a stool set at one side of the hearth, and drew closer to the fire, gratefully stretching his hands to its heat. When the front of him was steaming, he turned and warmed the back.

The heat was comforting—and dangerously seductive. Once his interview with Edward was finished, he would have to go back out into the storm, despite his dragging weariness.

At the thought of the interminable slog through mud and driving rain that lay ahead of him, Robert hunched his shoulders, clasping his hands behind his back, and glowered at the gray stone walls of the room. In the flickering red-gold light cast by the flames, they balefully returned his regard, like shadowy red-eyed demons come to mock his ambitions. And there, in the corner—

Robert started, then shrugged away the illusion.

That wasn't Jocelyn, peering out at him from the darkest corner of the room. Not his beautiful Jocelyn, dead in childbed these twelve long years. In spite of his sins against her, in spite of his plans now, she would not wish him ill or come to him like this, so angry and accusing. And yet . . .

With a muttered oath, Robert turned back to the fire,

but even as he stared at the flames he was conscious of the grim walls at his back, the stones like so many eyes watching him, waiting.

It was his weariness that made him fanciful, he told himself. Weariness and hunger and the remnants of the troubled dreams that had disturbed his sleep and dogged his waking hours this sennight past. Jocelyn came to him in the dreams, yet whenever he tried to grapple with them, they faded and drifted out of reach, insubstantial as cold river mist on a moonless night—and just as chilling to the soul.

Blame his uneasiness on the dangerous ventures upon which he had just embarked. All his life he had played for high stakes, but the stakes he played for now were the highest yet, with everything, including life itself, at risk. England was preparing to take up arms against itself, with a king and angry prince on one side, an army of barons and common folk on the other—and he had chosen to walk the dagger's edge between them, despite his allegiance to the prince, Lord Edward.

A burning brand rolled out of the fire and tumbled across the stone hearth. Robert kicked it back and watched as it flared bright red, then slowly crumbled, consumed in the flames.

He was like that brand, he thought, as he blindly stared into the heart of the blaze. He wasn't responsible for the fire, but if someone kicked him into it, he could as easily be reduced to cinders. He . . . and all those who depended on him to lead them safely through the troubles that lay ahead.

The sound of the door opening jerked Robert out of his grim thoughts. He straightened and swung around, but instead of the page he'd expected to see, a tall, handsome young man with blond hair, a full beard, and the broad, powerful shoulders of a warrior strode into the room like a king into his court.

The man stopped short at the sight of Robert, then causally shoved the door shut behind him. His penetrating gaze slid over Robert's mud-spattered boots, the rain-soaked cloak on the stool, the gloves on the table.

"Well, Wardell?" he said. His mouth curved into a mocking smile. "Have you grown so tired of your riches that you should venture out on such a night as this—and all for the pleasure of disturbing me?"

Robert cocked his head in answering mockery and bowed, relieved at the interruption to his thoughts. Heir to the throne of England Edward might be, but he was a man, and Robert knew how to deal in the world of men.

"I thought the rain might wash away my sins, milord," he said.

"Are your sins so great you needs must drown them?"

"No greater than yours, I think." Robert shrugged. "But certainly no less, either."

Edward laughed. "If matters stand that badly, my friend, you'd best get thee back into the night. Or to a priest." He crossed to the tall-backed chair set at the far end of the table and motioned Robert to the bench at the end nearest the fire.

"A priest would scarce answer my summons at this hour, milord," said Robert, taking the seat indicated. "Not unless he plucked a goodly number of coins from my pocket first. All for the glory of Holy Mother Church, of course," he added dryly.

"Of course," Edward agreed, amused. "If you like, I can have the chaplain roused from whatever doxy's bed he's warming and dragged here to confess you. Though God alone knows the damage he might do turned loose amongst us, deprived of his rutting and his rest."

"We've no need of a priest, milord, and there are more interesting matters to discuss than my sins."

"Indeed." Edward's gaze sharpened. "Then tell me, how fares London?"

"Troubled," Robert said curtly. "Simon de Montfort may be bound at Kenilworth with a broken leg, but his men hold the city and the Tower as securely as ever. There's much talk of a fight to come between your forces and his, with the merchants and tradesmen of London full ready to take up arms against King Henry. Already they speak of naming a constable and a marshal from amongst them, to lead them when they march against him."

Edward snorted in contempt. "Rebellious fools! Do they think they can stand against men who have spent their lives fighting instead of measuring silks and weighing out peppercorns?"

"They think their rescue of Montfort from your forces on London Bridge last month is proof enough of their strength. And there's no gainsaying they've good reason to back Earl Simon's cause against your father."

"Do you now turn against me too, Wardell?" Edward demanded angrily.

"Nay, milord, I do not. But the king has made no effort to endear himself to them. What would you think, and you an honest English merchant, if your king denied you the rights to which he'd sworn himself, and gave his trade and support to foreigners while you and your fellow merchants went a-begging?"

"I'd think me well suited to stand by my king and not some upstart baron who puts himself above the man God chose to occupy the throne of England!"

"You'd think yourself damnably cheated, and well you know it!"

Edward's head snapped up. He glared at Robert down the length of the table. "Direct as always, eh, Wardell?"

Robert met his prince's gaze unflinchingly. "I but speak the truth, milord. Henry has brought most of his troubles on himself by his poor choice of advisors and his support of foreigners at the expense of honest Englishmen."

"My father is the king!" Edward roared, slamming his

fist on the table. "He has the God-given right to govern as he sees fit!"

"Not fifty years ago God chose to back the barons at Runnymede when King John thought likewise, milord," Robert returned, unimpressed with Edward's display of temper, but well aware he trod on dangerous ground.

Edward's eyes narrowed. "Tell me, why do I let you speak so, Wardell? None other of your stripe dare so much unless they coat their words with honey first."

A knock at the door prevented Robert from replying. At Edward's peremptory command to enter, the latch lifted and the page entered bearing a tray with a pitcher, two wine cups, and a bowl covered with a clean linen napkin. He blenched when he caught sight of Edward.

"Your p-pardon, milord. I thought you still with my Lady Eleanor."

"You seldom think very well, Thomas, and then not for long. Come in, then, come in." Edward motioned him in, his irritation clear in his face. "At least you've brought wine."

"Yes, milord," the page said, cringing under his master's displeasure. "And food for M-Master Wardell."

The bowl's contents gave off a tempting smell of spices and meat that made Robert's stomach growl. He repressed a frown of irritation at being thus caught between an empty belly and an angry prince. He could not eat before Edward without permission, and if Edward granted permission, he would be at a disadvantage with his mouth full. Either way he lost, and he did not enjoy losing . . . to anyone, for any reason.

Edward lifted the napkin and sniffed. "Hmm. A common stew, perhaps, but—" He shrugged, then picked up the hunk of bread from the tray, tore off a piece, and dipped it into the stew.

Robert resolutely studied the patterns the firelight cast across the rushes on the floor.

"Ermmm," Edward said thoughtfully, chewing.

Out of the corner of his eye, Robert could see a gobbet of gravy on the prince's beard.

"Not bad." Edward waved away the page, adding in a bread-muffled voice, "Give it to Master Wardell, then. The man looks hungry enough to devour me if he's not fed. Go on, man," he added when Robert hesitated. "You're no good to me if you starve. You can talk, even with your mouth full. Never known a merchant yet who couldn't, and to the devil with good manners."

Robert dug his horn spoon out of the leather pouch on his belt. While the page poured the wine, he scooped out a good-sized chunk of meat liberally laced with the wine-and-spice-flavored gravy. He had a few seconds before the page left the room, at least.

"Well, then?" Edward demanded the moment the page had closed the door behind him. "I trust you came for some reason other than to insult the king. I've no desire to listen to you slurp your gravy if you've no interesting words with which to flavor it."

The problem wasn't finding interesting words, Robert thought, setting down his spoon. The challenge was not to give away the rest of the dangerous game with them.

He dabbed at his mouth with the napkin, then reluctantly shoved the bowl away. "Perhaps you would listen to the tune of five thousand pounds, milord . . . assuming those pounds were singing in your coffers and not Earl Simon's."

In a rush, the anger went out of Edward's face, replaced by satisfaction. "Then you have arranged for the loan as I instructed?"

"I have, and more. The money comes through me from a number of sources, all of whom are loyal to the king . . . and to you, milord. It but awaits your need of it, with more to come if necessary." He met the prince's eager gaze squarely.

Edward's right eyebrow quirked upward. "But . . . ?"

"But we want a guarantee. A writ of protection sealed with your own mark."

"And what is it you wish me to guarantee beyond the eventual return of your silver, master merchant?"

Robert breathed deep. What he asked was unheard of. "Among other things, milord, we want a commitment to future—shall we say—business relations? More important, your protection from the king's wrath when this is settled."

"You suggest my father would be unjust?" Edward's voice held a sharp note of warning.

"London has challenged the king. When the city is once more his, King Henry is like to forget that not all Londoners acted against his interests."

"And if Montfort and his scum-swilling barons triumph?" Edward let the question hang on the air between them.

Robert's jaw clenched painfully. He had considered that possibility, as well . . . and Jocelyn had returned to haunt him because of it. "I do not believe they will, milord."

"Do not? Or dare not, Wardell?" Edward asked with a mocking grin.

"Do not," Robert said firmly.

"You have that much faith in the king . . . and me?"

It was Robert's turn to grin mockingly. "I have that much faith in myself, milord. And in my judgment of you."

For an instant, Edward stared at him, caught between wrath and astonishment at Robert's effrontery. Then he tilted his head back and gave a shout of laughter. "God's teeth! You're an arrogant bastard, Wardell! I'd do better to have you hanged, and then confiscate your holdings and your hidden gold. To hell with your precious loans and writs!"

Robert's grin turned to a small, hard, satisfied smile. He could permit himself no more than the smile, but that, at least, he would have.

He had won the first round and had Edward for protection on one flank. If all went well with the priest he'd sent as emissary to Montfort's man, Sir Fulk Fitzwarren, baron of Colmaine, then he would have protection for the other flank as well. Between Edward and Colmaine, he would be invulnerable, and bedamned to dark fantasies and darker dreams.

At the thought, Robert's smile vanished.

It Begins

A ⌁ *Colmaine Castle, late February* 1264

WHOLE MORNING of watching spent for naught, Alyce Fitzwarren fumed as she raced up the steeply circling steps of the north tower. An entire *morning,* and all because she'd left her post for half an hour to lecture the steward, placate the head cook, and scold the two pages. Every one of them was as nervous as a rat in a barn full of hungry cats, and they bid fair to drive her mad before the day was out.

Well, who around the castle *wasn't* nervous? Certainly none of them had a better right to the feeling than she did, yet no one had found *her* falling into senseless, hand-wringing foolishness!

The slick leather soles of her new shoes slipped on the narrow steps. She stumbled and bumped her knee against the unyielding stone, then slid down two more steps, banging her knee a second time and soundly abusing her shins for good measure.

With a quick oath that a lady of her rank was expected never to use, Alyce scrambled to her feet and grabbed up the dragging hems of her kirtle and surcoat. Still grumbling, she raced up the remaining steps, heedless of the throbbing in her knee or her indelicate display of ankle and leg.

Old half-deaf Tadeus, the guard posted on the roof of
the tower, wasn't going to be looking her way, in any case.
His attention would be fixed on the riders whose approach
had just been announced with blasts of the olifants loud
enough to wake the dead . . . or old Tadeus.

Alyce burst out of the tower doorway, startling the pigeons strutting along the battlement into noisy flight. Directly across from her, a skinny male rump marginally
covered by a dirty green tunic occupied the crenel that
provided the best view of the main road leading toward
London. The skinny rump was attached to an even skin-
nier pair of shanks encased in baggy blue chausses. Alyce
could see the grimy, heavily callused soles of Tadeus's feet
through the holes in his shoes as he kicked and squirmed
and wriggled forward on his belly for a better view.

It was the pigeons flapping past his nose, rather than
the sound of her own undignified arrival that distracted
Tadeus from his efforts. The old man squawked and shoved
back out of the crenel faster than he'd gone in, then
grabbed for the crossbow he'd left propped against the
wall beside him.

He whirled about, bow up and pointed straight at her.
It might have been a problem if he'd remembered to put a
bolt in it first. His dried-apple face scrunched into a
toothless grin at the sight of her, and his eyes, half-hidden
in the wrinkled folds of his lids, sparkled with excitement.

"They be comin', milady," he said, setting the heavy
bow down and jiggling aside to give her access to the
crenel. "Fair gaudy, they be, and their bells janglin' to
fright the devil hisself."

Alyce couldn't help smiling down at the wizened
little man, but the olifants sounded again before she
could say anything. With a quick glance to assure herself
that the pigeons hadn't left any new offerings during her
absence—or that Tadeus had rubbed them off if they had—
she claimed the spot the guardsman had just vacated.

Leaning out across the broad gray stone of the crenel, she stretched as far as she could to get a good view of the road and its travelers.

Neither the road nor the travelers were hard to spot. The one wound down the hill and through the surrounding fields to the castle's gate like a placid brown stream, lazy under the late winter sun; the others sailed the stream like brightly colored barques brought out for a day's adventuring. The noise of their laughter and their horses' bells, while insufficient to rouse the devil, was surely more then enough to draw the attention of everyone in the castle and the small village beyond, assuming any of them had somehow missed the ringing call of the olifants.

She scanned the oncoming crowd, trying to pick out a stranger's face from among strangers. Her gaze fastened on one dark visage in the center of the group, the only one unsoftened by the gaiety that animated the other faces.

A hot, hard ball of doubt formed in her chest, somewhere just behind her breastbone and beside her heart. It was the distance playing tricks, surely, the distance and her own overactive imagination. No man who was going to his own wedding could be so grim-faced and silent. Not among that merry crowd, at any rate.

She tried to focus on the other members of the colorful cavalcade, but her gaze kept returning to the man who had first attracted her attention. Alyce frowned, futilely trying to make out details. The travelers were still too far away to pick out more than the boldest points. Of one thing she was sure, however—cost had not been a consideration when the riders and their horses had been decked out for the journey. Even the armed men who rode as escort were well mounted and well dressed, and the weapons they carried would make her father's armorer itch to add them to his stores.

To her dismay, any doubts Alyce might have had

about her identification of the dark man were laid to rest
when he held up his hand and the cavalcade drew to a halt.
He shifted in the saddle, as if to give instructions to
the man riding beside him, then set his horse into motion. The riders in front of him respectfully moved their
mounts to the side as he passed, like noblemen making
way for the king. Certainly he bestrode a mount fit for
a king.

Dappled gray with dark flowing mane and tail, the
creature paced forward with an eager, springing stride
that spurned the lesser animals that had hemmed it in. It
fidgeted and tossed its head, setting the silver bells on its
caparison ringing. Yet despite the palfrey's restless energy,
its rider sat erect and seemingly motionless in the saddle,
at one with the magnificent beast beneath him.

The man reined in the horse at a point in the road
where he had a clear view of Colmaine Castle. Head high,
one hand propped on his hip, he restrained his restless
mount and studied the scene before him.

Alyce's lips thinned at his arrogant perusal, but she
knew well what he saw, however little she liked to admit
it. An ancient stone keep with towers and walls in serious
need of repair. A crumbling curtain wall that wouldn't
withstand any serious attack for long—assuming anyone
cared to waste the time in trying. A shabby village com-
posed of a few huts and a tiny stone church, huddled in
the shadow of its larger neighbor.

There wasn't anything more.

And what there was, the dark rider clearly found less
than impressive. He shrugged—Alyce could see the dis-
missive gesture, even at this distance—then wheeled his
mount around and centered back to his retinue.

The travelers were too far away for her to hear any of
their conversation, and the dark rider's back was turned to
her so she couldn't see his face, but he must have said

something that amused the others. They burst into laughter and their heads bobbed as they commented back and forth among themselves.

Sheep. That's what they were, Alyce thought, studying them with disgust. Bleating and baaing and herding together as if afraid to move without another to command them.

And if they were sheep, then the dark rider, Robert Wardell, master merchant of London and the man she was to wed that night, was the dog who herded them.

Heat suffused Alyce's face. Her hands balled into fists, but her eyes filled with the same hot tears that had threatened to overcome her so many times since her father had informed her of the arrangements he'd made for her marriage.

Her marriage.

She dropped her head to glare at the flat gray stone lining the crenel. Its rough surface swam before her, blurred and watery and disconcertingly unfamiliar.

She'd always known her marriage would be arranged for her. The inevitable had merely been delayed by her father's unwillingness to provide her dowry, and the equal unwillingness of any family of rank to establish a connection, especially one through marriage, with such a feckless, impoverished minor baron. Even though most girls of her breeding were wed by the age of thirteen or fourteen while she was approaching her nineteenth year without betrothal, Alyce hadn't worried. Her father didn't want to pay for her dowry, but he was even less inclined to pay for her to be admitted into a convent where he would have no hope of gains through her dower rights and bridal gifts.

A husband would be found for her someday. She'd been sure of it. She'd just never expected he'd be a commoner, and a merchant.

With a determined sniffle, she blinked back the tears and scowled down at the man who was the cause of her present problems. He was leading his little army forward at a trot, as haughty as any lord and seemingly unconcerned that he was approaching the castle like an invader bent on conquest.

As if to render homage to his magnificence, the sun glinted off a jeweled ornament on his chest and flashed on the hilt of the narrow sword he wore at his side. His mount, obviously pleased at being freed from the former tight restraint, stretched itself into a ground-eating trot. Its hooves sent up small puffs of brown as they struck the ground; its tail streamed out like a dark banner, rippling with the breeze created by its forward motion.

Wardell himself looked neither to right nor left and made no effort to check his speed, not even when some of his followers lagged behind, unwilling to match his pace.

Irritated by the insolent tilt of that dark head, Alyce slid off the wall and bent to brush any trace of dirt from her fine new wool surcoat.

Crumbling it might be, but Colmaine Castle was a nobleman's castle, she reminded herself fiercely, and she was a nobleman's daughter.

If it weren't for her father's great need for funds and the enormous debts incurred when her brother had been knighted, Robert Wardell could never have dreamed of marriage with a woman whose lineage traced back to the Conquest and beyond. Yet even though Wardell's wealth carried the stench of trade, Sir Fulk had managed to stopper his nose when Wardell's representatives had presented his offer of a hundred pounds in silver pennies—an immense sum—not to mention the customary dower rights of a third of his entire estate—all in exchange for the hand of Fulk's daughter in marriage.

A hundred pounds! Alyce's hand closed around the heavy cloth of her surcoat. The amount still staggered her. It was almost equal to an entire year's revenues from all of her father's holdings combined. Who knew what her dower rights might be worth! Not that it mattered much now, for they would only fall to her on Wardell's death, and however little Alyce liked the thought of this marriage, she did not wish to be widowed soon.

She did not want to be married at all. Not to this proud man who claimed her in such haste, then mocked her and her family with his ostentatious display, as if he were intent on humbling them. Humbling her!

Alyce's grip on her surcoat tightened, but she forced herself to let go of the expensive perse fabric she had chosen with such care at the fair in Ayllesbury, then sewn and embroidered with even greater care over the past three months. She'd even gone so far as to pick out the gold thread of a crumbling belt that had been her mother's so that she might include it in the intricate design. It hadn't been easy, for the thread was worn and bent, and she'd had to place it with care so no one would guess at the purse-pinching stratagems to which she'd been reduced for her bridal clothes.

The effort had been worth it, though. The embroidery was exquisite, the surcoat elegant, as befitted her station. Merchant or no, she hadn't wanted her future husband to see her in her usual drab russet.

She certainly did not wish to give him any opportunity to sneer at her now. Bad enough to know that even costly clothes could not disguise her height or her thin, unwomanly frame.

Alyce smoothed the heavy cloth of her surcoat, running the heels of her hands over her hips and thighs, hoping to stop the sudden trembling of her fingers. Her palms left faint traces of damp on the bright blue wool. She glanced toward the crenel, wondering if Robert Wardell could somehow have seen her, then bit her lip, embarrassed by the foolish thought. He not only couldn't see her, she couldn't see him. From this angle, all that was visible was blue sky and a glimpse of the fields that lay at the edge of the horizon.

She stared at that small, familiar patch of land, desperately trying to memorize its shape and color and texture. She'd never noticed before how easily her own world disappeared from sight, just as it would on the morrow, when she left Colmaine as Wardell's wife.

"Almost to the gate, they be, milady," Tadeus announced with satisfaction and just a touch of concern. He'd been straining to watch from the crenel next to hers, but the angle wasn't the best and his face was flushed from his effort to stick his head around the obscuring merlon without plummeting over the edge. "Best ye go down now, so ye can greet 'em proper. Sir Fulk and yer brother have given up their tiltin' at the quintain and are already headed round to the front o' the keep."

Mention of her father, who had chosen to exercise his destrier and his strong right arm in a little weapons practice that morning, was enough to set Alyce in motion. As she scurried down the worn tower steps—she couldn't help muttering a few execrations on her sire's obstinate insistence that he'd no need to bathe and dress himself in all his finery.

He wasn't the one getting married! Sir Fulk had protested when she'd broached the subject a week ago. Christ's bones! A man would think he was about to appear before the pope, rather than merely attend his daughter's wedding, the way she wanted to disorder his life and his household with her ridiculous insistence on baths and cleaning and fancy show. And all for naught but a little blessing from the priest and a little bedding from a man who'd be paying dear enough for the right!

Alyce's brother, Hubert, had snickered into his ale, then sworn at her when she'd plucked a soup bone from the serving bowl and flung it at his head. The bone had bounced off his shoulder and fallen to the floor, where a snarling fight promptly ensued between the two hounds who'd claimed it.

Half the occupants of the hall had rushed to watch the fight, heedlessly tipping over benches and slopping wine across the tablecloths in their eagerness not to miss the fun. That had left Alyce seated alone at the high table, wadding her linen napkin in her hands and scowling at her father's broad back. Oblivious to her fury, he'd cheered on the dogs and placed bets that his favorite brindle bitch would emerge the winner.

When the bitch had fled with her tail between her legs, Fulk had sworn vilely, flung down the coins he'd wagered, and stomped off to work off his ill humor in sword practice with some hapless guardsman.

Alyce had decided not to pursue the matter of his dress further, no matter how much she wanted to. Nothing would be gained by antagonizing her father. In general, she was free to do as she liked where the castle and its management were concerned, but only so long as she didn't interfere with her father's comfort or bother his hawks or his hounds or his horses.

Unfortunately, all too many things fell under the heading of disturbing Sir Fulk's comfort. That wasn't usually a problem. Her father was away far more often than he was at home, and Alyce did as she liked during his absences. But Fulk hadn't left Colmaine for almost four months—not since he'd come home battered and bleeding from an early skirmish in the troubles brewing between King Henry and Simon de Montfort, to whom Fulk had so rashly pledged his allegiance. During that time much had been left undone that badly needed doing.

Alyce repressed a grimace of distaste as she stepped through the tower doorway into the great hall of the keep. One of the many tasks she'd been unable to undertake was the removal of the old rushes that matted the stone floor of the hall. Pulling up the packed mass of rushes, discarded bones, animal droppings, and whatever other vileness might have mixed in with the mess would have involved hours of heavy labor, then more hours of scrubbing the stone underneath. The rushes hadn't been changed since the last time her father had been away from Colmaine, and even if she'd dared pull in the stable boys and the kitchen scrubs to help the women who were normally responsible for such things, her father wouldn't have tolerated any disruption of his midday meal.

She'd had to content herself with placing a thick layer of fresh rushes sweetened with dried herbs over the old, decaying layer in hopes that Robert Wardell and his people wouldn't notice what lay beneath. It was just for one night, anyway, then they would be gone and—

Alyce stopped short. Her stomach heaved and she suddenly felt faint, oddly light-headed and unsteady on her feet.

One night. Her wedding night, when a man she did not know would have the right to claim her body, and then take her away from the only home she had ever known.

She squeezed her eyes shut and swallowed the bile that had risen in her throat, acutely conscious of the half-dozen curious faces peeping out at her from various corners and passageways, ready to spread the least scrap of gossip.

The lord's daughter didn't marry every day, and the castle folk had gladly set aside their usual conversational fare in favor of discussions of her coming nuptials, with any factual gaps conveniently filled by speculation and wild conjecture. Those not privileged to witness her present distress would be more than interested to hear how Lady Alyce had been so afraid of meeting her betrothed that she couldn't even walk across the hall without faltering.

Alyce breathed deep, then made a great pretense of

tucking an imaginary lock of her disappointingly red hair under her veil, of smoothing her wimple and shaking out her surcoat so it hung in graceful folds and the embroidery showed to its best advantage.

If she'd had the time, she would have diverted the servants' attention to less intriguing topics, such as the benches that had not yet been properly set in place or the unmended tears she could see in two of the cloths laid for the formal dinner.

She didn't have the time, though. Whatever was lacking or ill managed or unprepared would have to remain so, for she could hear the grumbling protest of the castle gates as they swung wide to welcome Robert Wardell.

Another deep breath, then Alyce crossed to the far end of the hall and the massive oak door that stood open, letting in the sun. She hesitated just inside the doorway where the shadows still held dominion, unwilling to go out into the light, clinging to the tiny details of the familiar world around her.

From the bailey she caught the cries of the guardsmen and the excited jabbering of the castle folk who had dropped their work and scurried over to watch the excitement. Dogs barked and horses snorted, and from somewhere deep in the stables, a resident whinnied a challenge. Harness bells clanged brightly as iron-shod hooves scraped and clattered over stone. Above it all, she heard her father's bellow as he swore at some hapless fool who had gotten in his way.

One more deep breath, and Lady Alyce Fitzwarren stepped out of the shadows and into the sun, carefully making her way down the outer steps toward the men gathering below.

2

SHADOWS IN
THE CHAPEL

"CHRIST'S TEETH, WHAT a wretched place!" Stout William Townsend brought his equally stout mare even with Robert's gray as they rode through the broad gate. "You should have sent me to negotiate with Fitzwarren instead of that lack-wit priest. I'd have had the girl for half what you paid for her—and gotten you a better dowry, besides!"

Robert glanced over at his friend and smiled. It wasn't a pleasant smile. "No doubt. But Colmaine wanted no dealings with a merchant, William. Any merchant."

"He was willing enough to sell his daughter to one." When Robert remained silent, he added between clenched teeth, "The priest was an ass, Robert."

"But nobly born."

"Then doubly an ass, for thinking he'd more to gain from Colmaine than from the commoner who paid him."

Robert shrugged, but he couldn't suppress a grimace of distaste as they rode past a shoulder-high mound of straw and manure from the castle's stables. "I tell you, William. If I were Colmaine, I'd have chucked my steward into the cesspits long since. I've seen cow byres that were cleaner than this."

"And slept in them too!"

That brought a real laugh. "And been glad of the lodging!"

The laughter died as a girl—grubby and ill-kempt, but as plump and fair and blue-eyed as Jocelyn had been—shoved her way to the front of the crowd and almost under his feet, startling Robert's palfrey. The beast snorted, then lunged forward in high-bred exception to the creature's presumption. Robert reined the gray in, but his hands trembled. It took an effort of will not to look back, not to seek the girl in the crowd.

Jocelyn was dead.

He'd wrapped her in her winding sheet himself. He'd spent a day and a night and half of another day on his knees beside her bier, too angry and full of guilt to pray, too numb to feel the cold stone floor or the ache of abused bone and muscle. Too empty to care about anything except that she was dead . . . and he was the one to blame for it.

"Smile, man! It's your wedding you're going to, not your funeral!" William's cheerful admonition slashed through the rabble's noise.

Robert's body jerked in reaction, and he inadvertently pricked his mount with his spurs. Indignant, the palfrey half reared, then dodged sideways, scattering the laughing, gaping crowd of peasants.

Glad of the distraction, Robert let the beast work out his displeasure, then drove him forward, toward the waiting crowd at the base of the keep and the bride he'd bought with a hundred pounds of silver . . . and his soul.

WHENEVER SIR FULK and Hubert—Sir Hubert now—returned from whatever campaign or adventuring they'd been engaged with, the bailey turned to riotous confusion, but Alyce couldn't remember any madness like the present.

Horses and dogs and people mixed and swirled and jostled in wild disorder, every one of them too excited to stand still and too befuddled to know what they ought to do next.

Yet a stillness dwelt in the heart of the milling crowd, like the dangerous center of a whirlpool. And in the heart of the stillness was Robert Wardell, tall and dark and gloriously gowned, his restless gray mount held in check, his head as proudly high as a king's. He turned, scanning the crowd, until his gaze fixed on her.

Alyce faltered, impaled mid-stride as if he'd run her through with his sword. Angry with herself for her reaction, and with him for his haughtiness, she braced herself against the cold stone wall of the keep and stared back defiantly.

Wardell seemed not to care. His eyes made dark holes in his face, but Alyce could read nothing in them. Not lust or curiosity or concern. Not even interest.

She tried to look away and found she could not. There was something so cold in his unblinking gaze, yet . . .

Her father's booming voice broke the trance.

"Ho! Wat! What mean you, man?" Sir Fulk angrily motioned to his stoop-shouldered head groom. "Stop gawking and take Master Wardell's horse, you fool."

Wat, jerked out of his lustful contemplation of the gray, jumped to obey. A wiry golden-haired youth in dark green livery took hold of the bridle first. At his touch, the gray bent its head, then shoved its nose into the young man's chest, sending him staggering. The youth laughed and cuffed the horse, who snorted and tossed its head as though amused by the game they played.

The gray's rider gave no sign he noticed. Wardell turned from his steely perusal of her, then dismounted in one graceful move and crossed to Sir Fulk, seemingly untouched by the noise and confusion of the turbulent crowd around him.

Alyce sagged against the wall, grateful to be freed of

his unsettling stare, then forced her shaky limbs to carry her down the remaining stairs. To her relief, no one had heeded her momentary weakness, not even the two small boys awaiting her. Like everyone else, the page, who held the jewel-encrusted silver cup that was her father's most precious possession, and the serving boy, who stood behind him with a pitcher full of wine, were watching Sir Fulk and Robert Wardell, wide-eyed with excitement.

Of the two men, only Sir Fulk seemed aware of the attention fixed on them, and he clearly relished it, sure of himself and his power within his domain.

It was as well that his manner proclaimed him lord, for his appearance did not. A rough reddish-gray beard grizzled his chin. Sweat and caked dust marked the lines where his helm had pressed. His practice armor showed the marks of long years of heavy wear, an image reinforced by the dirty tufts of wool padding poking through the tears in his leather gambeson. From the stained linen coif on his head to the battered, antiquated sabatons on his feet, he looked more like a penniless knight than a baron who held his lands directly of the king.

Wardell, in contrast, was bathed, shaved, and dressed in a short tunic and surcoat made of the finest scarlet. The costly red wool and its exquisite trim shone in the sun, bright against his dark skin. A jeweled brooch glinted on his chest. Gold and silver embroidery adorned the gloves tucked in his silver-mounted belt, and silver fasteners glittered on his fine leather shoes. He was tall, as tall as Sir Fulk, but leaner and more finely shaped.

Despite his costly trappings, Alyce could detect no hint of softness about the man. Certainly not in his face with its high cheekbones, thin-lipped mouth, and uncompromising jaw, nor even in the close-cropped black curls touched with strands of gray that brushed the tips of his ears. It was a hard, intimidating face, yet cleanly sculpted, arresting in its masculine power.

Alyce abruptly dropped her gaze and turned to the goggle-eyed page and the equally awed serving boy, neither of whom appeared to have moved an inch—or even breathed, for that matter—since Robert Wardell had ridden through the gate.

"Fill the cup," she commanded. "Have you both forgotten what is expected of you?"

The eight-year-old page, Edwin, jumped and nearly dropped the precious silver cup. A hiss from his companion brought him back to a clear sense of place and his proper duty. He gave Alyce a furtive glance laden with guilt, then scrunched his eyebrows into an intent frown as he extended the cup to be filled with wine.

With her heart pounding, Alyce crossed to where her father and Robert Wardell remained trapped in the throes of courtesy. Edwin, scowling in concentration as he tried not to spill the wine, followed dutifully at her side.

"Alyce! Daughter!" Sir Fulk's voice rang with false heartiness. Clearly, the strain of polite conversation with a stranger, and a merchant, was telling on him already. "My daughter, Master Wardell, the Lady Alyce."

"Milady." Robert Wardell bowed as gracefully as he seemed to do everything else.

Alyce kept her gaze focused on the ground six inches in front of her toes and sank into a curtsy. "Master Wardell." To her relief, the words came out stronger and steadier than she'd expected.

Head still bent, she rose and turned to Edwin, who stood behind her trying hard to see everything that went on without being seen himself. Her hands trembled, ever so slightly, as she took the cup from the page.

Once more she sank into a curtsy, but this time she extended the cup as an offering of welcome. "Castle Colmaine is honored by your presence, sir. Will you take our wine with our welcome?"

He was silent—a moment, no more—but to Alyce

the silence stretched endlessly, ringing in her ears more loudly than the racket around them. With her head bent, all she could see of him were his fine shoes, well-shaped legs encased in dark hose, and the hem of his tunic, but she was achingly conscious of his gaze, of his nearness and the smell of horse and sun and man that came from him, familiar, yet oddly tantalizing in its intimacy.

"I accept your wine and your welcome gladly, milady. I thank you." His voice shattered the stillness between them, as cold and hard as the rest of him.

He bent to take the cup she offered. Alyce looked up to find herself staring into fathomless black eyes.

It was deliberate, this coldness of his, she realized with shock. Because of her. Because of what she was.

His lashes immediately swept down to hide him from her. He took the jewel-encrusted cup from her nerveless hands, then straightened and lifted it to his lips to drink. Alyce could see the contractions of his throat muscles with each swallow he took, the shadow beneath his jaw, and the sunlight on his neck and shoulder and breast. Dark and light, and beneath it all the man himself, hidden from her sight.

Had it been her imagination, or had he hesitated, just for a heartbeat, when his eyes met hers? Were there truly such fires within him as she thought she had seen?

Her legs were quivering with the strain of maintaining her curtsy for so long, but she managed to stand without betraying herself. Managed to extend her hands to take back the cup once he'd drained it of its wine.

Her fingers brushed his as she reclaimed the precious cup. Not all coldness, she mused, for his skin was warm. But the fires she thought she'd seen within him were gone. His eyes revealed nothing.

"I thank you, milady," Wardell said. "And you, milord," he added, nodding at Sir Fulk. "Your wine is as fine as your welcome."

"Just brought in another few pipes from Bordeaux," Sir Fulk said, clearly pleased. If he noticed the dryness of Wardell's tone, he gave no hint.

Edwin, intent on doing his duty, stepped forward and solemnly offered Wardell a fine linen cloth to wipe away any trace of wine that might linger on his lips.

Alyce watched as Robert Wardell took the proffered cloth and blotted away the wine, uncomfortably conscious of a sudden heat low in her belly and a sharp, insistent ache lower still. What did wine taste like on a man's lips? Was it sweeter than wine from a cup, or did it carry a bitter tinge? Was it warm from the heat of his mouth, or—

Her grip on the silver cup tightened. Foolish, sinful thoughts. She had let her women's teasing and their constant, annoying chatter of men and marriage and babies corrupt her.

Once more she dropped her gaze, but not before another, and even more unsettling thought had formed—*you will learn soon enough, in any case.*

Hubert had been lurking at the edge of the crowd throughout, too proud to dismount to welcome a mere merchant, yet as curious as anyone else to inspect his sister's bridegroom. Five minutes spent watching a tedious exchange of civilities had worn on him, however. He swaggered forward and clapped Wardell on the shoulder with rough familiarity.

"You and your people are welcome enough, Wardell, but you'll scarce earn friends among us if you keep us from our dinner."

Sir Fulk roared out his version of a laugh. "True enough. Here, Alyce! Lead our guests in while Hubert and I rid ourselves of our armor and our dust. But don't begin without us!"

Alyce stiffened, but the only sign Wardell gave of recognizing the insult was a slight lift of his right eyebrow.

"I should be honored to have Lady Alyce escort me,

Sir Fulk," he said smoothly. "If you could direct my people
where to stable our horses . . . ?"

Heat scorched Alyce's cheeks and her hands curled
into fists. It was as well she no longer held the cup, for she
might have thrown the dregs in his face. Her father and
brother gained no honor by their crude manners, but
Wardell's suggestion that Sir Fulk concern himself with
such trivial matters as the stabling of a visitor's horses
went too far.

Sir Fulk was oblivious. "Wat will see to it." He
beamed with the expansive goodwill of a man who was
lord of the castle and whose annoying debts would soon be
a thing of the past. "Take Master Wardell up, then, Alyce.
Hubert and I will join you shortly."

With that, he turned and strode off, shouting orders
and setting a dozen servants scurrying in their haste
to obey.

Alyce forced her hands to uncurl. There was no help
for it, after all. "Will you follow me, then, Master
Wardell?" she said stiffly. "Your servants may go with
Wat."

Wardell eyed her. As if he were inspecting a bolt of
cloth or a mare for his stables, she thought, and felt her
cheeks grow warm again. Her chin tilted upward. "Your
friends may perhaps wish to refresh themselves first. There
is time before my father returns."

"My servants know what is expected of them, and my
friends . . ." He paused. One corner of his mouth curled
sardonically. "My friends are accustomed to hospitality
such as Sir Fulk's. I'm sure they will manage adequately."

He swept her an elegant bow and extended his hand
to lead her into the keep. "Shall we go in, Lady Alyce? I
shouldn't like to keep Sir Hubert—I take it that *was* your
brother?—waiting any longer than I have already."

Alyce flinched. Nothing in his words or his tone or his
manner betrayed his intent, yet he had pricked her as

surely as if he'd pulled the dagger hanging from his belt and sliced her flesh. If this was what the future held—

She cut the thought short. She had learned to live with her father's thoughtless cruelties and unintentioned slights. Robert Wardell was just beginning to taste them.

Head high, she placed her hand upon Wardell's and let him lead her into the keep.

NOW SHE KNEW how an ox felt in the marketplace. Inspected by everyone, talked about and argued over, ignored when it came to the bargaining, and without the slightest say in the matter, first to last. Wardell hadn't demanded to look at her teeth or feel her legs for soundness, but he might as well have done so for all the chivalrous effort he'd managed *not* to put into the affair so far.

Alyce dug her fingernails into the palms of her hands, fighting the urge to scowl, and the even greater urge to pour a pitcher of ale over the heads of her father and Wardell. The two sat at each end of the single trestle table that had been left in place after the dinner. A clean cloth had been laid and wine brought to ease the negotiations.

No, not negotiations, Alyce corrected herself scornfully. Discussions. The negotiations had been conducted a month earlier, when her father had agreed to trade her and three of his least productive manors for silver pennies. A lot of silver pennies.

Some of the coins now lay in glittering heaps upon the white cloth. The rest remained securely tied in leather pouches piled on the floor or dumped into the iron-bound chests that had been dragged from her father's sleeping chamber or brought up from the vault under the hall.

God knew it hadn't been a problem to find places to put Wardell's money, even a hundred pounds worth. Some of the chests had held bolts of linen or woolen cloth bought at the yearly fair and stored for future need. Most

had been empty—and would be empty again soon
enough, Alyce thought sourly. Sir Fulk would undoubt-
edly use some of the coin to pay his most pressing debts,
but she had no doubt that some, perhaps most, would be
spent on new armor or more horses or helping pay for this
rebellion of Simon de Montfort's that he'd engaged in
with so much enthusiasm and so little thought. There
wasn't a chance in heaven that he'd remember the money
was supposed to be hers.

Alyce glanced from her father, surrounded by his son
and his chaplain and his steward, to Wardell, who had his
own supporters respectfully arrayed behind his chair.

What would they say, her father and Wardell, if she
suddenly refused to go through with this marriage? She
had the right. She had always had the right. Consent by
both parties was required or a marriage could be ruled
invalid.

Alyce's breath caught at the mad thought. From her
chair, which had been set at one side, she had a clear view
of both Sir Fulk's and Wardell's faces.

It wasn't hard to imagine the consternation and anger
with which her father would greet such an announcement.
Sir Fulk had never been one to restrain himself. She'd seen
more than enough of his thundering rages to know what
she could expect if she dared overset his arrangements
now. It wouldn't be pleasant, but it would be endurable.

Wardell was another matter entirely. Alyce couldn't
even begin to guess what his reaction might be if she refused to marry him.

Although he'd shown no inclination to woo her, he'd
been courteous and considerate throughout the tedious
ceremonies and numerous courses of the formal dinner.
His table manners, unlike Sir Fulk's, were exquisite. Yet
underneath his polished courtesy lay a wintry reserve that
chilled her to the core.

Only once during the formalities had she seen him

display any emotion at all. As soon as the preliminaries were safely out of the way, he'd ordered his guards, who had remained with his heavily loaded sumpter horses, to bring in his "gift" for Sir Fulk. At sight of the men marching into the hall carrying fat leather money bags, her father had gleefully rubbed his hands together and made a crude joke about bridal gifts and bridal rights. For an instant, Wardell's upper lip had curled in scorn; then his features were as blandly unreadable as ever.

Now he sat with his right elbow propped on the chair arm and his left leg stretched out before him, as if to display the lean-muscled curve of his thigh and calf and the trim shape of his foot within his fine shoe. A ray of late afternoon sun lanced through one of the narrow windows to strike the back of his head and the square line of his shoulder, drenching him in dull gold even as it cast his face into shadow. Five fat wax candles set in the middle of the table in honor of the occasion softened the shadow without dispelling it. The flames wavered and sank, then flared again, tracing the arch of his brow and the sharp slope of his nose, but revealing nothing of his eyes except a hard glitter of black and white.

His gaze was fixed on Sir Fulk who sat, shoulders hunched, scowling down at the roll of parchment lying half-opened before him. All the eagerness with which Fulk had greeted Wardell's laden guardsmen had disappeared in the face of the complicated marriage charter.

Scrawny little Gilbert of Warbend, the castle's chaplain and chief record keeper, nervously smoothed the unrolled portion of parchment. "It's a record of the marriage charter, Sir Fulk. Among other things, it confirms that Lady Alyce's dowry includes the manors of Prestin, Mantock, and Little Drayeton, and lists the dower granted by Master War—"

Sir Fulk snorted in disgust. "All done in fancy Latin, I see. Got to keep the lawyers happy, eh, Gilbert?"

Gilbert twitched. If he could have, Alyce knew he would have stuck a finger in his mouth and gnawed on whatever remnant of nail he might have, but Sir Fulk terrorized him too much for him to risk it. "Yes, milord." He swallowed. His Adam's apple bobbed like a ball on a string. "You'll remember the difficulty we had over the land your good father willed to the abbey."

Sir Fulk's mouth twisted in derision. He shot an indignant look at Wardell. "Damned bloodsucking Abbott Baldwin took five good manors, and all because my fool of a father decided his immortal soul was at risk and signed some scrap of parchment when I wasn't here to stop him. Tried to fight it in court, but that weeviling priest waved the parchment in their faces and that was that."

"Good records are good business, milord," Wardell replied, clearly unimpressed by Sir Fulk's ire.

"And you'll make sure to get good records, eh, Wardell?"

Was it only her imagination, Alyce wondered, or did Wardell's eyes narrow slightly, as if in anger, or disdain?

"Of course. It's for your daughter's protection as much as for yours and mine, after all."

"Alyce?" Fulk's head jerked upward with his surprise. He glanced at her, then looked away dismissively. "She'd have been better off if her grandfather and his father before him had paid less attention to their souls and more to their heirs' future."

Wardell maintained an icy silence. Alyce fixed her gaze on the rushes beneath her feet, trying to ignore the indignant sniffs and sympathetic rustlings from her women, who were seated on stools to either side of her. Her father had always blamed *his* father and grandfather for his financial troubles, even though it was his own passion for grubbing every possible pence out of his lands that had plunged him into his present difficulties. Fulk's improvident habits, reinforced by his talent for antagonizing everyone who might have been of use to him, were what had left her unmarried for so long. And it was his own lack of concern for her future that had made her, in the end, willing to marry a merchant and to submit to this humiliating bartering of her body and soul rather than remain unwed.

When he received no response to his complaints, Sir Fulk bent once more to the task at hand. Using the dull red wax that he preferred, he carefully sealed and countersealed one of the two dangling strips of parchment cut from the base of the document, then did the same for a second parchment roll that would serve as Wardell's copy of the marriage charter.

Back and shoulders aching with tension, Alyce watched his every move. So many years of waiting, so many months of planning and wondering and worrying— all bound up in a piece of parchment, a blob of pressed wax, and the few words that would be exchanged at the castle's chapel.

Her gaze followed Gilbert as he carried the parchment rolls to the other end of the table and carefully laid them out for inspection.

Robert Wardell took no more time over the documents than Sir Fulk had, but from the way he scanned the writing it was clear he, unlike her father, could read as easily as Gilbert. He set his seal in yellow wax on the second dangling strip of the first parchment, then rolled the document and set it to one side.

Gilbert unrolled the second parchment and stepped back, hands respectfully crossed before him. Wardell poured the hot wax and picked up his heavy brass seal.

Alyce could *feel* the sudden, breathless stillness that claimed the hall's occupants as they watched. Her own breath stuck in her throat, a hard knot she couldn't choke down. Her hands trembled uncontrollably until she buried them in her lap.

Wardell swung the seal over the parchment. Alyce watched, frozen in place like a hare mesmerized by the fox's stealthy approach. A candle flared, glinting on the hard metal in his hand. A handsbreadth more and the seal would press into the soft puddle of yellow wax, reshaping it and changing the course her life would take through all the years that lay ahead.

At the last moment, Wardell paused. He raised his head and for the first time turned and looked directly at her.

Crowned in the light of the dying sun, he stared at her across the empty space that separated them. For one wild instant Alyce thought she could see the candles' fire burning in his eyes, but it was—had to be—a trick of the light and her own disordered senses. She laced her fingers together, desperate for something to hold on to, and stared back.

His lips parted ever so slightly, as if he wanted to speak, but could not force the words out. Then he took a deep breath and turned away from her. His gaze bent to the parchment and he pressed the seal into the wax.

It required only a moment more to affix the counter-seal, roll up the second parchment, and set it beside the first. Alyce could see the parchment strips at the bottom of each charter tangled on the table, their red and yellow seals tossed together like large, dull coins. They weren't as impressive as the pile of silver pennies at the other end of the table, but they were far more potent in their ability to reshape the lives of the humans they touched.

Sir Fulk slammed his hands down on the table and shoved back his chair, roaring with satisfaction. "A wedding, by God! We'll have a wedding, then!"

His words set loose the silent multitude that had gathered to watch the proceedings. Suddenly everyone was moving and talking and laughing, their noise echoing in the rafters overhead.

Everyone but Alyce and Robert Wardell. They sat mute, eyes locked on each other, with all the questions it would take a lifetime to answer hanging in the air between them.

THE WEDDING CEREMONY was held at the entrance to Colmaine's small chapel. The setting sun gilded the gray stones in a gentle benediction as the castle folk pressed close around them.

"I take thee Alyce to my wedded wife . . ."

The words seemed to Alyce to come from far away, as insubstantial as dreams, whispering on the air like soft mist at morning.

". . . from this day forward, for better or worse . . ."

Gilbert stood in the open doorway of the chapel, sweating nervously. She could see the tiny drops that had beaded on his high forehead in spite of the coolness of the approaching evening. Strange that she'd never noticed the fine lines that scored his brow. After so many years, she would have thought she knew everything about the people of Colmaine.

". . . in sickness and in health . . ."

Beyond Gilbert, she could see the glow of the candles on the altar. Their flames swayed and dipped, seeming to set the painted figures on the chapel's whitewashed walls into motion. Alyce couldn't tell if the familiar images that she had known since childhood were leaping in celebration of her marriage, or writhing at their inability to put their warnings into words she could understand.

". . . and thereto I plight thee my troth."

Alyce watched the dancing shadows in the chapel, waiting for whatever words would follow. Silence trembled on the air, an almost tangible thing.

"Lady Alyce?" Gilbert whispered. His gnawed fingers, laced together as though he were praying, dug into the backs of his hands.

Alyce frowned. She could hear the shuffling of feet as the people gathered around her shifted nervously. There was something she was supposed to say . . . Ah! She remembered now.

"I take thee Robert to my wedded husband . . ."

She got to the end without faltering, but she wasn't sure if she was truly speaking, or if someone else was uttering this strange litany that seemed so lacking in sense.

She heard a soft exhalation of air, as though someone beside her had been holding his breath. She turned and found herself looking up into a hard face made vulnerable by the naked emotion that shone in a pair of night-dark eyes. For a moment she stared, not moving, not even blinking, then this man, this stranger, bent to take her hand.

At his touch, awareness returned with gut-wrenching force. Alyce dragged in a searing breath. Not a dream, then, but reality.

With her left hand firmly clasped in his, Robert Wardell slipped an intricately woven gold ring over her first finger, then her second, and finally onto her ring finger as he spoke the words that would bind them, each to the other, forever.

"In the name of the Father, and the Son, and the Holy Ghost," he said, "with this ring, I thee wed."

3

A BLESSING...

FOR ROBERT, THE wedding mass passed in a dull haze, like something vaguely seen and heard at a distance. He knew where he was and what he was doing, but his mind insisted on tormenting him with the memories of another bride.

He could remember the day he'd first met Jocelyn as clearly as if it were yesterday.

He'd been a frightened, knobby-kneed boy of ten when his father had hauled him through the streets of London to present him to James Ancroft, alderman and master merchant. Master Ancroft had no sons and was in want of a likely apprentice who could help him in his business of buying and selling the costly fabrics that the wealthy craved. Robert's father had agreed to pay the steep fee for apprenticing his son to such a distinguished merchant, but the agreement was contingent on Robert being found worthy of so exalted a position. To that end, Robert and his father had been summoned into Master Ancroft's presence for an interview.

That morning, Robert had scrubbed his face until it stung, combed his hair thrice over, tied and retied his hose, then quietly thrown up his breakfast in the alley behind his father's house.

He'd tried to put on a brave front as he followed his father across London, tried to look bright and clever and trustworthy when he made his bow to the beak-nosed old man who sat huddled in a fur-lined cloak before the fire. He'd failed miserably at both. It hadn't helped that his father had been stern and not overly laudatory of his only son, saying that he, Robert, was hardworking and honest and reasonably sharp with his studies when forced to it, but somewhat overinclined to a bullheaded disregard for rules, and possessed of a lamentable proclivity for spending his free time wandering the docks or prowling around Newgate's stocks and gibbets instead of working at his Latin and his numbers.

Looking back, Robert suspected his father had been as nervous as he, anxious to secure the future of his beloved child, but unwilling to appear too fawning and indulgent. At the time, however, Robert had cringed in his new shoes and wished himself anywhere but where he was. Dead, preferably, or even bound to those same humiliating Newgate stocks. Anything rather than hear his transgressions detailed to a stranger.

Master Ancroft had leaned toward him, eyes black and beady as a hawk's, beaky nose quivering, and demanded he step forward for inspection. There'd been nothing left in his stomach, but Robert had felt his bowels gurgle unpleasantly and been terrified he would shit himself right there in front of God and Master Ancroft.

And that was when eight-year-old Jocelyn had walked into the room.

It was as though the sun had burst forth, or the Holy Virgin had appeared on the altar in the middle of mass. Robert's mouth had fallen open, the sour-faced steward who'd stood behind his master's chair had beamed, and in an instant Master Ancroft himself had been transformed from a ravenous bird of prey to a contented pigeon cooing at the feet of a golden saint.

Jocelyn had crossed to her father's side, sweetly oblivious of the dumbstruck boy who stared at her with the wonderment of a peasant privileged to look at the queen. Robert couldn't remember what small favor she'd begged of her father. It didn't matter. Whatever Jocelyn had wanted, she'd gotten, always. Had she asked for the moon, Robert suspected her father would have found a way to drag it down and put it safe in a treasure box, all for her.

Once her wish was granted and Jocelyn had thanked her father, she'd turned to study the unprepossessing boy who stared at her in gape-mouthed adoration.

"Who are you?" she'd asked, her blue eyes wide and guileless, her voice sweeter than the clearest bells.

"R-Robert Wardell, my lady, a-and it pleases you," he'd stammered as he sank down on one knee before her.

"I like you," she'd said. "Have you come to stay?"

And that had decided the matter. Robert had, indeed, come to stay.

Many things changed in the years that had followed. He'd grown from a spindly-shanked boy into a broad-shouldered, long-legged, confident man. His father had died, leaving Robert his small house and smaller savings. Jocelyn had blossomed into a delicate and glorious womanhood, while Master Ancroft had grown frail, withdrawing into his books and the pleasures of his daughter's company and leaving the running of his business to Robert's canny administration. The business itself had flourished. It wasn't long before the other merchants consulted and followed Robert's advice, not that of the old man who had taught him his trade.

But one thing didn't change—Robert's adoration of the radiant Jocelyn.

She had grown to love him as well, though it was a shy and gentle love that kept him at a safe distance, worshipful, yet unthreatening. Her world was bound up in her prayers and her father and her beloved garden, and Robert, like everything else she cared for, was relegated to the outer edges of her existence, treasured and trusted . . . and taken utterly for granted. At times, frustrated by her passionless, unworldly calm, Robert found himself envying her small lapdog for the kisses and caresses she so freely bestowed on the little creature, yet denied him.

It was only as Master Ancroft lay dying that he at last gave his consent for Robert to marry his daughter. Not because he wished to see his daughter wed, or because he thought Robert was worthy of her, but because the old man knew she would need someone to care for her and protect her once he was gone.

Robert had known, even then, that Jocelyn did not love him half so well—nor a tenth so passionately—as he loved her. He had thought it did not matter. Afraid as he'd been that she would enter a convent rather than wed, he'd been near delirious with joy when Master Ancroft informed him that he might take her to wife instead of seeing her given as a bride to Christ.

Only later had Robert realized she could never have endured the demands and limitations of convent life. Jocelyn loved her pleasures, loved being at the center of her own universe, the sun beside which all the stars about her paled to insignificance. She would not have tolerated having anything in her life that was more important than she. Not even God.

Their wedding had been a quiet affair, with Jocelyn's father borne to the church on a litter to hear their vows and the wedding mass, then quickly taken home and put to bed again, wheezing and gasping from the strain of it. There'd been no feast, no guests, no gifts.

Their wedding night had been a disaster.

Robert had sought to restrain himself, to control his aching, impassioned hunger for her. For delicate, sheltered Jocelyn, it had not been enough. His nakedness and his inescapable masculine arousal had frightened her. When he'd snuffed the candle and drawn the bed curtains around them, the darkness had made her whimper in terror.

He'd spent what had seemed hours soothing and kissing and gently touching her, trying to calm her fears and rouse a physical need in her to match the almost unbearable need in him. He'd tried every trick in his admittedly limited bag of sexual knowledge to prepare her, yet when he'd claimed her at last, she'd shrieked and beat at his chest and shoulders as if she fought a marauder bent on rape and murder.

By then, he hadn't been able to stop. Years of pent-up longing had exploded within him, shattering his self-control. He'd thrust into her, over and over again while Jocelyn—his sweet, fragile, beautiful, pampered Jocelyn—had lain limp and unresponsive beneath him, with only her sobs to accompany his agonized groans and anxious, hastening grunts.

The next morning, she had her maid move his few clothes and possessions back to the cubbyhole at the side of the hall that he'd occupied since he first came as apprentice, all those years before.

Her father died three days later.

For weeks after, Robert dared not touch her nor even speak to her. She avoided him, barricading herself in her room with her maid and refusing to respond to his anguished entreaties, his shouted demands, his tormented, whispered pleas. In the end, he gave up speaking altogether, bereft of words and any hope that they would pierce the solid oak of her bedchamber door or her wounded, frightened heart. Her meals were often sent back to the kitchen untouched.

But nothing, not even pain, lasts forever. Eventually she emerged, red-eyed and wan, to scurry to mass like a mouse forced out of its hole by hunger despite the cat that lurked outside, waiting to devour it. That was as far as she ventured. Even her beloved garden lay forgotten, left to the plundering pigeons and the rude mercies of the gardener and his helper.

Jocelyn could not keep herself walled up forever, though. Gradually, reassured by Robert's hard-won self-restraint and adrift without her father's familiar presence, she turned back to him for comfort and support. He, a disarmed knight left naked at her feet, blessed God and welcomed her back with tears starting in his eyes.

The day she first allowed him to kiss her, more than a year after their wedding, Robert charged out of the house and down the street to the church, exultant as a new-made king. He'd spent three shillings ten pence—every penny he had in his purse—on fat wax candles of thanksgiving. He could still remember how his blood had raced through his veins as he set those candles at the feet of Jocelyn's favorite velvet-robed virgin, how his heart had thundered in his chest as he carefully lit them, one after the other, then watched as their flames carried his silent prayers heavenward.

The pence and prayers were wasted. Jocelyn had dealt with the fright of her wedding night, not by coming to terms with it, but by forgetting it ever happened. Instead of eventually being welcomed back into her bed as he'd expected, Robert found he'd been assigned the role her father had left vacant with his death—he was allowed to serve as Jocelyn's protector and indulgent companion, to shower her with costly gifts and fulfill her every whim, but he was never, ever to be permitted the rights his marriage vows had given him.

Jocelyn never said it that clearly, of course. She simply drifted in her safe, secret world and ignored his existence except when it served her to remember it.

And he went mad because of it. That was the only word for it. He was a man, not a bloodless saint, and he loved as a man would love. He wanted Jocelyn. He *needed* her. She was the center of his dreams, the prize for which he'd striven all those years, the proof that his labors had been rewarded by something other than cold silver.

One night, after hours spent in the company of fellow merchants who had decided to hide their debauches under the guise of a guild meeting, the last, frail strand of his self-control snapped. Driven by a lust that made his bones burn with wanting her, he charged back through the nighttime streets, burst into his house—*her* house—and into her room. He physically threw her maid from the room, then locked and barred the door.

And then he took Jocelyn against her will, against her pleading and her tears and her prayers, against her desperate, panicked struggles to get free—and in the taking, he destroyed the thing he had most wanted to possess.

He never touched her again. She died in premature childbirth four months later, drenched in her own red blood and crying for mercy from a merciless heaven. He stayed outside her chamber through the long hours of her last agony, listening to her screams and her prayers and her curses, wanting to curse God, but knowing that he alone was responsible for the destruction of the frail and beautiful creature that had been entrusted into his keeping.

For weeks after, he'd longed for the release of death, but God gave him a far more painful penance—He forced him to live with his memories.

Robert found he wasn't even to be granted the relief of confession. Instead of exacting a harsh and painful penance as he'd expected—as he'd *wanted*—the priests to whom he crept, one after the other, assured him that he'd endured far more than a reasonable man should be expected to endure. Since neither he nor Jocelyn had ever taken a vow of chastity, it had been his duty, they said, to get a child on his wife, and hers to accept him into her bed. Perhaps he'd been too rough, too hasty, but she had sinned in denying him. Five Hail Marys, a candle for the altar, and a small contribution to the church in the name of the Son and His Virgin Mother would be more than sufficient. Go and sin no more, they said . . . and find yourself another wife who can bear you sons for the greater glory of God and Holy Mother Church.

Robert glanced at the pale, slender woman who knelt at his side, head proudly high, unblinking gaze fixed on the crude statue of the Virgin that hung above Colmaine's small altar.

It had taken him twelve years, but he had, at last, obeyed their injunction to take a wife.

THE GARDEROBE WAS not a place to which Alyce normally retreated for privacy, but now it served as her only refuge. At least she'd had the castle's gong man clean out the cesspits the day before. The dried herbs she'd had laid in the room sweetened the night air pouring in through the high, unshuttered window.

Perched on the edge of the broad stone seat of the privy, she stared out the window at the sliver of sky beyond and tried to bring some sense out of the turmoil within her.

The thump and roar of the merrymaking in the hall were muffled, muted by distance, thick stone walls, and the winding stairways between. A waning moon provided her only illumination—she had doused the tallow candle she'd brought. The wavering shadows it cast had reminded her all too clearly of the images in the chapel.

Alyce squeezed her hands into fists, but opened them instantly when her wedding ring pinched the fold of flesh at the base of her finger. She hesitated, just for a moment, then traced the metal band with the tip of her thumb, testing its hard curve and delicate detailing.

She was married. The marriage charter was signed,

the vows spoken, the mass celebrated in full view of her father, the guests, and the people of Colmaine. Tonight was her wedding night. Tomorrow she would leave for London in the company of a man she did not know . . . a stranger who happened to be her husband.

She pressed the ring hard against her finger, until it seemed to dig into the bone itself.

Robert Wardell had placed that ring upon her finger. He had taken her hand in his, and his touch, the heat and solid strength of him, had burned away the confused mists that had claimed her. She'd clung to him throughout the mass, and again when he had led her from the chapel to the keep, through the gathered well-wishers and the torchlit darkness.

She had endured a second feast, less elaborate than the first, but far rowdier as both guests and castle folk set aside restraint and drank deep of the ale and wine. They'd listened with respect while Taverel, the minstrel, sang songs of courtly love and chivalrous deeds, but they'd preferred the wilder antics of the jugglers and the dwarf that followed. Now they were dancing, and the evening promised to turn even more uproarious. From past experience, Alyce knew the wedding jokes were growing bawdier with each telling and the thought made her cheeks flush with heat.

She would have to return ere long. The newlywed couple was expected to leave the festivities early. There was the wedding bed—*her* bed—to be blessed, then her women would help her undress and make sure the small chamber that she usually shared with the two of them was ready to receive her new husband. And then . . .

Alyce pressed her hands against a sudden, uneasy tightening of her stomach muscles.

How would he come to her? Cold-eyed and inscrutable? Courteous, yet distant? Or would he risk revealing the man she'd seen so briefly before he slid the ring on her finger?

Had she really seen that flash of vulnerability, that need? She'd dreamed of wedding a brave and chivalrous knight, and now she found herself tied to a merchant almost half again her age. Whom had Robert Wardell dreamed of? What had he wanted? And why had he gone to such costly lengths to marry her?

Strange, she'd never thought to ask herself those questions before.

She had no chance to consider them now. A drunken curse echoed in the stairway, then another, jerking her back to awareness of the present. She caught the scuffle of shoes on the stairs and the rough scrape of metal against stone as someone staggered against the wall outside the garderobe. Clumsy hands fumbled at the barred door. When the door didn't open, the man thumped the wood in frustration.

For an instant there was silence, then another curse and the rustle of clothing, immediately followed by the splash of a small stream hitting stones as the unknown male gave up his struggle for self-control and relieved himself against the wall. He'd drunk deeply and well; it seemed to go on forever. Alyce tried, and failed, to shut out the sound of it. When he finally finished, he sighed with satisfaction, rearranged his clothes, then stumbled back down the stairs.

Alyce sighed as well, but not in relief, and reluctantly rose to her feet. Just as well whoever it was had interrupted her. She had to get back to the hall before someone noticed she'd been gone far too long.

She lifted the wooden bar that served as a lock and peeped out into the unlit stairway. No one was near, so far as she could tell. Her eyes were already adapted to the dark, but the stairwell, with only an occasional arrow slit in place of windows, was much darker than the garderobe had been. The stink of fresh, hot urine was sharp in the enclosed space.

Alyce scowled. Trust a man to piss on things, even when he had to work to get there to do it.

With one hand on the curving stone wall, she cautiously felt her way down the steeply winding steps, taking care to keep to the inside, away from the likely downhill path of her unknown visitor's contribution.

The stairwell eventually gave on to a short passage that opened into the hall itself. Just before Alyce rounded the last curve in the stairs, a distinctive deep voice coming from the passage stopped her.

"Trying to run away already, Robert?" the voice said. "Or are you going in search of your new bride?"

Alyce shrank back, heart racing. She recognized the voice. It belonged to one of the men who had accompanied Robert Wardell. She tried to think of his name. William. That was it. William Townsend. She had no trouble figuring out which "Robert" he was addressing.

"Neither, my friend," Wardell said lightly. "But you've been dipping rather deeper than I thought if there's now talk of my running away. You know me better than that."

"Christ's blood, man! Do you take me for a fool?" Townsend hesitated, then burst out, "What quirk of brain fever has brought you to this, Robert? This isn't your usual madness, and don't try to tell me it is!" He gave a harsh bark that, with him, must pass for laughter. "Not at *all* your usual madness. I'll wager even your wedding bed is amply supplied with fleas and lice and bedbugs!"

"I'll not take the bet," Alyce's husband replied. She couldn't miss the note of scornful amusement in his voice. "But whatever its deficiencies, it comes equipped with my bride and should be more comfortable than the bench you'll sleep on."

Townsend snorted. "Pray God I'm lucky enough to

grab a bench. I've no desire to sleep in those rushes. The top layer's fresh enough, but Lucifer himself would scarce have the courage to find out what lies beneath."

"It's for one night only. It seems your stomach has grown weak in your old age. I don't remember you being so muddle-brained and particular when we were younger."

His companion chuckled. "Aye, that's true enough. A comfortable bed and regular baths have unmanned me, but if fleas and filth are the price of regaining my manhood, I'll call it a good bargain and argue no more."

"And what think you of *my* bargain?"

"Your bride? I'd scarce call it a bargain. She's cost you a small fortune and at the end of it, she's no beauty. Not like Jocelyn was."

Silence, then, "No. She's no beauty." The sudden note of strain was unmistakable.

Townsend might have shrugged. Alyce could hear the dismissal in his voice.

"I can't grasp your thinking, Robert. I swear I've tried. What can you gain by allying yourself with this paltry nobleman? Baron of Colmaine? A fool could make a better jest than that! Fitzwarren's lands are poorly managed and his honors hardly worth the name. He has no real influence, not even with Montfort and his fellow barons, no matter how much he prates of it."

Wardell murmured something, but Alyce couldn't catch it.

Townsend snorted in disgust. "After this rebellion, the king and Lord Edward won't welcome him back—assuming they've won, of course. You've the connections *and* the money to buy your own knighthood. What can you possibly gain by this rash marriage?"

For a moment, the only sound was the merrymaking in the hall. "I'll gain what I want, my friend," Wardell said at last. "Have no fear."

"It's not I who's afraid, Robert," his friend said dryly, "but I can't help wondering who it is that should be."

I'LL GAIN WHAT I want.

Easy words to say—the devil knew he'd lived by them for long enough—yet never had they rung so hollow.

Robert crossed his arms over his chest, slumped against the cold stone wall outside the Lady Alyce's chamber, and stared into the dark.

On the other side of the wall was the bride he'd bought and paid for, just as he paid for the bolts of silk and samite and fine wool that were the heart of his business. He was a practical man and this marriage was a practical solution for what lay ahead.

A practical solution.

At the thought of the Lady Alyce, Robert winced. His grip on his arms tightened as he pressed back against the unyielding stones. His breath came faster, burning in his chest; his belly twisted in protest.

Through all these months of scheming, he'd thought of his bride as one more piece in the game he played, a token shifted to his advantage on the board whenever it served him, forgotten when there were other, more powerful pieces to be used. He'd thought to continue thus, but he'd been mistaken. It would never be that simple again now that he'd faced her, now that he'd touched her hand and heard her voice and looked into her eyes.

Especially not now that he'd looked into her eyes, green and deep and dark as a moss-bound stream. He'd seen the pride and the anger in those eyes . . . and the fear. The same fear that had shown in Jocelyn's eyes the day he wedded her . . . and again on the night he bedded her against her will, in spite of the fear.

Fourteen years since he'd taken his beautiful Jocelyn to wife—a full twelve since she'd died and left the indelible marks of her blood upon his soul—yet he'd thought himself safe against her protests to this loveless marriage.

He'd been wrong. If he closed his eyes, he knew he'd see her before him on the stairs, a golden radiance to mock his darkness.

Robert forced his eyes wider and stared into the black.

Not black. A faint dribble of light crept up from below, curving round the stairs. A tiny sliver seeped under the door of his lady's chamber, staining the stones at his feet. On the other side of the iron-barred oaken door was his bride, preparing to welcome him to his bridal bed, while the merrymaking in the hall below was like to make the foundations of the old keep tremble, so loud and frenzied was it.

Yet here he stood at the edge of light and warmth and noise, husband, merchant, master . . . and fool, to think he could so easily slip the bonds of the past.

Pace, Jocelyn, he murmured into the dark. Peace.

She was only a nobleman's daughter, after all. A nobleman's daughter and nothing more.

He would have her name to protect what he'd built and her manors to increase his own. He would have her to breed him sons.

That was all he needed of her. All he'd ever needed of anyone . . . save Jocelyn.

THE BED WAS blessed—Alyce could see the dark splotches of holy water on the pillows and covers—and the witnesses had returned to the hall below.

Robert Wardell stood outside her little chamber, waiting for Maida and Hilde to finish with the few tasks remaining—making sure the wooden shutters were closed, her clothes hung out of the way, and the few candles, especially the two on the tall iron stands near the bed, were lit.

As far as Alyce was concerned, he could wait until Lucifer abandoned Hell and the Holy Apostles came to dine at Castle Colmaine.

She huddled on the edge of the bed, naked and shivering, and glared at the sweet rushes on the floor—a floor of fresh-washed stone, should Master Townsend care to inquire! Here, at least, she could run matters as she pleased, and it had always pleased her to lay fresh rushes each week, just as she required that the servants regularly wash the bed linen and air the beds and blankets and furs. There were no vermin in her chamber and never had been.

"Come, milady. Under the covers before you freeze. No sense dying from ill humors in the lungs before you've seen the sights of London!"

Startled, Alyce glanced up to find fat Maida looming over her. That round, cheery face had comforted her through a hundred disasters, but Alyce found no comfort in her cheerfulness now. In fact, it seemed unbearably heartless of the woman to be so pleased with life, under the circumstances.

Little, wizened Hilde, bright blue eyes alight with excitement, gave a last pat to the clothes she'd hung with such care on their pegs, then bustled across the room and bent close to Alyce. "I saw his hands, milady," she whispered. "His thumbs, especially. Nicely rounded, they are, and solid. Very long fingers he has too, which is a good sign the Lord has blessed him."

Maida sniffed indignantly. "A wonder you didn't lift the skirts of his tunic, just to make sure."

Hilde instantly straightened, equally indignant. "As if you weren't just as interested, though why you think the thickness of a man's lower lip is any safe way to judge such matters, *I've* yet to understand." She turned back to Alyce. "You can judge by the size of the great toe as well, milady, as I've told you time and time. It's a sure sign, indeed it is."

Alyce, conscious of an uncomfortable heat in her face, couldn't help inquiring, "And have you seen his toe, then, Hilde?"

"No, milady." Hilde shook her head regretfully. "But I could see the bulge of it in his shoe, and it seemed promising!"

"By the time the Lady Alyce has inspected his great toe, she'll already have had a chance to inspect his tarse, Hilde." Maida's scorn would have been lethal for anyone less hardened than Hilde. "But she'll never have a chance to do either if you continue this senseless chatter and keep milady's husband freezing both tarse and toes in the stairwell."

At the pointed reminder, Hilde flushed. She glanced at the door as though she feared the expectant bridegroom might suddenly burst into the room, but she wasn't ready to give up yet.

"You remember what I've told you, now, milady. It's only the first time that hurts, and Master Wardell is of an age to know what he's about. Let him guide matters, at least at the first, and soon enough—"

"And soon enough she'll die of the cold and your wagging tongue," Maida interrupted. She leaned past Alyce and pulled the heavy bedcovers down. "Come now, milady. There's no sense trying to put off your new husband by listening to Hilde's prattling. A man's temper doesn't improve by being kept waiting."

Reluctantly, Alyce did as she was bid, letting her women plump up the thick feather pillows against the wall so that she was half sitting, half reclining, with the blankets pulled up over her breasts and her arms free. She clutched the covers tight under her chin when Hilde tried to pull them lower, then realized her hands were trembling—and not just from the cold.

Maida carefully arranged her braid so it lay on top of the covers. As she gave a final pat to the lustrous red-gold tresses, she blinked several times, fighting against tears. Her mouth compressed into a funny, twisted smile.

"Ah, milady," she said with watery maternal pride. "To think you're married at last." She squeezed her hands together under her vast bosom and sighed. "And such a fine, rich man who won't be spending all his time galloping around the country in search of another senseless fight like your lord father, may the saints protect him."

It was Hilde's turn to sniff indignantly. "*Now* who's keeping Master Wardell waiting, I'd like to know?" The little serving woman grabbed Maida's sleeve and tried to pull her away from the bed.

Maida jerked free of Hilde's grasp and bent to pat Alyce's hand. "God bless you, milady. You and your husband."

Hilde echoed the sentiment, then once more tugged on Maida's sleeve, more urgently this time. Alyce shut her eyes, hoping her own thoughts weren't as clearly written on her face as Maida's and Hilde's were on theirs.

She heard their rustling footsteps cross the floor and the creak of the door's iron hinges, but it was the cold draft of air sailing through the chamber that snapped her eyes back open.

Robert Wardell stood alone in the open doorway, stiff and proud and undeniably imposing. Candlelight flashed on the gold embroidery of his tunic. The fine scarlet cloth shone bright as fresh blood, vivid against the dull gray stone of the chamber's walls.

Perhaps it was the dark of the stairwell behind him, or a trick of the flickering candles, but his skin looked paler, his eyes more sunken and black as the night. His gaze flicked to Alyce, then away, scanning the small room as if he were seeing it for the first time.

And perhaps he was, Alyce thought. There'd been so many people earlier, when Gilbert had blessed their marriage bed, that it had been almost impossible to breathe.

Now there was only the two of them.

4

...AND A
BEDDING

THE SIGHT OF a wide-eyed and wary Alyce, half buried under the mounded covers of her shabby bed, stopped Robert in the doorway. His hands tightened around the small tray with the two crude earthenware cups and the jug of wine he'd brought.

He'd gone hunting once when a nobleman, in a fit of drunken good cheer, had insisted on dragging half his guests along with him. Robert remembered it vividly. They'd coursed for what seemed like hours, until the deer had stopped at last and turned to face them, legs trembling, too exhausted to run farther.

Despite its terror, its head had been high, its eyes wide and dark and alive. Its coat had gleamed in the sun, rich red against the dark forest.

An instant later the dogs had dragged it down and ripped out its throat.

Alyce watched him as that doomed doe had, terrified, defiant, yet resigned to her fate. He'd had no hand in the slaughter then and he had no taste for the slaughter now, but it was too late to retreat. He'd sicced that dog of a priest on her, hunting her down for his own purposes until he'd finally brought her to bay. Now he needs must end it, whether he would or no.

He could feel the muscles in his shoulders tighten and an ache that wasn't passion stir somewhere deep in his belly.

It would be best if he did it quickly, and as gently as he could. She was nineteen, a goodly age to still be a maid. God grant that would not make matters more difficult than they already were.

With careful deliberation, Robert set the tray on a nearby chest and turned to shut the door.

ALYCE'S GRIP ON the covers tightened. She thought his hand trembled, but decided it must be a trick of the light. Robert Wardell was not a man to let so slight a thing as a cold draft affect him. She wasn't fool enough to think he was nervous.

Without speaking, he poured out the wine he'd brought. As he walked to the bed, he carried a cup in each hand.

"Milady," he said, extending one toward her.

Alyce eyed the cup, uncertain. She remembered all too clearly the way his fingers had brushed against hers when she had offered him the wine that morning.

Her rejection didn't seem to bother him. Still holding both cups, he claimed the edge of the bed as a seat. The frame creaked as the leather webbing beneath the heavy wool-stuffed mattress adjusted to his weight.

Alyce swallowed nervously. The bed frame never made this much protest except when fat Maida shared the bed with her. It seemed Robert Wardell was more solidly built than he appeared.

"Come, Lady Alyce," he said gently, extending the cup once more. "It's only wine. The same red wine you gave me in welcome this very morning. Surely it hasn't soured so quickly that you would refuse my offer of it now."

Reluctantly, with one hand still clutching the covers

to her breast, Alyce took the cup from him. In her effort not to touch him, she almost spilled the wine. She dropped the covers and grabbed for the cup. For one agonizing instant, she feared she'd lost both, but somehow modesty and wine survived.

She could tell by the faint twitch at the corner of Robert Wardell's mouth that her dignity had not.

As heat suffused her face and throat, Alyce buried her nose in the cup and tried to ignore him. Her ploy didn't work. How could she ignore a man sitting so close to her, especially when he was clothed and she was not?

She lowered her cup to find him watching her. His gaze dropped to her neck, then to her shoulder and the freckle-blotched white skin above her breasts that she'd inadvertently revealed when she'd let go of the bedcovers. His gaze slid lower, then lower still to her hand and the cup of wine she held.

Before she realized what he was about, he rubbed his finger across the soft web of flesh between her thumb and forefinger, blotting up the drops of wine that she had slopped over the edge of the cup with her clumsiness.

His touch was as feather-light as it had been that morning, and just as unsettling. An odd tingling swept through Alyce's hand and up her arm; her lungs struggled to take in air. Worse, down between her legs something contracted with startling force, shooting a strange new heat through her belly and thighs.

Seemingly unaware of the effect his touch had produced in her, Robert Wardell licked the traces of wine off his finger. Alyce watched, enthralled. Watched his tongue curve around his finger and over the top, once, twice, then a third time. Watched the way he held his hand—the hand that Hilde swore bore promise of other, more carnal pleasures. Watched the way his mouth opened and his lips moved. Watched the line his teeth made, white against sun-browned skin.

And with each stroke of his tongue, each subtle twist of his hand, the heat in her veins increased and the ache between her legs grew, then grew again, disorienting in its intensity.

He finished his catlike efforts at cleaning, then let his hand drop to the covers only inches from her leg. As he took a sip of his own wine, he watched her over the rim of his cup.

Except for that one light brush of his finger across her skin, he hadn't touched her, yet he held her trapped against the pillows nonetheless, breathless and heated and aching, crushed beneath the weight of the covers she clutched so firmly to her chest.

Her fingers tightened their grip on the covers and her cup of wine. Her lungs burned with the effort to breathe. She tried to look away from that dark, unsettling gaze and found she could not. Dared not.

Was she mad or was he a sorcerer? No one, not even Hilde, had ever told her that such things were possible. The rough wooing and even rougher swiving she'd seen among the castle folk and the animals they tended had yielded no hints of it, despite the number of times she'd peeked—or outright stared if her curiosity grew too great for her good manners and there was no one to catch her at it.

She stared at Robert Wardell, wondering and half afraid. Of herself, perhaps, as much as him. And he stared back unblinking, a demon or mayhaps one of the ancient gods, cast in gold light and black shadow, hard and unreadable, yet dangerously alive and *aware*. Of her. Of her awareness.

A small, wry smile curved one corner of his mouth. "Three hours wed and we've scarce had a moment to talk. I had not mean to be so . . . inattentive, Lady."

"No," said Alyce. "I mean, I did not think you inattentive, sir. We had no opportunity to—to talk, or to say anything . . . umm . . ."

A muscle at the corner of his mouth quivered. "Anything . . . interesting?"

She nodded.

"Or useful? No time to get to know each other as man and woman before we became man and wife."

"No. I mean, yes!" She blushed and looked down at her hands, knotted around the covers and her wine cup in a grip that should have strangled them both. She forced her fingers to relax and sipped more wine. "You must think me a fool."

"Nay, Lady, never that." He smiled again. "Young, yes, but time will remedy that condition, I do assure you."

The smile transformed his face, softening the harsh-cut features and warming the cold, dark hardness of his eyes. But only for an instant. His smile vanished, and with it the fleeting warmth.

"I will not harm you, milady. On my honor, I swear it. You've no cause to fear either me or what lies ahead."

Alyce jumped, startled by his unexpected fierceness. Her grip on the covers tightened once more. "I didn't think you would. And I don't. Fear you, I mean."

He didn't look as if he believed her.

"I've known what a man's parts look like," she said defensively, "and what he does with them, since I found one of my father's guardsmen tupping the laundry maid when I was six. A nun couldn't live at Colmaine without learning, sooner or late, and I—"

The tender, protected place between her legs throbbed. She could feel the heat spreading. The muscles in her stomach tightened.

"And you . . . ?" he prodded gently.

"And I never wanted to be a nun," she said, letting her gaze drop. His hand rested on the much-mended coverlet, only inches from her thigh. A strong, shapely hand, with long fingers and a well-shaped thumb.

His gaze followed hers, then slid higher, up the mounded covers that hid belly and breast until he met her gaze once more.

"The priests teach that it's women who have the carnal instincts in greatest measure, milady. That they would devour men with their cravings, if they could." He breathed deep. "I have found that is not always true."

Alyce hung on that indrawn breath, waiting.

He let out his breath. "I do not wish to rush you."

"No," she said, as if on a prayer.

In truth, now he was there, she thought he was taking a damnably long time about it. She'd waited nineteen years to learn a woman's secrets firsthand. Robert Wardell might not be the man she'd dreamed would reveal them to her, but he was her husband, and she did not care to wait any longer.

With the easy grace that seemed so much a part of him, he bent and placed his cup of wine on the floor, then straightened and plucked her cup from her unresisting fingers. He glanced down at the cup, then back at her. With tormenting deliberation he lifted it to sip from the side where her mouth had touched, then slowly ran his tongue over his lips to lap up any lingering drops.

Alyce watched, breathless, utterly incapable of looking away.

This time, when he bent to place the second cup beside the first, he didn't straighten. He leaned forward and gently kissed her.

Alyce didn't move. She was afraid to. She'd never kissed a man before, certainly not like Robert Wardell was kissing her. Yet some instinct within her whispered that she *should* kiss him. That she would like it, if only she would try.

Instead, she curled her fingers tighter around the bedcovers and hung on, as if they were a rock that could somehow anchor her to the simple world she'd always known.

He kissed her again and traced the curve of her lower lip with the tip of his tongue.

Alyce's lips parted.

He kissed her a third time.

Alyce moaned and opened her mouth wider, but when he claimed what she had so unthinkingly offered, she gasped and jerked back, frightened by her own ready response.

This close to him, she could see the individual strands in his thick sable brows and lashes, the tracery of silver through the dark, close-cropped curls on his head. The flame from the candle beside the bed reflected in his eyes in drops of molten gold, etched the sharp, unforgiving line of nose and cheek and chin, cast shadows at the corners of his mouth.

Vaguely, she remembered she'd been angry with him, that he was cold and hard, but it was difficult to remember for very long. He wasn't cold now, and his mouth was soft and warm and infinitely tempting. It caressed her chin, the hollow of her cheek, the angle of her jaw. He kissed her neck and traced the line of her shoulder with his tongue, leaving damp heat in his wake.

Alyce closed her eyes. Licking her lips, she tasted wine. That morning she had wondered what it would taste like on his lips. Now she knew. Sweet. Sweet and hot with the heat of him. The richness of it lingered on her tongue.

And still he rained kisses on her. He kissed her fingers and her wrist and the soft, sensitive flesh at the inside of her elbow. He kissed her shoulder once more, and the curve of her throat.

Then he pulled back from her and the bed shifted under his weight, protesting the withdrawal.

Alyce opened her eyes, suddenly bereft.

His own eyes were shut. His head was thrown back and he was breathing hard, nostrils flared, mouth compressed in a tight, forbidding line. The jeweled brooch at the base of his throat sparked fire in rhythm with the rapid rise and fall of his chest. A muscle in his jaw jumped, as if he'd ground his teeth together. He looked like a man on the point of rage, just before self-control snapped and rational thought became impossible.

For an instant, she thought of fleeing, but then his eyes opened as he took a deep, shuddering breath. With sudden resolution, he rose and proceeded to strip off his clothes, tossing the costly garments onto the floor as if they were so many useless rags, until he stood in his braies and nothing more.

He might as well have abandoned those too, for the fine linen hid very little, and failed completely to disguise the jutting, rigid length of his tarse.

Alyce couldn't help herself; she shifted slightly so she could peer over the edge of the bed.

Hilde had been right—in this case, at least. Robert Wardell possessed an impressive great toe. The thought wasn't very comforting, considering the intimidating proportions of the man.

He settled on the edge of the bed once more. For a moment he studied her, as if he wanted to be sure he knew exactly who it was he was bedding and exactly what she looked like. When he spoke, his voice was tight with strain. "It will hurt, you know. At first."

She dragged the covers back under her chin. "I know." Her own voice sounded very small, even to her.

"Sometimes . . ." He stopped and his eyes went blank, like a man remembering something he had tried to forget. "I'll be as gentle as I can, but I can't do anything about the pain."

Why didn't he just begin instead of talking? Alyce wondered. Then it would be over with and the pain would be over with and—

She cut the thought short, conscious of a pang of regret that everything might end so soon. Hilde had warned her of men's tendency to take their pleasures quickly, but she'd never imagined just how frustrating that tendency might be.

To her surprise, Wardell made no effort to douse the candles and climb into bed with her, even though his skin was pricking into bumps that made the dark hairs on his arms and legs stand on end.

He didn't kiss her either. Instead, after a moment's hesitation, he picked up the end of her braid where it lay on the covers, just above her hip.

Alyce drew in her breath sharply, startled by her body's quickening response to so chaste an act.

Carefully, head bent and his eyes fixed on his self-appointed task, he untied the blue silk ribbon that bound her hair, then slowly began to unweave the heavy tresses. Inch by inch, he undid the intricate braid until he could spread the shining mass of red-gold hair out on the blankets like a length of rare silk, bright against the dull brown covers. Just as slowly, he dragged his hand down the length of hair, pressing lightly over her breast and belly and hip as he smoothed out the crinkles the braid had left.

Despite the thick covers that divided him from her, Alyce moaned and arched into his touch, helpless to prevent the wanton, revealing motion or suppress the heat that was consuming her. Once more he traced the fall of her hair, then again, and again, and again. At the moment when Alyce thought she could bear it no longer, he dragged the covers away, swept her hair to the side, and let his mouth and tongue trace the same tormenting path over her breast and down her side and back again.

And where he touched her, bright fire bloomed.

•   •   •

ROBERT SUCKED IN his breath, startled by his new wife's eager response. She flared like tinder beneath his touch, light to his dark, white gold to his black iron.

He had thought her thin and unappealing and plain, but he'd been wrong. Her great green eyes glowed with an inner fire that was all the more startling because it was his touch that had roused it.

Her hair spilled over the pillow and across her breasts and belly, red-gold and copper, russet and roan and a dozen shades for which he had no names. The strands clung to his fingers and caught in the dark hairs of his arms like silken cords, binding him to her.

She tasted like dark gold honey, her hair and skin perfumed from the herbs and dried flowers she'd used in her bath, and heavy with the first trace of a woman's musk.

He had promised himself he would be gentle and patient and understanding of her maiden's fears. He hadn't been prepared for the hunger that drove her to arch against him in an instinctive demand for more than he had thought to give. More than he had *wanted* to give.

Yet he could no more refuse her than he could stop breathing. The fire already burning within him would permit no such cowardice. He slid his hand down her belly to cup her, then delicately probed with one finger. She gasped and arched again, squeezing her eyes shut against the power of her response.

She was ready. More than ready. All she lacked was the knowledge of what came next.

"Open your legs to me, Alyce," he said. "Milady. Like this. Yes. Yes." His voice sounded strained, even to his ears. His tarse tautened until it was a glorious, almost painful ache between his legs. His breath burned in his lungs.

Gently, he told himself, and gritted his teeth. *Gently.*

He shifted above her, spreading her legs farther,

stroking the inside of her thighs. Up and down and up again, then across her belly and back to her thighs, just brushing the dark red curls. She moaned and opened farther still.

He glanced up to find her watching him, eyes so wide they seemed to consume her face. She was chewing on her lower lip, and her chest rose and fell in rapid, shallow grabs for air. She clutched the bed linens on either side of her as tightly as if she was afraid of falling if she ever let go, yet she did not look away or plead for mercy. There was more fire in her than fear, and he had the sudden, sure sense that even if the fear had reigned, she would not have yielded to it.

He shifted to kneel between her legs, then leaned forward, sliding his hands under her hips, up her back, then down again, lifting her and pulling her into position. Taking a deep breath, he thrust forward, careful of her untried flesh, but implacable, giving her no opportunity to wrench free of him.

Halfway in, the unseen membrane barred farther passage. He shoved harder, testing it, unwilling to thrust too hard for fear of tearing her, yet fighting against his own urgent need to plunge deep, sucked in by the exquisite tightness that held him in her heat. He could feel the sweat beading on his brow. The muscles of his hips and thighs trembled with the effort at self-control.

Alyce whimpered, arching in protest at the pain. The involuntary movement opened her to him. He thrust again, harder this time. The barrier ripped apart and he plunged home.

Robert groaned, a deep rumble to her sharper cry, then he slid his hands up her back again, holding her against him as he kissed her breast, her throat, the side of her mouth, waiting, stilling the heat within him while her body adjusted to his rude invasion.

"Be at ease, lady," he soothed, though his own body

was strung tight as a bowstring. "It will be better in a moment. Just a moment." He nipped at her earlobe, then ran the tip of his tongue around the ear's outer curve, touched the inner well.

She sucked in her breath. He could feel the muscles that gripped him relax under the distraction of this new wonder. Like a swimmer clinging to her last, best hope of rescue, she let go of the bed linens and wrapped her arms around his shoulders, drawing him against her. His chest hair grazed her nipples, stirring a pulse in him that made her tense again. Her eyes were wide with wonder.

He began to move inside her, slowly at first, letting her learn the rhythm while he explored her mouth, her chin, the carved line of her neck and shoulder. Her hair tangled and slid between them, a delicate, erotic brushing that teased at his heated senses. His blood was racing, thundering through his veins and pooling with mindnumbing force in his tarse, making him ache and throb, relentlessly driving out all thought of her innocence in the desire to carry her with him, to never stop, to go on and on and on.

He forced himself to slow even as she tried to match him, but his rising hunger consumed him, swallowing his self-restraint. She dug her heels into the bed on either side of him, trying to find her balance against his greater weight and power. Tried and failed. He plunged deeper, harder, at the very instant that she cried out in pain and tried to pull away.

Robert froze, still deep inside her, breathing hard and shaking with desire and a stabbing shame. "I'm sorry. I didn't mean to hurt you."

She blinked back tears. "It's all right. I didn't know . . ." She hesitated, then moved beneath him. "It hurts, and yet . . ."

He stroked her hair back from her face, willing his breathing to slow. "And yet . . . ?"

"Don't stop," she whispered, arching into him. "Please, *please* don't stop."

He had been prepared for tears, for pain and fear and anger. He had even been prepared for hatred, but not for this naked, eager need or the unschooled hunger that demanded more of him than he had thought ever to give. That demanded more of him than he *had* to give.

For one mad instant, he considered pulling out. In the next instant, he knew he could not.

This time, when he bent his head to kiss her, she kissed him back. This time he was more cautious, moving slowly, insistently, bringing her with him. The long, exquisite torture made him burn with the effort at control, building until her breath came quick and shallow, hot against his sweat-slicked skin.

"Please," she said again. She laced her legs around his thighs, instinctively gaining the leverage she needed to push her hips into his, to deepen their joining. *"Please."*

"Patience, milady," he murmured, thrusting deep, suddenly eager himself. "Patience."

"No," she gasped, and pushed again. She beat at his shoulders and dragged her nails down his skin. Her fingers dug into his back. Her legs trembled with the effort of holding herself tight against him.

This was how a butterfly felt when it first slipped its cocoon, he thought—desperate to fly, even though all its frail, damp wings could do was beat up and down in the sunlight, going nowhere.

His hand slid between them, his fingers claiming her just above their joining. He rocked into her, then out, then in again, his fingers rubbing and stroking in time to the beat of his body against hers.

She sucked in her breath and clung to him until he thought they would both shatter, until thought was impossible and only sensation remained, until Alyce cried out and arched against him, her body seized, then set free, wings spread wide to catch the sun.

Unlike Alyce, he did not soar. He stiffened suddenly, like a hart as the arrow strikes home, his body shaking with the force of his release. Then he groaned and slowly crumpled onto the bed beside her.

And then he rolled away.

5

FAREWELLS

HER HUSBAND AWOKE long before dawn. Alyce feigned the sleep that had eluded her through the past hours, wondering if he would claim her.

He didn't touch her. Instead, he quietly slid out of bed, then fumbled about on the floor to gather his discarded clothes.

Though she couldn't see him in the shuttered, predawn dark, she could hear him—the rustle of rushes beneath his feet, the soft in and out of his breathing, the whisper of his clothes as he pulled them on. Each sound pricked her like a needle, drawing blood.

He didn't want her, even on this first morning of their life together. Last night he'd claimed her, then rolled away and into sleep without a word, leaving her to stare into the dark alone.

He had bought her and bedded her and that, for Robert Wardell, was enough.

It wouldn't be long before everyone else in the castle knew it too.

The wooded bar on the door scraped against the stone as he lifted it. Alyce, rigidly still beneath the covers, sensed him hesitate, as though he feared to have awakened her. When she remained silent, he propped the bar against the wall, pulled open the door, and noiselessly slipped out of the room.

Only when he was truly gone did Alyce bury her face in the pillows and give way to the tears burning inside her.

A COCK CROWED as Robert crept down the narrow, winding stairs, even though the strips of sky visible through the arrow slits were still dull black and speckled with stars. No one else was on the stairs, yet the back of his neck pricked with cold and the unnerving sense that someone watched his descent in silent condemnation.

He stopped at the foot of the stairs, stretching to ease the tension in his shoulders, knowing he'd really stopped in defiance of the guilt that had dogged his heels down each stone step that led from the Lady Alyce's chamber. He turned to glance behind him. There was nothing but darkness. When he looked ahead again, a faint glow from the hall beckoned him onward.

In the frail light of a guttering fire, the great hall looked like wreckage left in the wake of a battle. The difference was, the stains on the bodies strewn about in the rushes were of spilt wine and ale and urine, not blood. Robert's nose told him that as plain as his eyes could. The discordant chorus of snores and snorts and ungodly whistles, male and female alike, said there'd be some thick heads to deal with once the assemblage awakened.

He couldn't see William or any of the others of his party, but it would be easy to miss them in the dim light. It didn't matter. He didn't need them immediately, and he had no desire to waken the castle folk by looking for them.

Moving with care, he picked his way among the sleeping bodies. One man muttered in his sleep and rolled over, almost tripping him, but no one else so much as stirred. The outer door was properly barred and, for a wonder, the guard seated on a stool beside it was awake, though he reeked of wine like all the rest. The man leaned forward to peer into Robert's face.

"You be the merchant, be'nt you?" he demanded thickly, squinting hard in the dim light.

Robert compressed his lips in distaste, irritated by this new obstruction in his path. "I am."

"Arrr." The rough sound of acknowledgment rumbled in the guard's throat. He nodded, then leaned closer still, his face screwed up like a gargoyle's. "Why be you about so early, then? Din't the Lady Alyce—"

Robert heard nothing else as rage exploded within him. He seized the guard by the collar of his tunic and dragged him to his feet, then slammed him against the wall. The man, too thickheaded to resist, squirmed in his grasp, then froze as the tip of Robert's dagger pressed against his belly.

"One word more about the Lady Alyce," Robert said between clenched teeth, "and I'll geld you where you stand. Before God, I swear it."

The threat registered, even in the guard's wine-fuzzed brain. "Meant no disrespect," he wheezed, eyes bulging.

It was the stink of his breath, not compassion, that induced Robert to release him. "Keep your mouth shut, then." He shoved the man away. "And open the door."

The guard hastily complied, bowing and cringing and muttering what might be apologies—or curses. The instant Robert was through the door, the guard slammed it shut and rammed the bar into place.

Free of the fetid air in the hall, Robert breathed deeply, shaken by his unexpected rage—and the knowledge that he would have done just as he'd threatened had the guard uttered another word. His hand trembled as he slid the dagger into its sheath. He took another breath, then another. Even the sweet, mist-damped air of early morning couldn't clear the bitter aftertaste of anger and self-scorn.

He'd meant only to slip away from his own dark thoughts. He hadn't considered what his too-hasty abandonment of his wife's bed might do to *her* reputation.

His wife.

Robert let out his breath with a groaning whoosh. Not a day married, and already he'd sinned against her. Again.

He shook off the thought and looked about him. A few folk were already stirring among the stables and workshops that pressed against the castle's curtain wall; the three guards he could see on the ramparts appeared alert enough.

Robert smiled grimly. Not everyone, it seemed, had celebrated the Lady Alyce's wedding.

A drowsy kitchen drudge on her way to the well provided Robert with a tallow lantern. He ignored her fulsome wishes for his good health and his lady's, but he was acutely conscious of the speculative look she cast after him as he crossed to the stables at the far side of the bailey.

He found his apprentice where he'd expected to find him, wrapped in his cloak and burrowed into the hay near where Robert's palfrey was tied. An ear and a shock of gold hair were all that was visible of the boy.

Robert nudged him with his foot. The boy stirred, groaned, then curled even more tightly into the cloak.

Envy stabbed at Robert. He remembered what it was to be sixteen and able to sleep without dreams.

He hadn't been sixteen for a long, long time.

He bent and grabbed the boy's shoulder, giving it a good shake. "Piers? Piers! Wake up!"

"Mmrmph?" The bundled cloak tried to burrow deeper still into the hay.

A corner of Robert's mouth twitched upward. "There's a wench here to see you, and her father right after."

The cloak sat up abruptly, then was thrown back to reveal a handsome, wiry youth with wide blue eyes and hair that stood in disordered tufts all about his head. "What wench?"

Robert laughed. "We've been here but one night. Is there more than one already?"

The boy blinked, then looked about him suspiciously. "There's no wench," he said at last in grumbling accusation.

"Not now," Robert admitted, setting the lantern down on a shelf. "Get up. I want my cloak that you so carefully guarded for me . . . and that I'll warrant you've been using for a pillow all the while. It's damnably cold out."

"And early," Piers said, dragging out the wadded-up cloak and handing it to Robert. The words were casual, but the glint in the boy's eyes said his thoughts were straying down the same path as the guard's and the kitchen drudge's.

"There's work awaiting for us in London, and five days' hard ride between here and there," Robert said, taking the cloak.

Piers tossed his own hay-flecked cloak aside and rose to his feet. Like a cat, he stretched, working out the cramps from his makeshift bed. His gaze never left Robert's face.

"There's much grief at milady's leaving," the boy said at last.

Robert froze, then shook out his cloak and swept it about his shoulders. "Her father gave no hint of it."

Piers shrugged. "My lord baron, it seems, grieves for naught but spilt wine and a bad hunt. But the others here about, they speak well of the lady and will miss her sore once she's gone."

Robert studied his apprentice. Even in the weak light of the lantern, the boy's eyes sparked with an adult's understanding.

"And from whence had you this intelligence?" Robert

demanded, conscious of a sharpness in his voice he could not control.

"From my neighbors at table and the stable folk and—and anyone else who would talk."

"And the anyone else would be . . . who?"

Piers grinned, unrepentant. "A plump and pretty wench who told me all in exchange for good wine and a better roll in the hay." His grin turned wicked, teasing. "She was my lord baron's leavings, but sweet for all that, and more than willing."

Robert shrugged and turned away.

"You'll be well rested then and can rouse the rest," he said, his voice harsh. "I want all in readiness for milady. We depart as soon as might be once morning mass is done."

"I'll take this bundle with me," Alyce said, patting the small leather pack that lay atop her pillow. The pack held her embroidered surcoat, the ivory comb her mother's father had given her when she was a child, and the jeweled necklet and gold brooch that had been her mother's—everything of any value that she owned. Every possession she treasured and could not bear to leave behind.

It was a very small pack.

Hilde frowned and straightened from tidying the bedclothes. With ready understanding, she'd avoided undoing Alyce's careful arrangement that hid the dark redbrown stains that marred the once-pristine sheets.

Time enough for the world to see the stains once she was gone, Alyce thought, and bedamned to her father's mockery.

Hilde eyed Alyce's pack, then Alyce, then the pack once more. Her frown deepened. "Now, milady," she said with patent disapproval. "It's not seemly for you to be carrying your own bags and bundles, no matter what's in them. I'll warrant Master Wardell's people will be careful enough if it's your things they're handling. They've tended to all the rest, after all."

"Everything's loaded?" Alyce asked, ignoring Hilde's objections. She rested her hand protectively on the bundle, fighting against the urge to snatch it up and hold it tight against her chest so no one would dare take it from her. Unseemly it might be, but having the pack close would be a comfort, a reminder that she was not leaving *everything* behind.

From the darkling expression in Hilde's eyes, Alyce suspected her old friend understood quite well why she wanted the pack.

"Aye, they're loaded," Hilde said briskly. "I sent old Thorleigh down to check. And Maida right after him, just to be sure. It won't take those two long, even if they was to count it all thrice over."

Alyce nodded. In truth, there was little enough. She should have had more, as befitted a bride of her station, but her father had begrudged every penny she'd pried out of him. No matter. There were other things to worry about now. "You gave my old kirtles to the laundress and the scullery maid and—"

"Aye, milady. And the shoes and everything else." Hilde beamed. "Pleased they were, and grateful. They'd not expected such stout clothes . . . or such generosity."

"It was little enough, and I . . ." Alyce drew in a deep breath. "I didn't want to arrive in London gowned in russet."

"I should think not!" Hilde's face pinched tight in disapproval. "A sin it is that you ever had to wear such coarse, common cloth at all, let alone be wed to a merchant! And having to pinch purse for your brideclothes when you're a baron's daughter! It—it's indecent, that's what it is!"

Alyce couldn't help it. She burst out laughing. The laughter, however, had a sharp, almost panicked ring to it. "I would that Master Wardell might hear you. From the way he eyed my gown at dinner yesterday, I suspect he thinks his bride a spendthrift."

"A spendthrift! And you pricking your fingers raw with the needlework, then scrimping to buy Maida and me the cloth for those lovely new surcoats and kirtles, as if you'd no needs of your own to be worrying you! Why—! Well—!"

The protests died away in a series of soundless huffs. It was too much. Hilde's wizened face crumpled. She sniffled, then sniffled again, wrinkling her nose in an effort to draw in air and choke back the tears she was too proud to shed.

"The kirtle's as nice as any I've ever had, milady," she said, "but I'd gladly have forgone such finery if we could have kept you safe here with us. Or gone with you to London, as you asked."

"However would the castle go on without you and Maida?" Alyce said, as lightly as she could. Her eyes burned, but she didn't want to cry any more than Hilde did. It had been hard enough to erase the traces of her early morning tears.

"Well enough." Hilde snorted, then angrily dabbed at her eyes with her sleeve. "The only reason your father forbade us to go with you is he likes Maida's ale better than the brewster's."

"And your hedgehog pie."

Hilde gave her a wavery smile. "Aye. Well, there *is* that!"

"Perhaps in time I can convince Master Wardell to fetch you."

"You mean, pay your father to release us."

"Hilde." Alyce tried to sound stern, but the smile she couldn't repress betrayed her.

"A wicked man, your father is," Hilde said fiercely. "Wicked and ungodly and mean, even for a nobleman. Always has been."

She glared at Alyce, as though daring her to contradict her judgment. "I've a good mind to put a dose of soapwort in his soup when he's too drunk to notice! One strong enough to put him in the garderobe for a week, so it'd clean out some of that meanness he's so stuffed with."

Hilde's eyes brightened at the thought. "If it weren't that he'd fart like a drunken dog for another week after, I'd do it too!"

SIR FULK HAD decided to honor them by delaying his weapons practice long enough to see them off. The previous night's debauch had left him bleary-eyed and ill-tempered, though the three stout drafts of ale he'd downed since waking had helped ease the morning's pangs. He'd risen in time for early mass, but hadn't bothered to change his linen or wash his face. Bits of straw stuck out of the rat's nest of his hair, remnants of at least one roll in the rushes the night before. His clothes reeked of spilt wine.

He stood in the middle of the bailey, scowling and scratching his beard, head cocked as he studied the gray mare that Master Wardell had brought Alyce as a wedding gift.

"The beast's well enough as a mount for a woman, I suppose," Sir Fulk growled at last, begrudging even in his praise. "Never survive a campaign, though. Look at her feet. Too small. Never hold up to a *real* horse."

Alyce barely stopped herself from growling back. The mare was beautiful, delicate and graceful and perfectly mannered. Compared to the lumbering, stone-mouthed beast Alyce had been riding for the past few years, the mare might as well have wings.

Wardell ignored Sir Fulk's surly temper. "I trust the Lady Alyce will find her acceptable," he said smoothly. "A gift, milady," he added, bowing to Alyce. "In celebration . . . and in thanks."

His finely sculpted features gave no hint that he was aware of the castle folk who had crowded round to see them off. His slight smile was for her and her alone . . . or so it must seem to those who avidly watched them.

Alyce turned to study the mare. Wardell's smiles might be for her, but there was no warmth in them. His eyes were unreadable, almost inhuman in their dark and distant stillness. It didn't matter. The smiles were enough to fool the rest, and for that she was grateful

"She is . . . exquisite. I thank you—" She stopped, blushed. "Sir."

She had almost said "milord." A foolish slip of the tongue, but it would have shamed her to make it. He was Master Wardell, nothing more, and she no longer the Lady Alyce Fitzwarren, but Mistress Wardell, a merchant's wife.

"Why are you standing about, then?" Sir Fulk roared. "I've better things to do than stare at two love-besotted fools and a damned useless horse. Have done and be gone, the two of you!"

It was a jest, but a cruel one. Alyce's face flamed scarlet. She straightened, drawing herself up to her most impressive, unfeminine height. "Master Wardell?"

"Milady?"

"I believe we have my father's blessing. Shall we away?"

Wardell's gaze locked with hers. Slowly, almost imperceptibly, his smile softened and his eyes warmed. "I but await your command."

Alyce tilted her chin upward. "Then let us be gone. I've an urge to see London as soon as may be!"

Wardell's smile widened. He turned and snapped his fingers. Like an obedient dog, the golden-haired youth led the mare over. Wardell took the reins from him and offered them to Alyce.

"She is yours, milady. May she carry you swiftly and well."

Alyce's cheeks grew warm again. His smile was so . . . unsettling. And unexpectedly kind.

She gathered up the reins and stepped closer, ready to mount. She'd long ago learned to mount on her own, despite her long skirts. It was either that or be left behind— neither Hubert nor Sir Fulk ever waited for anyone. To her consternation, Wardell went down on one knee and extended his linked hands.

Her hesitation lasted a heartbeat, no more. Like a princess accustomed to such attention, she put her foot into his hands and let him throw her into the saddle.

At the sudden weight, the mare danced away, then meekly came back to hand, the silver bells on her caparison jingling merrily. Delighted at the beast's ready response, Alyce laughed, settled her feet into the stirrups, and set her to dancing once more. The mare jigged sideways, then spun around on her heels and sidled back, coming to a head-tossing halt beside Wardell.

"She is enchanting. Magnificent! I—" Alyce laughed again and impulsively bent down to offer him her hand in thanks. "Never have I ridden one such as this!"

Wardell's hand closed about hers. His skin was warm, his fingers firm and strong. With easy grace, he raised her hand to his lips and pressed a light kiss against it.

For a moment, the world stopped.

"Milady," he said, and the moment shattered. He bowed, then released her and turned to take his horse's reins.

Alyce watched him mount, too stunned to think, too inexperienced to find the words that might come easily to another. She was afraid to look at her hand for fear she would find her flesh aflame.

As if sensing her disquiet, the mare fidgeted, shifting around until the crowd that hemmed them in seemed to spin like a whirligig. For a moment, there had been only herself and Robert Wardell in that great press of people. Suddenly faces swam out of the dizzying mass, each one as familiar and precious as the breath in her body. There was Edwin the page, grim Hertha, the dairy maid, and old Wat. She spotted fat Maida and little Hilde, both smiling bravely in spite of their tears.

Every one of them a friend she was leaving behind, perhaps forever.

With a sharp cry, Alyce reined in the mare.

Before she could regain her wits, her father's voice cut through her confusion as easily as his sword cut through flesh. "Ho, Wat! Where are you, man? My horse! I've better things to do this day than watch a pack of idiots prance about in the bailey as if they were playing May games! Hubert! We're off!"

The crowd split apart as Sir Fulk shoved his way through, then shattered altogether as Wardell's people moved to find their own mounts and make one last check of their packs and belongings.

Alyce sat her horse and watched it all break apart around her. If her father had a word of farewell for her, it was lost in the stir and bustle. Even Maida and Hilde disappeared, swallowed up in the chaos.

For a moment, panic claimed her, but only for a moment. The world shifted, then coalesced around the dark, lean figure of her husband as he rode up beside her.

Wardell glanced down at her . . . and as quickly turned away. Before she could say a word, he threw a swift look around at his followers, then set his horse forward into a trot.

It might have been a trick of the light or her own

fevered imagination, but Alyce would swear that in that instant's glance, his smile had died and his eyes had once more gone hollow and distant.

Her fingers tightened on the reins. Her skin still burned where his lips had pressed.

With an oath, she set the mare into a canter after him.

To the accompaniment of wild shouts of farewell, a hundred jangling silver bells, and the clatter of iron-shod hooves on stone, Alyce Wardell rode out of the gates of Colmaine at her husband's side . . . and never once looked back.

6

LONDON...AND
HOME

ROBERT LED HIS little band away from Colmaine with a clatter and stir that brought the villagers
from their fields and a flock of tattered boys, whooping
like demented crows, hot after them. A pack of dogs
snapped at their heels, and a hen who'd rashly ventured
into their path barely escaped being trampled under the
speeding hooves. She fled, squawking and flapping in indignant protest, leaving two tail feathers spinning in the
dust. From somewhere in the village, a donkey brayed
farewell.

The boys gave up first, but the villagers, hands raised
to block the morning sun, remained staring after them
until they were almost out of sight. The yapping, panting
dogs were the last to abandon the chase, but Robert set too
brisk a pace even for their love of sport.

There were other beasts at Robert's heels that drove
him far harder than those gaunt mongrels—chief among
them disgust and contempt and a pressing need to breathe
air untainted by drink or filth or dung.

Most of all there was anger for the offhand cruelty with
which Sir Fulk had bid good-bye to his only daughter.

Robert could still see how she'd looked when her father had roared for her to be gone. Her cheeks had burned

and her mouth had drawn thin and tight, but she'd borne herself with a pride that belied her pain. And he could still feel the way her fingers had trembled in his when she'd leaned down to thank him for the gift of the mare, the way her eyes had glowed with gratitude and with relief that he, at least, had not shamed her before her people.

Given his earlier abandonment of her, the gratitude stung.

His companions' willingness to match his pace did not last long. Colmaine had scarce disappeared behind them when, one by one, merchants, servants, and guards dropped from a teeth-rattling trot to a slow jog, and from a jog to a droop-shouldered walk. Only the guards made any effort to look alert, but their gray, tight-lipped faces betrayed what their attention to duty was costing them.

Robert recognized the signs—they were all, servants and masters alike, suffering the penalties of having drunk overmuch and slept scarcely at all. The morning's pint of ale and day-old crusts of bread had scarce been enough to allay the pangs of hunger, let alone the miseries of a night's overindulgence.

The only ones not yet called to atone for their sins were Alyce, Piers, and himself, and the Lady Alyce seemed no more inclined to idle conversation than he was. That left Piers to fill the silence.

The boy, who had somehow insinuated his mount between theirs, plunged into the task with ready goodwill, pleased as a curious jay for any excuse to while away the time with chatter and what gossip came to hand. It seemed the boy had become a partisan of his lady wife. It stung to think she might have need of one.

"A beautiful day, milady," Piers said, with the air of one making a gratifying discovery. "Cold, to be sure, but the sun is bright and the sky blue enough to rival the Virgin's cloak itself."

Out of the corner of his eye, Robert saw Lady Alyce

glance at Piers and smile, then, more hesitantly, turn her gaze on him.

"If the wind will but keep the clouds from hiding such blue, then its cold is welcome," she said. "We've scarce seen the sun for more days than I'd care to count, yet out it came yesterday, meek as a dog at heel. It is a good omen, I think."

Robert shifted to stare at her, surprised. There was a stiff-spined dignity about her that said she still smarted from the wounds her father's words had inflicted, yet it wasn't the past she was thinking on, but the future.

Another, prettier woman might have offered him a beguiling smile designed to tempt and conquer, or might have cringed under his attention like a frightened mouse that had ventured too far from its hole. The Lady Alyce was too proud to resort to either wiles or whimpers. She met his startled gaze as a man would have—direct and un-blinking.

But not, he thought, unafraid.

His respect for her rose another notch.

"The people of Colmaine must be grateful for the winter's passing, as hard as it's been these past months," said Piers, with the air of one oblivious to everything but the satisfying rattle of his tongue against his teeth.

"Myself," he went on, "I've a hankering for Champagne, in France, or for Castile. I named your mare Graciella after a girl I met there, you know." He smiled, like a conspirator sharing secrets. His wicked charm drew an answering smile from Alyce. "Master Wardell took me on one of his trips last year. None of your gray, misty days there! It's all sun, and the wine as sweet . . ."

His apprentice's words faded from Robert's awareness. All his attention was fixed on the proud creature he had taken to wife with such careful thought to the advantages, and no thought whatsoever to the woman herself.

She bore his gaze unflinchingly. Her green-gold eyes

seemed dark and still in her cold-reddened face, her thin golden lashes invisible even at this small distance. Wrapped in the sharp whiteness of her matron's wimple and the dull green of her hooded woolen cloak, she seemed all eyes and carved bone and mouth. Not a beauty, but strong, compelling in a way that startled him for being so unexpected.

Robert blinked, and found he could not bear to face that straightforward, questioning gaze any longer. As he looked away, her smile faded. She ducked her head and turned to gaze out over fields that were rapidly giving way to winter-bare woods. Even over the muted thud of hooves and the jingle and creak of harnesses, he could hear the faint clack-clacking of dry branches striking against one another in the chill breeze. Like mourners bidding fare-well, he thought, then frowned at the grim fancy.

There's much grief at milady's leaving, Piers had said. The words seemed to echo hollowly in the breeze, keeping time to the woodland's clattering good-byes.

To ALYCE'S RELIEF, Robert called a halt at midday. He chose a spot beside a stream that spilled down a rocky hillside and into a quiet pool, then ran burbling over the road and into the willows below. Grass, dry and brown at this time of the year, cushioned the banks of the stream; a low ridge cut the chill wind that had followed them from Colmaine. In the spring, or the full flowering of summer, it would be a beautiful spot; in the dull, dead end of win-ter, it was merely grim and cold and gray.

No matter. Alyce dismounted gratefully to find one of the guards waiting to take the reins. As he led the mare away, Alyce turned to seek Robert among the milling merchants and servants and guards. She hadn't far to look. In his clothes of finest scarlet, he stood out from the more drably gowned men like a cock pheasant in a flock of brown hens.

Not that he needed fine, bright clothes to set him apart from his fellows, she thought, watching as he conferred with one of the servants who were unloading the sumpter horses. Robert Wardell could dress himself in rags, but he would never be able to hide the arrogant tilt of his head or the square, straight back that, she suspected, bent to few men, and then never readily.

Unlike her father, who roared and cursed and kicked when giving orders to his underlings, Robert spoke softly, yet those around him leaped to do his bidding like eager hounds on a hunt. It did not surprise her. Not a full day had passed since he first rode through the gates of Colmaine, but one thing she had learned—Robert Wardell gained with respect what others might demand with force, yet never obtain.

A commoner he might be, but he was a strong man, and kind, and respected by his peers and servants alike. A man to reckon with . . . and to trust. It wasn't a bad basis on which to anchor the rest of her life.

With a curt nod, he finished giving instructions to another of his men, then turned and walked toward her.

"I came to ask if you would prefer to take your midday meal on the streambank, milady, or up there, under that old oak."

Alyce stretched to see where he pointed. The tree, a gnarled and venerable specimen of its kind, was bare of leaves, but its broad trunk would provide shelter from the wind. The grassy area at its base—the only part not knobbled with roots or rocks—would comfortably seat two. Three would fill the space to overflowing.

"The bank, I think. Thank you." The image of the two of them in that small, sheltered space was all too vivid. She was accustomed to dining with men, but a private meal taken with *this* man, while all his friends looked on and judged her . . .

Alyce shuddered at the thought.

THE SERVANTS COVERED a packsaddle with a blanket to make a chair for her. Everyone else sat on the ground around her, or took their meal away with them to perch on rocks or eat standing, eyes alert for any trouble that might come down the road or out of the woods.

Alyce didn't worry about unwanted fellow travelers. She'd eaten little the day before and nothing at all that morning. Right now, even the simpler travelers' fare that Robert's people had spread on a cloth on the ground in front of her made her mouth water.

The bread and ale were from Colmaine, of course, but the wine and cheese and dried meats had been brought from London. Alyce nibbled her way through a little cheese and meat, wondering at the new tastes. She'd never dreamed there could be so many variations of goat cheese, or that dried meat could be so flavorful without choking her with too much salt or an overstrong taste of spices. The wine was sweet, heavy and silken on the tongue. She took a sip and held it in her mouth for a moment, savoring the richness.

Clearly, Robert Wardell's provisioners were far more talented than even the best cook at Colmaine. The thought troubled her even as it stirred an unexpected pride that this new husband of hers could command such luxuries—seemingly without any thought that they *were* luxuries.

She ducked her head as if to study the bits of dried meat she'd shredded into her napkin, but instead glanced at him out of the corner of her eye.

Robert sat on the ground to her left, legs crossed like a boy's, dark head bent over the task of spreading a pungent mustard sauce on his meat and bread. Not for the first time, she wished she'd been blessed with thick, dark lashes to hide the direction of her gaze. Lashes like his, she thought, so long and thick that he might as well have shutters to hide his eyes.

From this angle, she could see nothing of his expression beyond the firm line of cheek and mouth and chin. His eyebrows drew together ever so slightly as a blob of mustard sauce slipped off the tip of his knife. The sauce hit the lip of the little earthenware sauce pot with a splat, spraying dark yellow droplets on his hose and the white cloth spread on the ground.

Robert swore. Softly. Alyce hastily stuffed an overlarge strip of meat in her mouth to muffle the giggle that threatened.

Unaware he was being observed, Robert set his jaw, then scooped out an even larger portion of mustard and plunked it on his meat. He spread the spicy sauce with liberal abandon, then folded the meat in a piece of bread and, with the air of a man who had triumphed over his adversary and was determined to make sure of his victory, took a good-sized bite.

His cheeks bulged, his jaws strained as they worked up and down, then he swallowed hard and let out a great gust of air from his nose. Very much, Alyce thought, like a contented bull set loose in a grain bin.

Her lips twitched in spite of her. She must have made some small sound for his head came up and his eyes fixed on her.

Seated as she was on her packsaddle throne, her head topped his by a good two hand spans, perhaps three. He had to tilt his chin to look up at her. The movement—and the faint smile that went with it—gave him a boyish air that belied the lines at the corners of his eyes and the strands of gray that were mixed in with his raven curls.

A dab of mustard adorned the corner of his mouth.

"You missed a bit. There," she said, leaning to point, and barely stopped herself from touching the tip of her finger to his mouth. She drew back, embarrassed by her boldness, and curled her hand into her lap, the wayward finger pressed tight against its neighbors.

His tongue flicked out to catch the errant bit of sauce. She could see his throat work as he swallowed, then he ran his tongue over his lips a second time to remove any remaining trace.

Alyce followed the motion of his tongue with her eyes, entranced, yet puzzled why so ordinary a gesture should suddenly be so . . . intriguing. Or have such an oddly stirring effect on her pulse.

Slowly, with deliberation, Robert Wardell winked at her.

She blinked, startled, then hastily fixed her attention on her own food, uncomfortably conscious of the heat rising in her cheeks. From somewhere to the side she heard a soft snort, hastily stifled. One of Robert's friends had no doubt caught the little exchange between them and was trying not to laugh.

She glanced at the men gathered in a ragged circle around the food, embarrassed and resentful as each of them suddenly found an overwhelming fascination in the food in front of him.

She caught three of them sneaking glances at her and Robert. Just as if they were two-headed sheep at the fair, she thought, and grimaced, then ducked her head and savagely bit off a chunk of meat.

There were two heads in this marriage, indeed, but she was damned if she'd be anybody's sheep.

THEY WERE FIVE days on the road. Five long, hard days with little rest and less comfort. They spent the nights sleeping on the floors of manor halls that were barely large enough to accommodate the people of the manor itself. They had no privacy, and only Alyce had the comfort of a straw-filled pallet and good wool blankets to keep out the cold. Robert had seen to that.

He had seen to a great many things, ensuring she had a comfortable seat when they stopped for the midday meal, the choicest bits of meat, the first sip of wine. But for all his careful attentions, she no more knew what thoughts lay behind his black eyes than she had when he'd first ridden into the bailey at Colmaine.

She watched him furtively, teasing at the edges of the puzzle that was her new husband, looking for what hints and insights she might glean.

His friends thought well of him, she knew. They clearly looked to him for leadership—not as her father's men looked to Sir Fulk, out of duty and obligation, but as free men who had chosen the man they would follow. More than once William Townsend whiled away the hours on the road by recounting wild tales of Robert's exploits. Even under the generous larding of exaggeration, Alyce caught traces of the man himself, and what she caught, she liked.

Intelligent and bold. A strong man not afraid to carve his own path in dangerous woods. A stern but fair master, a generous if somewhat distant friend, a respected man of business. He was also arrogant, though that came as no surprise, and impatient, and perhaps too quick to anger, though that fault didn't trouble her overmuch either. She wasn't the easiest-tempered creature herself and she'd had too much experience with her father's and Hubert's quick tempers to be unsettled by another's.

He was discreet as well. Not by so much as a raised eyebrow had he commented on the disgrace of a lady of her rank being sent off with only a few bundles of clothes and no woman to keep her company. She had learned to be grateful for his restraint, as grateful as she was for his thoughtfulness in the bailey or the gift of Graciella.

Sometimes, she caught him watching her as furtively as she watched him—long, thoughtful looks when he believed no one would notice, or darting glances when someone was likely to spy him out. He gave no hint of what he thought or the conclusions he'd reached about her. She hoped his impressions of her were as favorable as hers of him . . . and prayed she hadn't disappointed him too much on their wedding night.

Her only disappointment was that they'd had no chance to be alone since then. The farther they rode from Colmaine, the sharper her memories of her wedding night became. Heated, lustful, troubling memories that made her ache and burn despite the cold. She'd even tried to rub herself against the saddle to relieve the worst of the need. The wanton act had shamed her but done little to assuage her need or quiet the carnal imaginings that plagued her waking hours.

By the afternoon of the fifth day, however, her lust had turned toward thoughts of hot water and a fire and a night spent on a soft, clean bed that didn't rustle every time she rolled over, and even those concerns fell away in the excitement of coming at last within sight of the great walls of London.

Alyce fought to keep her restless mount under control while she tried to take it all in—the motley, noisy, bustling people, the vendors' stalls and the narrow houses and shops and wide kitchen gardens that lined the broad road, the familiar smells of man and beast overlaid with more exotic scents appropriate to England's greatest city. Most of all, she found herself staring at the massive towers that framed the great stone arch of Cripplegate, and the crenellated city walls that stretched away on either side of them.

London! She'd never been farther south than Ayllesbury. That town's yearly fair always seemed a brawling confusion, yet it couldn't begin to match the workday jostle and roar that engulfed her now. Robert had said that nearly twenty thousand people dwelt in the city and the suburbs and settlements like this that pressed so close against its walls. She'd thought it a jest, but now she wondered if he hadn't lost a few thousand somewhere in the count.

They were less than a quarter mile from the gate itself when they found their way blocked by an ox cart with a broken wheel.

The cart had spilled half its load of old straw and manure across the road and traffic had come nearly to a standstill as the carter tried to get his balky oxen to drag the cart to the side. Passersby made matters worse by stopping to gawk, and to shout insults and advice in equal measure. The carter shouted and cursed, the oxen bellowed, and the cart went nowhere.

"Ye'd best kill the beasts and have done with it," jeered one bystander. "Ye'll never get them to move it that way."

"Set fire to the straw and we'll roast them right here!" shouted another, who grinned and bowed when his audience laughed in approval.

"Not like that, man! Ye'll ruin the wheel *and* the axle, and then where'll ye be?" shouted a third, abandoning his own cart to offer unwanted help.

Stunned by the din and the press of people about them, Alyce pulled her horse to a halt while Robert's guards tried to force a path through the crowd.

"Give way! Move, you clutter-headed lump, *move!*" One of the guards, a man named Henley, leaned out of his saddle to poke at a hulking villein who had stepped in front of him.

The villein cursed and shoved at the guard's horse, the

guard swore, and only the confusion of the moment and a comely maid passing near them prevented a fight from breaking out.

Bypassing the villein, Henley slowly made headway against the crowd, though he was forced to cut his path through the mounded dung and straw to do it. Alyce glanced over her shoulder. Robert had disappeared in the press of people and animals that jammed the road behind her. She heard William Townsend's angry roar at finding his way blocked, but the rest of their small band seemed to have vanished in the crowd.

She turned back to follow Henley, only to find another rider forcing his way in ahead of her. Before she could move out of his path, a peddler with clanking tinware strung from a pole dodged between them. Alyce's palfrey snorted in well-bred contempt, but stood her ground.

The other rider's mount squealed and reared back, then plunged to the side, neatly unseating the rider and dumping him in the muck. The crowd shouted its approval and pressed closer for a better view.

"Come back here, you sheep-swiving whoreson!" the hapless rider roared at the peddler. Surging to his feet in a shower of straw and dung, he lunged after the cause of his indignities—too late. The peddler had disappeared into the crowd.

Frustrated, the man snatched at his mount's trailing reins, then roughly dragged the snorting, wild-eyed beast to a stand.

"Quiet! Damn you! Stupid beast. And you!" He turned on Alyce like a dog on its tormentor, lips drawn back in a snarl. "What mean you, blocking the road like this? I've a good mind to sue—"

"Sue and be damned, Hensford. A man with your length of leg ought to be able to keep his seat better than that."

Alyce jerked round in the saddle, startled by Robert's

sudden appearance at her side. His sharp challenge brought approving laughter from the crowd, which moved closer still, excited by the prospect of a quarrel.

Hensford's head snapped back as if he'd been struck. Hate flared in his pale eyes. "Wardell!"

"The same." Robert eyed the man's soiled garments with an insulting air of interest. "I might have known I'd find you knee-deep in a dung heap."

Hensford's face turned a blotchy red. "And I'm not surprised to find you master of it."

"You should never be surprised by finding me on top, my friend. Not ever." Robert glanced at the mounded mix of dung and straw, then back at Hensford. His mouth curled up in a taunting smile.

With a score of curses for his nervous horse and another score, riper still, for the carter and his oxen and cart, Hensford plowed his way to the edge of the odorous heap in which he was bemired.

Robert made to move his own mount out of the way, but Hensford grabbed the reins and pulled him to a halt.

"Have you heard the news, Wardell? That fine prince of yours broke his sworn oath at Gloucester and held the city to ransom. His sworn oath!" Hensford ostentatiously turned and spat.

Henley, who had halted at the commotion behind him, tried to drive his mount back to Robert's side, but the crowd was pressing in close, straining to hear what was said and blocking all movement.

Hensford was too caught up in his quarrel with Robert to heed anyone else. "Now there's word they're raising Henry's dragon banner for war, and all the countryside trembles at the thought of Edward loose upon them." His mouth twisted in an ugly sneer. "As well trust that leopard the king keeps chained at the Tower as trust the king's son, for there's no beast more treacherous, and none so apt to change his spots."

Robert stared down at him, his expression hard and mocking. "Do you tell me, then, that Montfort's forces cannot defend what they've already taken?"

"I do not! Montfort is not so weak, nor his men such fools! They'll have their own back, never fear. And *we'll* have the justice the king denies us!"

"Justice?" Robert snorted dismissively and pulled his mount's reins out of Hensford's grip. "I'd rather have peace. I can't make money when the land's in turmoil, and neither can you, Hensford, nor any of these good people here, who need that profit to put a roof over their heads and food on the table."

He leaned down to glare directly into his opponent's face. "And I tell you this, it isn't Montfort who can give us peace. In the game of power, it isn't Earl Simon's honor that will triumph in the end!"

The people of London crowded closer still as the argument waxed hot. There were a few who shouted support for Robert's views, but the majority jeered and flung curses at him, and with each curse they grew more belligerent. Even the carter who was responsible for the confusion in the first place joined in the shouting, evidently having decided he might as well have a little diversion along with the rest.

Alyce snorted, disgusted. Damn all men and their damnable politics! Five days on the road and a good meal and hot fire within reach, and they were balked by a quarrelsome acquaintance and a crowd of fools who had nothing better to do than to listen to arguments they'd no doubt heard a hundred times before. Well, she was having none of it.

She tried to edge out of the press of people. No one gave way. They were so close-packed even the horses didn't have room to kick, though a couple of them clearly wanted to try. Robert was as hemmed in as she was, and Hensford was enjoying his audience too much to let the

debate die. At this rate, she'd be lucky not to be shut outside the city when the gates closed for the night.

She rose in her stirrups, scanning the crowd and the
buildings beyond, looking for some way to divert the people's attention. Half of the stalls and peddlers' carts on either side of the road stood untended, their proprietors
evidently having abandoned them to join in the shouting. The folk who'd stayed to guard their wares were little
better—everyone was craning to catch the brewing fight,
and no one was watching his property.

Alyce smiled. There was a way.

"Look!" she cried, taking care not to point. "Is that a
thief?"

The people standing nearest her were the first to take
up her cry. The warning traveled through the crowd like
waves from a stone thrown into still water.

"Thief? There's a thief?"

"Where?"

"There!"

"No, *there*!"

"My stall! There's a thief in my stall!"

The crowd split apart like rotten cloth. Merchants
and workers scattered, each more anxious than the next to
catch the wretched dog who was robbing *him*. Suddenly,
the road ahead was clear all the way to Cripplegate.

Alyce gestured to her astonished guard. "Follow me! I
want someone who can lead me home if the rest of them
prefer to stay and argue!"

She didn't wait to see if Henley obeyed. Cripplegate
lay ahead and for one sweet, swift moment, she was free.
At her command, her restive mount willingly plunged
into a gallop, dirt, dung, and dank straw kicking up from
beneath its hooves.

Those among the crowd who still lingered leaped
out of her way as Henley yelped and spurred his mount
after her.

．　．　．

ROBERT HAD WATCHED the walls of London grow until they loomed over the houses and shops that lined the road to Cripplegate, uncertain if he was more relieved or worried to be at his journey's end.

On the one hand, he was eager to continue his bride's education in the subtle—and not so subtle—arts of making love. They'd had no chance for intimacy since leaving Colmaine, and for five days he'd been plagued with the memory of their wedding night and her quick, untutored response to his touch.

On the other hand, the thought of her as wife and mistress of Wardell House was more unsettling than he'd expected. The Lady Alyce Fitzwarren, now Wardell, was not a woman to be put in a corner and forgotten until it was convenient for him to remember her. She'd earned his respect with her calm, uncomplaining acceptance of the discomforts of hard travel, but every now and then he'd caught a glint in her eye, or an unexpected proud lift to her chin, that warned she was not so tractable a creature as she seemed.

Finding Alan of Hensford ankle-deep in dung and swearing at his wife had provided the perfect release for his roiling emotions. Deep in hot-tempered argument, he'd ignored Alyce's cry of thief, just as he'd ignored the taunts and catcalls of the crowd that hemmed them in.

He couldn't, however, ignore the sight of his wife galloping toward Cripplegate like a sinner with all the demons of hell at her heels.

Robert sat bolt upright in the saddle. "Alyce! Milady! Wait!"

If she heard him, she paid him no heed. She dodged an unwary bystander and kept on going, full tilt, with that idiot Henley hard on her heels and a yapping mongrel dog hard on his.

Robert swore and spun his horse about, regardless of Hensford or the crowd still gathered about them. Hensford, however, was not so willing to abandon the quarrel.

"You'll regret your support of the king, Wardell!" the man shouted after him. "It isn't Simon de Montfort he wars against, but the good Englishmen he robs to fill his pockets, and the people of London know it! You'll regret having chosen the wrong side! Wardell? Wardell!"

Whatever else he might have said was swallowed up in the thunder of iron-shod hooves on the road as Robert raced after his errant wife.

He caught up with her in the shadow of the great gate. The guards at the gate—Montfort's supporters and scarce better than untrained rabble—stirred to uneasy life at this unexpected charge on their position. Robert ignored both them and Henley, whom he'd just passed. His attention was fixed on Alyce. He leaned out of his saddle, grabbed her horse's bridle, and pulled her to a plunging halt under the shadow of the arch itself.

"Have you gone mad?" he demanded, furious. "You can't race into London as if it were the bailey at Colmaine! What were you thinking?"

Her head was up and her eyes blazed emerald fire. "I was thinking that you have a fine way of welcoming your wife to London, sir. Crow like a dung-hill cock if you like. I'll not waste my breath to stop you—nor my time to listen either!"

"What!" His horse jibbed away, startled by the fury in his voice.

The guards at the gate snickered loudly and relaxed their hold on their weapons, glad of the entertainment. Henley, on the other hand, had drawn his horse up at the far side of the broad stone gate and was dutifully pretending to be both blind and deaf to the world around him.

Robert let go Alyce's bridle and brought his mount

ruthlessly back to hand. "A dung-hill cock, am I? By my faith, I'd not expected a wife who'd be so ready with her insults!"

"Nor I a husband given to quarreling in the streets like a drunken peasant, though it seems I shall learn the trick of it quick enough. Only my father ever made such an ass of himself!"

Robert's jaw dropped. Alyce set hers.

A rough voice cut in before either had a chance to say another word.

" 'Ere, then! Enough o' yer carryin' on, you two! The gates is still open an' here you sits, a-quarrelin' like fish-wives over flounder an' blockin' the road so there ain't a mouse small enough could get past!"

A grubby laborer stood glowering at them from behind a handcart piled high with charcoal.

Robert's mouth snapped shut. He glared at the char-coaler.

The charcoaler glared back, unimpressed. "Ye'd think ye was the king 'isself an' there no hardworkin' folks a-waitin' t' get by! Have a-done, do, and let a workin' man pass!"

Robert glanced at Alyce, then back at the man behind him.

The charcoaler more closely resembled a wine cask on legs than a man. He was dirty and shabby and ugly and poor—and he stood there as haughtily as a king, sure of his rights as a citizen of London and unwilling to concede an inch to anyone who dared infringe on them.

Robert couldn't help it. He threw back his head and laughed, startling Alyce and the charcoaler, both.

"We'll have done, good sir," he said, fishing a coin out of his purse, "but only if you'll agree to drink a toast in welcome to my new wife!"

He tossed the coin to the startled man, who snagged it out of midair, scraped it with his thumbnail to be sure he wasn't being made fool of, then thriftily stashed it in the leather pouch on his belt.

"A wife, is it? Bah!" he said, and spat. "Troublesome creatures they be, with no end to their wailin' an' wantin'. Ye'd do better to get yourself a clean doxy. That way ye could throw her out in the street whenever ye was tired o' her."

With that, he shoved his cart into motion, grumbling and muttering and forcing Robert and Alyce to back out of his way. Still muttering, he trudged past them, straight down the middle of the road, through the gate, and into the city, oblivious to the scowling guards or the hostile glares and angry imprecations from the passersby who had to move out of his way or risk being run over.

Alyce watched him go, then burst out laughing herself. "I'm well served, I suppose, for calling you a dunghill cock. But beware, Master Wardell, if ever you try to find out whether a doxy's truly better than a wife! I've sharper things handy than my tongue!"

"And know how to use them, I'll be bound!" Robert felt an unexpected surge of pride in his new wife. Without warning, his cock stirred to life.

He shifted uncomfortably in his saddle and glanced back along the road into London. The others had finally worked their way free of the crowd and were coming toward them at a sedate pace. Henley had drawn the guards aside, no doubt to learn the latest news. No one else was close by.

They had a few moments of relative privacy left, then.

"Tell me, lady," he said, trying to ignore the stirring in his braies. "*Was* there a thief? The truth, now," he added, grinning.

"The truth?" Alyce grinned back, unabashed. "There might have been, given the crowd and all the merchants who were neglecting their stalls. It's more likely than not."

"And you've no worry that some poor soul will be accused of a crime he did not commit?"

She shrugged. "There's little chance of that. In the confusion, everyone will be running hither and yon, and no one able to say who or where or what exactly happened."

His grinned widened. "I see I shall have to tread with care, madam. First you cause a respected merchant of the city to land in a pile of dung, then, with but a word, you break up a hostile crowd when armed men were unable to act. And all because they blocked your road! God forfend I ever rouse your ire in earnest!"

Her smiled faded. "*Can* he sue? Hensford, I mean? For something so trivial as falling off his horse?"

"He can't sue, but I've no doubt he'll make complaint of me to the guild, or that I'll be held in mercy for a shilling four pence if he does." Robert spoke lightly, even as he cursed himself for having raised the subject at all.

"A shilling four pence! So much?" Alyce frowned as another thought hit. "How can you be so sure your fine will be precisely that? Have you quarreled with the man before?"

"I?" Robert flicked his fingers dismissively. "He's the one who quarrels with me, but as I am so often at odds with the guild, it's I who generally pays the fine."

"That's—that's unfair!"

He shrugged, amused by her indignation. "Hensford has never got over his father—a mere second son of a miller from Kent!—having gained the freedom of the city, and he spends a great deal of time and money defending his dignity. I'd swear half the courts of London have heard his suits at one time or another. If he's not suing the baker over shortweighting the bread, he's suing his neighbor over drainage from a latrine, or a foreign merchant for cutting cloth inside the city walls instead of bringing it in already cut. And he—" Robert cut himself off.

"Yes?"

He hesitated, then shrugged. He'd gone too far to retreat now.

"Hensford and I have been at daggers drawn for years, ever since we were apprentices to rival masters." And rivals for Jocelyn, though Alyce need never know that. "The man would gladly do me an ill turn if he had the chance. And I would just as happily return the favor."

Alyce frowned. "So it's not just your support for the Lord Edward that's the trouble between you?"

"I am a merchant and my support for the king and Lord Edward are well known . . . and not at all appreciated here, when London itself has thrown its support behind Montfort."

He gave her a wry smile. "Did you think that marriage to a merchant was any simpler than marriage to a quarrelsome knight? If so, you needs must think again, lady."

"Best not think at all, milady," William's booming voice interrupted. He drew up beside them. "When it comes to marriage, the less attention you pay to it, the better off you are."

" 'Ere, then!" cried a shrill voice. "Think the gates o' London is only for the likes o' you?"

This time it was a scrawny old woman driving a fat pink sow who stood glaring at them. The woman was dressed in a much-patched kirtle and dirty shift, yet she seemed not one whit more impressed by their wealth and position than the charcoaler had been.

"Stop yer jawin' an' move along so's respec'able workin' folk can pass!" she demanded, brandishing the long stick she used to drive the sow.

The sow turned a sharp, piggy gaze on them, then grunted and abruptly sat in the mud in the middle of the road, blocking William's path into London.

Alyce giggled. William swore.

Robert's laughter swelled. "Welcome to London, lady wife. May it bring you joy!"

They passed under the broad stone arch of Cripplegate together, still laughing, with the others trailing after in a ragtag string. Alyce didn't bother to look back. Robert was at her side and that was all the assurance she needed.

She was in London!

The experience was almost overwhelming, for if the road outside the city had seemed noisy and crowded, the streets of London were thrice that. People flowed around them in a seemingly endless stream, talking and swearing and hawking their wares, apparently oblivious to the sheer wonder of it all.

There were Jews with their pointy caps, and churchmen in the robes of a half-dozen orders, peddlers and housewives with shopping baskets over their arms and ragged urchins darting through the crowd. An old woman cried out offers of miraculous potions while another picked her way down the side of the street, two squawking hens dangling by their feet from each hand, wings flapping wildly. A band of jongleurs shouted insults and jokes as they passed, inviting them to stop for a show if they had a few pennies to pay for the privilege.

Impossible to see it all! Impossible to sort out the sights and sounds and scents into a coherent whole. Even the martial notes that rang so discordantly beneath the din—the armed men in the street and the wary look on strangers' faces at the sight of Robert's guards—were not enough to quell her excitement. Stunned, deafened, and defenseless, Alyce stared about her in openmouthed wonder.

It was only when Robert touched her arm, drawing her attention back to him, that she remembered what had brought her to this strange new world in the first place. She started to stammer out an apology, but he smiled and shook his head, stopping her before she began.

"There, milady," he said, pointing. "That's Wardell House."

Alyce looked where he pointed, and sucked in her breath in shock.

She'd expected to find her new home was much like the homes of the merchants in Ayllesbury—a long, narrow two-storied structure of timber or stone with a stall out front, or possibly a large shutter that could be pulled up during the day, and a broad wood shelf where Robert would display his merchandise. A practical, solid house filled from cellar to roof with servants and apprentices and whoever else a merchant might keep in his employ. In her more optimistic moments, she'd hoped there'd be a garden in back, but her imaginings never got beyond that.

She wasn't prepared for the grand stone edifice that ran from one alleyway to the other, as arrogantly superior to its less imposing neighbors as its owner was to lesser men. It was two stories high, with six costly glass-paned windows on the upper floor and two barred and shuttered windows on the ground floor. Between the two lower windows was a single vaulted gate with broad, iron-strapped oak doors that opened inward.

A small boy slouched on the ground to the side of the open gate, idly pitching pebbles at a mud hole in the middle of the street. He looked up at the sound of their horses, then leaped to his feet, eyes wide with excitement.

"Master Wardell! Master Wardell!" he shouted, waving and jumping up and down like a demented frog.

Robert raised his hand in greeting. That was all it took. The boy flung down the rest of his pebbles and raced through the gate, shouting the news of their arrival.

They were hard on the boy's heels. The horses broke

into a trot, eager for their stable. No one bothered to rein them in. With Robert in the lead, they swept through the gate and into a small stone-flagged courtyard.

From that vantage point Alyce could see that the main building which fronted the street was L-shaped and newly built. Not so the hodgepodge of other stone and timber buildings jammed one right next to the other, forming, with the main house, a rough square around the courtyard. Alyce caught a glimpse of a garden through a narrow opening between the buildings, but she didn't have a chance to see more. They were scarcely through the gate when heads started popping out of various windows to call greetings and people came flying out of doors to flutter around them, clamorous as pigeons after corn and just as much underfoot.

Robert swung out of the saddle and threw his reins to the boy who'd announced their arrival, then crossed to her.

"My home," he said, indicating the buildings with a grand sweep of his hand. "Now your home as well, milady, and welcome."

The courteous words of thanks that Alyce had practiced for just this moment died on her tongue unspoken.

Her home.

The words had a curious ring of finality about them, as sharp as the words that had pronounced them man and wife. She nodded instead of speaking and let him help her dismount. Her stomach churned. Her knees sagged like wet rushes. Her palms were coldly damp inside her gloves.

Something of her distress must have shown on her face, for Robert took her gloved hand in both of his and leaned close to whisper, "It will be all right, milady. Truly."

His grip was strong and sure. His gaze singed her with its heat, yet she could read nothing of what lay behind it. His features had once more fallen into that sharp-drawn stillness she was coming to recognize as his way of keeping his thoughts as well hidden as the emotions they brought with them.

"There's no one here will harm you," he insisted, "nor treat you with less than the respect that is your due. I swear it."

She tore her gaze from his face to scan the unfamiliar buildings and unfamiliar faces that surrounded her. Something in her stomach knotted painfully.

Dutiful respect!

It was a cold, gray thought for a cold, gray day. Pray God the fire, at least, was warm!

7

UNCERTAIN
WELCOMES

ROBERT LED HER up the stone steps, through
a narrow screens passage, and into the main hall, which
occupied the short end of the main house's ell. The hall
wasn't anywhere near so large as Colmaine's great hall, but
it was far more welcoming. Instead of a fire set on an open
stone hearth in the middle of the room, it had two broad
modern fireplaces, one at either end. Fires blazed in both,
brightly welcoming. In Robert Wardell's house, evidently, no one counted the cost of firewood. The stone
floors were clean, the rushes freshly laid, and the linen
cloths on the trestle tables were pristine white, unmarred
by stains or ill-mended tears.

Alyce removed her gloves while she stared about her,
acutely conscious of being the center of attention. Curious
faces peeked out from doorways and around odd corners,
but the pair that caught her eye were two women, one short,
fat, and sour-faced, the other tall and broomstick thin. They
stood stiff and straight at the far end of the main table, like
regal servitors who had grudgingly condescended to wait
on rabble. A squarely built, well-dressed man of middle age
stood in front of them, keeping his eye on everything and
almost quivering with the effort to look as if he weren't anxious to be presented to the new lady of the house.

When she thought no one was looking, the broom-stick twitched a corner of the tablecloth into place, then smoothed away nonexistent wrinkles. The effort earned her a scowl from the dour woman and a warning hiss from the man, who Alyce guessed was the steward.

Alyce pressed her lips together to keep from smiling in relief. She'd lived with the quarrels and petty jealousies of a castle's staff all her life, so the sniping jealousy between the two women was comfortingly familiar. Life here might not be so very different from Colmaine, after all, despite the luxuries that surrounded her.

She turned and caught Robert glaring at the fretful threesome. There was no mistaking *that* look either. It was the same one she gave the pages at Castle Colmaine if they indulged in personal squabbles whenever guests were at table.

The tightness in Alyce's shoulders eased still more.

Piers, who'd been sent on ahead earlier in the day to alert the household of their coming, danced up to them, eyes alight with mischief.

"Welcome, milady," he said, gracefully extending a fine silver goblet filled with red wine. "Master Wardell said I should make sure all was in readiness for you. Since the fires were lit, the tables set, and the cook had chased me out of the kitchen, the only thing I could be sure of was the wine."

"And you sampled it first, just in case?" said Alyce, amused and grateful for a familiar, welcoming face.

"Aye, milady. Though not from *your* goblet, I assure you! I'd fear a beating and I ventured so far."

"You'll have need to fear *my* wrath, scamp, if you don't draw me a cup of that as well." William Townsend, divested of cloak, gloves, and spurs, had come up behind them, leaving the others to gravitate to the fires at either end of the room.

"Only a cup?" Piers pretended shock. "You aren't sickening, are you, Master Townsend?"

"Hah!" said William, grinning. "Bring me a pitcher, then, and I'll have at it while Robert's too distracted to notice what I'm about."

As Piers darted off to do his bidding, William let out his breath in a gusty snort, stuck his thumbs in his belt, and looked around him. "Traveling's damned thirsty work. Be glad you've such comforts to come home to, Robert."

Robert's lips twitched. It was only as the tension in his own shoulders eased that Alyce realized it had been there at all. She couldn't decide if it was comforting or worrisome to know that he had been as uncertain of her homecoming as she was.

Just the word "homecoming" was enough to bring her tension springing back.

"Pray God Mistress Townsend doesn't hear you say so, my friend," Robert warned. "She'd scarcely thank you for valuing her housekeeping so low."

William snorted dismissively. "If you think my good wife would take insult, you haven't listened to her babbling on about 'Robert's new hall' and 'Robert's new solar' and all the details about 'Robert's' damned new tile floors—and that in spite of this new babe in her belly to distract her! Tell her how often I may that Robert's money chests are better stuffed than mine, she'll have none of it. Ah, thank you, lad!"

He took the huge mug Piers offered and saluted Alyce. "Milady!"

Alyce could see his Adam's apple bobbing up and down with the great gulps he took. He didn't stop until he had to come up for air.

"Ah! That helps ease a man's sufferings, indeed it does."

"Too much like that," said Robert, frowning, "and you'll feel nothing at all, and we won't see the back of you until tomorrow."

"And risk a hiding from an angry wife? I think not!"

William lowered the mug. "You'd best get on with the introductions, Robert. Your good steward is like to pee himself from being so eager to be the first to welcome your lady, and judging from her scowls, Erwyna might well poison your ale and you don't put her second. And that's not counting the rest of us, half-starved and three-quarters frozen, wondering if you mean to send us on our way with nothing more than a sip of wine as thanks for having stood by you through your ordeal these past few days."

Alyce considered the possibility of dumping her own wine down the front of his tunic. Ordeal, indeed!

She glanced at the three who stood at the main table watching her like ferrets at a mouse hole, then at the servants who were moving among Robert's guests with cups and pitchers of wine, trying not to reveal their intense curiosity about their new mistress. Every one of them, she knew, would be impatient to be presented and avid to gain an edge over their fellows in her favor, if they could—or keep her firmly in her place as an unwelcome upstart, if they couldn't.

She took a fortifying sip of wine. Five days in the saddle and the wet and the cold. Her clothes were stained, sagging with damp and hemmed in mud kicked up by the horses' hooves; her wimple was wrinkled and had long since gone from white to a blotchy cream; her face was chapped and raw from the cold and had turned an unbecoming red. She didn't need to look in a mirror to know it was so. And this was how she was to be presented to the people who would call her mistress.

Ordeal might be the right name for it, after all.

JOHN RARETON WAS the steward's name. His welcome was florid and pointedly conducted in the finest of court French. An honest man, Alyce thought, and puffed up at having a baron's daughter as mistress.

The broomstick, Margaret Preston, was cook. She'd come from a knight's household, she said with condescending dignity. *And woe to anyone who intrudes in my domain.* She didn't need to say the words for Alyce to catch the challenge. It didn't worry her. Dame Preston would be vulnerable to flattery, respect, and a discreet touch of arrogance, regularly applied.

The stout, sour-faced woman was Erwyna, alewife, housekeeper, and mainstay of the household—or so she informed Alyce. "I've been here since before Master Wardell was apprentice to *his* master, milady. There's none other as can say that, nor knows the way of things better than I."

She shot a challenging look at Margaret Preston, who frowned at the rafters with the air of a woman who saw cobwebs, but was too well bred to mention the matter in public.

Alyce mumbled a polite response. Erwyna was clearly the bully of the Wardell household and not pleased at having a new mistress—*any* new mistress. She wouldn't risk outright defiance, but she also wouldn't hesitate to make Alyce's tenure as difficult and unpleasant as possible. The battle lines were being drawn.

Erwyna reluctantly yielded to Joshua, the gardener, and Haim, the head of Master Wardell's stables, and to undercooks and a half-score of maids and boys who had somehow found a place in the house's hierarchy. Their names jumbled in Alyce's head, but their faces stood out clearly. Nervous or sly or boastful, intelligent or slow-witted and dull, they were each of them an individual, each a part of this new life of hers with the power to welcome her or make her life a misery, as they chose.

The last to be presented was a little brown mouse of a maid whose voice quavered so she was nigh unintelligible.

"Githa, milady, and your serving woman, if it please you." She sank into a curtsy so deep she almost disappeared beneath the rushes. Judging from her expression, she expected Alyce to have her tossed into the street without so much as a word of farewell.

Alyce bent impulsively and clasped the girl's hand in both her own, drawing her to her feet. "I'm sure it will please me very much," she said. "Master Wardell was most thoughtful to bring you to me."

Erwyna looked as if she'd just taken a bite of rotten eel, but the little maid flushed with relief as she stammered assurances of devotion.

As Githa retreated, Alyce studied the people gathered before her. Altogether, not a quarter the number of Colmaine's people, but a goodly number still. She turned her head and caught Robert watching her, brows drawn together in a questioning frown.

She gave him the only answer she could . . . she smiled.

Robert couldn't control what his people thought, but he had promised her their respect, and Githa had sworn her good service.

There were, she thought, far worse ways to begin.

WHERE *WAS SHE?*

Robert drummed his fingers on the table in front of him. He wanted this dinner over with and his friends gone, which was a less than gracious thanks for their having stood by him these past several days. That didn't matter because he *still* wanted them gone . . . and they couldn't even get started if Alyce wasn't here. Githa had led her away as soon as the formal introductions were over, and she hadn't yet reappeared.

How long could it possibly take for a woman to use the garderobe and wash her face and hands?

William spotted her first. He'd already drunk deep of his wine, but his eyes were bright as he leaned over and poked Robert in the ribs. He gestured toward where Alyce stood at the entrance to the screens passage, looking about her with the air of a woman who wondered if demons lurked in the rushes.

"There she is, Robert," William said, grinning wickedly. "You can give off worrying that she's left you already or decided to hide under the bed where you can't reach her."

"I wasn't wor—"

"The devil you say!" William's grin became a leer. "I'd think you were distempered did I not know it was just a case of you with a new filly and no chance to try her paces."

"Damn you, William! I'll thank you to keep that vulgar tongue of yours between your teeth. And I'm *not* distempered," he added fiercely.

"Hoh! Tell that to the one-eared beggar! He might believe you, for I certainly won't. I've two good eyes in my head and I can tell when a man's cock is beginning to twitch in his braies."

"My cock be damned!"

"No doubt, and every other man's besides." William's grin faded. He tugged thoughtfully at his lower lip as he watched Alyce cross the hall toward them.

"Damned if I don't like the wench, Robert. She's no beauty, but she's no fool either, nor yet a coward, as she proved in that crowd this afternoon. And despite five days in the saddle, I've yet to hear a word of complaint from her. She might serve you very well, after all. And not," he added with a knowing wink, "just in bed, though I've a notion you found her a bit more to your liking there than you'd expected."

Robert glowered at his friend. "You know, Townsend, I'd cut off your balls and boil them if they weren't so damnably large and hairy."

William threw back his head and laughed. "They are

that, but my wits are well polished, my friend, have no fear." One bushy brow quirked upward. "And since when have you taken to vulgarities?"

Robert scowled.

William leaned closer; his voice dropped. "You've done well for yourself, little though I thought it when we rode through the gates of Colmaine. I begin to think you might have found as good and true a mate as I, and I'd not say that lightly. Quick-tempered and shrewish she may be, but my Mary is a wife worth having."

He raised his voice once more, this time in greeting. "My Lady! Welcome! Here's Robert chafing at playing host, and the rest of us near faint from hunger. Much longer and I'd have come to fetch you myself, before I grew too weak to manage all those stairs!"

She blushed. On her pale, freckled skin, the effect was startling, and strangely attractive. "I beg pardon. I thought you would begin without me." She made her way around the table to them, glancing up in astonishment when Robert rose and pulled out the chair on his right hand for her, the chair between him and William.

"William will survive a few minutes' hunger, milady, little though he likes it," Robert said, again taking his seat beside her. There was something different about her, something . . .

It took a moment for him to realize that she'd discarded her travel-stained wimple. Instead she'd drawn her veil forward and over her shoulders to disguise the change. It was wasted effort. A long lock of her hair had worked its way loose to curl around her slender throat. The dark green of her tunic showed brighter against her white skin, with the merest hint of her linen shift visible beneath, its edge worked with delicate green stitches as though she'd planned the pieces to be worn together.

He hadn't realized how long her neck was, or how

graceful. He could see the pulse that beat in the hollow of her throat, and the delicate tracery of veins beneath the surface.

The direction of his thoughts was suddenly diverted by an imperious twitch in his braies. Robert frowned and dropped his gaze to the table.

Judging from the way William was claiming her attention, he'd noticed the change in Alyce's garb as well. Or perhaps his old friend, amused by his earlier jest and fueled by too many cups of wine too quickly drunk, did it just to annoy him.

Disgusted, Robert signaled for the simple meal to be served. The sooner William and his friends were fed, the sooner they'd be gone, leaving him in peace . . . and alone with Alyce.

William jumped to his feet and snatched up his cup. "A toast!" he roared, raising his cup high. "To Robert and his lady wife. May their union be blessed"—the assembled company waited, cups half raised—"and Robert have the strength to keep it so!"

Robert's friends roared their approval. Alyce's face flamed scarlet. As soon as good manners permitted, she snatched up the silver goblet she shared with Robert and retreated behind it.

Under cover of the confusion of the meal, Robert scanned the room, studying the faces of his friends. Beneath the laughter and the hunger, they were all of them tired and worried by the news that Hensford had so eagerly shared from his stinking dung heap.

King Henry and Earl Simon drew ever closer to outright war. Edward's attacks on the towns that had supported Montfort only drove the people more firmly to the earl's side and widened the gulf between the two camps, until there would be no bridging it except with the heaped-up bodies of dead Englishmen.

Every man in the room had accompanied him to Colmaine out of friendship, but more than friendship was at stake. On his word, his vision, each of them had joined with him in lending support—and money—to the Lord Edward. They had as much riding on his marriage and the political connections it brought him as he did.

And all he wanted was for them to be gone.

Robert picked up the goblet of wine and drank. As his lips touched the cool metal rim where Alyce's had pressed, he thought of the cup they'd shared at Colmaine . . . and of what had followed.

The memory brought the twitch in his braies to painful, aching attention. He carefully set down the goblet.

Tomorrow he would deal with the questions of trade and the threat of war. Tonight . . .

William had been right, after all.

Tonight, all he wanted was to be alone with Alyce.

WHILE THE SERVANTS cleaned up the remains of supper and Robert was closeted with his steward, Githa led Alyce upstairs. Because she hadn't wanted to keep Robert waiting when they first arrived, Alyce had straightened her clothes in the garderobe on the lower floor, and washed her face and hands in a basin Githa brought to her there.

This was her first sight of the upper floor. The long solar had been built above the house's main gate. During the day the glazed windows along the outer wall would flood the room with light and provide a good view of whatever might be passing in the street below. That night, however, the shutters were closed and the only light came from a small fire in the fireplace built into the wall opposite the windows. Two uncurtained beds for senior members of the household occupied the end of the room closest to the stairs. Several tall chests lined the walls, storage no doubt for pallets and blankets for those not lucky enough to merit a spot in the beds. A single chair and scattering of stools stood beside the fireplace.

Alyce didn't have a chance to do more than glance around the room, for Githa immediately led her across the solar to Robert's private chamber at the far end.

Hers and Robert's.

Alyce stopped short at the open door. It was a small room, especially after the much larger solar, but it had its own fireplace—to Alyce, an unheard-of luxury—and a fine curtained bed and two of the glass windows she'd seen from the street outside. A square dark chair stood to one side of the fireplace, a low stool at the other. Two leather-bound trunks, one at the foot of the bed, one at the side, bore tall candlesticks and fat wax candles instead of crude little pots of wicked tallow. Painted canvas cloths covered the two unbroken walls, providing decoration as well as insulation from cold stone.

"What are those cloths on the floor?" Alyce demanded, startled by the red and black patterned squares of woven cloth that covered much of the stone floor.

Githa swelled with pride. "Carpets, milady. Brought all the way from Spain. They say the Lady Eleanor, Lord Edward's wife, brought such as these with her at her marriage, but only the very richest households have copied her. Very fine, these are, and far softer and warmer beneath your feet than rushes."

"Carpets," said Alyce blankly. She tentatively probed one with her foot, then stepped onto it. The thick-woven cloth gave beneath her feet. Even through the still-damp leather soles of her shoes, she could feel the difference between it and the cold hard floor. "Carpets!"

"And hot water for your bath, milady," Githa added shyly, indicating the wooden tub that had been set before the fire and the steaming, covered wooden bucket on the floor beside it. "Master Wardell gave orders to have real soap from Castile for you, and sweet-scented oils, and fine new towels from Lincoln. I've set the towels to warm in front of the fire. See?"

Alyce murmured her thanks and rapidly shed her travel-stained clothes, then stepped into the steaming tub. The water flowed around her legs, then up to her waist as she sank into its heat. A pity she couldn't linger. Though John Rareton had insisted on a word with Robert, she didn't expect her husband to delay overlong on business details that would be the same come morning.

Her husband.

With a washcloth she squeezed the sweet-scented water over her shoulder, relishing the slide of it on her skin as it poured over her chest and down her back. She dragged the thick cloth along the path the water had coursed, over her breast and ribs and down her belly, into the scented water, then up again to squeeze more water over her shoulder, then down, then up again.

There was a languorous, erotic feel to the familiar actions, and if she shut her eyes she could imagine it was Robert's hand that held the cloth, his touch that trailed over her skin, his gaze that followed the rivulets as they traced their wayward paths down her body.

Perhaps someday she could invite him to share her bath, or offer to share his. Would he like it? she wondered, then thought of the way he had touched her on their wedding night and decided he would.

But how would they manage, a little tub like this and the two of them? She pictured the tangle of legs—long legs, her pale skin against his dark—and the possible physical combinations, imagined the way the water would slosh and how warm and slick his skin would feel against hers, how hard—

Alyce forced her eyes open and bent to scrub at her

toes, trying not to grin like a fool. There were, it seemed, more things to learn about married life than just how to manage a merchant's household.

Thank God she was an apt pupil.

While the kitchen scullions took away the water and the tub, Alyce donned the heavy linen shift and light cloak that Githa had laid out for her, then sat on the stool in front of the fire so Githa could comb out her tangled hair.

The combination of warmth and the feel of clean clothes against clean skin was comforting, the steady stroking of the comb through her hair as soothing as a lullaby. Heavy-eyed, Alyce wrapped her arms around herself and stared into the fire, letting her thoughts drift until they seemed to merge with the flames, insubstantial as light.

As if from far away, she heard a door open as the last scullery maid slipped away, felt a draft of colder air, saw the flames duck and flare. None of it roused her from her drowsy dreams. Robert would be here soon. Soon.

She closed her eyes and sighed with pleasure as the comb once more resumed its slow stroking through her hair, over her crown and down her back in a simple, sensual rhythm that lulled and teased her both. She murmured something, she wasn't sure what, and tilted her head back, into the hands that held her.

Her hair crackled in the air around her like a live thing. Loose strands clung to her face and throat, and to her hand when she tried to brush them away.

"Did you know your hair is like fire?" a soft voice whispered in her ear.

Her heart gave a panicked thump and landed in her throat. She spun around on the stool. "Robert!"

He laughed, the sound of it like warm honey over her skin. "That I am, milady. I trust you expected no other?"

He'd bathed, shaved, and donned a plain black tunic, loosely belted at the waist, that made his lean body seem even leaner. He was kneeling behind her, her comb in one hand, her hair in the other, twisted like a thick, soft rope. Strands of it clung to him, threads of pure red light against the black sleeve of his tunic.

Lust flashed through her, melting her bones. Imagination couldn't begin to compare to the temptation of the man himself.

"I didn't hear you come in."

He smiled and tapped the tip of her nose with the comb. "I slipped in when the last of the maids were leaving, and sent Githa away with them."

She could see the firelight reflected in the black of his eyes. His hold on her hair was the only physical connection between them, but she could have sworn she felt a heat in him to match the rising heat in her. He leaned closer.

"After five long days," he said, very soft and low, "I found I wanted to be alone with my wife."

Alyce gave a small, choked cry and wrapped her arms around his neck. Their lips met.

Dimly, as if from far away, Alyce heard the clatter of bone against stone flooring as he tossed the comb aside, then he was coiling her hair around her back, binding her to him as he drew her with him, off her stool and down onto the wondrous red carpet from Castile.

8

UNANSWERED PRAYERS

ROBERT DIDN'T REPEAT the mistake of abandoning his lady's bed before cockcrow. He roused to light and the muffled sounds of people in the street. At first, he wasn't quite sure what was different about the morning, then Alyce stirred, nestling against him with the soft murmurs of a sleeping child, and he came awake with a gasp.

The air was unpleasantly chill. The fire had died long since, but firewood was liberally stacked at one side of the chimney and there would be live coals beneath the ashes. He'd never bothered with a morning fire before, but this morning he wanted one in spite of the work awaiting him. He told himself it would be more pleasant for Alyce if she woke to a warm room, but truth was, he preferred to remain snugly in bed with his wife rather than spend the next few hours with John Rareton, poring over inventories and accounting rolls.

Moving carefully so as not to awaken her, Robert slipped out of bed and, naked, crossed to the hearth, his skin pricking with the cold. He was acutely conscious of the change as he stepped from carpet to cold stone, then back again. The feel of the heavy wool beneath his feet stirred tantalizing memories of the night before.

A few puffs from the small bellows that hung beside the chimney was all it took to rouse the still-warm coals to glowing life. The flames caught at the dry wood, crackling and flaring in a cold draft that circled the room. Robert shivered and rose to his feet.

He turned to find his wife lying on her side, her head propped on one hand, the blankets drawn up to cover her breasts. She was watching him with the sleepy-eyed look of a satisfied woman. He could see a small red mark on her neck where he'd nipped her, and was reminded of the scrapes on his back where her nails had raked him in her ecstasy. Her hair flowed over the tumbled covers like a shredded silken banner claimed from the field of battle.

His blood warmed and his cock twitched, in spite of the cold.

Her mouth curved into a faint smile. "A fire?" Her lower lip quivered with the effort not to laugh. "It's true, then, what they say. That life in London is softer than elsewhere."

"Is that what they say?" He plunged under the covers.

She squealed when his toes brushed her leg, but obligingly rolled into him, nonetheless. "That's what they say. And that there's gold and silver for the taking in every street."

"The gold and silver is a fantasy, madame, and I do assure you that not everything is soft."

Her eyes widened as he pulled her close against him; her mouth quirked in a smug little smile. "It seems there have been more fires lit than just the one on the hearth."

"Indeed." He propped himself up on one elbow and rolled so his belly pressed against her side, savoring her warmth. "And you, madame, and I mistake not, have a liking for the heat."

She curved into him so that her breast brushed against his chest. Robert felt a tightening in his scrotum as his own nipples hardened in response.

"I do find it agrees with me," she said, unabashed. Under the covers, her hand stroked down his side and over his hip.

He couldn't disguise the pleasure that rippled through him at her caress. His skin burned where she touched. He shifted so that his legs tangled intimately with hers. With his free hand, he captured a wayward lock of hair that had fallen across her cheek and tucked it behind her ear, then slowly traced the length of it over her throat and across her breast, his gaze following the path of his finger. Alyce sucked in her breath at his touch.

His gaze flashed back to her face. His grin widened as he curled the hair around his finger. "Perhaps it is this fire you wear when you wear nothing at all. It seems to cover a temper that's hot enough for two."

"You mean at Cripplegate?"

He nodded.

She frowned and ran her hand up over his chest, spreading her fingers so the soft, curling hair would sift through them. "I am not usually provoked to temper."

"Indeed?" He grinned. "I swear, it flared hot enough yesterday."

He'd meant to tease her, but his words fell amiss. Her frown deepened.

"I have lived with quarreling and fighting all my life. I had thought—hoped—that marriage to a merchant might be more . . . peaceable."

His smile was wry. "Did you think it was only your father who had quarrels with his neighbors?"

"Since my father quarrels with everyone, even Earl Simon, to whom he's sworn allegiance—"

Her hand froze in the midst of its tantalizing exploration. "That's why you married me, isn't it? Because you support the Lord Edward, while my father is allied with Simon de Montfort. And I . . ."

"And you?"

"Was available, and could serve as balance between the two camps," she finished unhappily.

For answer, she had only his silence. It was enough.

"That *is* the reason you married me, isn't it?"

"Yes," said Robert, wary and treading with care. "That's why I married you." He hesitated, but found he could not lie to her. Not when she stared at him so wide-eyed and unflinchingly. His Alyce was not a woman who would appreciate lies.

"For that," he said at last, "and for the manors you brought me. They lie near my own property at Wincham, and though they're not in good state, with time and care they can be made profitable again." His gaze hardened. "And I intend to make them *very* profitable."

Her gaze dropped as her hand fell away from his chest.

"Surely you knew all that," he said irritated now. "Neither your father nor I made any pretense it was otherwise."

"So that's what I'm worth? Three manors and the dubious value of my father's ties to Montfort?"

"And a hundred pounds in good silver, milady," Robert said coldly. "Your money, now, though I doubt you'll ever see it."

"No." She pulled away from him and sat up, drawing her knees to her chest and clutching the covers as if they were a shield against the world—a shield against him. She leaned forward to wrap her arms around her legs. Her hair fell around her, hiding her face.

Robert's gut churned. Dark memories roared at him, reminders of another woman who had turned away and wrapped herself in silence, shutting him out forever.

He beat the memories back as he fought to keep from touching Alyce.

Her hair had fallen so that her shoulder was exposed, satiny pale under its tracing of freckles, reminding him how soft and warm her skin was.

He remembered how carefully he'd traced the line

from throat to shoulder the night before, over her breast and down her side. He remembered, all too well, how she had drawn in her breath at his touch and arched against him, wanton and wild and sweet. Even now, the memory stirred the fire within him.

He jerked upright, shaken by the unexpected surge of need. It was one thing to take a wife for practical and eminently rational reasons, quite another to be ensnared by emotions he'd buried twelve long years ago.

Alyce hunched her shoulders at his abrupt retreat and tightened her hold on her knees.

"You're right," she mumbled to the bedcovers. "I'll never see that hundred pounds. My father will have spent it all ere long."

"Is that why you agreed to marry me, milady? Because of the silver?" A harsh laugh escaped him. "You speak as if none of your noble blood ever married for advantage, yet I swear, from the way your father bargained, he'd have tied you to a mad Welshman if needs served—and been pleased with his bargain, to boot!"

Alyce flushed, but refused to meet his gaze.

With difficulty, Robert swallowed his anger, forced his voice to a calm he was far from feeling. "Come, lady. I'll swear it's not I who has all the gain of this marriage. Nor even the greatest part."

For an instant, he wasn't sure if she was going to attack him or run away.

She did neither. Instead, she fell back on the heavy feather pillow and stared up at the curtained canopy above her. She still clutched the tumbled covers, but he could see her right breast peeping out from beneath the folds of white linen, the dusky-rose nipple pricked to a tempting point.

His groin tightened as his body roused to the sight of her. In the silence, the snapping of the fire seemed unpleasantly loud.

"No," she said at last in a small, tight voice. "It's not you who has the greatest gain of this marriage, Master Wardell. It's not you at all."

Because of the pain he heard in her voice—because he could not help it—Robert reached to touch her, to reassure her.

Too late. In one rough motion, she threw back the covers and rolled away from him and out of bed.

The instant her feet touched the carpet, Alyce regretted her hasty abandonment of Robert's bed. She was too proud, and too much the coward, to apologize however. Especially not when she was naked in the cold and he was still decently covered by the bed linens.

She snatched up the shift she'd briefly worn the night before and whipped it over her head, then grabbed for the clean woolen kirtle and retreated to the warmth of the fire to finish dressing.

She hadn't had the luxury of a fire in the morning since she was a child, but still she flinched as her bare feet hit the cold hearthstones. She gritted her teeth. She would *not* step back on the carpet. Robert had taken her on that carpet last night, and now was not the time to be reminded of their fierce coupling, nor the joy it had brought.

Blindly she tugged at her kirtle, fumbling for the sleeves, conscious of Robert in the bed behind her. Too late she realized she hadn't yet tied the laces on her shift. It slid off her shoulder and down her arm, baring her breast and swallowing her hand. Irritated, she pulled it up, but lost the opening to her kirtle sleeve in the process.

Her hair was as much an obstacle as her unlaced shift. It was a wilderness, so tangled and tumbled that it fell about her in a froth of unmanageable curls, spilling over her front and back and getting in the way of her dressing. She tried and failed to toss it back. That was a two-handed job and at the moment her hands were entangled in the mess she'd made of her clothing.

Behind her, the bed creaked. Alyce swore softly under her breath.

With one last desperate heave, she dragged the kirtle over her head and, wriggling and swearing, found the sleeve openings, shoved her hands through, and tugged it down. She still hadn't properly laced her shift—its sleeves were balled up to her elbows and her hair was caught between the two garments—but at least she was decently covered.

"Do you always fight getting dressed, milady?"

Alyce jumped. She hadn't heard Robert cross the room.

He tugged at her kirtle, pulling it into place. "Is it me?"

His hand curved over her shoulder as he bent toward her; his voice lowered seductively. "Or is it just that you're loath to forgo another pleasuring?"

She stiffened. "I'm not one to lie abed in the morning, sir."

He leaned closer, so close she could feel his breath on her hair. "Not even with me?"

She shrugged free of his hold and swung around to face him. Too late she realized he hadn't bothered to don even his braies. The sight of his long, muscled body, fine as a coursing greyhound's, sent an unsettling bolt of heat through her.

She turned back to stare at the fire, face flaming. As she fumbled with the lacing at the neck of her shift, she was achingly conscious of him so close behind her. She'd seen naked men before, but not one of them had ever stirred her blood the way Robert did. She closed her eyes, willing herself not to think of it.

It wasn't enough. Her treacherous mind provided the images that her eyes had shut out—the dark, springing hair that softened the hard lines of chest and belly, the nest of black curls at his groin that contrasted with the meaty

red of his thrusting sex, the coarser black hair that darkened his thighs and calves.

Despite the layers of linen and wool that divided
them, she would swear she could feel the animal heat of
him at her back.

Without speaking, he gently lifted the tangled mass
of her hair, tugging it free of her kirtle and dragging it
back over her shoulders. She could feel the weight of it
shift under his hand as he gathered it together at the nape
of her neck.

"I would not have us begin the day with harsh words
still between us, lady."

"No." She would swear there was regret in his voice,
and, deeper than the regret, a dark, troubling anger, scarce
repressed.

"Then come back to bed with me. Now." Like a boy
playing with a string to distract himself from worrisome
thoughts, he twisted the tail into a heavy rope.

Alyce stiffened, fighting against the urge to melt into
his hands. "I will not be ordered into your bed, sir, wife
or no."

His grip on her hair tightened—she could feel the
pull of it at the back of her head. Another twist and his
hold on her would turn painful. He sucked in an angry
breath.

"It was not an order, madame."

"It sounded like one."

He tensed—she could feel it, even though the only
contact between them was his hold on her hair—then he
abruptly let go and stepped back, leaving the twisted rope
he'd made to unwind of its own accord.

"You are proud, lady. Proud and cruel."

"I'm not cruel." The words caught in her throat.

"Proud, then."

A braver woman would have confronted him in all his

nakedness. She stared blindly at the stones of the fireplace. "I have the right to it, whether my father bargained me away or no."

"Would you let that pride divide us?"

She kept silent. Her breath burned in her lungs. The popping of the fire was the only sound in the room. Though she did not turn to look, she sensed Robert's struggle to master his temper.

His finger brushed her cheek as he looped a wayward strand of hair back over her ear. "I would not have us quarrel this way," he said at last, not on a note of apology, but of regret.

"Nor I."

"Well, then?" He bent and pressed a kiss against her throat, soft as a feather's caress.

She wanted to give in. Oh, how much she wanted to! But he was right. She *was* proud. Far too proud to go to his bed just because he bid her. Too proud to give in, even when her blood burned and her body ached for his touch.

Proud, not for her name or her rank or, God knew, the beauty she hadn't been granted, but for herself, for her own value as a woman and a human being.

She had watched the women her father had kept after her mother's death, pretty creatures who thought their charms sufficient protection against being cast aside before they had secured their place within Sir Fulk's household. They had all been wrong, and Alyce had learned early the lessons their fates had taught her.

Because of them, and because she could not do otherwise, she'd fought to protect the fragile sense of self-worth lodged deep within her. She'd taken pride in her ability to run Colmaine despite her father's mockery and the obstacles he'd placed in her way, foolishly hoping that marriage would bring the respect her father had never granted her.

Now marriage—a marriage arranged on a shrewdly calculated exchange of land and coin and connections, as she'd known it would be—had claimed both her name and her rank. She would not, *could* not, let it claim her sense of self as well. She would not give herself for Robert's amusement only, for amusements palled, and she had no desire to be forgotten as her father's companions had been forgotten.

"What of your work?" she asked, searching for a way out of the impasse. "Surely you have better things to do than lie abed with me, sir?"

"My work will wait."

"And mine?"

He laughed. "You, milady, have nothing to do but please me."

Anger exploded within her. She spun to face him.

"Nothing but please you! Is that what you think, now that my lands and name are yours? That I lack the wit for anything other than to warm your bed and tease your flesh? That I'm no better than a lapdog, to be petted one moment, then kicked into a corner and forgotten the next?"

"No, I—"

"If so, you much mistake me! I am no moonling child, sir, nor a whore in all but name, and I will not tolerate being treated as such!"

"I didn't—"

She shoved past him to snatch up her shoes, then crossed to the door and threw it open. The half-dozen people gathered in the solar froze like sheep at sight of the shepherd, mouths agape and eyes bulging. Alyce spared them one scornful glance, then turned back to brandish her shoes at Robert.

"And should you treat me as an idiot lapdog, in spite of all," she added hotly, "be warned! I have teeth, Master Wardell—sharp teeth—and I will bite!"

With that, she turned and, hair flying like a battle flag, swept across the solar and out the door beyond.

Robert stormed after her, but was too late. By the time he reached the door to the solar, she had disappeared.

The silence was deep enough to drown dogs, but even the presence of six slack-jawed witnesses, including his red-faced steward, his grinning apprentice, and his outraged housekeeper, wasn't enough to deflate the erection that waved so arrogantly in front of him.

The bug-eyed kitchen maids and the stable boy, whom Erwyna had set to cleaning the windows and scrubbing the floor, clapped their hands over their mouths to stifle their giggles.

Rareton cleared his throat and pointedly turned away to study the far wall. His hands were clasped behind his back, but Robert could see his fingers twitching.

Piers's gaze dropped to the front of his own tunic, but not before Robert caught the same speculative gleam in his eyes that shone there every time the boy compared the merits of two different bolts of cloth.

Erwyna simply stared at his crotch with the disgusted look of a fishwife inspecting an underweight eel. Robert had a sudden, gut-twisting image of her with a fish knife in her hand. His erection drooped.

"What?" he demanded angrily, glaring at them all.

The kitchen maids' eyes crossed from the effort to keep from laughing out loud. John Rareton cleared his throat while Piers stared at the floor, whistling under his breath, and nudged the bundle of parchment rolls that sat at his feet as if to remind Robert of the work that awaited him.

Erwyna settled for cuffing the stable lad's ears and sternly ordering him to haul away the buckets of dirty water and to bring up fresh—quick!—before she flayed him for his foolishness.

Robert stepped back into his room and slammed the door behind him. Through the heavy wood, he could hear the sound of the maids choking on laughter.

Good! he thought savagely. Let them choke. As soon as he was dressed, he'd find work enough to keep them busy till the next saint's day, and then some. *All* of them!

HER SHOES WERE on her feet, her shift was decently laced, and her kirtle was properly adjusted by the time Alyce ventured out of the garderobe almost a half hour later. To her relief, there was no one in the passage or the solar, and Robert had dressed and gone, leaving her in sole possession of the upper floor.

The instant she was safely in her chamber, she shut and bolted the door behind her. Her temper had cooled long since, but she didn't yet feel like facing the curious stares that would await her once she went downstairs. She fastened her belt, then settled on the stool before the fire to comb out her tangled hair.

The familiar task took on an unsettling intimacy. With each stroke, she could feel Robert's hands gathering the tumbled mass, twisting it until it became a cord that bound her to him.

She was a fool for having said anything about the marriage agreement he'd reached with her father, triply a fool for having let his comments trouble her. A woman in her station of life—most women, in fact, if they had any property worth disposing of—married for political and financial advantage. In some ways, they were little more than property themselves, first of their fathers, then of their husbands. Their desirability lay in what they could bring to a marriage more than in their beauty or wit or skill. Only a widow had much ordering of her life.

Such was the way God had arranged things. As far as Alyce was concerned, He hadn't done a very good job of arranging, no matter what the priests said about His judgment.

The fire popped and spat a burning ember at her feet,

as if to remind her of the penalty for her arrogance in questioning God.

Chiding herself for her foolishness, Alyce kicked the ember back, then bound up her hair and donned a clean veil and wimple. Hard work was what she needed, no matter what Robert thought. It had been her escape and her salvation in the past, the rock on which she anchored herself.

But to what would she anchor herself now?

The question rang in her head, chillingly blunt.

What, indeed? At Colmaine she had overseen the daily drudgery of baking and mending and cooking and brewing. Though her father had never seen fit to give her the authority she needed to manage his affairs as they ought to have been managed, she had connived, cajoled, and bullied to get the essentials done. She could keep accounts and manage farms and oversee the provisioning of a castle, even hold it in time of siege if necessary.

But what could she do here? From everything she'd seen, the household was well run and Robert's people more than capable of managing on their own. She knew nothing of a merchant's life or the ways of a merchant's household, and even less of the demands of living in a city like London.

Alyce chewed on a torn fingernail, considering. What could she offer Robert beyond the lands he had already claimed in the marriage settlements, or the coupling they shared in their marriage bed? Where was she to cast her anchor now that she'd been thrust into these turbulent and unfamiliar waters?

No answer came to her.

Give it time, she told herself. Whatever there was to learn, she would learn. If Robert wouldn't teach her, she'd find others who would. But first, there was morning mass and penance to be paid for her show of temper.

And an apology owed Robert for her defiance.

Alyce sighed and got to her feet. His laughing dismissal of her still rankled, but despite her occasional flares of temper, she preferred peace to constant brangling, and she had learned long ago that if she didn't smooth over the quarrels, no one ever would.

After a quick check to be sure the fire wouldn't flare up, and an even quicker, involuntary glance at the tumbled bed in the corner, she threw open the door and went to find Robert.

"WITH THE PRESENT troubles, pirates are growing bolder along the coast, threatening the safety of our shipments. Worse, the local dockworkers stopped another ship, the one carrying our latest purchases of cloth from Venice and Lucca. That makes three so far this month."

John Rareton paced in front of the head table in the hall as he worked his way through his litany of troubles, too anxious and nervous to take the chair Robert had pulled out for him. Even the embarrassing incident in the solar had been forgotten under the pressure of more urgent matters.

"The workers are still refusing to give alien ships access to the city's docks. They refuse to let the duties go into Henry's coffers, and the city council are backing them, in the main, despite the damage they're doing to the merchants. The captain of our ship was forced back to the Cinque Ports to see if he could unload there, but the ports are under Montfort's control at the moment, so who is to say if that will serve? The captain was going to try for Rye or Romney, to cut our costs for transport overland, but God knows the ports are so backed up he may go all the way around to Hastings and back to Sandwich and *still* be waiting, even if the fools don't refuse him anchorage. And we haven't yet gotten that second load out of Dover!"

Robert grunted to show he was listening, and toyed with the string of wooden tally sticks that lay on the table before him. He ran the notched and polished sticks through his fingers over and over and over. The mindless, repetitive act and the delicate clicking sound the sticks made were strangely soothing.

He had to force himself not to look into the flames of the candles that stood on the table before him. Twice already he'd found them leading his thoughts off in other, more carnal directions.

"As things stand now," Rareton continued, breaking in on Robert's thoughts, "we can't get our wool out or our cloth in. Not unless we pay to have it transferred to English ships or carried overland. And *that's* not counting the duty the gatekeepers are putting on goods taken across London Bridge. For Montfort, they claim, though I take leave to doubt the earl has seen so much as a penny in the pound of what they've taken!"

As he paced, the steward fidgeted with the silver ring he wore as if it were some magic talisman against the troubles that threatened to engulf London.

For the last half hour Robert had listened to Rareton bewail the growing problems for English commerce as the quarrel between King Henry III and Simon de Montfort moved England inexorably toward war. Given what was at stake, he should have been straining every nerve to see through the dangerous thicket of political turmoil that was closing in around him, yet this morning he was finding it curiously difficult to concentrate. His thoughts were caught in a different thicket, and no matter how much he plucked and pulled, he couldn't seem to work himself free.

What was it about this plain, proud witch he'd taken to wife that robbed him of his wits, yet so readily teased his cock to eager attention? Who would have thought a skinny, flat-chested woman with little to recommend her but her family name would prove so damnably distracting? Who would have thought she would be possessed of such a temper? And just what was it he'd said to set it off in the first place?

Her hurt at the terms of her marriage settlement and her anger at his teasing were unreasonable and unjust . . . so why was *he* the one suffering from guilt? And why—

"Master Wardell?"

Robert glanced up, startled, to find his wife standing at the end of the table. He hadn't heard a whisper of footsteps in the rushes.

"My lady?" he said, and tried to ignore the immediate stirring of arousal.

She wore that damned wimple and veil again. Now wasn't the time to tell her he preferred her wild red locks to those matronly garments, but one of these days . . .

"I wished to apologize for my temper."

She kept her voice calm, her head high, but there was no mistaking the glint in her eyes. The Lady Alyce wasn't nearly so sure of her welcome as she tried to appear . . . and she wasn't anywhere near as penitent either.

"I also wondered when it would be convenient for you to accompany me to mass. The morning marches apace and I would not care to arrive too late."

"Mass?" He frowned. "I had no plans to attend mass this morning."

Her spine stiffened. "But we've spent five days on the road and had only Gilbert's faint blessing when we left Colmaine. It's scarcely an auspicious beginning to a— To our marriage. Surely you want your priest to bless us as well?"

Roberts fingers tightened involuntarily on the fragile tally sticks. He had followed the priests' guidance in the matter of his first marriage. He wanted none of their preaching in his second.

At the thought, one of the tally sticks snapped under

his fingers with the sound of a cracking whip. He flinched and carefully laid the sticks aside, uncomfortably conscious of his steward's presence despite Rareton's absorbed fascination with the rushes at his feet.

"I possess no tame priest, madam, but I am sure we can find one who will bless us as well tomorrow as today. If you would hear mass now, Piers can take you. There are churches enough round about, and priests past counting who'll be more than willing to grant your blessing in exchange for a coin or two."

Alyce flushed, but held her ground. "You take what some might call a dangerous view of the matter, sir."

"I take no view of the matter at all," he said coldly, fighting against another stab of irrational guilt.

He picked up the account roll that lay closest to hand and rolled it out on the table before him. "Now, if you will excuse me, madame, I have work to do."

He watched her walk away. Her head was high, her gait unhurried. To all outward appearances, she was as calm as a nun at prayers.

He could feel her anger from halfway across the hall.

John Rareton must have felt it too, for he coughed, cleared his throat, and shuffled his feet.

Robert's fingers twitched with the urge to strangle the man.

THE CHURCH WAS small and stark, but either the priests had aspirations for greater things, or the place had a wealthy benefactor, for the altar was covered with a richly embroidered cloth of gold and flanked by two massive bronze candlesticks that topped her height by a full hand's span. The huge beeswax candles they bore cast a flickering golden light that softened the hard lines of the stone and glinted on the bright paint and gilded ornamentation on the statues of the saints, the Virgin, and

Christ that occupied the stone niches in the apse behind the altar.

Yet not even the candles' clear light was strong enough to illuminate the stone arches overhead, or soften the line of choir stalls that crouched on either side like so many dark, boxy demons lurking in the shadows. Alyce could feel their presence, as though unseen monks filled the stalls, watching her with condemning eyes. The muscles across her shoulders tightened involuntarily.

Piers had willingly accompanied her to mass, and as willingly agreed to wait for her on the porch steps while she prayed afterward, when she could have the church to herself. To Alyce's relief, he'd made no mention of the incident in the solar.

She pushed aside the thought of her quarrel with Robert, crossed herself, then carefully arranged her skirts to pad her knees as she knelt. The cold in the place made her shiver. She clasped her hands, bowed her head, and tried to pray.

Nothing came. No words, no release, no comfort.

This was not the familiar, shabby chapel at Colmaine with its peeling paintings and crude statue of the Virgin. The priest who had celebrated mass that morning was not thin, nervous Gilbert, who chewed his nails, and squeaked when he laughed, and knew her every quirk . . . and loved her in spite of it.

Perhaps her prayers only worked in Colmaine. Perhaps she would have to learn new ones to fit this new life of hers. Perhaps—

Alyce threw off the troubling doubts and reluctantly conceded defeat. She would not find any peace in her prayers this morning.

She crossed herself once more, then rose to her feet and turned to leave, only to stop short at the sight of the priest who stood in the shadows at the side of the nave.

His shoulders were hunched, his hands buried in the

sleeves of his white robe so that he seemed more like carved stone than living flesh. Assured that she was finished with her prayers, he stepped out of the shadows toward her. The heavy skirts of his robe swayed with his motion, but his sandaled feet made no sound on the stone paving.

Alyce sank into a curtsy to hide her irritation at his intrusion.

He was close enough now so that the light from the altar candles revealed his fine, patrician features. By the look of him, he was wellborn. A younger son, perhaps, for whom the church offered the best hope of advancement. He studied her incuriously.

"You pray for guidance, daughter?"

She nodded.

He waited.

Alyce drew in her breath, impaled on that flat, unwavering gaze. Suddenly, like a stream released from the winter's ice, words poured out of her in a tumbling, incoherent rush. She told him about her father and about Robert, about Robert's reasons for marrying her and her anger at so bald an admission of the truths she had always known. She told him of her marriage, her doubts, her hopes for the future, and her uncertainties about the present.

The only things she didn't tell him about were the fire that Robert's touch set alight within her and the soaring wonder of the secrets that lay between husband and wife.

Eventually, the torrent of words eased to a trickle. The trickle stopped, leaving her mouth dry, her palms damp. She felt dizzy; the muscles in her legs seemed too weak to hold her upright. She sucked in a breath and fell silent, dazed by the odd sense of release the confession had brought.

"And so you've come here," the priest said softly. "You are seeking guidance."

"Yes. I—I wish to be a good wife, Father."

The priest nodded. "That is well."

He studied her, as if weighing her worthiness for the role allotted her. "You know that it is a wife's duty to serve her husband, to follow his commandments as the Lord's, and to give her body unto him?"

"Our family priest instructed me, Father, reminded me of my duties."

"Then what troubles you, my child? The . . . unequalness of your estates?" He frowned. "Surely your father would not have given you in marriage thus had he not thought it best?"

Or profitable. "No, of course not, Father."

"Then what?" He seemed truly puzzled.

"I—I don't know." It was a cry from the heart. "I wanted to be wed, wanted to have children, but . . ."

"But?" he prompted when she remained silent.

"But I had thought to marry within my own rank, Father. I know how to be a good wife to a knight, but I know nothing of a merchant's life or the world he lives in. I don't know his people. I don't know *him*. I have no skills, no knowledge—"

"Your husband will teach you," the priest cut in sternly. "Learn from him. It is his duty to guide you, to teach you what you must know."

Alyce drooped, defeated. How could she possible put what she felt into words, especially when she didn't understand it fully? How could she think to carve a place for herself when all the world knew her place was at her husband's side, doing as he bid her?

"Of course, Father."

"Remember that God gave woman to man that he might guide and protect her."

She nodded.

"The sinful nature of your sex must yield to the stronger call of duty and obligation, my daughter. Obey your husband in all things so that you may be strong against the temptations to idleness and gossip and error that are woman's constant enemies."

She stared down at her clasped hands. Her nails dug into her skin, but she didn't dare ease the tight grip she was maintaining on herself.

"Follow his guidance, so that your household is at peace," the priest continued, as unfeelingly as if he were reciting a lesson from a book. "Heed your husband's counsel and take care not to provoke him to beat you. Yet if he should beat you, remember that it is for your own good, to teach you your rightful place and how you should act, and to guide you for your soul's sake. You must learn to profit therefrom."

"Yes, Father."

"Then go, my child, with God's blessing. Prayer will guide you. Prayer and your husband. See that you attend to both."

"I shall, Father. Thank you." What use in asking guidance of a priest, after all?

He made the sign of the cross over her bowed head and murmured a few words of blessing, then turned away to kneel before the altar, her existence already forgotten.

9

MISTRESS OF THE
KEYS

ALYCE TRAILED BACK through the crowded streets, too wrapped in thought to heed the people and the noise that swirled around her. Piers walked beside her, as silent and watchful as an obedient dog. Twice he had to grab her arm to prevent her from stumbling into some particularly foul muck. Each time Alyce thanked him, and each time she carefully avoided meeting his troubled gaze.

Once through the front gates, she released him to his work, then slowly climbed the shallow stone steps that led to the hall. The courtyard was empty and no one of the household in sight, yet she sensed a hushed expectancy in the air, as if Robert's people were collectively holding their breaths, waiting to see what she would do next.

The screens passage was empty as well. The soft *grit-grit-grit* of her footsteps seemed to echo in the confined space. She stopped, guiltily realizing she'd forgotten to scrape the caked dirt and mud off her shoes before she'd entered.

She turned back to rectify the oversight, but stopped short at the sight of her muddy prints cutting across the tile floor, dull brown blotches against the yellow and red patterned tiles. The sight made her tsk in disgust. She would have to find one of the scullery maids and have her sweep away the evidence of her carelessness. And a good coating of wax on that floor wouldn't be amiss either.

The hall was empty. The table where Robert had sat earlier had been taken down and set against the far wall, ready to be put up again for the next meal. Alyce untied her cloak and laid it on the nearest bench. The smell of roasting pork and cooking vegetables teased her nose, faint, yet rich with the promise of a delectable meal. She drew in a deep breath, and with it, a new resolve.

Whatever else might lie ahead, she was now the mistress of Wardell House. She might not know anything about a merchant's life or what was expected of a merchant's wife, but she *did* know about cooking and cleaning and managing a large household. If she was going to take over the responsibility for the running of it, there would never be a better time to start than now, and she could think of no better way to begin than with a full frontal assault on the very heart of the household.

She took a deep breath, carefully wiped her palms on her skirts, and set off to storm the kitchens.

ALYCE'S STRATEGY WASN'T at fault, but her timing was off.

She caught the murmur of voices before she was halfway along the main kitchen passage. At the foot of the stairs, the passageway turned right and ended at a wooden screen placed to block any draft that might harm the cook's handiwork. The screen had a convenient crack, perfectly placed for spying.

The cook, Margaret Preston, sat on a stool with the kitchen cat on her lap and a small army ranged in a respectful half-circle around her—the undercook, the scullery maids, the kitchen boy, and the thin old woman who served as pantler. Opposite them, Erwyna sat on another stool with the gardener, the head stable man, the maid who served as butler, and one of the stable lads who helped out in the garden seated on either side of her.

Between the two camps, the guard, Henley, was engaged in draining a sizable mug of ale while regaling his assembled listeners with tales of the trip from Colmaine.

"Aye," he said with the air of a man who was regretfully coming to the end of his tale. " 'Twas as cold and miserable a ride as ever I've known, but never a peep out of our lady did we have. She kept up with the master and still had a kind word at the end of it for the man as took her horse or carried her bundles."

He swigged more ale, dragged his sleeve over his mouth, and belched. The scullery maids giggled.

Erwyna, more mindful of the dignity of the house, frowned at them, then at Henley. She leaned forward, her hands on her knees, her elbows akimbo. To Alyce she looked like nothing so much as a bulldog disdainfully eyeing a rather stupid bull.

"Is it true that Master Robert and Alan of Hensford had words on the road? Outside Cripplegate, Newton said."

Newton was a thin, surly guard who'd accompanied Robert to Colmaine and who looked as if he'd never met a man or had a meal that agreed with him. Since he'd told his tales to Erwyna first, Alyce didn't have any trouble figuring out which camp *he* was in.

Henley nodded. "Aye, that's so. I've heard there's bad blood between the master and that Hensford fellow, though I can't say as ever I heard the cause of it."

He glanced at Erwyna hopefully, but she showed no sign of wanting to enlighten him.

"What happened?" she demanded instead. "*Did* they exchange words?"

"Aye. Said so, didn't I? Turrible sharp words. Drew a nasty crowd, they did."

With only a few embellishments, he told them the tale of the broken cart and the man with the string of pots and Alan of Hensford's abrupt descent into the dung heap. The assembled listeners nodded encouragingly, then laughed outright at Robert's insult to Hensford. Robert Wardell's people had clearly taken his enemies as their own, whatever they thought of his wife.

Erwyna looked grim. "And did she really cry thief outside Cripplegate? Newton swore 'twas true." Her mouth screwed up disapprovingly, as if at the taste of something foul. "Just like a common shrew from the sounds of it, and no thought of her dignity or Master Robert's."

No one needed to ask which "she" the housekeeper meant. The expressions around the circle turned disapproving—all but Henley's. He nodded and looked smug.

"Aye, she did. But Newton is fair and far off if he says it were so bad as that. Packed tight as dried fish in a barrel, the crowd was, and yellin' for the master to have at it with Hensford, or Hensford to have at it with him, and no sign they'd have budged till they'd had their fill of fightin', bloody noses and all. And there was me, fair stoppered with tryin' to think how to get her out of it, knowin' it'd be my head did I let anything happen to our lady."

"And rightly so." Margaret Preston looked around the assembled listeners with an expression that said *she,* at least, understood what was owed a lady's dignity. "Though I'd not claim such behavior is appropriate to a lady of her rank, it's as well she had her wits about her. It's obvious no one else did, or even thought to get her free of the tangle they'd got her into!"

She frowned at Henley, then transferred her disapproving stare to Erwyna. Erwyna glared right back.

Alyce gnawed at her lip as she studied the two women. There were, it seemed, sharper divisions in Robert's household than she'd expected, and while Margaret might welcome a baron's daughter as mistress, Erwyna clearly resented being displaced in the house's hierarchy. Worse, she seemed eager to rouse her followers to an equal resentment.

"Could be the master hadn't all his wits about him," Henley said, "or not enough to be thinking of such things, at any rate." He gave the cook an exaggerated wink and a smirk. "I'd wager my new shoes the master's fair taken with her. Not that she's much to look on, mind, but I know a man with an itch in his drawers when I sees one, and the master—"

"Can do without your peeping and prying," snapped Erwyna, clearly displeased with the guard's assessment of the situation.

A quiver of pleasure ran through Alyce. She'd never had a man with an "itch" for her. In spite of the embarrassment, it was oddly gratifying to think that Robert not only had one, but that others had noticed.

"No prying about it!" Henley protested. "A man'd have to be blind not t' notice! Not that he started out that pleased, mind, but he do seem to have changed his views a bit, now he's bedded her. May be she's a lady, but ain't nothin' says she don't know a few tricks to tempt a man regardless."

He cackled and snorted, mightily amused with himself, and took another hefty swig of ale just as Erwyna leaned forward to poke him in the ribs.

Henley choked and sprayed his listeners with ale, who squealed in protest and backed out of range. He slammed down his ale pot to mop at his chin.

"Why'd you do that, then?"

"You keep you tongue between your teeth, you dirty-minded old fart."

"A man's got a right to speak, you *bloody*-minded old witch, whatever you think!"

"Don't forget what happened in the solar this mornin'," one of the scullery maids exclaimed.

Alyce felt her cheeks grow warm. The snickers and leering looks said that tales of that confrontation had already made the rounds of the household, to everyone's great amusement.

Erwyna angrily rounded on the girl. "Didn't I tell you to keep your tongue between your teeth about that?"

"Wasn't me!" the girl protested, shrinking away from the housekeeper's ire.

"The master was more that a mite addled over supper last night, don't forget," another said, quick enough to divert Erwyna's temper. "Frettin' and fidgettin' till Githa brought his lady back, an' couldn't hardly take his eyes off her once she'd sat down beside him!"

"But she's plain as a post!" protested the gardener.

"All cats look alike in the dark."

"Githa says as how she's got bright red hair. An' red's the color o' temptation. Ain't that whot the priests say?"

By craning a little, Alyce could see it was the wizened pantler who spoke. What was her name? Bondig? The woman was old enough to have flirted with Noah, but the glitter in her eyes said she hadn't forgotten the trick of it.

A murmur of agreement swept through the assemblage.

"Well, then!" Bondig said with satisfaction. "Stands t' reason t' master'd be wantin' back in 'er bed. She was *born* with the secrets for seducin' a man, no matter her looks!"

Erwyna scowled. Margaret Preston sniffed and looked interested. Only the cat seemed unimpressed. It stood, arching its back and stretching, then hopped off the cook's lap and strolled out of the kitchen.

"Enough!" Erwyna levered her stout figure off her stool. "There's work to do and you"—she poked Henley's arm with an accusatory finger—"you've had quite enough ale for one morning. Be off with you, and the rest of you too. The mistress will be back soon enough and here we are with the morning's work not done. I'd best see some feet scurrying or I'll know the reason why!"

Alyce just had time to retreat up the stairs she'd come down before the others, grumbling and chattering among themselves, began to disperse.

Halfway up the stairs, she halted. She couldn't hide from their curiosity, no matter how much she'd like to. Eventually something or someone new would come along to draw their attention away from her, but in the meantime . . .

Reluctantly, she turned back. To someone coming up from the kitchen, it would appear she was just coming down, and if she walked slowly enough, the cold in the unlighted passage ought to banish the flush from her cheeks before she reached the kitchen.

A moment later, one of the kitchen boys and the pantler Bondig came around the screen and started up the stairs. They didn't see her immediately since she was in the darkness above them. Alyce moved down three steps.

Bondig stopped, gaped, then almost mashed her nose against the step above her when she sank into an awkward curtsy. She did bang her knee, which caused her to squawk in pain and start to tumble backward on top of the boy who followed at her heels.

The boy swore and shoved at her skinny rump, then froze as he realized why she'd stopped.

"M-m-milady!" he stammered, and tried to bow and back down the stairs at the same time. He missed his step and half staggered, half fell down three steps at once.

Alyce couldn't help smiling. She hadn't caused this much excitement since she'd set fire to the pigeon coop when she was five.

At least this time she wouldn't have as much trouble sitting down to dinner afterward.

Her smile widened. She nodded graciously as the be-fuddled servants shrank against the passage wall to let her pass, then continued on her way to the kitchen.

ROBERT'S STRONG ROOM was a chill, windowless cell built into the undercroft below the hall. The thick stone walls muffled sounds from outside and there was nothing to look at besides the table in front of him and the iron-strapped chests that held his money and his most costly silks and satins and samites. It was the perfect re-treat for a man of business who wanted to escape distrac-tions and concentrate on his work—or so he'd thought.

Today, the silence rang in his ears. He hadn't bothered to start a fire in the iron brazier that stood next to his work-table, but he didn't even notice the cold. The chamber's shadows and its intimate closeness reminded him of an-other chamber and another hour altogether, and the memo-ries heated his blood until he had no need of a fire.

Alyce might as well have been on the other side of the table glaring at him for all the good it had done him to come here.

When he'd first taken Alyce as his wife in body as well as name, he'd intended nothing more than to make her transition into womanhood as easy as possible. Never had he thought to find her so willing, or so swift to rouse to his touch. And last night—

His belly muscles tightened at the memory of last night.

In the twelve years since Jocelyn's death, he'd had his share of women, but they'd been pretty, practiced doxies who were more than willing to trade their favors for the comforts that a man of his position could provide them. When he tired of them, as he inevitably did, it had been easy enough to smooth the parting with a purse full of coins. A couple of them, cleverer than the rest, had eagerly accepted his offer to set them up in business, and now they had their own little shops. One had even married.

They'd been good women, and company for the long nights when business kept him in London and his own bed grew too cold and empty. Yet not one of them, despite their skills and their manifest charms, had ever stirred him to the eager, lustful interest that Alyce did. Even the guilty memory of Jocelyn that had dogged him on his wedding night had faded in the heat of their coupling.

He wasn't sure he liked it—he didn't like being at the mercy of anyone or anything, not even his own body—but he was beginning to realize he liked his wife.

When she wasn't glaring at him or humiliating him in front of his servants, that is.

He cursed and threw down his pen.

He *hadn't* been unreasonable, and it was damned unreasonable of her to think he had. What had she expected? A besotted lover out of some damned French tale? She ought to consider herself lucky her father hadn't married her to some swaggering knight who'd have swived her, and beat her, then abandoned her to bear his snot-nosed brats in some damned drafty ruin of a castle while he went off on his damned—

Robert swept aside the account roll that lay open on the table. The stiff parchment rolled up with a soft *thup-thup-thup* until it rolled right off the table and onto the floor.

Damn, damn, *damn*!

He stood abruptly, knocking over the chair he'd been sitting on and jarring the worktable so hard that another account roll obligingly plunged over the edge.

With a snort of disgust he snatched up the remaining rolls, then walked around the table to retrieve the two that had fallen. To hell with all of it! Rareton could tally the accounts as easily as he could, while there were a dozen things he'd put off because of his wedding, things he ought to be attending to instead of hiding in this damn room like a hermit in a damned cave.

He yanked open the nearest chest. It wasn't the one he wanted—of course.

He cursed again and started to slam the lid down, but stopped as a flash of color caught his eye—the end of a bolt of velvet. It had been wrapped carelessly so that an edge hung free of the protective linen wrapper.

He knew that particular piece of velvet well. He'd bought it in Ypres on his last trip, thinking to make a gift of it to Queen Eleanor. Henry gave his favor to alien merchants, paying no heed to the protests of the English merchants he scorned, but Robert had thought he'd be more willing to listen if it was his beloved queen whispering a suggestion or two in his ear. The velvet, like his loan to the Lord Edward, was an investment for the future. Only the political troubles had delayed its presentation.

It wasn't the thought of the queen and the favor he hoped to curry with her that made Robert stop, however. The lustrous moss-green cloth was the color of Alyce's eyes—when she wasn't angry—right down to the gold tints cast by the candle's light.

Again Robert started to slam the lid shut, yet again he hesitated. Then he threw down the rolls of parchment he held, flung open the chest, and pulled out the length of cloth. He pulled away the linen wrapper and spread the velvet on the table, full in the candles' light.

Exactly the color of Alyce's eyes.

Slowly, fingers spread wide, Robert ran his hand over the precious cloth. Even in the chill room it seemed warm against his skin, shifting under his hand as though it were alive and as responsive to his touch as Alyce was.

Her hair would be like fire against the green.

Closing his hand on a fold of velvet, he savored the weight of it, the way it gathered in his hand. He lifted it up, then let it fall and watched it pool in lush verdant ripples on the tabletop—a fitting gift to tempt the favors of a queen.

He could give it to Alyce instead. Not as a bride gift, but simply for the pleasure it would give her . . . and the pleasure it would bring him to see her in it.

The thought caught him like a blow to the belly.

Pleasure? He frowned at the velvet, then roughly rolled it up again. This marriage was a practical arrangement, for both of them. He'd do well to remember that.

He picked up the bolt of cloth, then slowly set it down, considering possibilities.

A merchant in his position often appeared at public gatherings and displays. Since the world judged a man's standing in part by how well his wife was habited, Alyce would literally be wearing his honor on her back. It behooved him to ensure that she was appropriately dressed for such occasions.

Not that the embroidered surcoat of perse she'd worn on their wedding day wasn't appropriate—a queen might have coveted it—but it hadn't taken him long to figure out it was the only fine garment Alyce possessed. He'd taken half a dozen extra sumpter horses with him to Colmaine, and planned to send a carter for the heavy stuff later, yet Alyce's possessions hadn't made a full load for even two horses. If she was to represent him well, she would need another tunic or two, a second surcoat, perhaps a golden hair net to bind up her hair rather than hide it under that damned wimple and veil.

He smoothed a wrinkle in the velvet. An eminently practical gift, when he thought of it that way. A good, sound business investment for a man who made his living out of the threads that men and women wore. As politically useful, in its way, as giving it to the queen.

And there was the color—

"Master Wardell! Master Wardell!"

The heavy oak door to the chamber slammed open and his apprentice burst into the room.

"Come quick, master. You *have* to see this."

PIERS, EYES SPARKLING wickedly, barely gave Robert enough time to blow out the candles and lock the strong-room door before he dragged him up the steps, along the passage, and across the hall to the doors that opened into the buttery and pantry.

The pantry door stood partly open. Robert could hear voices from within, though he couldn't make out the words. Two of his servants were pressed against the wall nearby, trying to peer in without being seen themselves. At the sight of him following Piers, they scuttled away like mice at the entrance of a hungry cat.

Before Robert could say a word, Piers put a finger to his lips to indicate silence, then gestured for him to take the spot the servants had vacated. Puzzled, and not a little irritated, Robert did as he was bid.

As he got closer, the voices resolved themselves into Alyce's and Erwyna's. Robert craned to see through the half-open door.

Alyce, tall, thin, and outwardly serene, stood at one end of a waist-high locked chest. At the other end of the chest stood short, stout Erwyna, clutching an iron ring of keys and bristling like a dog over a knuckle bone.

"There's naught but old linens in the chest, milady," said Erwyna. "Nothing to trouble yourself about, I'm sure."

"I'm sure you're right," said Alyce, and smiled and held out her hand.

Erwyna hunched her back and drew in her chin until her head seemed to merge with her shoulders. "Wouldn't you rather take a look at the garden?"

"On such a beautiful day? Of course I would! But I don't dare be so lazy and self-indulgent when you're so dedicated and hardworking. What would you think of me?"

Erwyna's head lowered even farther. "I don't want to put a burden on you, milady. I'll warrant you were never troubled with so much as a napkin at Colmaine, let alone a pile of old linens."

A subtle shadow crossed Alyce's face, but her smile never wavered. "I wouldn't wager so much as a clipped half-penny on the possibility, if I were you."

Robert thought of the worn and patched tablecloths at Colmaine and the shabby covers on Alyce's bed. For the first time he wondered if Alyce had been as oblivious to Colmaine's shortcomings as he'd thought.

"If you're worried that I might be troubled by finding that not all the linens at Wardell House are in perfect shape," Alyce continued, "I should tell you that I'd worry about wastefulness if there weren't a few old linens around, rather than about your housekeeping skills."

Erwyna straightened indignantly, eyes blazing. "Wastefulness! There's never a stitch of cloth wasted in *this* household, milady, and so I take leave to tell you!"

She whipped a key from the ring she held and, fat fingers fumbling with her haste, shoved it into the heavy iron lock.

"You see?" she demanded triumphantly, throwing back the lid of the chest. "*Lots* of old linens!"

Alyce leaned forward. "Why, so there are," she said. "And all neatly cleaned and folded and ready for use when they're needed."

Erwyna looked smug as she closed the chest. Alyce murmured her admiration of Erwyna's management, but the instant the lid was down, she deftly turned the key in the lock, pulled it out, and dropped it into the leather pouch that dangled from her belt.

Piers snickered. "Foxed again."

Robert turned to find his apprentice standing on tiptoe just behind him, craning to see around him. Piers edged back toward the hall, gesturing for Robert to follow.

"They've been at it for the past hour and more, master," the boy whispered when they were safely away from the door. "And that was only after milady wrapped old Maggie around her finger by cooing over the pigeon pies she served last night and telling her thrice over how lucky you are to have so talented a cook in your kitchen."

Judging from the grin on his apprentice's face, Piers had been a highly appreciative observer of the encounter in the kitchen, though Robert doubted that any of the combatants had been aware of his presence. The boy knew more peepholes than a mouse, and made far better use of them.

"Erwyna's been trying to keep from handing over the keys to milady," Piers continued in an eager whisper, "and milady just keeps smiling and saying nice things about the housekeeping and the floors and isn't it wonderful the way the rafters have been swept clean of cobwebs until Erwyna's got no reason *not* to hand over another key. And if that doesn't work, then milady says something to get Erwyna riled so she *has* to do what milady wants just to prove she's right and milady's wrong, and all the while milady looks as innocent as a newborn lamb. By the time Erwyna realizes she's been had again, they're on to the next thing, and milady's chattering on about just how well Erwyna's managed *that* too."

Piers flashed another grin. "The Lady Alyce may look thin enough to blow away in a high wind, but she's cleverer than a cat and stubborner than Erwyna and the bishop's mule combined!"

Before Robert could dredge up a reply, a glowering Erwyna emerged from the pantry. She scowled at him and Piers, glared at the hall, where the work of setting up tables and benches for dinner had been abandoned, half done, then without saying a word, stumped off toward the kitchen.

A moment later, Alyce emerged from the pantry, smiling. It was exactly the sort of smile she might have worn if Erwyna had offered their the crown jewels instead of truculently refusing to hand over a set of iron keys.

At the sight of him, her smile vanished. Her chin came up as she walked toward them, the keys clanking in the leather pouch at her waist.

You have nothing to do but please me. His own words echoed in Robert's mind.

What in the hell had he expected her to do in the interim? he wondered suddenly. His Alyce was not a woman to sit by the fire while the world went whirling past her. Had he truly been so foolish as to think he could put her away as he'd put the velvet away? That once safely out of sight, she was also safely out of mind? Had he really been that much of a fool?

She stopped two paces from him and looked up, eyes dark with an unspoken challenge.

Robert sucked in his breath, shaken.

He'd been right. The velvet was *exactly* the same color of her eyes.

10

A GAME
OF FOOLS

T
HE DAYS FELL into a rhythm, different from
the days at Colmaine, but no less familiar. Erwyna, still
grumbling, had eventually offered a reluctant truce,
though not in so many words. Alyce had had copies made
of the household keys, then returned the originals to the
gratified, yet puzzled housekeeper, who once more went
about with them clanking officiously at her waist.

Alyce didn't tell her that she'd never intended to take
over her duties, that she'd only wanted to assert her own
position as mistress at the start, before it became impossible to do so. The old woman wouldn't appreciate the
subtleties of political maneuvering. To her, life was simple
and direct, an all-out battle to protect her standing in the
household and defeat the twin demons of dirt and slothful
servants, no quarter asked, none given. At times, Alyce
found herself envying that straightforward view of the
world.

Her own new world was not so simple.

She missed Colmaine and Maida and Hilde and all the
old friends she'd left behind, but she refused to dwell on
it. Her life was in London now. Impossible to change that,
and when she lay with Robert and felt him move within
her, she knew she would not change it even if she could.

London, late March 1264

It was only in the long, bright hours twixt dawn and dark that she doubted herself. However eager Robert might be at night, outside their marriage bed he offered her not one soft "thee" or "thou," nor any hint of what he thought or felt. He was always courteous, but distant as the moon. She could have understood curses and quarreling far more easily. At least she was familiar with them.

Yet no man could have been more generous. Her mare was only the first of many treasures. He had given her cloth for new clothes—a fine brown velvet, a length of green wool, and another of saffron rayed with blue—bought her a fur-lined cloak, a silver brooch, a comb, three silken hair nets, another pair of shoes even finer than her bridal pair.

Never had she known such wealth or owned such finery. She and Githa had make up the cloths into new gowns; she'd proudly worn the cloak and brooch and shoes. Only the hair nets lay where she'd put them at the bottom of her small chest of clothes. Despite Robert's generosity, she couldn't bring herself to give up the safe, familiar veils and wimples that covered her so well.

It might have been easier if Erwyna hadn't taken such pains to tell her about Robert's first wife, Jocelyn. A radiant beauty, according to Erwyna. Fair of face and figure, blue-eyed and golden-haired and with the sweetest voice in all of Christendom. A saint. A glorious creature. An angel among women.

Alyce had never felt her own imperfect humanity more acutely.

It didn't matter that Jocelyn Wardell was twelve years dead—in childbirth, Erwyna said, with a dark look to suggest that there was more if only she cared to tell. Alyce hadn't pressed for details.

She hadn't asked Robert either. She had no desire to rouse old ghosts, assuming they even lingered in the house. Robert never spoke of his first wife and Alyce had found no gowns or trinkets or jewels hidden safely away like memories.

She hadn't looked very hard. The secrets of the past could remain with the past. All she wanted was to secure today and all the days to come.

But how?

LONDON WAS AN armed camp. Despite the broken leg that still hadn't healed enough for him to ride, Simon de Montfort was in and out of the city as boldly as a king. He held the Tower and plotted strategy, and all London cheered whenever he passed in his great wagon.

Robert watched and listened to the warlike talk from men passing in the streets and tried not to think of the bodies that would be heaped in the fields if Montfort and the king ever met in battle. Edward had been right all those months ago. Men who spent their lives measuring cloth and weighing out peppercorns could not stand against heavily armored soldiers who'd spent those same years learning the subtleties of bashing in their opponents' heads.

As always when there was talk of war, business was good for armorers and metalworkers and provisioners, but poor for men such as himself. Which didn't mean there was no business at all. Great ladies still had need of silk, and powerful priests had their robes of office. Men must clothe themselves, after all, and the weavers in Flanders still needed English wool for their looms. He kept busy.

But not quite busy enough.

The green velvet remained buried in the chest, wrapped tight in its protective cover and hidden under half a dozen other cloths. He'd put it back himself, then pulled the heavy chest into the farthest, darkest corner of the room where he couldn't see it unless he twisted uncomfortably round in his chair.

Out of sight, however, was far from out of mind.

Try as he would, Robert could not forget it. The thought of it would prick him at odd moments, as when he caught Alyce laughing with one of the stable lads over the antics of a kitten, or found her, hands caked with mud, chivying Joshua and his helpers over the planting of a patch of herbs.

Not the sort of behavior appropriate to the daughter of a baron nor what he'd expected of his wife, yet he was grateful for it. It made it easier for him to focus on his work, knowing Alyce fit so well in this new life he'd brought her to.

No, that wasn't right either. She didn't fit. She changed it utterly, seemingly without trying.

She was like a March wind that blew through London, bringing April in its train—sometimes tempestuous, ofttimes sweet, but never still for long. The talk of war might be roaring in the streets, but whenever he was with Alyce, the roaring faded to a faint and distant rumble. She tugged and teased at him, swirled round him like an errant, agile breeze, left evidence of her passing in his changed and tumbled household, then flitted away, always out of reach, unfettered and impossible to hold.

It was his fault she kept her distance, pointedly going about her self-claimed duties as if her soul depended on the good completion of them. Perhaps it did. He'd willed her into a box and she'd refused to go, and now she roamed free about his house and in his life, changing both in ways he was only beginning to guess at.

It wasn't that his house was any cleaner or his food any better prepared—sullen, foul-tempered Erwyna had always managed the household well, and Margaret ruled the kitchen with a stern, yet artful hand. No, it was subtler things he noticed, small differences in the people about him, a new cheeriness that clung to them like invisible cobwebs, softening their outlines in unfamiliar ways.

Even Erwyna, who resented having another set over her, did no more than glower and grumble when she thought he wasn't looking.

More than that, he no longer had to listen to the litanies of complaint that had been brought to him so often in the past, nor see to the ordering of the house accounts, nor think of anything other than his business and the growing troubles that threatened it. Without a question of how or where or why, Alyce had taken up a burden he hadn't known he carried and claimed it as her own.

It was . . . unsettling. It wasn't what he'd planned, though he couldn't remember ever actually thinking about the changes a wife would bring into his household and his life.

He'd given her several fine pieces of cloth for new gowns and thought that would be enough. Yet without intending it, at least at first, he found himself searching out small gifts he thought might please her—a comb, a length of ribbon, a silver brooch to pin to her cloak—and found a pleasure in the giving that he had never known before. Unlike Jocelyn, who'd taken such gifts as no more than what was due her, or the women he'd kept, who'd always calculated the cost and weighed his value to them thereby, Alyce accepted each small gift with a simple joy that made the gesture all the sweeter, as though the gift had less value to her than the giving of it.

To his disappointment, the only gifts she refused to wear were the hair nets, each woven of a different-colored silk. When he'd bought them, he'd pictured how her hair would shine in the morning sun, how her long, graceful neck would look once freed of its enveloping wimples, and found the pictures pleased him. The hair nets hadn't pleased her, however. She'd thanked him as sweetly as she'd thanked him for all his other gifts, but she had never worn them.

He hadn't asked her why. He hadn't dared. They put

on their best court manners when they met during the day, and though he often burned at the memory of their nighttime joinings, she seemed not to remember them, as though, once risen from her bed, she put the experience aside as neatly as a dust rag when its usefulness was ended.

They met seldom enough. His work often took him from the house, and she managed, by chance or design, to keep well out of his way when he was there. It wasn't until he found himself making excuses to seek her out that Robert began to wonder if this was some new madness that had claimed him.

He refused to call it love. He'd known love once and didn't care to repeat the experience, or bear again the guilt he'd earned for wanting to hold it so close and tight that he'd destroyed it in the end. As well put Alyce on a chain and lead her to her destruction! The nights they shared had to be enough. He would not encroach. Suffice, in times like this, to keep his business without venturing into such lunacy!

Yet still he could not stop himself from watching for her, or listening for her quick, light step, or thinking of the long, sweet hours of the night when he ought to be attending his accounts. He looked forward to the evenings after supper when they would sit before the fire in the hall and she'd regale him with tales of her adventures about London, face aglow in the firelight and eyes wide at the latest wonder—a six-fingered beggar, a donkey that could count to ten, a dancing dog, a reliquary containing a saint's dried penis that was famed for curing impotence and aiding barren women.

She didn't tell him so, but he knew she'd paid the ten pence the priests exacted for the privilege of touching that shriveled member. She'd been disappointed when her woman's courses came for the second time since they'd wed, while he had breathed a silent and heartfelt sigh of relief.

Not that they hadn't tried! Whatever barriers stood between them vanished once their bedchamber door swung shut. He sometimes wondered if he'd grown young again, so eager was he to teach her the secrets of the marriage bed. Never had he known a more willing pupil, nor one so naturally inclined to those intimate pleasures.

In the dark, with the bed curtains drawn against the world, whatever tension of rancor had risen during the day faded and whispered away into silence. In the dark, they met, joined, flared hot with a physical need neither could resist.

A need of the body, Robert told himself, over and over again. Nothing more. The prospect of Alyce pregnant wasn't something he was ready to face yet, but he wanted sons, and even Holy Mother Church did not deny him the pleasure of begetting them so long as it was within the bonds of matrimony. Yet sometimes, as he slipped into sleep with Alyce curled warm and soft beside him, he found himself dreaming of daughters—red-haired daughters with secret moss-green eyes.

What Alyce dreamed of, she never said. Before dawn even teased at the corners of the shutters, she rose and left him, dressing in the cold and dark, then slipping away to mass with Piers or one of the guards as her escort. Though he had always been early to rise in the past, he never accompanied her. He remained in bed instead, soaking up her lingering heat and wondering what madness had hold of him.

Curse or blessing, he was not sure, but he had wedded and bedded a woman who could not be ignored and would not consent to remain discreetly to one side, and nothing would ever be the same.

"MEN ARE ALL the same. Hard enough to deal with at the best of times. Turn them into merchants and it's all a body can do to keep up with them. Worse than noblemen and their quarrels, I swear!"

Mary Townsend patted her swelling belly and winked at Alyce, a fellow conspirator in the great female effort to keep the males of the world firmly in their place. Alyce, seated on the stool at the other side of the Townsends' hearth, couldn't keep from smiling back.

William's merry, tart-tongued wife had welcomed Alyce into her home and her family with the same warmth and lack of pretense that she might have shown a long-lost friend. After several strained encounters with other merchants' wives who either pretended to a dignity they lacked or were stricken into uncomfortable silence, Mary's unassuming friendship was a treasured gift.

"Mind you," Mary added, clearly trying to be fair, "your Robert is as canny as they come. But he's run unbridled for more than half a score of years, so he'll want a little breaking in. Didn't I tell you, first time we met? Watch that man of yours, I said, or there's no telling what mischief he'll be into next!"

Alyce's smile widened. Mary was short and as squarely built as her husband. With the added burden of an enormous pregnancy that was nearing its term, she seemed almost as round as she was tall. She was also outspoken, gruff, and made a great show of keeping William under her heel, but it hadn't taken Alyce long to realize that Mary's shrewishness was as much a sham as William's pretensions of being abused. The two were deeply devoted to each other and to their four rambunctious children, and more than once Alyce had found herself envying their loving give-and-take.

"That's what you said," Alyce replied. "But what you failed to tell me is exactly how I was supposed to do that. I *told* him I didn't want a wedding feast. More than once too! Especially not with the threat of war hanging over us.

What else can I do except bar the house to his guests to make my point?"

"Not much." Mary awkwardly shifted a pillow behind her back, then propped her feet on the footstool that Alyce slid over for her. "Ah, thank you, my dear. I wish this babe would come and be done with it, but if it's like all the rest, it won't bother until it can be sure to inconvenience everyone in the process, and me most of all! That's the way of the little beasties, so you'd best be prepared for it."

Alyce frowned. "I wouldn't mind a little inconvenience."

"Now, there, don't waste your breath on foolish worrying. Give it time." She hesitated, then, in a lower voice, added, "And though it's all silly superstition, I know a woman who swears that powdered eagle's dung is as good for opening the womb to a man's seed as it is for making the babe come out easier afterward."

Alyce grimaced.

"Aye, it's not what I'd care for either. But you *might* try sleeping without a pillow. And refrain from eating foods with vinegar. There's some as say it will turn your womb bitter."

"I've heard of such," Alyce admitted. "Yet one of my women would have it that eating pickled rampion is a sure cure for a barren womb."

"Hah! As well stand on your head to make sure his seed settles into place! It's likely to be as useful, though not near so foolish."

Alyce laughed. "Surely no one's ever suggested that."

Mary's round cheeks grew rounder still as her smile widened. "They have. Indeed they have! Besides, you can scarce call yourself barren when you're not two months wed."

She leaned toward Alyce, eyes twinkling. "Though with enough imagination," she added in a conspiratorial whisper, "you and Robert might manage almost the same while you do it. The standing on your head, I mean. There's no one to say you can't have fun and a little good exercise in the trying!"

"That's all very well," said Alyce when she finally stopped laughing, "but it won't solve the problem of this feast Robert's so set upon."

"Aye, well." Mary flicked her hand dismissively. "You know as well as I it's more a case of politics than aught else. There's no man ever thought of such but what he wasn't calculating the gain to be had from it. And there's no denying," she added with a significant tilt of her head, "that you're a prize such as few men can boast of. Merchant men, anyway."

Alyce sighed. "It's not me he's showing off but his connection to my father."

Mary shrugged. "It's all the same. Having you as wife will help keep his enemies at bay. He's supported the king, and the king's laws have harmed the other merchants and their businesses. They'd be more than willing to rend him limb from limb if they could—and my William along with him, if it comes to that—but they'll not dare to risk Earl Simon's wrath by harming the daughter of one of his men. And there's no denying they'd harm you if they brought Robert down."

She pursed her lips and shook her head thoughtfully. "No, there's naught you can say that will stop Robert from having his show, so you'd best resign yourself to it—and see what fine clothes and new jewels you can get out of the bargain!"

Alyce gasped. "Clothes and jewels! At a time like this? He's already spent more on gifts than I—"

She stopped. Not even to Mary would she reveal the emptiness of her jewel box or the shabby state of her wardrobe before Robert's generosity.

"Besides," she added, retreating into indignation, "just feeding all the guests he's invited is likely to bankrupt us. He wants peacocks. At *this* time of the year!"

"He has to make a show! It's the same for him as it is for any fine lord. Look and act like a strong and wealthy man and all your enemies will keep a respectful distance. Show them weakness, even in something so foolish as a simple meal, and they'll come ravening like wolves to a kill."

If Mary had any other pearls of wisdom to offer, she didn't get a chance to share them because four scruffy, towheaded boys chose that moment to burst into the room.

"Mother, come quick!" cried the tallest and the obvious leader of the pack. "Earl Simon's passing! *And* his men!"

"They say they're off to fight the king, Mama!"

"There's war-horses, Mama! Great, tall beasts! And knights and bowmen and soldiers too!"

Alyce met Mary's troubled gaze above the four shaggy heads. This didn't sound like some minor force. If Earl Simon went out with bowmen and foot soldiers in his train, then he expected to need them.

"May we go with them, Mama?" cried the fourth and smallest, bouncing up and down on his toes with excitement. "Just to the city gates? May we? Huh? May we?"

"Of course not! Foolish boy. Like as not you'd run under the hooves of those great horses and then where would I be? Having to patch you up and fetch and carry for you till you healed, that's where. And me with a belly out to here!"

Threats of bodily harm weren't sufficient to quell the younger Townsends' enthusiasm. They pulled and tugged at their mother until they levered her, protesting and scolding, out of the chair and dragged her to the door.

Alyce followed unhappily after. Such martial show was becoming almost commonplace in the streets of London.

She ought to be used to it by now, but all it did was string her that much tighter between her father's allegiances and her husband's.

Both sides had good arguments for their stand, but to her way of thinking not one of them was worth a man's life, let alone the hundreds that would be lost in the fighting and the inevitable disruption that war would bring. A pity women didn't have the ordering of things. For all their quarreling, women never yet laid waste a town or slaughtered an innocent for the sake of a few words on parchment.

Useless thoughts, and useless her worrying over them. Robert had chosen his path, her father had chosen his. She must make the best of it, regardless.

Alyce hurried after the eager boys and their mother. She didn't care to miss the pageantry either, no matter how little she liked the reason for it.

The Townsend house and shop were located on a busy side street that led directly to East Cheap, one of London's main thoroughfares. The street was filled with people, all of them hurrying in one direction. East Cheap itself was jammed on either side as everyone crowded close to watch the spectacle that was slowly wending its way past them.

While Mary and the two servants who'd followed them kept an eye on the excited boys, Alyce found a stone stoop that gave her a decent view, yet let her remain safely out of the way. The main streets of London had been built wide enough to accommodate a dozen or more knights riding abreast, but between the crowds and the piles of muck on either side, it would be all too easy to be pushed under the feet of those enormous destriers that so entranced Mary's sons.

The cavalcade was enough to fire the imagination of any boy who'd listened to the old heroic tales—armored knights on snorting war-horses, grim-faced men marching side by side with grinning youths puffed up with the

adulation. No boy bent on glory would waste time thinking of the shovels loaded on the wagons with the tents and
cooking pots, shovels that would be used to dig new
graves as well as latrines. They'd scarce notice the priests
who rode with the soldiers in order to give absolution before the battle, and to say a prayer over the dead afterward.

It was a show Alyce would have preferred never to
have seen. She scanned the crowd, half repulsed by their
fury and the festive air, only to draw up sharply at the
sight of two men who were trapped by the press of people
on the far side of the street. She stretched on tiptoe, straining for a better view.

The two men exchanged a few words, then the shorter
one nodded curtly and disappeared into the crowd, leaving the taller, lankier one to shove his way through the
people blocking him and stride up a narrow side street.
He never once looked to right or left or so much as glanced
at the passing army. Alyce watched for as long as he remained in sight, then slowly sank back, perplexed.

What was John Rareton doing talking to Alan of
Hensford, Robert's enemy from the dung heap outside
Cripplegate?

She didn't have a chance to do more than wonder.
Sunlight flashing from the armor of one of the passing
knights caught her eye, drawing her attention to more immediate matters.

She stood frozen a moment, staring, unsure of what
she'd seen. There was no mistake. She plunged into the
crowd, pushing and shoving as she tried to work her way
to the street. "Hubert!"

Her brother was already to the next cross street by the
time she broke free of the crowd. *"Hubert!"*

He drew his horse to a snorting, restless halt, craning
around the restrictions of the new armor he wore to see
who had called him. She'd been right about where
Robert's hundred pounds would be spent, Alyce thought

as she edged to the side so she wouldn't come within reach of the stallion's hooves.

"Alyce!" Hubert swung his mount out of the line of soldiers, heedless of the people who had to scramble to get out of his way.

Alyce kept a respectful distance as well, craning to look up at him. She scarcely recognized him. He was freshly shaved and barbered and that, added to the fine new armor and the magnificent stallion he bestrode, gave him a bold, brave look that would make more than one maiden's heart beat faster.

"What are you doing here, Hubert? Where's Father? How long have you been in London? Where are you headed? Why—"

"Stop. Stop!" He laughed. "It seems London and a husband have loosed your tongue, sister. I don't remember you being so full of questions before you wed."

"I didn't expect to see you here. When did—"

"We've been at the Tower for the past nine days. Father was in council with Earl Simon and—"

"Nine days? And you sent no word?" She drew back, hurt.

"We'd more important things to concern us, as you ought to know." His great horse fidgeted and champed at the bit, impatient at the restraint.

Alyce let his comment pass. "But where are you headed? Are you— Are you off to war?"

"Not yet. We go to help garrison Northampton. Earl Simon sees us only to the gates of the city, though I've no doubt he'll soon be joining us. And once he does, we'll show the king and that bastard Edward the folly of taking counsel of foreigners rather than good Englishmen! I tell you, Alyce, it will be something grand. You know we've the right of it and God on our side. We can't help but win!"

Since Alyce had never known Hubert or her father to

fight for anything other than amusement and self-interest, and she wasn't at all sure their cause would triumph, she let that pass as well.

"Surely you've time to take a meal with us. A cup of wine, at least, and tell me how the people of Colmaine fare."

"Dine in a merchant's house? Now *that's* a fine jest. Though I must say," he added, eyeing her up and down, "being a merchant's wife seems to agree with you. You're still skinny as a post, but I've never seen you dressed so fine."

Because Father always begrudged the money for anything finer than workaday drab!

She managed not to say it.

"It's a fine house," she said instead, "and the wine far sweeter than anything Father ever had in his cellars. Surely you can linger that long?" The need to talk to someone familiar, someone from Colmaine, was suddenly overwhelming. "Just one cup?"

"Hubert! What are you about, man, to be— Alyce!" Sir Fulk brought his roan stallion to a halt beside Hubert's. He eyed the noisy crowd with disfavor, then frowned down at Alyce.

"What are you doing, girl, standing in the road like any commoner? This isn't Colmaine, you know, and you're not some common slut to be going around thus, unescorted! What's that husband of yours thinking?"

"I—"

"And still as flat as a stone. Hasn't Wardell the balls to breed up babies? Get to it! I want grandsons, even if they are a merchant's brats!"

Alyce's face flared hot. Her hands curled into fists. She had to bite her tongue to keep from answering back.

"Get home, girl! You've our name to honor, you know. Get home." He scowled at his son. "And you, you damned fool! Think you can preen like a peacock now I've bought you that horse and armor? Well, think again! And while you're thinking, get your arse moving or I'll prick you to make sure you do!"

He dragged his mount around and trotted off, forcing foot soldiers and bystanders to scatter or be run over.

Hubert grinned, then shrugged and gathered up his reins. "Another day, sister. Until then, you'd best feed that man of yours more oysters if you expect to grow a belly and a brat."

He spun his mount about, then kicked him into a thundering trot, leaving a furious, red-faced Alyce to get out of the way of the passing soldiery as best she could.

"THE LORD EDWARD asks too much. It's no good slaughtering the cow just because you want more milk!"

Robert's angry words cut the air like knives. The man who sat across the table from him quirked one eyebrow upward; his lips thinned to a faint intimation of a sneer. In the windowless strong room, with only the frail candle-light to push back the dark, the expression seemed satanic in its mockery.

"You can always refuse Edward's demands, you know."

Robert didn't answer. He didn't have to. They both knew he wouldn't challenge the Lord Edward or refuse to do his bidding. Not now.

The man shrugged as though to say he'd given Robert a way out, and that it was on Robert's head if he refused to take it. "Montfort sends men to reinforce the garrison at Northampton, though he himself remains in London. The bishops of Oxford treat with the king in Montfort's name, but while Earl Simon might be willing to concede some points, he'll not give an inch on his refusal to allow the king to name foreigners to his council. And Edward—"

Robert's visitor glanced at the door of the strong

room. It was firmly shut, but he lowered his voice and leaned closer across the table, nonetheless.

"The Lord Edward's harshness with those who defied the king has earned him more enemies and reinforced the resistance from the barons. Edward's clever, and he's brought a number of Simon's followers back to his side, but there are those who doubt it will be enough. England rallies to Simon's calls, not to Henry's or his son's. The great nobles will survive, come what may, but the rest of us . . ."

He shrugged again and sat back, shaking his head. He didn't need to finish the thought. They both knew how steep a price might be exacted of the losers if Earl Simon and his barons gained the day. They also knew that even those who chose the winning side could be trampled and forgotten by the powerful men whose victory they'd helped obtain.

Robert dropped his gaze to his cup of wine. The liquid showed black and thick in the flickering light of the candles. He lifted the cup to his lips and took a sip, then slowly and deliberately set it down again.

"England has been known to be fickle in her loyalties. Whatever the justice of Earl Simon's cause—and I'll not deny he has it in fair measure—in the end, England will not abandon its king. I say Henry will triumph."

"I'm not so sure of that."

Robert met the man's dark gaze with an equally direct one of his own.

"There is little sure in life," he said harshly, "and nothing sure at all when men like us meddle in the affairs of kings and fools." He shook his head, more in weary resignation than negation. "I tell you straight, this game we play is a game of fools, and it will leave widows and orphans in its wake."

His visitor's mouth twitched with wry amusement. "I thought it was only the game of love that fools played at."

Robert's fingers tightened around the cup. "That too."

"You've grown cynical in your old age, Wardell."

For an instant, their gazes locked. Then Robert roughly shoved his cup aside and got to his feet. The sound of his chair scraping across the rough stone floor sounded like the cries of the damned.

"Tell the Lord Edward I will do what I can to meet his demands. I cannot promise more than that."

11

STAKES OF THE GAME

ROBERT DIDN'T BOTHER to see his visitor out. He held the strong-room door for him, then swung it shut behind him. The candles on the table flared and dipped with the draft, setting the shadows dancing. The sound of the man's footsteps on the stone steps came through the thick oak door, muffled, fading into silence.

With an angry grunt, Robert leaned back against the door, head bent, arms crossed over his chest, and studied the room before him.

He'd had it built when he built the new hall and solar and the new kitchens at the side. He'd needed a place to store his coin and his precious cloth, a place safe from thieves and the ravages of fire. He'd gotten what he wanted. The king himself would welcome the security this room offered. There were no windows to break the thick defenses of walls and ceiling and floor, and only narrow air holes against dead air and damp. The room's sole point of vulnerability was the iron-barred door at his back, and it was as strong and stout as man could make it.

But even stone walls and iron-barred doors weren't proof against the threat of destruction from within.

Robert had no illusions. Edward's demands for new loans could destroy him as easily as fire and thieves and the pillaging of war. Even if Edward won—and there was no guarantee of that, nor any assurance he would even survive the conflict—his victory would mean nothing if Robert's business had already crumbled under the combined pressures of princely demands and the staggering strains that came with a country at war.

If it were only himself, it would not matter so much. He could rebuild again, if he had to.

He had not acted alone, however, and if he fell, others would be crushed beneath him, unable to rise again. His friend William might recover, but not Richard Tennys. Not John Byngham, nor Hugh Giffard, nor Walter Gournay, nor any of the others. Good men, every one. Men with families. Men who had trusted him, followed him, though he'd warned them—God! how often he had warned them!—of the risks they ran, the dangers they faced.

Yet still they had insisted on following him, believing he must be in the right of it just as he had been in the right of so many other things over the years. They had trusted him in the past and their purses had grown heavy as a result. They trusted him now, when there was the risk they would lose not only their purses, but everything else that mattered to them as well.

The danger didn't lie on one side of the balance only. If Montfort triumphed, he wouldn't destroy the king or the Lord Edward, but he could easily reward those who had supported him by giving them the wealth of Edward's vanquished followers to fatten on. If the king won, and Robert had refused these new demands for funds, Edward was capable of forgetting that there were other, older debts he owed. He might even go so far as to exact revenge for having been denied the funds he needed now—and a proud prince's vengeance could be terrible when it fell.

Robert shook the thought away. He would not fail. He was sure of Edward's eventual triumph, just as he was sure he'd judged the risks and the rewards aright.

Truth was, what troubled him most wasn't Edward's demands or the dangers they brought with them. He'd known from the start that such were possibilities. What he hadn't expected was that the thought of Alyce, of what she might suffer if he failed, would press at the back of his mind, coloring his every word, his every thought. The green velvet in the chest behind him had seemed a live and speaking thing while he'd met with his visitor, its message clear, its presence inescapable.

This was madness. He'd wed for reasons of strategy and because he needed to beget heirs. His marriage was a business proposition, nothing more. He'd gained a toe-hold in the opposing camp, and Alyce had gained a husband and a life that was far more comfortable than what she'd led shut away in her father's crumbling castle. The physical pleasures of their union were simply a bonus, pleasant, to be sure, but unessential.

He had to keep his distance from Alyce, and from his growing need of her. Once, he'd clung too tight, needed— *wanted*—too much. He would not make the same mistake again.

At the thought, Robert swore. How many times must he remind himself of that?

He shoved away from the door, irritated with himself and his troubled thoughts. He couldn't afford such indulgences. Not now. Perhaps not ever.

In the meantime, there was still his business to be run—wool to ship, cloth to buy and sell. He had a shipment of wool for Flanders for which he'd arranged passage. Arranged, of course, meant bribed the captain and the workers who would load the ship and paid the puling weasel of a port official who drew his pennies from the government, then turned around and claimed his pounds from the merchants he squeezed on the other end. There was nothing new in that. The only difference these days was that scarcity had driven the price of the bribes higher.

Whatever the cost, the wool must go out that day. Too few ships were docking in London these days, and the need to sell the wool accumulating in his storerooms was more urgent than it had ever been.

He'd already paid for it, and there'd be no chance of recouping his investment, let alone making a profit, until he got the wool out of England and into the hands of the weavers in Flanders. And if he couldn't make a profit, he wouldn't have the money to buy the wool from the next shearing, which would hurt everyone who depended on it. People starved when markets collapsed, as they threatened to do now.

At the other end, with shipping curtailed, the Flanders weavers ran the risk of seeing their looms idled for lack of wool. They would pay premium prices for high-quality wool like his and be glad to get it. If he then delivered his wool to the markets that needed it, Robert could make a considerable profit, a profit that would provide a hedge against the Lord Edward and his demands and still cover the next year's purchases.

But he had to get it to Flanders first. Business did not end even with the world turned upside down.

HENLEY HAD ESCORTED Alyce to the Townsends' and he escorted her back, but he led her down side streets and through narrow, fetid alleys to avoid the militant crowds that lingered in the wake of Earl Simon's passing.

Alyce scarcely noticed her surroundings. She was still vibrating to the blows her father and brother had struck on her soul.

They wouldn't stoop to dine in a merchant's house! They wouldn't even take his wine! It was Robert's money that had put that fine armor on Hubert's back and that even finer stallion under him, but not by so much as a nod would they admit their debt to him . . . or to her.

Inwardly she raged and cursed and cried. Outwardly, she was cold and silent. Henley felt it, she knew. He kept throwing nervous glances at her over his shoulder as if he expected her to shatter suddenly, or explode in fury.

She refused to do either. She wouldn't put her pain on show for the world's entertainment. Maida and Hilde would have understood, but there was no one in all of London to whom she could reveal her wounded heart. Not Mary or Githa. Not Robert.

Certainly not Robert.

She closed her eyes against the vision of him that suddenly hung in the air before her. It was a wasted effort—his face pursued her into the dark behind her lids.

If it were night, she could creep into bed beside him and lose herself in his heat and strength. Her shoulders ached to feel his arm around them. No matter that he didn't love her or that he kept her at a safe distance once she'd risen from the bed they shared. She craved his reassuring presence, his certainty. From them she might draw enough confidence to reclaim that part of her that Hubert and Sir Fulk had so carelessly trampled into the mud of East Cheap.

But when they turned into the street that ran in front of Wardell House, the first thing she saw was a pack of schoolboys clustered beside the closed gate, snickering over something that one of them was scrawling on the wall with chalk. Henley shouted, but Alyce had already kicked her horse into a gallop, furious at the insult to Robert and to her house.

The boys spun around, wide-eyed, then scattered like startled pigeons before a cat. Alyce chased after them—too late. They dodged down alleyways and up narrow side streets, laughing and jeering, knowing she couldn't catch them. Henley swore and charged after a pair of them, anyway.

Alyce reined Graciella to a plunging halt in the middle of the street. The mare snorted and half reared, excited by the race and eager to keep at the game.

One of the boys, bolder than the rest, poked his head around a cart, then darted into the street in front of her, tongue out, fingers flapping in an obscene gesture. "Nyah nyah! Nyah nyah!"

Henley, emerging from the side street empty-handed and furious at being balked, roared an oath and set spurs to his horse.

"Try and catch me," the boy cried, delighted at the fury he'd roused. "If you can!"

He dodged out of Henley's path, then slipped between the cart and the wall of the house behind it, disappearing up a path so narrow it wouldn't even qualify as an alley. Henley was on the point of swinging out of the saddle when she called for him to stop.

"Your pardon, milady," he grumbled when he reluctantly rejoined her. "I should've grabbed one of those gallows birds at least. Nothin' but trouble they've been. Shows what comes of teachin' 'em to read and write. Gives 'em ideas above themselves, it does."

At the sight of what the boys had scrawled on the wall of Wardell House, both of them stopped short. Henley might not be able to read the insults, most of them written in French or misspelled Latin and all of them vulgar, but there was no mistaking the meaning of the crude stick figures that sprawled across the stone.

There was Robert, kissing the bare backside of an old man wearing a crown who was trampling little stick figures—the citizens of London, no doubt—beneath his feet. In another, a squint-eyed woman sat with her hands on a money bag and her legs splayed wide, her skirts indecently rucked up above her scrawny ankles. She didn't normally squint, but Alyce had no more trouble identifying herself than she'd had recognizing Robert.

There was worse, but she turned away, stomach churning.

Henley shook his head in disgust. "Erwyna will be in a right fury at having t' scrub the walls again."

"Again?" Alyce glanced at him, startled out of her shock. "They've done this before?"

"Oh, aye, milady. Two, three times at least. It's the boys from the grammar school down the street. Merchants' sons, the lot of 'em, who've heard their fathers cursing Master Wardell for his support of the Lord Edward." His brow furrowed, his shaggy eyebrows meeting above his nose, as he scowled at the filth on the wall. "I ever catch 'em, they won't be able to sit for a week, and that's a fact."

"Oh," said Alyce weakly. She glanced again at the wall. As she stared at the scrawled words and the rude, awkward figures, the sick feeling in her stomach vanished, replaced by a growing fury.

How dare they? How *dare* they?

All the tensions and insults of the day blended into one maddening rage that swept through her like fire, burning away the uncertainty and self-doubts that had held her.

She leaned out of her saddle to pound on the gate with her gloved fist. As soon as it swung open, she pushed through, ignoring the eager greeting of the stable lad who held it.

Heads appeared at the windows and from behind doors as she rode into the yard and dismounted.

"Where's Master Wardell?" she demanded, handing the reins to the boy who had opened the gate.

The boy's eyes widened in startlement. "Gone, milady."

"Gone!"

" 'At's right. Down to the docks."

Alyce pushed aside the irrational irritation that Robert wasn't there when she wanted him. She gestured to one of the scullery maids who'd poked her nose out to see who had arrived. "Get brushes and buckets and scrub down the outer walls."

She didn't have to explain why, a fact that only added to her anger. "Is Master Rareton about?"

The maid shook her head and scurried away, anxious to be out of the reach of her anger.

"Master Rareton's at the docks with Master Wardell." Alyce turned, startled, and saw Piers walking down the hall steps toward her. "At least," he continued, "that's what Master Rareton planned. He wasn't about when Master Wardell left so I can't say for sure where he's got to."

Reading Alyce's blank look aright, he added by way of explanation, "We've some wool being loaded for Flanders today."

"How long will they be?" she demanded, more sharply than she'd intended.

"There's no telling, milady. Master Wardell had a visitor this morning, so they were late getting off. Since Master Rareton hadn't returned, he said I was to finish my work here, then join him at the docks."

"Why didn't he just send Master Rareton? Or you?"

"He was afraid there might be trouble with the workers on the river, milady. Refusing to let the boat dock, or load the wool, or let our people do it in their place. Dumping things in the river and letting them float away. Spilling oil on the best wool sacks. Whatever would cause the most harm. You know Master Wardell's no favorite with them of late. Surely he—"

"Yes, yes." Alyce had no intention of revealing that Robert hadn't mentioned a word about his business or how it fared. The knowledge that he hadn't stung almost as sharply as her father's earlier words. "Can you take me to him?"

"Take you to the docks? But—" Piers looked troubled. "There's naught for such as you there, milady. Truly."

"Such as I?" Alyce stared at him.

What was she, then? A merchant's wife who was ignorant of his business? A baron's daughter whose father ignored and insulted her? A mistress whose own servants feared to tell her of the insults and mockery of unruly schoolboys?

For an instant, the small yard seemed a vast and empty place, and she but a speck lost in the middle of it.

"Ride double with Henley if you must," she said, reclaiming Graciella's reins from the stable boy. "I want you to take me to Robert, to Master Wardell, *now*."

"WHAT DO YOU mean, you won't load the ship?" Robert's fingers twitched with the urge to throttle the smug bastard who stood before him, to dig his fingers into that thick, filthy throat and squeeze until the man's eyes rolled up in his head and his lying tongue stuck out, as purple and swollen as a hanged man's.

Overhead a gull wheeled, keening in protest. The ship tied up to the quay shifted impatiently at its moorings, restless on the tide that would soon turn and run back to the sea. Its masts creaked and a loose flap of canvas slapped at the rigging, a hard, sharp sound against the heavy-throated murmur of the great river itself.

The familiar sounds seemed oddly loud when there was not so much as a whisper from the dockworkers who stood on the strand, eyes narrowed, bodies tense, and hands hovering near whatever clubs and knives were within easy reach. The sailors watching from the deck of the ship were just as silent. It wasn't their fight, but Robert knew they could easily be drawn into it if given an excuse.

"We had an agreement, Pykct," he said to the leader of the dockworkers. "You and your men were well paid for your . . . assistance."

"Well, now, maybe we 'ad an agreement, an' then agin, maybe we din't. As fer bein' well paid . . ." The burly riverman cocked his elbow upward and scratched under his armpit, grimacing with the air of a man mired in serious thought. "Now that's a matter of opinion, wouldn't ye say?"

"Damned if I will!"

"Wardell!" The ship's captain, as sleek and sharp-nosed as the rats in his hold, eyed Robert with patent disfavor. "Your quarrel with this man is no concern of mine, but the tide *is*. If you can't load your goods, there's others who can, and I can't wait. I've trouble enough shipping English goods these days without getting mixed in an Englishman's quarrels." He eyed Pyket with distaste. "Especially not yours."

"It's not a quarrel, Hoeke," Robert said. His eyes narrowed dangerously. "It's a matter of dealing with thieves and cheats."

"Thieves, is it?" The riverman bristled. "I'll show you thieves—"

"No need to show him. Wardell knows all about thievery."

Robert's head snapped around at this new interruption.

"Hensford!" Robert glared at the lanky man standing at the top of the steps that led from the quay to the warehouse above. "What brings you here?"

"What brings me here?" Hensford laughed. He came down the steps with the arrogant swagger of a man who knew he was the center of attention and relished the knowledge. "Why, the same thing that brings you, Wardell. A ship." He waved toward the one moored behind Robert. "Captain Hoeke's ship, to be precise."

He didn't look at the ship or its captain. His glare was fixed on Robert, his face drawn taut with the avid look of a predator that sees its prey almost within its grasp. "It will serve admirably to transport my wool to Flanders."

"Your wool!"

Hensford smiled. "My wool, Wardell. Ask Pyket."

The burly dockworker shifted unhappily. It was one thing to cheat a man whose money he'd taken, quite another to have his treachery revealed by the man who'd suborned him in the first place. Had it been a matter between the two merchants alone, he might well have backed off. Unfortunately, there were witnesses, and he had his position among the dockworkers to protect. The angry muttering of his men gave fair warning: they wouldn't take kindly to any move that jeopardized their future illicit earnings from anxious merchants and ship captains with cargo to load.

"Did you take Hensford's money to ignore me and load his goods instead, Pyket?" Robert demanded.

"Well, not to say 'instead.'" Pyket's head sank lower on his neck. He glared at Hensford. Hensford stared back, one eyebrow arched in a silent warning that wasn't lost on the unhappy docker. "Master Hensford had work fer us, is all. Nothin' wrong with that."

"Not unless it required you to break your agreement with me."

Robert's own men shifted uncertainly. The dockworkers outnumbered them, even counting the two men guarding the wool-laden carts on the street. If the sailors joined in the quarrel it would be three to one, and though his guards carried swords, which gave the advantage of an extended reach, a heavy club could easily shatter the bones in a man's sword arm in a single, well-placed blow.

Robert cursed silently. He should have waited for Rareton. He should have brought Piers and old Joshua and the stable lads with him. It would have taken longer, but they could have loaded the ship while he and the rest of his men stood guard.

Too late now to worry about all the things he should

have done. He'd been worried about the damned tide and distracted by Edward's new demands, but tide, treacherous cheats, and old enemies alike wouldn't stand between him and his goal. He wouldn't let them.

"My men will load my wool, Hoeke," he said without taking his eye off Pyket and the other dockers. "After that, if there's time and space left in your hold, then Hensford can load his."

Pyket hesitated, uncertain how to deal with so direct a challenge.

"Go ahead, Pyket," Hensford sneered. "Load the wool of a man who'd rather kiss the king's arse than support those who fight for his fellow Londoners."

Pyket wavered. His men muttered and edged forward, faces hard and grim.

"The devil take you quarrelsome English!" Hoeke exclaimed angrily. "I'll find cargo elsewhere." He spun on his heel and would have stalked away, but Robert blocked his path.

"The devil may well take us, Hoeke," he said softly, "but you'll take my wool in the meantime. We had an agreement. Despite Pyket's greed, that hasn't changed. My men—"

Pyket cursed and whipped out his knife. Before he could advance a step, a cry from the street above snapped them all around.

"My lady! *No!*"

Like a warrior angel at the call of battle, Alyce suddenly appeared at the top of the steps above them. Her head was defiantly high. Her eyes flashed fire and her cloak flared about her like wings.

Robert gaped, then cursed. His hand dropped to his sword, but he dared not draw it. Not yet. Not until he had no choice.

Without hesitation, Alyce set her mount to the

descent. One step. Two. Then the mare launched herself from the steps in a soaring leap to land on the stone-flagged quay, iron-shod hooves scrabbling for purchase. Men on either side jumped out of Alyce's way, too startled even to curse. Pyket backed up a step, eyes rolling as he tried to face this new threat and keep watch on the old.

If she'd brandished a sword of burning fire, Alyce couldn't have cowed them more.

She pulled her mount to a snorting, dancing halt not a foot from the gape-mouthed captain. Hoeke instinctively dodged back. She spared him one haughty, withering glance, then scanned the other drop-jawed men assembled on the quay. Her lips thinned and her eyebrows rose in disdain. She paid no heed whatsoever to Piers and Henley, who were cautiously making their way down the steps after her.

Robert's stomach twisted with fear and a futile rage. At her for coming. At Piers and Henley for letting her. He would string them both up for not keeping Alyce safe—right after he throttled her for recklessly plunging into danger. Proud, hardheaded fool! What did she think she could accomplish by so mad an act? And what in hell had brought her there in the first place?

One of the laborers, a hulking black-haired beast of a man—more bear than human by the looks of him—eyed Alyce narrowly, then wet his lips. Robert's hand tightened around his sword hilt. He'd skewer the first man that dared so much as lay a hand on her bridle.

The mare half reared, but Alyce quickly brought the beast to hand. "Master Wardell!"

Robert's jaw set. "My lady?"

"I am come to tell you," she said with an unaccustomed arrogance, "that my father has left London at the head of the forces Earl Simon has dispatched to Northampton. Sir Fulk sends his regret, but he and my brother could not stay to dine."

Robert twitched. For an instant, anger consumed him. She had put herself at risk for this? For a stupid, useless— Then his brain started working.

She wasn't a fool, but he was acting like one. He gulped in air and forced his hand to drop from his sword, his legs to straighten from a fighting crouch. He felt dizzy, almost light-headed, and a sudden stirring in his braies warned that more than his brain was coming alive.

"I am sorry to hear that—for your sake, dear wife," he said, and hoped the rest were still too stunned to wonder at the residual quaver of fear in his voice. "But in times such as this, Earl Simon's claims on his barons must be greater than ours. I trust Sir Fulk will be free to grant us a few hours of his company the next time he is in London."

Their little play lacked polish, but it was enough. Pyket's men muttered uneasily among themselves. It was one thing to take money to betray a man they thought had betrayed all London, quite another to fight him if he'd wed the daughter of one of Montfort's barons.

"You will forgive us, my lady," Robert went on, "but there is still some unfinished business to attend to here and the wool to be loaded on the good captain's ship." He stared pointedly at Pyket.

The man blinked. He opened his mouth, then closed it, slipped his knife back in its sheath, and nodded sullenly.

"Come on, then," he growled at his men. "Let's get to it."

Hoeke snorted and looked grimly amused. Hensford turned bright red. He glared at Pyket, then at Robert, then he spun on his heel and stalked off, retreating to his horse and cart on the street above.

For herself, Alyce didn't budge an inch.

From the look on his face, Robert would happily have pitched her in the Thames or sent her home trussed up in one of his wool sacks. So much for gratitude. First her father and brother, now her husband. And not one of them with so much as a thank you in his mouth.

She stared down at Robert, fighting for calm. Her heart hammered painfully in her chest. It had almost stopped when that beetle-browed dog had pulled a knife on him.

Robert glared back at her. "I suggest you let Piers and Henley lead you home, milady."

Her upper lip curled in anger. Lead her home! He made it sound as if she were a packhorse to be stabled and forgotten.

Before she could say something she'd regret, she turned away. A dozen pairs of eyes were fixed on her, coldly hostile, avid, dangerous.

Disgust and fear shuddered through her. She'd been right. They *had* meant Robert harm, Robert and his men. And Hensford!

She glanced up at the tall, stiff figure that stood at the top of the steps, watching them like a crow watched a dying rat, waiting for the chance to swoop down and pick the meat off the creature's bones.

"Milady! Alyce!"

She swung back to face her husband.

Her father would have cursed and threatened to beat her for having plunged in where she was not wanted. Robert looked as if that, for him, would be no more than a beginning.

"You should go home," he said. "It would be far more comfortable for you there."

And safer, she thought. She knew her presence could turn to liability if violence broke out. He didn't need to put it into words.

"We haven't even started loading and it will be some time before—"

"I'll wait," she said, and turned her head to watch the first of the laborers walk by, back bent under the weight of the bulging, bulky wool sack he carried on his shoulder.

She would not leave. Not now. Not yet. She couldn't bear the thought of sitting uselessly in the solar, waiting for him to return, and her pride wouldn't let her slink away like a whipped dog just because he said she ought. Besides, she'd never been on the river before, never seen a ship being loaded. Sheer curiosity was enough to keep her there, no matter what.

Head high, spine prickling with her husband's angry scrutiny, she guided Graciella to the side where she would be out of the way, yet able to see everything that went on. Piers and Henley unhappily followed after.

"You need not keep me company," she assured them. "I don't intend to move from here until Master Wardell is ready to leave and I'm sure he—"

"Would string us up for crow bait if we dared so much as stir from your side, milady," Piers said. "Were he any other master, I'd fear a beating for having let you get so far."

Henley nodded agreement with that assessment as he stationed himself at Alyce's right side.

"But *I* ordered you to bring me. Surely Master Wardell needs you more than I. With all those sacks—"

"There's men enough to load them," Piers told her, claiming the post of left-hand guard. "Any more and they'd just trip over each other's feet."

He was probably right. Now they'd started, Alyce could see the rhythm of their work. A man would climb the stairs to the carts above, hoist one of the wool sacks, then carry it down the steps, across the quay, and up a narrow plank that shifted with the shifting of the ship and bowed beneath them with each step they took. Though the sight of that unsteady plank made her stomach squeeze unpleasantly, it bothered the men not at all. Despite the enormous weight of the wool they carried, they went up the plank as nimble as goats, tossed the wool sack to someone out of sight in the bowels of the ship, then descended by another plank to return to the carts for another load.

It was a smooth, well-practiced system, and after the first few minutes, thoroughly boring to watch. Almost—*almost*—Alyce wished she'd agreed to return home as Robert had demanded.

After that first angry suggestion that she leave, he'd ignored her utterly. He stalked at the side of the endless circle of men like a hungry wolf eyeing a flock of sheep for any sign of weakness. The laborers felt it, too—the anger, the will to control, to rule, to *win,* whatever the cost. It made them wary. It also made them dangerously resentful that he *had* won, and at their expense.

However little Robert liked her being there, Alyce didn't doubt that her arrival had turned the scales in his favor. True, she'd plunged down those steps without thinking, but her father and brother had taught her a few tricks. She wasn't helpless and she was mounted, an advantage in itself.

That was hindsight speaking, of course. At the time, all she could think of was Robert and the need to reach him, to stand by him.

For all the thanks he'd offered afterward, she might as well have gone for a swim in the Thames.

Yet hot as her resentment was, it was a pale, cold thing beside the heat stirring within her at just the sight of him. Even Hubert, in all his armored finery, could not match her husband's commanding presence. He was—

"Not very exciting," Piers said. "Watching them load wool sacks, I mean. Gets boring pretty quickly, don't you think?"

Piers's comment dragged her out of her thoughts. Alyce glanced at him, irritated. Neither the prospect of a brawl nor Robert's anger were enough to deflate his natural optimism for long. He was jauntily seated cross-legged atop his horse, watching the workmen lumber past and clearly in the mood for talk.

"It's interesting to me," she lied. "I've never seen a ship loaded before."

Her attention wasn't on the workers, however, but on Robert. She watched as he strode up the plank, quick and graceful as a cat, then disappeared into the belly of the ship. He didn't once glance her way. When he didn't re-appear, she reluctantly turned her attention back to the talkative apprentice.

"And what do you think of the riverfront, now you've seen it, milady?" he asked.

In her haste to reach Robert, Alyce had paid scant heed to her surroundings. She swept her gaze along the riverside, then up to the jumble of warehouses, inns, ale-houses, and workshops that crowded along the waterfront and the narrow streets that led away from the river. The noisy, bustling warren stank of fish and hides and what-ever else moved into and out of London on the back of the river. Robert had said that shipping was down because of the present troubles, but to her it seemed an anthill alive with busy, quarrelsome ants.

Beneath the smells was the heavy, damp scent of the Thames. Under the shouts of the men and the creak of the carts and clatter of the horses was the low, dull susurration of the vast river flowing past, oblivious to the humans that swarmed on either side of it.

"Ever been on the river, milady?"

She shook her head again.

"I know a waterman would take you," Piers said. "He'd take you under the bridge too, if you asked, and not get so much as a drop of water on you."

She studied the long arc of the bridge that stood per-haps a quarter mile to the east of them. With the houses and shops built on top of its broad back and its solid stone piers spaced at close intervals along the span, it looked like nothing so much as a huge, hump-backed centipede working its way across the river. So far, she'd had no excuse to set foot on it, but it was impossible to live for long in the city and not be aware of the great stone link between London and all that lay on the opposite side of the river.

"A riverman who'll take me under the bridge?" she said at last. "Why should that be so exceptional?"

"Hear that rushing sound?"

Alyce frowned. Beneath the nearer sounds of carts and horses and the cries of busy men, she could hear a steady roar that hung just at the edge of hearing. "Surely so large a river—"

Piers shook his head. "It's not just the river. That's the sound of it pouring between the piers of the bridge. It's dangerous, you know. Lots of people won't go under the bridge, nor anywhere near because of it. People drown every year, even the rivermen, when they get caught and overturned in that."

"People can drown in a duck pond, if it comes to that," Alyce said.

"It's more than that. Master Wardell explained it to me once. How the piers cut off so much of the river's flow that the water rushes faster through the space that's left. Sucks you down as easy as sucking an oyster out of an oyster shell, they say. *Thurrp!* Just like that!"

He laughed with the ghoulish delight that all boys seemed to take in mayhem and disaster. Henley snorted, frowning at the massive stone beast that dominated the horizon.

Alyce studied the churning waters where the great river split to run between the massive piers. Even at this distance it looked cold and hungry.

"I've been under the bridge before," Piers informed her with pride. "It's all froth and roar, like a dragon that wants to swallow you whole, and the water pushed so high against the stone on either side sometimes that it towers over you. I stood up in the boat once, just to see, and it was taller than I am!"

Henley frowned and muttered something about bloody-minded care-for-naughts.

Piers laughed, his face alight with remembered excitement. "Old Brugher clouted me so hard after, my ears rang for a week. Said I could have tipped us over and we'd both have drowned."

"He was right, and if I'd known you'd tried that stunt, I'd have made sure your ears rang for another week!" Henley growled. "I saw a body fished out of the river once. Floated down from somewhere else, it did, but one of the watermen spotted it and dragged it ashore."

He grimaced in distaste. "It were a man. A big man. He'd turned white as a flounder and gone soft, like bread soaked in milk, and the fishes had taken bites of his nose and feet and—"

"*I* saw a fellow drown!" Piers broke in, eager to top Henley's gruesome tale. "He was trying to row across to Southwark when a floating tree limb snagged his boat. He fell in trying to get free, then got caught on the limb. We could see him flailing and thrashing, but by the time a boat put out from shore, he'd slammed into the bridge and been sucked under."

Alyce fought against a sudden queasiness in her stomach. "I don't think—"

"They dragged him out just beyond the Tower," Piers added, clearly pleased with the effect his story was having. "I saw him later. Had half his face scraped off and—"

"Enough!"

Piers jumped, startling his horse. He glanced at Henley, who returned the guilty look. They shrank under Alyce's glare. "Beg pardon, milady."

"As well you should. *Both* of you!" She shuddered. "And don't ever stand up in a boat again! You're not immortal, no matter what a boy your age may think."

"No, milady." He tried, and failed, to look properly abashed. "But it *was* fun. And I still ride the river. There's more'n one traveler who gets off on one side of the bridge and walks around to the other, but *I* never have!"

"You haven't a scrap of good sense either," Alyce said tartly. "Enough talk of the river," she added, cutting off his protest. "I want—"

She stopped, her attention caught by the sight of John Rareton picking his way through the dockworkers and down the steps to the quay.

"Why, there's Master Rareton!" Piers exclaimed. "Now, where could he have been to be so late?"

HE HELD HIMSELF in check as they made their way back through the streets of London, but the instant the door of their bedchamber slammed shut behind them, Robert exploded.

"What the *devil* did you mean, plunging in amongst so many armed and angry men? Have you no idea how easily they could have taken you hostage? How easily they could have hurt you? Could have *killed* you?"

Alyce's head snapped up. Her eyes flashed green fire. "The daughter of the Baron of Colmaine? Not once they knew! They wouldn't have dared!"

"But they didn't know! And they might not have given you the time to tell them!"

The muscles of Robert's shoulders and arms quivered from the force of his pent-up fury and fear for her. His hands curled into claws against the urge to grab her and hold her safe against him.

"Bah!" she replied. "What good are your sword and your armed guards if you could let them harm me?"

"What good would my sword be if Pyket had pulled you from your horse and put his knife to your throat?"

"You act as though I were some meek and fragile creature to be wrapped in wool and put away in a box, or an idiot incapable of rational though. I am your wife, sir, and I expect to be treated as such!"

"And how might that be, my lady? By dragging you to the docks with me like any common whore?"

She gasped, outraged.

He swept ruthlessly on. "Tell me in what way I failed to accord you the honor due you as a lady, and my wife. Have I beat you? Mocked you? Ill-treated you in any way?"

"You've set me to the side as if I lacked the brains of a mouse," she snapped. "You've refused to take me into your confidence."

"What would you know of trade?"

She drew in a sharp breath at that.

Shame stung him. He sucked in air, then let it out, forced his voice to gentle. "You see, my lady," he said, "I do not forget that you *are* a lady born."

"And can do more than tend a garden and see to the mending of your hose. Robert!" she cried, hands outstretched, suddenly imploring. "I would be a wife to you in all things, if only you would trust me, share your worries with me."

"My worries? I have none, lady," he lied.

"None?"

He shook his head, fighting against an urge to tell her everything. That would be madness. Already she'd claimed more of him than she had any notion. More than he cared to admit, even to himself.

"What of today, at the river?" she demanded.

It was his turn to brush her concern aside. "Men like Pyket have always tried to cheat the merchants who need their services. There's nothing new in that."

"What of your steward?"

"Rareton? What of him?"

"I think he betrays you."

"What?"

"I saw him this morning, talking in the street with Hensford. It was only a glimpse, but they acted like men who had arrived at some sort of agreement between them."

Robert opened his mouth, then closed it on his protest. His steward had no reason to so much as nod hello to Hensford, let alone talk to him openly. And Rareton *had* been late to the quay.

He shook his head. "Rareton wouldn't turn traitor. Not for money. And certainly *not* with Hensford."

"There are other things than money that can drive a man to treachery."

Robert met Alyce's angry, unflinching gaze. His own fury was stirring again. "I'll not condemn a man who's served me well for no more cause than a chance encounter in the street."

Her chin lifted. "Yet you would doubt me."

Had he not been looking directly into her eyes, he would have missed the flash of vulnerability beneath her anger and her pride. It was gone in an instant, but it took his anger with it.

He brushed the back of his hand across her cheek. "I would keep you safe, my lady." The words came soft, more plea than promise, heavy with fears even he would not admit to.

She jerked back from his touch. "That's what all men say, yet the truth is, they'd rather keep women ignorant of the dangers into which they drag them, for fear they might protest."

Robert flinched. The lady placed her barbs with uncanny accuracy.

He started to turn away, but spun back instead, closing the gap between them and pulling her into his arms. Because he had to. Because he could not stop himself.

He'd been burning to hold her from the moment she'd come flying down the steps of the quay. Even as he'd trembled with rage and fear, he'd thought of kissing her, of stripping that damnable veil from her head and the clothes from her body and making such passionate love to her that they both collapsed and died of it.

She tried to pull free, stiff-backed, but he folded her to him. He took her chin and forced her head up so she had no choice but to look at him.

Her body softened, then arched against his. Her eyelids fluttered over eyes grown dangerously dark and deep. She slid her arms around his neck, tangled her fingers in his hair, and drew him down to her.

He cupped her cheek. "I know you, lady," he said softly, his mouth only inches from hers. "I'd not dare to drag you anywhere you had no mind to go."

And then he kissed her.

The kiss flared like oil thrown into the fire. All thought of quarreling vanished as she matched him kiss for hungry kiss. Their angry words, their quarrel, the world beyond their chamber door, all lay forgotten. Somehow they rid themselves of cloaks and tunics and belts and shoes, flinging each cumbersome item aside as they made their twisting, staggering way across the room. Clad only in shift and shirt and braies, they tumbled into bed.

"I swear, milady," Robert gasped, "there are times I think I wed a sorceress rather than a woman of flesh and blood."

"You're mad." Her breath came quick and shallow and eager. Her shift was pulled off her shoulder and rucked up to her waist; her hair spilled over the sheets in heedless, wanton display. Just the sight of her was enough to set his blood to burning.

He breathed deep, fighting for control, and traced the curve of her shoulder with his palm. "How else explain this? One moment we're quarreling like dogs over a bone, the next I can think of nothing save bedding you."

She shifted beneath him impatiently. Her hands slid over his chest, down his sides, up his back and arms, making him tremble. "It's no sorcery, only you and that second nose you wear stuck out so straight and hard that it's impossible to ignore!"

Robert burst out laughing. He pressed his hips against her and felt her arch to him in involuntary response. "A second nose, is it? Beware, lady, for it's found your scent and would go a-hunting!"

Her mouth curved upward with delight. She knotted her hands in his shirt and pulled him closer still. Her breath was warm against his skin, her lips only inches from his. She squirmed beneath him in deliberate provocation.

He tweaked a wayward lock of hair that had drifted across her cheek. "Whence comes this vulgar talk, sweet Alyce? I swear not even Joshua, deep gone in drink, is half so blunt!"

She laughed. "It's your ill influence, sir," she said, and nipped at his neck. "You make me lust and set my bones aflame, even when I would be most angry with you. I can neither think nor mind my manners when you tempt me so to other things."

She shifted, pulling free, then twisted so it was she who was on top, astraddle him, and he who looked up at her. He slid his hands up her long legs, savoring the length of her, the flesh that warmed so temptingly beneath his hand.

"Was it not you told me it's women have the carnal instincts in greatest measure?" She rubbed against him even as she unfastened his braies. "Remember? On our wedding night, as you tried to worm your way into my bed?"

He gripped the exquisite curve where thigh joined hip, digging his fingers into the firm, yet yielding flesh. "Worm, was it?" he said, and shifted so that he pressed against the soft core of her.

She gasped, then giggled and rocked her hips against him. "Aye, a measly little worm, sir. And I—"

"Had best take care," he said, toppling her back onto the bed, then rolling over so that he was once again on top. "This nosy worm of mine is like to take insult, and then what would you do?"

"Do? Why this!" she said, working her hand between them even as those wondrous legs of hers wrapped round him, drawing him more tightly against her. "And this. And—"

Robert groaned and plunged into her, and whatever else he'd meant to say fell away, forgotten.

"TEACH ME," ALYCE said. "Share your knowledge with me, Robert. I'm no fool. I can help, if only you'll let me."

She knelt atop the tumbled covers with only her tousled hair to cover her. She knew he liked to see her thus, liked the freedom to touch and kiss and suckle, but this time, when he reached for her, she shoved his hand away. The memory of the day's events was too fresh to be put aside any longer.

He sat up, scowling. His hair was mussed from the violence of their lovemaking. Alyce sternly repressed the urge to touch those wild curls, to trace the scattered strands of silver at his temples, smooth away the creases in his brow.

"I won't drag you into trade," he said. "I'll not turn my wife into a . . . a—"

"A merchant's wife?" she said tartly. "But that's what I am, for better or for worse."

"It's not meet for you to tend accounts and measure silks and haggle over the price of wool," he insisted, his scowl darkening. He looked ferocious and, she'd swear, a little frightened.

He also looked damnably compelling.

She scowled right back. "What do you think I did at Colmaine? I tended accounts and haggled over prices and worried about the state of the castle's cesspits. Compared to that, measuring out silks would be a boon and not a burden!"

He snorted dismissively. "Then you didn't tend your duties very well. I haven't forgotten that great mound of dung and straw in your bailey, even if you have."

She drew back, stung. "I'd ordered it spread on the fields. It was my father refused to give me authority over his steward. If I'd had my way, we——" She stopped short; her eyes narrowed. "You're trying to distract me. And speaking of stewards——"

"That we won't!" Robert grabbed his braies, which Alyce had pulled off him and flung aside with such reckless haste, and swung off the far side of the bed.

"I wasn't lying!" She rolled off the end of the bed so that she was between him and the rest of his clothes.

"I didn't say you lied." He glared at her, then tugged at one corner of his braies. In her haste, she'd left them in a tangled knot with odd ends and lacing strings sticking out in inappropriate places.

"You don't seem to believe me either."

He stopped, one hand poked through an opening in his underwear, and stared at her. And as he stared, his gaze softened, warmed, and slid inexorably downward.

Alyce blushed and took a half-step back. Yet when his inspection lengthened, an angry pride took the upper hand. She tossed her hair over one shoulder, baring her left breast, the curve of her waist and flare of her hips, the dark red cluster of curls between her legs.

Robert's mouth opened on a sigh—a short, but very heartfelt sigh. He blinked, forcing his gaze back to her face, then shook his head emphatically. "No. No! I—"

He stopped, as if the words stuck in his throat. Alyce brazenly propped her hands on her hips and didn't say a word.

He tried again. "This has nothing to do with John. I don't want you meddling in my work, wife or no. I don't want to teach you what you weren't born to know."

"Not born to know? I wasn't born to wed a merchant!" she shot back. He flinched, which pleased her. His pain was some small balm for hers.

He didn't want to share his life with her. His bed, yes. His house, his wealth, his name, but not the center of it all, not the work that anchored him and formed him, the work that was at the heart of his existence.

Anger swelled again, forcing out the hurt. She shoved her shoulders back, straightened her spine.

"I can't offer you wealth or beauty, Robert. You knew that when you wed me. But that doesn't mean I can't offer you my wits and my education and my loyalty. You *have* a housekeeper! You don't need another one. I can serve you better in your business than any other woman you might have wed. If only you will teach me. If only you will let me learn!"

He drew back as if struck. "Serve me!"

"Help you, then. Is that too much to ask? To have the right to help you?"

He stared at her as if she'd gone mad. The braies dangled from his hand, forgotten.

She stared back, determined. Usually the sight of his lean body was enough to distract her from everything but lustful thoughts and yet more lustful yearnings. But no man, not even Robert, could lay any claim to grandeur when he stood stark naked with his underwear in a knot in his hand.

He opened his mouth, then shut it without speaking and threw up his hands, defeated. The gesture might have been more effective if his drawers hadn't flipped upward with the motion.

Alyce grinned. Her anger faded as an odd sense of power stirred within her.

"Other merchants' wives work beside their husbands," she said, emboldened. "And merchants' widows often run their husbands' businesses. They even start their own. I know they do. I've seen them."

He glared at her. "But you're not any merchant's wife."

"No," she said. "I'm yours."

He sucked in air, then let it out in a groan of frustration. As if drawn, his gaze dropped to her breast, then lower still. Like a beast waking from a nap, his tarse twitched, then stirred to eager life.

Robert frowned, obviously irritated, and turned away. His choice of direction was unwise. His gaze fixed on the disordered bed and the discarded garments that spilled off its edges. His tarse strained higher, harder.

He swung back to her, an almost maddened light of desperation in his eyes.

Alyce's nascent sense of power swelled to giddying proportions. He wanted her. Not just her body, *her*.

She took a step toward him, deliberately provocative. He flinched and his grip on the tangled braies tightened until his knuckles shone whiter than the linen he held.

Alyce bent and took the braies from him. "Why is it a man can conquer the world but he can't get his clothes untangled without a woman to help him?" she asked on a pleasant note.

A strangled, choking sound came from somewhere in the back of Robert's throat.

"Women, on the other hand"—she deftly pulled one end of the garment free—"manage to bear children, run a house, and *still* keep a business or a castle going. And they don't get their underwear in a twist to do it either." She smiled at Robert and neatly undid a knot in the lacing strings.

Robert growled. His gaze was fixed on his braies, but his body betrayed the direction of his thoughts.

"There!" she said, and smiled. "See how easy it is?" She held the now-untangled braies in front of him, just close enough to touch his erect tarse. Waving the garment in the air, she pretended not to notice when it brushed against his straining flesh. "It's a wonder you ever get anything done without me there to help you out."

Once more he threw up his hands in defeat and backed away, out of reach. "All right! I'll teach you the business. But if you find it's not to your liking, milady, don't blame me!"

She grinned, glanced at the bed, then back at him.

"I won't," she said. She tossed his braies aside and stepped forward, closing the gap between them. "Besides, I have other things in mind. For the moment."

ROBERT STROLLED OUT of his chamber, jaunty as a jay and humming like an overlarge, contented bumblebee, but the farther he got from Alyce, the faster his good cheer bled away.

Teach her a merchant's secrets? Work with her by day as well as sleep with her by night? Make her so inextricably a part of his life that he would never again be able to tell where one part of it ended and another began?

The prospect unsettled him. He'd spent most of the past dozen years carefully separating the pieces of his life. He thought he'd managed rather well—until he'd wed Alyce.

Once, he'd let Jocelyn consume him. Everything he'd done, every hope he'd had, had centered on her, on the life he'd dreamed of building for her. He sometimes thought that his dreams had destroyed her as much as his lust had. Perhaps if he'd wanted less, loved less, been more willing to let things go, he wouldn't have been so quick to take what she hadn't cared to give him . . . and wouldn't have destroyed her in the process.

After Jocelyn's death, his work had filled his life, given it the only meaning he could find in the endless round of days and nights that had echoed with her absence. The women he'd kept in later years had been dispensable—pretty, pleasant companions to while away the time when he wasn't working or traveling, good company and good bed partners and nothing more. Some had been his friends—a few still were—but they hadn't intruded into his work and he hadn't allowed his work to lap into the narrow corners he'd allotted them in his life.

He wasn't eager to see all those years of careful effort undone. He'd given in to Alyce's demand against his better judgment because his blood had been roaring in his ears and his brain had moved south to his tarse, but the more he thought of his concession, the more troubled he became.

Not that he doubted Alyce's intelligence or her willingness to work. She'd already demonstrated both in the way she'd taken over the running of his household. No, what troubled him was that she was creeping ever deeper into his life, inch by subtle inch, until he was having trouble imagining a day without her in it, until there was nowhere he could turn that wasn't colored by her presence, by her very existence.

He could think of nothing he could do to stop the process either, and for the first time, the very first time, he wasn't sure he even wanted to try. And that thought troubled him most of all.

His head awhirl, Robert slowly crossed the inner courtyard to what had been Master Ancroft's house and now served as workroom and warehouse. England might be at war and his personal life turned arse in the air, but cloth was still cloth and work could still offer the solace of escape. There was the day's shipment to be recorded in the accounts and correspondence he'd left unfinished because of his unexpected visitor that morning. There were Edward's new demands to consider, plans to be made to deal with the dockworkers the next time he needed their services— Robert was as sure there would be a next time as he was that they would be more than eager to get their own back again in retribution for his winning that day. There was—

He cut that thought short. Suffice that there was more than enough to distract him for the hour or so until the evening meal was served and he had to face Alyce again.

His thoughts churning, he climbed the narrow stairs that led to his workroom on the upper floor.

John Rareton was there ahead of him. The steward sat at the single table with a pen in his hand and the account rolls spread out before him, golden-yellow in the late afternoon light streaming through the unglazed windows. At Robert's entrance, he raised his head, blinking with the blind, fumbling air of a man pulled out of his troubled thoughts.

Robert could tell the instant Rareton's mind registered his presence—his chin snapped up and his lower lip twitched as if at the taste of something unpleasant.

I think he betrays you.

Alyce's warning seemed to hang in the air like a dust mote caught in the slanting sunlight. From the wary look on Rareton's face, he seemed to hear it too.

Robert casually crossed to the table. "Already hard at work, I see."

Rareton swallowed. "The inventory, you know. The records of shipment." He gestured at the account rolls.

"Yes," said Robert, "I know." He frowned down at the table, then flicked the edge of one of the rolls. "You probably heard that Hensford tried to steal that ship out from under me."

"Yes." The single word sounded half-strangled, as though Rareton had forced it out against his will.

Robert looked up to find his steward staring at him like a cornered rat. Bile rose in Robert's throat. He'd told Alyce she was mistaken, sworn that Rareton would never betray his trust. He didn't like to think he'd been wrong.

"What kept you, John? I'd expected you at the quay before we started loading."

Rareton's gaze dropped to the account rolls. His quill pen twitched in his fingers as he stared at the closely written figures like a man who hoped to find his answers written there. "I was . . . detained."

"Detained?"

Rareton hesitated an instant, then set down his pen and raised his head to meet Robert's questioning gaze. "I met with some members of the guild, supporters of Earl Simon."

Robert stiffened.

"By chance!" Rareton added hastily. "Purely by chance. I ran into them on the street as they were on their way to a meeting. They—they insisted I come with them, that they had information you would want to hear."

"Did they?"

Rareton flinched at the cutting cold in Robert's voice. "They are . . . concerned." His jaw worked as if he were chewing on the words, trying to grind them into something that would be easier for Robert to swallow. "They're afraid that you're undermining their efforts to gain concessions from the king, to gain protection for English merchants and English goods. *Our* goods."

"They've said that before."

Rareton didn't respond. The silence stretched.

"And you?" Robert said at last in a quiet, dangerous voice. "What do you think?"

Rareton breathed deep, then pressed against the edge of the table as though he needed its support to stay upright. "I think they're right. I've told you so often enough."

"And now you've decided to work for Hensford? You've decided to—"

"No!" Rareton leaped to his feet. "No! I never— I . . . I wouldn't betray you like that."

Robert eyed him narrowly. "I don't tolerate lies or treachery, John. You know that."

"No, I mean, yes, of course I know. I've never lied to you, you know that."

"I thought I did."

"I haven't!"

Again the silence stretched. Rareton wilted under Robert's sharp gaze, but he neither looked away, nor tried to argue for his innocence.

In the end, it was Robert who turned away. He stared out the open window, across the stone-paved yard to the house he'd built, the fine house that was meant to show the world just how far Robert Wardell had risen.

Despite its solid appearance, he knew there was no guarantee the house he'd built would stand. It could fall from rot or burn from fire. It could be pulled down by anyone with the will and the means to do it.

Well, he'd never asked for guarantees. He'd built as well and as strongly as he could, made provisions against fire and theft, built iron-barred gates and thick, strong walls to protect them all from attack or riot. He'd done everything that could be done to keep what he'd built safe against any threat from without.

He glanced again at John Rareton.

This was the first time he'd ever thought of needing protection against the threat of treachery from within.

MINDING
BUSINESS

London, early April 1264

"AND THAT?" ROBERT demanded, shoving a length of close-woven purple wool in front of her. "How was it made and where? What would you pay for it if you were a clever merchant? What would you expect to sell it for, and where?"

Alyce sighed and stretched, trying to ease her aching back and look abused. It wasn't hard to look abused. A day spent scrubbing floors couldn't be more exhausting than one spent trying to learn the subtleties of cloth under Robert's exacting tutelage.

"Well?" he asked. "What do you think?"

"I think it's time for dinner," she grumbled under her breath.

When he showed no sign of relenting, she wearily leaned forward and squinted at the cloth. She rubbed it between her thumb and finger, stroked along its length to feel its nap, tugged at it to test the firmness of the weave, then held it up to the light streaming in the open windows to judge the sheen and the evenness of the coloring.

"Lichen dyed," she said at last, reluctantly. She's been wrong nine times out of ten that morning. "A worsted twill of wool with linen threads mixed in. Eight shillings a cloth with perhaps forty ells to each cloth. I'd buy it in

Lincoln and could sell it here in London for perhaps eleven shillings a cloth."

She set the fabric down, then glanced up at him to see how closely she'd hit the mark. His frown told her she'd missed by a fair amount.

"It's worsted twill, all right, but with silk, not linen. And it's dyed with French woad mixed with madder to deepen the color. You'd pay twelve shillings a cloth, perhaps thirteen, and you'd ask one pound four pence to cover your profit and the cost of transporting it from Douai, though you'd accept one pound and might go lower still for a good customer. As for the length . . ."

He pulled it free of the other cloths that were heaped on the table in front of her and rapidly measured it out, looping the cloth from hand to elbow for each ell of fabric.

"Thirty-six ells."

She glared at him. "It would be closer to forty if it was *my* arm doing the measuring!"

He nodded, still frowning. "And a great deal less than that if the government ever sets the standard of thirty-six inches to the ell as the guild has asked. But you have to be prepared to deal with the differences in measurements from one merchant to the other."

"I knew that," Alyce snapped. She rubbed her aching temples. "I wonder I ever managed to buy an inch of fabric for Colmaine without running us into bankruptcy," she added peevishly, and his frown eased into a crooked smile of amusement.

She slumped back in Robert's chair, exhausted. Her back ached from bending over the table for hours on end. Her eyes burned from squinting and peering as she desperately tried to see the nuances of color and texture and weave that distinguished one cloth from another, even if, at first glance, they looked to be twins. Most of all, her head throbbed from the effort of trying to learn in a week what Robert had spent most of a lifetime mastering.

Be careful what you ask for, Hilde had often told her. She should have listened while she had the chance.

She'd already spent three days in the darker, colder storerooms on the lower level of the old house learning about raw wool and its markets. She'd thought it bad enough to be immured with mounds of wool sacks and the woolfells that Robert had rolled out on the floor like so many dirty, bramble-starred rugs. In the closed storerooms, the stink of the unfinished skins had made her head ache and her nose stop up, but at least she'd known the answers to some of Robert's questions as to the quality of the wool or the fineness of the fells. But this!

She looked around the upper workroom where Robert had moved his "school." He'd hauled out every length of cloth from every trunk and chest and bundle in Wardell House. The finest, most costly cloths buried the table in front of her or spilled out of the chests that Robert had ordered brought up from his strong room below. The more common cloths were heaped on linen dropcloths spread against the walls, or spilled out of the cruder leather chests where they were normally stored.

Alyce couldn't even begin to name them all. There were cendals and burnets and brocades and plunkers, cloths dyed in grain—which she'd learned was made of the shells of lice and not from grain at all—four kinds of scarlet, three kinds of samite, ells and ells of perse, even more ells of silks that were rayed or figured or plain, velvets in a dozen jeweled colors, cloth of gold from Constantinople, fine canvas and linen from Paris and Rheims, black says from Lincoln, rays of Stamford, blues of Beverly and Leicester, damasks from Damascus, cloth of Arras, and yet more silks from Venice and Lucca. Alyce's head spun at the sight of them all.

It hadn't helped to know that few merchants ever carried half the inventory that Robert did. Unlike the majority of merchants, Robert sold to other merchants as well as to buyers, and he sold English cloth on the Continent as often as he brought the finer pieces from abroad to sell in England.

As he'd spread out each length of cloth, he had lectured her about its provenance, about its warp and woof and the tightness of the weave and the techniques and skills of the weavers who'd made it. He'd quoted the price he'd paid for it and the price he expected to get in return. He'd pointed out the differences between similar pieces, and explained the tricks that dishonest weavers and merchants used to pass off a poorer quality cloth as a more expensive one.

Alyce threw a wry glance at the closest mound of what Robert called mere common cloth. He had heaped the cloths there, dismissing them even as he'd shown them to her. Yet they were often a finer quality than what she'd been accustomed to at Colmaine. She sighed and shook her head as she scanned the jumble about her.

"Have you had enough for one day's work, milady?" Robert asked, shattering her daze.

She looked up to find him watching her, his dark eyes unexpectedly soft and warm and . . . troubled. The concern disarmed her, pushing out her irritation.

"I've worked you hard," he went on, and frowned. "Too hard. I'm sorry."

She gave him a slight smile in return. "I did say I could keep up with whatever you might throw at me." She glanced at the cloths, then back at him, and sighed. "I just didn't expect you to throw it all at once."

"There's much to learn and little time to learn it in."

"Little time! You speak as if the world will end tomorrow and I run the risk of damnation if I can't tell the difference between one length of perse and another."

"Aye, well . . ."

He reached to touch her, to lay his hand on hers as if to

comfort her, but at the last minute pulled back. Instead, he sighed as well, and dropped onto the stool beside her. Alyce curled her fingers into the cloth beneath her hand, fighting against the tingle of disappointment that spread across the back of her hand and up to her heart.

It wasn't the work he'd given her that troubled her. Ever since he'd agreed to teach her the secrets of his business, she'd sensed a distance between them, as if he'd put a thick but invisible wall back up.

"Perhaps I *have* been too hard on you," he admitted. "But you said you wanted to learn . . . you should have said something sooner."

"Said something! I've been grumbling and complaining for the past three days and not once have you paid me any heed!"

His smile lightened, quirking upward at one corner. "And for every grumble and complaint there were three more questions to tax my skills. I've seen starving men who were slower to grab for bread than you are to grab for knowledge. You're as quick with numbers as Piers—quicker than I am, if the truth be told—and behind those green eyes I love is as shrewd and calculating a brain as any man might wish."

Her breath caught in her throat. He loved her eyes!

"The bits and pieces, the knowledge of the cloth—they'll come. Give yourself time."

"I feel a fool," she admitted. She lightly ran her palm over one glistening silk on which golden dragonflies flitted among a wealth of brilliant flowers. "I've been to the fairs near Colmaine, yet never have I seen cloths such as these."

Robert's right eyebrow arched. "They're not the kind of thing you would find at any local fair."

"But who would possibly buy all this? Something like this"—she gently lifted a corner of the silk—"would cost a quarter of a year's revenues from one of my father's smaller manors. Maybe more. Who would have such wealth, or spend it on something so—so *useless?*"

"Who?" He laughed, but Alyce thought she heard a hint of mockery in it. "Anyone with wealth enough to pay me for the cost of them, and for a goodly profit besides."

He sprang to his feet and crossed to the window. For an instant, his finely shaped body was outlined against the light, then he swung back to face her, his expression unreadable.

"I've sold cloth to the king and his master of the wardrobe," he said. "I've sold it to the queen and to her daughters and to the king's sister, who is Earl Simon's wife. I've sold it to half the bishops and all the archbishops of England, to barons and knights and minor lords with a yearning to make a fine show. I've sold it to the richest grocers and goldsmiths and aldermen of London. I sell to other mercers who prefer a narrower profit to the risk of travel and the need to deal with alien weavers and merchants."

He paused, dark eyes glittering, then added, "There is always someone with money to spend on luxuries, and I'll sell to *anyone,* providing he has the coin to pay me for it."

Alyce watched him, breathless at the arrogant, confident power of the man, troubled by the hint of angry mockery that lingered in his voice. Chance of birth and fortune had cast him in the mold of merchant, but it was Robert's own brains and daring and sheer hard work that made him what he was.

He leaned forward and carelessly lifted a length of heavy silk. The threads of gold woven into it glistened in the sun pouring through the open windows.

"The quarreling of great men doesn't put an end to our business, milady. It never has and never will. There are those, I swear, who would fret about their fine robes if they

stood at the gates of Hell itself, and there are men like me
who are more than willing to service them even as those
gates swing wide for all of us."

He frowned at the cloth as he spoke, turning it first
this way, then that as the sunlight played across its surface.
Alyce had the sense he'd almost forgotten her, that he was
speaking not to her, but to some doubting phantom that
sat beside her. The thought troubled her even more than
the hint of mockery had a moment earlier.

He'd said she was quick with figures. It wasn't
true, not entirely, but she was good enough to know that
the cloth heaped in this room was worth a fortune, far
more than her father's yearly revenues from all his manors
combined.

Robert had agreed to teach her about his business, but
he'd refused to show her his account rolls or tell her precisely how his finances stood. She'd tried to figure it out
for herself, but without records it was impossible to make
sense of the tangle of contracts and connections with
weavers and wool growers and the merchants of a dozen
cities spread from Lincoln to the Levant.

Now, listening to him, seeing the shadows lurking in
his eyes as he watched the flash of sun on gold and silk, she
couldn't help but worry that England's troubles had created more problems for Robert than she knew of. Far more,
perhaps, than he was willing to admit, even to himself.

He jerked her from her thoughts by suddenly leaning
forward and draping the golden cloth across her shoulder
and over her head. He cocked his own head, studying the
effect, then leaned closer still to lay the edge of the fabric
against her cheek.

"Green velvet suits you more," he said.

She blinked up at him, too startled to pull away, too
shaken by the heat that flared within her at the unexpected intimacy to ask him what he meant.

He flipped the costly silk off her head and tossed it

aside dismissively. It billowed on the air, then drifted into a dozen sunlit folds atop the mounded silks in front of her.

"Promise me you won't wear a veil and wimple for your welcome feast."

She gasped. "Not wear— But why?"

His gaze locked on hers, holding her. What did he see in her eyes? she wondered. Why couldn't she read the secrets hidden in his?

He hesitated. "Because I ask it," he said at last as he straightened and stepped back, away from her.

She continued staring up at him, bewildered. Her cheek still burned with the remembered feel of the silk, the remembered brush of his fingers against her skin.

She raised her hand to touch where he had touched her. In that instant, in the pause between one heartbeat and the next, she knew—knew beyond the faintest of faint doubts—that she had fallen utterly and completely in love with her husband.

Something must have shown in her expression. He drew back as if she'd stung him.

"Never mind," he muttered. "Never mind."

A moment more and he was gone, leaving her alone, blindly staring at the discarded length of silk, its golden threads still glittering in the sun.

"SO THERE'S THE roast peacocks, the veal and raisin pasties, the hare in ale with saffron, and the gilded hens. They'll do well enough for the main course so long as we take care to have sufficient sides of cheese pies and spiced beef and whatnot, though it's not anywhere near so much as is due a feast in honor of *your* marriage, milady."

Margaret's gaze swept the hall. At the moment, the space was empty except for the two of them, but Alyce knew the cook was picturing it as it would look two days hence, crowded with London's most powerful merchants and officials and their wives, all of whom had been invited to the feast that Robert had decreed necessary to honor his new wife. No one had refused the invitation. In these uncertain times, people were more than eager to forget their cares in a grand show of finery and goodwill . . . especially if someone else was paying for the food.

But even the prospect of political gain wasn't enough to keep Robert at home. He'd turned the household on its head, then ridden off—called away on business, he'd said, though Alyce suspected his motives included a large dose of male cowardice. He hadn't wanted to endure the discomforts of a house in upheaval even though he was the cause of it.

She hadn't slept well since he'd left. She'd had Githa spread her pallet on the floor at the side of her bed rather than outside the door of their chamber, but even the maid's presence wasn't enough to dispel the emptiness of the big bed when Robert wasn't there to share it with her.

"I do wonder, though," said Margaret, pulling Alyce's thoughts back to the matter at hand, "if eel soup will do as well as carp and leek. And Master Hitcham's cook made an almond and chicken mold for his wife's saint's day, I hear—Master Hitcham's wife, I mean—though I'm sure it wasn't nearly so fine as *mine* will be."

"I'm sure your almond pa—"

"Still, perhaps I should prepare a tart of pickled fish, instead."

The cook leaned toward Alyce and lowered her voice confidingly. "Master Townsend's wife has begged me I know not how many times for the secret of my pickled fish. I've told her it's in the quality of the salt, which must be fine and white and fair, but I suspect she tries to save a pence or two by using salt fit only for the larder. And if she does, what can she expect when her fish lacks the flavor of mine?"

"Pickled fish would be fi—"

"I've ordered up the peacocks and the hens and veal and beef, and I sent Huetta out for eggs today. Sixteen dozen, at the least, I said, and all of them large and fresh, though I doubt not I'll have to send her to return half and demand better, for the silly wench has fallen in love with the grocer's son, and say what I will, whenever he's about she hasn't the wit of a half-wit goose."

Margaret's long nose twitched disdainfully. "Last month it was the baker's lad. Thank God we've ovens of our own or we'd have starved while she mooned over a boy with more spots on his face than our best speckled hen."

"Girls are prone to that, but I—"

"Mind, I'll have to order up the trenchers from old Garrick, for there'll be no space in our ovens to bake fresh when I've the pies and pasties and tarts to see to and—"

She stopped short. Her eyes widened and her nostrils flared as the scent of roasting mutton wafted up from the kitchens.

"I *knew* I couldn't trust Flyta with the mutton!" she cried. "She's set it too close to the fire, for it's too soon to be smelling it otherwise! Not this far from the kitchen!"

She was halfway to the door before she remembered that Alyce was still standing where she'd left her. The cook spun about and sketched an ungainly curtsy.

"Your pardon, milady, but I can't risk the mutton, and I think I've a good enough idea of what you want for the dinner that I needn't bother you further."

What *she* wanted! Alyce slumped into Robert's chair, glaring at the ceiling.

She didn't want this damn feast in the first place, but there! When had men ever listened! Robert wanted it and he'd willingly set the house in an uproar to get it. Margaret had been given free rein and a deep purse from which to draw, with the result that for the past few weeks she'd been lost in dreams of trouncing Master Hitcham's cook's pretensions and scarce heard a word Alyce said.

Erwyna, for her part, was caught in such a passion to clean and polish and wax and mend that no place in the house was safe from her. Robert had agreed the housekeeper might have free use of the stable lads and gardener's boys for her rafter-to-cellar housecleaning, but the scullery maids were strictly off limits. Their labors, Margaret had insisted, were required in the kitchen. The two women had glared at each other until Alyce had been forced to intervene, siding with the cook. Erwyna had held a grudge ever since, and she'd made sure Alyce knew it, grumbling and muttering and pushing Alyce's patience almost to the breaking point.

The temporary loss of his stable hands had irritated the stableman, and Joshua, the gardener, hadn't been any too pleased either, for he had counted on the lads' help with the work in the garden. When Alyce had overruled them as well, the two had retired to their respective kingdoms, muttering and grumbling about the foolishness of women and the unreasonable disruption they caused in a reasonable man's life.

Only John Rareton seemed untouched by the tumult. His work carried on regardless of the rival merits of pickled fish and almond paste. He kept busy enough for three—or so it seemed.

Though Robert had dismissed her warnings, Alyce continued to watch the man. It frustrated her that she couldn't follow him whenever he went out, or set Piers or one of the stable lads to do it in her place. She wanted to know what he was about, and why, and with whom. That everyone else took his comings and goings for granted only made her all the warier.

She didn't have much freedom to worry about it, though. She was far too busy worrying about the feast.

The thought of a hall full of strangers made her stomach churn, but she knew as well as Robert did the political advantage to be had from so public a show of his new connections to Earl Simon's camp. She'd proved it herself, that day on the quay. But as the bills mounted, she worried about the wisdom of so lavish and costly a display.

Alyce got to her feet with a sigh. Hilde would have scolded her for being a grim little please-me-nothing, and Maida would have suggested a half hour's prayer and three hours' work with the laundry to clear the ill-humors from her head.

Just the thought of the lye and boiling water of the laundry tubs was enough to get her stirring.

She was halfway across the hall, heading for the stairs to the solar, when Erik, the gardener's boy who had waited at the gate the first day she'd come to Wardell House, poked his head around the outer screen. "Milady?"

"Erik?" Alyce smiled. The boy was an imp, but a clever one, and she'd grown fond of him.

The boy edged around the screen. "It's about them tablecloths, milady. I got an idea, see, an' I thought you might had want t'hear it."

"Indeed."

He nodded, then glanced back in the direction he'd come. Assured that no pursuit was in sight, he set his jaw, and, bristling with determination, crossed to Alyce.

"Didja know there's a calendrer on Cornhill Street, not far from Saint Anthony's hospital, milady?"

"A calendrer, hmmm?" Alyce signed. She had a good idea where this discussion was headed, but she liked the boy too much to cut him off short. "No, I didn't know there was a calendrer on Cornhill Street."

"Well, there is. A good one too! Name's Grudwell. Grudwell of Lyme. He takes them ol' tablecloths an' does *all* the washin' 'n starchin' 'n pressin' 'n stuff 'n brings 'em back done better'n anything! Timeo"—Timeo was the stable lad who had been drafted into Erwyna's provisional army—"he says ol' Grudwell is the very, very, *very* best there is. Better'n anybody in London!"

"And you think we should send the table linens out to be pressed instead of doing them ourselves, do you?"

He nodded solemnly. "A calendrer, he can do it easy. Better'n with a slickstone, milady. Fair an' far better."

Alyce had to purse her lips to keep a smile from sneaking past her self-restraint. Timeo and Erik had both been assigned to rub slickstones over the freshly laundered tablecloths and napkins to flatten them and smooth out the wrinkles. It was dull, drudging work, but necessary if the banquet table was to be set as befitted the honor of Wardell House.

Necessary, that is, if one didn't use the services of a calendrer. Alyce never had, for the simple reason that there were none within a three days' ride of Colmaine.

"And what does Erwyna say?"

His face fell. "She says we've more'n enough arum root ground up for starch, an' that me'n Timeo might as well be starchin' 'n rubbin' those cloths as payin' a stranger to do it."

"I see."

"She says we—Timeo'n me, I mean—she says we'd only be gettin' into trouble if she din't keep us busy. But"—Erik's expression turned crafty—"Timeo says there's all that work in the stable 'n the garden 'n old Joshua's grumblin' 'n saying' the garlic's gotta be planted 'n the ground dug for that new herb bed you wanted an'—"

Alyce help up her hand. "I see your point."

She also remembered what it was like to slick down a tablecloth just as clearly as she remembered what it was like to wash it in the first place. Maida had made sure she knew about *all* the work that went into running a nobleman's household. On the other hand, Maida had also made sure she knew how to run a frugal household, and Alyce was quite sure that hiring the services of a calendrer didn't qualify as frugality.

"He'd do a real good job, milady. Honest!" Erik stared up at her anxiously, eyes wide and innocent.

"I'm sure he would. But I'll have to talk to Erwyna first"—the boy's shoulders dropped—"and perhaps to this Grudwell of Limn—"

"Lyme, milady."

"Grudwell of Lyme. I'm not sure—"

"Master Byngham's wife uses 'im, milady. An' Mistress Cantrell down the street. An' Mistress—"

"Whoa, whoa!" Alyce held up a warning hand. "It's Mistress Wardell's house I'm concerned about, not Mistress Byngham's or Cantrell's."

"But milady—"

The boy's protest was cut short by the sound of quarreling coming from the kitchen stairs.

"Tempted him away, I've no doubt, all because you want to plant garlic and haven't a thought as to the work—"

"It's the mistress's garden we be talkin' of, woman, not any odd patch o' weeds!" Joshua's deep voice echoed in the stairwell, a grumbling counterpoint to Erwyna's shrewish tones.

"Weeds, garlic, whatever. The way you tend that garden it's hard to tell one from the other at times!"

The two stumped up the last of the steps from the kitchen, too intent on their argument to notice Alyce or the boy. Erwyna's head was down, her shoulders hunched, and her elbows cocked skyward as she held her skirts up. Her stocky body swayed from one side to the other as she heaved herself up each step with Joshua growling at her heels like an irritable, toothless old terrier.

"Can't tend a garden without boys to weed and hoe and carry water," the old man protested.

"Weed and hoe! When I've tablecloths piled to the rafters and—"

"If you'd washed 'em proper the first time round—"

"What! I'll have you know my tablecloths are *always* washed and properly mended and slicked!"

The two combatants were so engrossed in their quarreling that they were halfway across the hall before they noticed Alyce. Erik had slipped around the screens and out the door the instant he'd realized Doom was headed his way.

"Is that boy around?" Erwyna demanded.

"Boy?" said Alyce.

"Erik. Supposed to be helping out with the linens, but he's scooted off for who knows where and left my women to do it all alone. If I get my hands on him—"

"You leave him alone. Timeo too!" Old Joshua glared at Erwyna. "I told you! The lads have better things to do than spend their time head down in a tub full of tablecloths as if they were maids and not men."

"Men, hah!" Erwyna retorted. "Scarce old enough to piss standing up, those two, and *you* let them—"

"Enough!" Alyce's sharp command neatly cut through their quarreling.

Erwyna's spine stiffened. "There's work to be done if we're to be ready for this feast of yours, milady, and I need those boys to do it."

"And *I* need my lads to work the garden, milady!" Joshua said. "There's too much work for me to handle all alone."

"There wouldn't be if you'd do more than—"

"I said, enough!" Alyce glared first at Joshua, then at Erwyna, who glared right back.

Alyce's temper flared. She was tired of the constant quarreling over preparations for this accursed dinner. Frugality be damned. "Send the tablecloths to a calendrer," she said.

"A calendrer!" Erwyna's face turned bright red.

"I know you've enough work for ten, Erwyna," Alyce said, more calmly than she felt. "With all that yet remains to be done, it only makes sense to send the cloths to a calendrer."

"I'll not!"

Alyce's temper snapped. "If you won't, I will."

"You can't do that!"

"I can. I'm mistress here, in case you've forgotten!"

Erwyna set her fists on her broad hips, shoulders hunched and chin thrust out like a bulldog's. "You may be mistress, but it's me has the work of running this house, milady. I wouldn't trust my tablecloths to the master of the king's wardrobe, come to that!"

That did it. Alyce had had her share of quarrels with truculent retainers, but no one, ever, had dared defy a direct order.

In the end, Erwyna didn't either. She gave in and agreed to do as Alyce said, but Alyce knew, as she watched the old woman stalk off in one direction and Joshua stroll off, triumphant, in the other, that she had just made an enemy.

She closed her eyes and breathed a heartfelt prayer for patience. She was well and truly in love with Robert, but if he were within reach right then she'd happily string him up by his heels and leave him to dry. And that was just for starters.

ROBERT RODE THROUGH Newgate and breathed deep of the pungent odors that were an inescapable part of London. He'd been gone six days, and they'd been six of the longest, hardest days of his life, days further darkened with the news that Edward had moved against the garrison in Northampton where Alyce's father and brother were.

Yet despite the news, the hardship of the journey, and the near impossibility of rousing more financial support for the king and the Lord Edward, he hadn't passed an hour of those six days without thinking of Alyce. Not even in his sleep.

What sleep he'd gotten. Barely two months married, yet he was already accustomed to having her in his bed. He'd even found himself missing her cold toes and the way she curled into his warmth in her sleep.

It troubled him, this growing need for her, the way she wound through his thoughts like thread through cloth. Yet if he tried to pull her free and set her to the side, then all the rest of it unraveled, leaving him with a tangle and nothing more. If he—

"Wardell! If I didn't know better, I'd think you'd gone blind and deaf. You didn't use to ignore me thus."

Robert jerked around in the saddle, startled by the familiar voice. "Marion! I didn't hear you." He smiled at the dark-eyed, elegant woman who'd ridden up beside him.

"Nor see me either, even though you rode right in front of me. Thrice now I've waved and called your name, yet I might as well be baying at the moon for all the good it's done me."

Her laughter flowed over him as easily as it always had. "If it weren't for that grim-faced lump of a guard behind you, I could have picked your pocket and you'd have been none the wiser."

Robert grinned at the woman who'd been his mistress, several years before. "Newton has his uses."

She glanced back at Newton, then leaned out of her saddle toward Robert. "It's well he does," she said with a saucy smile, "for I can't imagine keeping him for the pleasure of his company! From the looks of him, his mother's milk was curdled in the breast."

"You, on the other hand," said Robert gallantly, "would tempt a saint to sinning."

Of them all, she'd been his favorite. Marion Naismith, now Marion Mychet, was a kind, good-humored, eminently practical woman who knew how to make a man comfortable. She'd been good company, in bed and out of it, and the only one who hadn't tried to snare him into a marriage he hadn't wanted. When they'd parted, she'd shrewdly accepted his offer to set her up as a vendor of cloth, then even more shrewdly wed an old man whose business, added to hers, gave them a fair stature among the mercers of London. Robert still sold her cloth for her shop and advised her on business matters from time to time, and she still shared the street gossip that came in useful every now and then. Their friendship hadn't gone beyond that for a long, long time.

Robert swept her with his gaze. "It seems that marriage agrees with you."

She nodded, smiling. "It does. Old Mychet is creaky in the joints and full of wind, but he's a good man and treats me well, and he doesn't meddle in my business."

"Then your business goes well, even in these dark times?"

"Well enough, thanks to you. I always put you in my prayers, you know."

It was his turn to laugh. "Your prayers! You *have* become respectable. First it was a husband, then a maid to follow you about like a pet dog. Now prayers."

She shrugged, eyes alight with merriment. "I long ago decided that God is rather like a husband. He's more inclined to listen if you aren't forever droning in His ear."

They'd drawn to a halt at the side of the street, with Newton and Marion's fat maid in disapproving attendance at their sides.

Marion cocked her head, studying him. "I'm not so sure marriage agrees with you, however. You're thinner than you were the last time I saw you, and you've never had an ounce to spare."

His smile vanished. "Both marriage and my wife agree quite well with me, I thank you," he said stiffly.

She laughed. "Oh, ho! Turning fierce, are we!"

He simply glared at her.

"I've seen her, you know," Marion went on. "Walking in the street. Rather plain, I thought, though there's something about her that catches the eye all the same." Her eyebrows arched in inquiry. "They say that she's a baron's daughter."

"A baron's daughter and a lady," he said, more stiffly still, "and no doubt wondering what's keeping me."

"I take your meaning," she said, clearly amused. "But let me at least send her a gift. She needn't know it's from me," she added quickly. "Something simple, but pretty. Frivolous, perhaps, the sort of thing that women love and men never think to give them."

Robert forced his shoulders to relax. He felt a fool for being so quick to defend Alyce, especially since there wasn't a drop of malice in Marion. On the other hand, though he wasn't any expert on etiquette, he couldn't imagine that a gift from a former mistress was quite the thing to bring home to one's wife.

Marion leaned closer still and laid her gloved hand on his arm. "Humor me, Robert," she pleaded. "Let me give her something. You were kind to me and I truly do wish you well in this marriage of yours."

Robert gave in in the end. With Newton and the maid as their grim-faced escort, he accompanied Marion to the narrow, two-storied building that served both as house and shop for her and her merchant husband.

The awning was up and the broad shelf that served for display during the day, then was folded away behind the front window at night, was open and covered with an array of neatly folded lengths of cloth. Marion catered to the prosperous middle-class merchants and tradesmen at this end of town, men and women who normally bought good, stout woolen cloth that befitted their station in life, but who occasionally wanted a more expensive length of silk or velvet as proof of their success. She also offered a selection of trinkets and finery for the ladies, things that weren't readily available elsewhere.

As he threw his reins to a frozen-faced Newton, Robert decided that he would look for a gift of his own to give to Alyce, something that would serve as apology for having left her to manage the preparations for their marriage feast alone. He said as much to Marion as he helped her dismount, then followed her into the shop.

"You left her to deal with all that on her own!" she said, aghast.

"It's just a dinner!" Robert protested.

"Just a dinner, he says!" This was directed to the squint-eyed apprentice who'd been left to tend the shop while she was out. The boy grinned weakly back, then disappeared into the back of the house when she shooed him away.

"You men are all alike!" she said. "Even the brightest of you is an ignorant fool when it comes to such matters, and you're no exception, Wardell. Your wife deserves a golden necklet, at the very least!"

As she scolded him, she rummaged in a waist-high chest that stood against the far wall, emerging with a couple of small wooden boxes and a broad, shallow tray that was divided into compartments.

"There ought to be something in all this that will suit," she said, setting the tray and the boxes down. "A purse to fasten at her belt, perhaps, or an embroidered handkerchief?"

Robert, his brow wrinkled in concentration, studied the items laid out in the tray's compartments. "She has a purse. *And* a handkerchief."

Marion picked up a small comb carved from polished bone. "A new comb, then?"

"I gave her one of ivory."

"A silver ring?"

He shook his head. "She refuses to wear any rings except her wedding ring."

Marion's face lighted with interest. "*Does* she?"

He frowned at her, then turned his attention back to the merchandise arrayed before him. He opened the first box, but it was filled with nothing but ribbons, so he set it aside. He opened the second box, then froze at the sight of what it contained.

Marion mumbled something. He looked up, distracted. "What? What'd you say?"

"I suggested a bit of Venetian licorice, something sweet for your sweet lady."

Robert glanced at the hard candies she'd spilled into her hand. The delicacy was as costly as the flavored twists of sugar that came from Spain, and even more uncommon.

"I never thought to give her sweets," he admitted, conscious of a twinge of guilt. Alyce was fond of sweets.

"Then *I* shall!" Marion declared. She tipped the candies back into their cloth pouch, then craned to see what had caught his attention. "What have you found?"

"This," he said, and pulled a crumpled net of golden silk laced with pearls from the box.

"A hair net?"

He nodded as he gently untangled the thing. The pearls glistened in the light.

"She has red hair," he said softly. "Glorious red hair, and a long neck as white and graceful as a swan's."

"*Does* she?" Marion murmured.

Robert nodded, dazed by the thought of how the pearls and golden silk would look against Alyce's wild red hair. "Beautiful white skin that almost glows in the candlelight."

Marion laughed. "Take the net, then, with my blessing." She cocked her head, studying him as if he were some intriguing new trinket to be put into her tray and offered to the public. "Methinks you're well and truly caught at last, Wardell."

"Caught?" he repeated, still dazzled at the thought of Alyce's white skin.

"Aye, caught, my friend." Marion's eyes twinkled with delight. "I wonder if she even knew she'd cast her net when you got tangled in it."

No one was there to greet them when they rode in the gate of Wardell House, and no one appeared to take their horses. Newton led their mounts away, grumbling under his breath, while Robert trotted up the steps and into the hall.

He almost turned around and walked back out again. Erwyna and her army had taken over. They swarmed like ants, dusting the rafters and scrubbing the floors and enthusiastically polishing everything in between. In the center of it all was Erwyna, her veil askew, her wimple sagging beneath her fat chins, her broad face bright red as she irritably exhorted her minions to work faster, faster, faster.

She swung on him, brow beetling in warning as he started across the still-damp floor.

Robert eyed her warily. "There are only two things I want," he said before she could start scolding. "A pot of your good ale and my wife. Surely someone can be freed long enough to fetch me the one, and you can tell me where I can find the other?"

She grunted, snapped for someone to fetch a pot of ale, and pointed toward the stairs that led to the solar. "Last I saw, the Lady Alyce was headed that way. I'm too busy to keep track of her, and now that your wife has made sure that I'll be mending tablecloths on top of it all, I'll have even less time than ever!"

Robert declined to investigate the obscure reference to tablecloths and took the stairs to the solar instead. One at a time at first, to preserve his dignity, then, once he was out of sight, two and three at a bound. The net of silk and pearls was like a thing alive in his purse. The frustrations of his unproductive mission over the past week were forgotten in his eagerness to see his wife.

She wasn't in the solar, but the door to their chamber stood open. He crossed to it, his heart thudding in his chest.

She didn't see him at first. She was in the far corner of the room, her back to the door and a broom in her hands, industriously attacking the dust that had had the temerity to lodge there. She was wearing some sort of drab worka-day gown he'd never seen before, and instead of her usual veil and wimple, she'd tied a kerchief over her hair. He could see a trace of red peeking out beneath the edge and, when she turned, the curling tendrils that had escaped at the sides.

At the sight of him, she stopped, hands curled tight around the broom handle. "You!"

He blinked and stopped short in the doorway. "Er, yes. I just got back. Did you . . . did you miss me?"

Her eyes narrowed and her eyebrows did their best to meet over the bridge of her nose. "Miss you? Hah!" she said, and went back to sweeping, determinedly working her way around the end of the bed toward him.

"Oh," said Robert, deflated. "Well, good."

What, by all the saints, had he done to deserve this frosty homecoming?

Alyce kept on sweeping. With every stroke she came closer to the door, and to him. She stopped just out of arm's reach.

"You're in my way."

He considered debating the issue, then politely stepped aside. One foot closer and he could snatch that kerchief off her head, grab that broom out of her hands.

"I'm delighted to see you too."

"Hah!" she said, depositing her little pile of dirt in the middle of the doorway, precisely where his feet had been.

She left the pile where it was and turned to attack the floor on this side of the bed, flipping the edges of the carpets back to sweep under them, then flipping them back down once she'd passed. It didn't seem a very thorough way of sweeping, but he was in no mood to debate the finer points of housekeeping.

He edged around her to claim the chair that stood at the far side of the hearth. If Alyce could sweep around the carpets, he decided grumpily, she could just sweep around him too.

"Gone not even a week," he muttered, "and this is the welcome I get? I've seen felons on their way to the gibbet get a warmer reception from the crowd."

"Isn't that just like a man?" Alyce demanded of her broomstick. "He sets the entire household on its ear, then runs away and leaves me in the middle of the quarreling and the mess. And *then,* when we're trying to put everything back together again, in he strolls, wanting attention."

"Wanting attention! I walk into my house—my house, mind you!—to find everything in an uproar. No one to take my horse, no meal waiting. Not even a cup of ale. I can't walk across the floor of my own hall without being treated as though I were a stable boy, and now my wife tells me it's all my fault!"

He scowled at Alyce and her broomstick, then settled deeper into the chair, crossed his arms over his chest, and stretched his long legs out before him.

"And what are you doing sweeping the damned floor, anyway?" he added peevishly. "We have servants to do that."

For an instant, he thought she was going to hit him with her broom.

FOR AN INSTANT, Alyce considered thwacking him over the head with her broom, but chances were his hard head would do more damage to the broomstick than the broomstick would do to him.

Instead, she relieved her feelings by informing him in vehement detail of the disruption caused by his feast. The quarrels between Erwyna and Margaret that had rocked the household over the past several days; the perfidy of the butcher who had promised the plumpest geese and delivered tough old ganders instead; the uproar caused by Huetta the kitchen maid's new infatuation with the wine-seller's apprentice, which had led her to forget the sparrow tarts in the oven, a transgression for which Margaret had soundly boxed her ears and caused the girl to spend half the day in sniffling lamentations; Joshua's outrage at having his lads taken from him and the needling he'd given Erwyna when he'd gotten them back; and everything Erwyna had done to make his and everyone else's life as miserable as possible because of it.

One after another, the week's grievances spilled out of her like wine from a broken jug, yet even as Alyce ranted, she knew that at the bottom of it all lay her anger and hurt and confusion that she had fallen in love with Robert, and that he had gone away in spite of it.

He listened to it all without speaking. But as her list of complaints lengthened, his expression of surly irritation gave way to one of unholy amusement, which didn't help her temper in the least.

"At least when my father ordered a feast at Colmaine, he didn't expect me to serve peacocks! Not at this time of the year he didn't!"

Robert burst out laughing. "That's my Alyce. Practical to the pence."

She eyed him with disfavor, then thrust her broom under his feet. "Best someone be if you're going to upset the household for silly triflings like a wedding feast, Master Wardell."

He grabbed her broom and pulled her to him. "Triflings, lady wife? *Triflings?*"

His gaze held her, made her dizzy with wanting him.

Alyce clutched her broom, the only solid, familiar object in reach. He tugged harder, pulling her off balance, over the arm of his chair and into his lap, broom and all.

"I'll show you triflings, milady," he murmured. He twitched off her kerchief and tossed it aside, then bent his head and nipped her ear.

She squeaked in protest.

He drew back, frowning at her with mock ferocity. "Quiet, woman."

She set her jaw and glared up at him.

"It's your duty to obey me," he said, fiercer still. "Didn't the priests tell you that?"

She snorted and tried to wriggle free. An impossible task, what with his arms wrapped so close around her and her legs dangling indecently over the edge of the chair and the broomstick knocking against her knees.

He bent again and whispered into her ear, "Besides, trifles can be by far the most profitable things in one's pack." His voice dropped lower still, a warm brush of words, teasing her senses. "I'm a merchant. I know."

She blinked, bewildered, then gasped as his tongue darted into her ear and out again. Fire shot through her. Her grip on the broomstick tightened, every muscle in her body tensed. It was almost a week since he'd gone away, a week without his kisses, his touch, his warmth. A week without his making love to her.

The broomstick fell on the carpet at his feet. Robert kicked it away so hard it clattered and thumped on the floor before coming to rest against the foot of the bed.

Alyce scarcely noticed. She twined her arms around his neck, stretching up to claim the kisses he offered.

He fumbled at the hems of her tunic and kirtle, pushing them up her legs and over her knees until they bunched in her lap. He slid his hand back down, over one knee and the inner swell of her calf, dragging at her hose so the soft wool scraped against her skin, making it burn. His hand slid down to her ankle. He fumbled at the fastening of her shoe one-handed.

She didn't help him. She was too engrossed in the pleasant task of kissing his jaw, his cheek, the corner of his eye, in tracing the curve of his ear with the tip of her tongue. The growing tightness in her midsection and building heat in her veins were made all the more demanding by the past week's abstinence.

Robert tossed aside her shoes, then slid his hand back up her leg until he reached the knot at the top of her hose. Even as his fingers tugged at it, he turned his head to claim her mouth with his. Her lips parted; their tongues met, curled against each other as his fingers brushed against the tender flesh of her inner thigh, making her suck in her breath.

Somehow he undid the knot on one stocking and pulled it free, then slowly, tormentingly, dragged his fingers back up the length of her leg, tracing the curve at the back of her knee, the line of her thigh, higher and higher and higher, until—

He pulled away abruptly, cursing, and fumbled at the hem of her skirt, trying to pull it back over her knees.

Too late. Alyce followed the direction of his gaze. One

of the kitchen maids stood in the open doorway with an enormous mug in her hand. Her mouth stretched in a wide, delighted grin.

"Erwyna says you wanted some ale," she announced in a tone that said she, at least, could see they wanted something else entirely.

"Put it down," said Robert, frowning. "There. The chest. No, that's fine. That's *fine*! Just put it down and get out."

The maid tittered, set the heavy pot of ale atop the chest nearest the door, but made no effort to get out. "Erwyna says to tell you, she'll send up supper in a bit for she don't want no mess in the hall, but you can take it in the kitchen if you'd prefer since that's where—"

"Get out!"

She turned and fled, giggling.

"And shut the door behind you!" Robert roared.

A moment's pause while she retraced her steps, then she poked her head back in. "Should I maybe tell Erwyna—"

"*Out!*"

The door slammed shut. Alyce burst out laughing.

Robert growled. "Impertinent wench!"

"Her?" Alyce teased. "Or me?"

"Both." He frowned at her. "One day, you know, that saucy grin will get you in trouble, and then where will you be?"

Her smile vanished. She met his gaze unblinkingly. "Here," she said, very softly. "With you."

THE FIRST THING Alyce noticed about Robert's guests was that they were far better mannered than her father and his friends had ever hoped to be. They'd bathed, for one thing, and donned fine, well-brushed clothes for another. They'd brought no hounds or hawks into the hall with them, didn't grope the serving maids, used napkins to wipe their fingers when they ate and the lip of their cup after they drank, and no one showed any inclination to stage wrestling matches in the hall as had one of her father's more memorable visitors.

Unlike the sorry wedding feast at Colmaine, when she had blushed for the plain fare and the much-mended tablecloths, this feast was fine enough to please the king. Margaret had outdone herself in the kitchen, though she'd driven everyone mad to do it. Old Grudwell of Lyme had disappointed Erwyna by returning the tablecloths properly pressed and starched and without so much as a pinprick in them, but nothing else had fallen short of her expectations, not even Erik, who had been thoroughly washed and scrubbed, then dressed in his finest and put to work carrying away empty serving plates and running errands for the guests.

Alyce's stomach had been tied into knots and her knees had been shaking when she'd received the first guests, but she'd put on a brave front and a smile, and tried to look as if she were accustomed to this sort of thing. Even the lack of news from Northampton, where Edward had engaged the baron's forces, was not permitted to intrude. Not today.

She *was* the Lady Alyce, after all, and daughter of the Baron of Colmaine, and this feast that Robert had offered in her honor had drawn half the notables of London to their hall. Whatever deficiencies Robert's guests might find in her face or figure or family connections, she was determined they would find none in her manner.

They hadn't, as far as she could tell. In fact, she'd drawn more than one admiring glance from the men and not a few envious glances from the women. Some of the guests were simply impressed with her name and lineage, of course, but others were clearly impressed with *her*. The unfamiliar admiration and envy were heady stuff.

Lord knew, she'd done her best to look like a baron's daughter and a rich man's wife. She'd worn the surcoat she'd embroidered for her wedding, and her mother's jeweled necklet, and her fine new shoes. After much hesitation, she'd even put aside her customary wimple and veil and done her hair up in the exquisite hair net that Robert had given her—*after* he'd bedded her so eagerly and well that she'd scarce been able to lift her head from the pillow.

The thought made her smile, and lifted her chin a fraction of an inch higher. Robert had been right. The gold and pearls made a striking contrast against her red hair. The pride that had shone in his eyes when she'd emerged from their chamber that morning, before the first guests arrived, had been as precious to her as any jewel he might have offered.

"More wine, milady?"

The polite query pulled Alyce from her thoughts. As the highest-ranking guest, Thomas Fitz Thomas, the lord mayor of London, had been seated on her right. Despite his political differences with Robert, he'd proved to be an entertaining dinner companion and more than once had made her laugh with some dry sally or scandalous bit of gossip. With Robert on her left, she actually found herself enjoying the meal that she had dreaded.

"No wine, I thank you, sir." she said, smiling. "I've had more than enough to content me for the nonce."

"God knows there's enough of it, and all of the finest. But then, Robert has always been known for demanding the best of everything." The twinkle in the mayor's hooded eyes was unmistakable. "It doesn't surprise me that he's managed to gain such a fine wife to go with all."

He lifted the silver goblet they shared in a salute, smiling at the flush that stained Alyce's cheeks, then took a sip of the rich red wine. With his napkin, he wiped the goblet where his lips had pressed and set it down between them.

"I confess, my lady, I am grateful for this feast, and not just for the pleasure of meeting you." He scanned the crowded hall, his expression becoming grim. "The division between the king and Earl Simon has divided us all. Anything that can bring us together is welcome, even if it be for only a day."

Alyce studied the faces around her. The mayor was right. Today, for a few hours at least, quarrels had been set aside in order to share in the merrymaking. William and Mary Townsend were seated just below the salt, but Alan of Hensford, whose standing in the guild of mercers was too great to ignore, had a place of honor at the head table. The presence of Robert's political opponents, of his outright enemies, only strengthened the advantage he gained from the gathering, proof of the power he wielded in London and among London merchants.

"You're Earl Simon's man, are you not, my Lord Mayor?" Alyce asked.

He nodded. "I am. Montfort promises what the king will not, and he has no more liking for the king's foreign advisors than do we. Henry's policies have harmed us, and if we do not stand against them now, they might well destroy us." He paused, then added, "No matter what your husband thinks."

"Master Wardell follows his own path," Alyce said mildly. "It seems to have served him well enough in the past."

Fitz Thomas's mouth quirked in a smile. "He was always a clever bastard. Who'd think he'd manage to wed a baron's daughter, let alone one whose father is pledged to Earl Simon."

Alyce merely smiled, but beneath the cover of the full tablecloth, her hands twisted her napkin as if it were a rope coiling about a felon's throat.

"I met him," Fitz Thomas went on, "when he and your brother lodged at the Tower a few weeks past. Your father, I mean." The mayor's face gave no hint of what he'd thought of Sir Fulk.

"No, I didn't know," said Alyce. She forced herself to stop tugging at her napkin, afraid he would notice the nervous gesture. "No doubt my father forgot to mention it."

She hesitated, but Robert was deep in conversation with the mayor's wife and wouldn't be likely to hear. "Is there— Have you had any word of Northampton, sir? My father and brother are part of the garrison there and I—" She faltered, then tried again, fighting for calm. "It's difficult, you know. The not knowing."

He shook his head. "There's been no word beyond that first intelligence, that Edward had moved his forces against the city. Earl Simon has gone to aid them. We must hope the city can hold out until he gets there."

"Yes." She shouldn't have asked. "Would you like more peacock, sir? There's a fine slice of the breast still left."

The roasted peacocks, carefully redressed in their feathered skins with their tails fanned out, had been a hit. There'd been ten of them, each brought in on a separate platter for display, then hastily returned to the kitchen to be stripped and carved and brought out again, ready for eating. A cluster of the long, brilliant tail feathers lay on the table beside her. Every woman at the dinner had been given at least one as a momento.

The dark look in the mayor's eyes vanished as he laughed. "No, no more of the peacock, I thank you. I can't remember when I last saw so grand a feast, my lady."

He graced her with a roguish smile. "Your husband has grown vain indeed to flaunt his newest jewel with such a show. I wonder he hasn't claimed all those peacock feathers to thrust into his own hat and parade before the world."

Alyce laughed and resolutely turned the conversation

away from politics. There was more than enough to talk about, and Fitz Thomas, his tongue loosened under the influence of Robert's wine, was more than willing to tell her tales of life in London and his own adventures as a young merchant.

As the afternoon advanced, some of the guests began to show the effects of too much food and wine. If it weren't that the benches were so crowded, Alyce suspected a couple of the guests would have toppled over altogether, or crawled beneath the tables and gone to sleep.

For herself, she was more than ready for the long afternoon to be over and the hall emptied of guests. Her head ached. Her ears buzzed with the constant roar of conversation. She'd been careful not to drink too much, but even with only nibbles from each course, she'd eaten far more than was good for her.

She longed to lie down and go to sleep with Robert warm and solid at her side. Instead, she smiled and laughed at the mayor's jokes and continued to keep a sharp eye on the proceedings despite Erwyna's watchful presence at the back of the hall.

Beside her, Robert entertained the mayor's pretty wife and lifted his cup in recognition of the occasional and increasingly drunken toasts that were offered on his behalf. If the hours of drinking and eating and talking had affected him, Alyce couldn't see it. Perhaps his eyes were a little brighter than they usually were, his manner more relaxed, but that was all.

She was sampling the baked pears in honey that the mayor had offered her from the serving bowl when a sudden stir at the side of the hall caught her attention. People craned to see what was toward. A murmur of voices rippled outward from the screens passage, growing louder, drawing still more attention to whatever was happening outside.

Henley, who had been posted at the hall entrance,

strode into the hall, his face set in grim, hard lines. As he circled behind the crowded tables, working his way toward Robert, the room fell into a tense and waiting silence. A moment later, Newton and one of the lord mayor's guards appeared in the doorway, a lanky stranger wedged between them.

Alyce couldn't hear what Henley whispered into Robert's ear, but she couldn't miss the sudden tension in Robert's features as he listened.

"The messenger is for you, Fitz Thomas," he said, gesturing to the trio in the doorway. "Your guard vouches for him."

His voice was low, calm, controlled, yet in the expectant stillness, it carried clearly. Another murmur swept through the crowd. Even those who had drunk and eaten overmuch seemed shocked into alertness.

Everyone turned to watch the lanky man unsteadily making his way toward the head table. "My Lord Mayor." The man swayed on his feet, eyes wide and face pasty white. "Northampton has fallen!"

An instant's shocked silence, then the hall erupted in a roar. Whatever else the man had to say was lost in the tumult.

Fitz Thomas angrily shouted for quiet. "Whence had you this news, man? Montfort and his men can't have reached the town this quickly."

The man shook his head. "They had word of it before they'd got far from London, my lord. Earl Simon's turned back. He'll be in London again before nightfall. I was at Cripplegate when the news reached us, and was sent to find you and tell you of it."

Another roar, as sternly quenched. "What of Northampton's defenders? What of its people?" Fitz Thomas demanded.

Alyce would swear he glanced at her from the corner of his eye. She was dimly conscious of Robert's hand on her arm, but her attention was fixed on the man who stood in front of them. Her fingers curled into her napkin like claws.

The messenger grimaced and shook his head. "The lords and knights who defended the city are all dead or taken prisoner. Edward has trampled the city under his feet. There's naught but rape and burning and pillage, the messenger said, and not one hand lifted to stop it."

This time Fitz Thomas didn't bother trying to call for silence. The roar as everyone burst into speech rocked the hall to its foundations.

DEAD OR PRISONER! Her father, her brother—dead or prisoners of the Lord Edward.

The words seemed to echo in the silence, though Alyce hadn't spoken them out loud.

She'd waited until the last of their guests were gone, then, while Robert had escorted them to the gate, she'd driven the servants from the hall as well. They could clean tomorrow, she'd said, and the look in her eye had convinced even Erwyna not to argue.

The instant Robert returned, Alyce had pounced on him. He had to use his influence to find out what had happened to Hubert and Sir Fulk, she'd said. He had to arrange for her brother's and father's freedom if they were alive, or the return of their bodies if they were dead.

Robert had refused. She pleaded, begged, argued, and demanded, but still he refused to help her.

"Why?" she asked, stunned. "Why can't you send to the Lord Edward for news of them? Why can't you ask for their freedom?"

"I can't, I tell you. It's as simple as that."

He sat, chin sunk on his breast, his hands curled over the arms of his chair like a hawk's talons digging into its perch. His gaze fixed on her across the width of the table and the wreckage of their marriage feast that divided them. She saw no compassion in his dark eyes, no hint of grief to match the grief in her.

She stood before him, her head high, her hands curved into fists at her sides. She would not beg, but she would fight for this. No matter that Sir Fulk hadn't loved her, that Hubert had teased her and the two together had mocked her all her life. They were her family. They were her father and brother. They were her *blood*. That was enough.

"You mean," she shot back, "you can use my family and its connections to your gain, but you can't use *your* connections to aid them when they need you?"

"I mean," he said, "that there is nothing I can do! My money bought future trade concessions and special rights, nothing more. Do you think a few thousand pounds of silver is enough to bend a prince to my will?"

"A few thousand pounds of silver?" There was a sharp edge to Alyce's laughter. "You talk as if it were a penny tossed to a beggar!"

Robert's smile held no trace of mirth. "The Lord Edward would scarce thank you for comparing him to a beggar."

She slammed her hands down on the table, too upset to control her fury. "They are my family, my father and my brother. You have to act for them!"

Robert leaped to his feet. "I don't *have* to do anything, my lady. Not even when you demand it."

He shoved aside the wooden plate that sat on the table before him, heedless of the way it crushed her peacock feathers. Planting his fists on the table, he leaned toward her, his eyes gleaming as hard as obsidian in the waning light.

"Edward won't return good fighting men to Simon's side no matter who asks it. Not now. Not while Montfort and his barons still run free. If your father and brother live, they will be honorably treated as befits their rank. If they are dead . . ."

He stared at her, then shrugged and straightened, starting to turn away. His gaze caught on the peacock feathers. He picked them up and slowly ran them through his hand. Alyce couldn't help but watch. It was as if he held her, as if his hand stroked her. Once, twice. The colors of the feathers shifted as the delicate vanes compressed between his fingers, then sprang free, still beautiful despite the broken quills.

His hand abruptly closed in a fist, crushing the feathers unmercifully, twisting them beyond redemption.

"If your father and brother are dead," he said at last, "then only God can help them now."

Tears burned her eyes, her face twisted with her pain, but Alyce refused to cry. She also refused to give up.

"Have you no pity?"

His head snapped up. "I? Not for them! It's the poor of Northampton I pity. The washerwomen raped beside their laundry tubs and the cradles of their babes. The laborers cut down like dogs in the street for no more crime than trying to defend the hovels that are their homes. Why should I pity men like your father and brother, who would have raped and killed the same as Edward's men if they had been the victors?"

"They are my *family*!" Alyce said.

"And *I* am your husband!" Robert roared.

His roar echoed, beating against the walls on every side of her, then faded into silence.

Alyce breathed deep. Her body trembled and her tears spilled, burning down her face.

"Not anymore," she said. She didn't roar or shout, yet her words hung upon the air as clearly as his. "From this day forth, Robert Wardell, I'll not have you in my bed nor be your wife in anything but name."

Her gaze locked with his, as unbending as steel. "If

you dare touch me, I swear I'll slice off that cock that you're so proud of and feed it to the pigs, and then—"

She drew in her breath; it seared her lungs just as her tears had scored her face. Fury shook her, but still she refused to look away.

"And then, Wardell," she said, "I'll leave what's left of you to rot. I swear it."

He was still standing, straight and stiff and unmoving, his gaze fixed on the broken peacock feathers he held, when Alyce stalked out of the hall and up the stairs to the chamber that would now be hers alone, forever.

⟶ London, late April, 1264

ROBERT LED HIS men through the silent, empty streets, past churches that loomed like monsters and shuttered shops and houses half-hidden in the fog that was swallowing London.

He'd never been a man much given to grim fantasy, but to his straining senses it seemed as if they traveled an abandoned city. Their horses' hooves striking against the ground sounded muffled and distant. The light from the single torch his steward carried reflected back from the mist, surrounding them in a dull-gold nimbus as though they were minor saints lost in some dark corner of a forgotten chapel. The creaking of the cart wheels reminded him of the groaning of a gibbet as its human burden slowly twisted at the end of a rope.

His companions must have shared his thoughts. They hunched under their cloaks as they peered into the dark on either side, nerves on edge to catch warning of any enemies who might be lurking unseen.

It was well they were alert. He broke no law that night, betrayed no man's confidence, but for what he was about to do, all London would be his enemy.

·   ·   ·

ALYCE ROLLED ONTO her back and stared into the dark above her. The bedclothes were tangled about her, their weight pressing her into the bed, which had never seemed so large with Robert there beside her. Not anywhere near so large.

They hadn't slept together—had scarce conversed as man and wife—for nigh on two weeks, and even the knowledge that he was out tonight on the Lord Edward's business wasn't enough to ease her sense of loss and pain.

If it hadn't been for the stir he and his men had made leaving at such an unaccustomed hour, she wouldn't have known he was going out at all. He'd greeted her appearance with a frown and a stiff, straight demeanor that betrayed his intentions as clearly as if he'd shouted them for all the world to hear.

She'd challenged him, accused him of sending aid to Edward even though her father's and brother's fates were still unknown. He neither denied nor admitted it, just coldly advised her to return to her bed, safe out of the cold and damp.

Instead, she'd watched from a window as his men had loaded a small, obviously heavy chest onto a horse-drawn cart, buried it under sacks of wool, then ridden out of the gate and into the night with only the creaking of the cart wheels and the ring of shod hooves on stone to show where they had gone.

Only once the last echoes of their leaving had vanished in the mist had she retreated to her chamber, drawing the door closed behind her and creeping into bed like a thief frightened of being caught in the midst of his thieving.

Anger and loss warred within her, but it was fear that triumphed in the end. Fear for her father and brother. Fear for Robert, for the risks he ran. Fear for herself that she would lose everything just when she'd thought it was within her grasp.

A shiver shook her; she drew the covers up close beneath her chin. Was this what it was to be in love? To worry and wonder and try to divine secrets from the most fleeting of glances, the faintest of clues? She'd never fretted over Hubert and Sir Fulk this way, not even when they'd come back bloodied from some quarrel or other. Not even now, when she knew nothing of their fate. But Robert—

Alyce closed her eyes and burrowed deeper into the pillows, ears alert to catch the first hint of his return.

"DAMN THE FOG. Damn the cold too." William Townsend hunched his shoulders against the weather and drew his cloak tighter around him. "And damn *you,* Robert, for dragging me out on a night like this and for such an errand. Weather like this bodes no good."

Robert didn't answer. He stood motionless at the end of the quay, staring into the mist. Nothing showed except the diffused glow of the torch reflecting off the sullen gray waters of the Thames. No sound came except the slap of the river against the stone. The thick mist hung about them like a pall, shrouding the night.

When Robert remained silent, William transferred his ire to John Rareton, who stood to one side, holding the torch. "And you! Make sure you don't fail us, do you hear?"

Robert's steward flinched, making the torch bob. The flame hissed and shivered, then steadied as the man tightened his grip and stared silently back.

William turned again to Robert. "My wife threatens murder and I leave her again, what with the babe so close to its time and London as unsettled as it is. I've not told her what we're about for fear she'll make the child a fatherless orphan ere it's breeched."

Robert shrugged. "It's only a few hours I've asked of you."

William snorted and stamped his feet, then turned

to peer anxiously upriver. There was nothing to see in the mist. "A few hours and another loan to the Lord Edward! I'd think it a madman's errand except it's you who asks me."

"You'll be glad of it eventually, William. You and all the others."

William huddled deeper into his cloak, unconvinced. "The others were right, Robert. This new loan is good money after bad." He shook his head. "Montfort will win this pissing match, regardless. After the butchery at Northampton, all England calls for Edward's blood."

Rareton nervously shifted his grip on the torch. The whites of his eyes gleamed a sickly gray beneath the shadow of his hood.

Robert was silent, listening to the Thames rushing past. His thoughts were too much like that cold race and swirl of water, but he could no more divert their path than he could bend the river to run tame at his command.

"Perhaps," he said at last, reluctantly. "Perhaps Montfort will win . . . in the beginning." He met William's angry gaze squarely. "But *only* in the beginning. In the long run, it will be Edward who triumphs, no matter how many are clamoring for his head now. I'm as sure of that as I am of these stones beneath my feet."

William snorted. "Those stones are cold and wet and treacherously slick, my friend. Take care where you tread!"

Robert shrugged. "What would you? There's no sure footing in any of this. Not for us and not for the king and Lord Edward. Not even for Earl Simon. We can but do our best, and I say this is the better dance."

William didn't reply, just stood there frowning at him with an expression grim enough to frighten demons.

"Would you rather have joined the merchant rabble that swears they'll march in Montfort's train, my friend?" Robert demanded, pricked by his friend's doubts. "Think you that would be safer than this bloodless risk of coin?"

William turned away to stare again into the drifting mist. John Rareton, who had followed the exchange with the strained intensity of an anxious dog uncertain of its master's humor, drew his cloak more closely about him. Even in the wavering torchlight, Robert could see his hand tremble as he clutched the edges of the cloth.

Robert let his gaze drop to the iron-bound chest that sat on the stones at his feet. He nudged it with his boot. It didn't move an inch. He hadn't expected it to, not with the weight of French gold coins and English silver that it held. His gold and silver, in the main. He'd had no time to seek more support from his English contacts in France and Flanders, and many of those Londoners who'd followed him at first had grown uneasy with the passing weeks. They'd preferred to risk the Lord Edward's ire rather than their coin, leaving him to fill the breach. In the end, he'd managed, but even Rareton did not know how sorely it had taxed his resources.

The faint splash of oars snapped his head up. He tensed, straining to see through the mist. Torchlight shone dimly, seemingly adrift on the restless river.

"Ho, the shore!" came a muffled call.

"Ho, there!" Robert replied. He snatched the torch from his steward's hand and waved it back and forth.

Like a monster from the depths, a slender barque slid out of the mist, looming sleek and dangerous in the dark. At a hushed command from a man standing in the prow, the oarsmen shifted the craft so it slowed, then swung sideways to the quay. The current carried it the rest of the way in.

Before it touched, the man sprang onto the quay, immediately followed by two of his crew with ropes to hold the craft against the river's pull. The man blinked, then frowned, shading his eyes against the glare of the torch in Robert's hand.

"Wardell?"

"I'm Wardell," Robert said, returning the torch to Rareton and stepping forward.

The man squinted, studying Robert's features as if trying to match them with a description in his mind. Evidently satisfied, he handed Robert a sealed roll of parchment, then glanced down at the chest that lay on the stones between them. "You have it? All of it?"

Robert glanced at the image pressed into the wax seal. It was Edward's seal, as promised. He nodded.

"All," he said curtly, then gestured to William. "My friend Master William Townsend and my steward, John Rareton. He'll go back with you and the gold."

"That's not necessary."

"He goes with you," Robert said evenly in a tone that brooked no challenge. He beckoned Rareton forward. "I trust the Lord Edward will send him safe back again."

The man grunted, clearly displeased but unable to find a reason to refuse. "Very well."

He gestured to the crewmen, who picked up the chest between them and, grunting and swearing, handed it to the men in the barque. The craft bobbed and swayed and edged back into the river, making the crewmen scramble to grab the ropes again.

Robert paid them no heed, but turned to Rareton instead. "Do not forget to seek out news of Sir Fulk and Sir Hubert."

"No," said Rareton. The man met his gaze unflinchingly. "You can trust me that far."

"And further, I think," said Robert. The choice of Rareton had been deliberate. Despite his steward's doubts about the wisdom of this course, despite Hensford's efforts to subvert him, Rareton would not betray the trust placed in him. Robert was sure of it.

He returned his attention to the boat.

Once the craft was brought back to heel, Rareton handed the torch to William, then gingerly climbed in. He settled himself in the center of the barque, his feet propped on the chest he was to guard and his cloak drawn tight about him as if it could keep out more than just the cold and the mist.

Without a word of farewell, the man in command of the barque leaped into the prow, then gestured to his crew to shove off.

"God be with you," William called as the craft eased away.

Rareton lifted his head in acknowledgement, but said not a word. His face shone pinched and hollow in the torchlight.

The man in the prow laughed. "God rides with the king and the Lord Edward," he said, and turned to face the darkness. The words were almost lost in the splash of the oars and the creaking protest of the barque as it fought to swing around against the insistent current.

Robert said nothing, just stood and waited. When the last faint sound of their passing was swallowed up in the swirling fog, he turned and strode back up the quay.

William willingly followed after, holding the torch high to light their way against the dark.

THE POUNDING AT the gate brought Alyce out of bed, heart racing.

"Open up! In the name of Simon de Montfort, open up, I say!"

Again the pounding, this time accompanied by cries and sleep-befuddled curses from the solar.

Alyce fumbled for her cloak where it hung on the wall. Shoes she would have to do without; hers were lost in the dark. Her thoughts churned. Robert. Where was Robert? Where in God's name was Robert?

"Milady? Milady!" A panicked Githa tumbled into

the room when Alyce threw open the door. "There's men at the gate and—"

"Yes, I know," Alyce snapped. "Run to the stables and alert the lads and men. Tell them to grab what weapons they can and meet me at the gate."

In the dim glow from the banked fire, the solar resembled something out of a nightmare, with bodies shrieking and running about in confusion.

Alyce raised her voice in what she hoped would be reassurance. "Don't worry. Whoever they are, there's naught they can do. They've no right of entry and the gate is stout. You men, come with me. The rest of you wait here or in the hall where you'll be out of the way."

She didn't pause to find out if her orders had been understood, but swept across the solar, elbowing aside someone who stumbled into her path. The stairs were invisible in the dark, but Alyce made her way down them as quickly as she could, one hand on the wall to guide her descent. Behind her, the solar's occupants broke into a frightened gabbling, but a few apparently still had their wits about them. She could hear footsteps following in her wake.

To Alyce's relief, by the time she reached the yard Newton was already halfway to the gate, a tallow lantern in one hand, a short, stout sword in the other.

"Get back," he snarled, and gestured with his sword.

"Who else is here?" she asked, falling into step beside him.

"There's naught but me."

Alyce winced. With no walls to muffle sound, the pounding and shouting were terrifying. The gate's heavy iron hinges groaned in protest at the assault.

"What about Joshua? The stable lads?"

He spared her one contemptuous glance. "Old men and boys, of use to no one. Stop your hammerin', then!" he bellowed. "I'm comin'!"

The pounding stopped. The sudden silence was almost more frightening than the racket that had preceded it. The very air seemed weighted with menace.

Alyce stayed back, out of sight, as Newton peered out of the barred window set in the gate. "God rot you all and all your bastard sons," he swore. "What do you want?"

"Wardell. Where is he?" The voice had the ring of authority in it.

"Gone to the devil. You're welcome to follow after if you've a mind to see him."

"Not before I've sent you there myself!"

"You and how many others?"

Alyce had heard boys exchange such insults. Somehow it didn't seem so amusing when it was between armed and angry men.

She pressed her back flat against the stone wall of the entrance, shivering in spite of her heavy cloak.

THEY STORED THE wool sacks in a warehouse for which William had the key.

"At least this damn fog's kept Montfort's men indoors," William said. "I don't envy your steward, out on the river in weather such as this."

"No." Robert did not care to speak of John Rareton. He peered into the faceless night. "Watch yourself, my friend. I'd not care to have Mistress Townsend accuse me of having mislaid her husband."

William laughed and kicked his horse into motion. "It won't come to that. When a man has a comfortable home to return to and a good wife waiting for him, he's not likely to go astray. Not even on such a night as this."

Robert watched as his friend disappeared into the mist. Behind him, his men shifted restlessly, anxious to have done with this night's work. He wished he were as eager. The pallet in his workroom was not near so comfortable as his good feather bed, and without Alyce to warm it, it was damnably cold as well.

Reluctantly, Robert set his horse to a walk. He didn't look to see if his men followed after.

IT DIDN'T TAKE long for the men and lads of Wardell House to arm themselves and assemble at the gate, but one look at them and Alyce's heart fell. Newton had been right. They were boys and old men. They knew nothing of fighting and their weapons—staves, shovels, an ax, a length of iron from the fireplace spit—were no match for the swords the men in the street were sure to have.

They stared at her, eyes wide, a mix of eagerness and fear and fury on their faces. In the heavy mist and the dim light from Newton's lantern, they looked like gargoyles come down from the church eaves to answer the soldiers' angry summons.

And the soldiers were growing angrier by the minute.

"Open up, I say!" their captain roared. "We come at Montfort's order. Delay any longer and we'll break the gate down!"

Alyce squared her shoulders and motioned Newton away from the gate's barred window.

"Who dares threaten my house and at such an hour?" she demanded loudly.

"I'll give you to the count of ten. *One* . . ."

Montfort's men had brought torches, but the small opening restricted her vision to a narrow square. A helmeted head filled most of it, though with the light behind him, she could make out almost nothing of the man's features. She could see two mounted soldiers and had the impression there might be half a dozen more. Impossible to tell. Enough to make good their threat to break down the gate if they chose.

"Two."

"By what right do you drag us from our beds like this?" she asked.

"*Three.*"

"Even the king has no right—"

"*Four.*"

He was up to eight when she cursed and finally gave in.

"All right, all right. I'm coming out with one of my men. Back away."

The gate opened inward. If they chose to rush it once it was unbarred, there was little anyone could do to stop them.

Alyce motioned her makeshift army back, away from the gate. "Do *nothing* unless I tell you," she ordered them in a hissing whisper. "Understood?"

Joshua opened his mouth to protest, but she forestalled him. "Nothing! The first man to disobey me will be looking for a new master come morning."

Newton eyed her doubtfully, but something in her face must have convinced him she knew what she was doing . . . or that she at least meant what she said. He handed the lantern to whoever was nearest, shifted his grip on his sword, and nodded for someone to open the gate.

For the first time since she'd come to Wardell House, Alyce found herself grateful for his presence.

The gate opened a crack, enough for Newton to slip through. She followed hard on his heels, head proudly high. Barefoot and in her shift she might be, with her hair rapidly working free of its heavy braid, but she was a baron's daughter, for all that.

It didn't feel like much when she heard the bar fall back into place behind her and found herself facing an armored knight with a dozen armed and mounted men behind him. At the sight of Newton, two of them dismounted and moved nearer to the gate.

The knight glanced at Newton, then eyed her up and

down with the bored air of a man checking the points of a mare. He snorted dismissively. "If this is what the citizens of London send to defend their homes, I wonder the city still stands."

Alyce glared haughtily back. "It stands in spite of men like you." She could feel the damp beading on her skin and in her hair and had to fight against the urge to brush it away. Would that she could brush him away as easily.

"I am the Lady Alyce. By what right do you roust honest folk from their beds? And in such a manner too!"

"Lady Alyce?" His left eyebrow shot mockingly upward.

"Daughter of Sir Fulk, Baron of Colmaine."

Beneath his heavy mustache, his mouth twisted in amused contempt. "And wife of Robert Wardell. Or so they say," he added in a tone that barely avoided outright insult.

Alyce wavered. It wasn't quite so easy to put up a bold front when even her name provided no protection. "What do you want?"

"Where's Wardell?"

"Not here."

"When will he return?"

She shrugged. He grabbed her arm and yanked her to him. His leather-and-mail mittens dug into her flesh, even through her cloak. Newton started forward, sword upraised, but one of the mounted soldiers moved to block his way.

"Pride is a fine thing, milady," the captain snarled, "but were I you, I would take more heed of where and when I permitted myself the indulgence of it."

Alyce spat in his face.

He almost jerked her arm out of its socket in return.

She cried out at the sudden pain and would have gone to her knees except for his cruel hold on her. She twisted, trying to pull away, but her bare feet slipped in the mud of the street. Her anguished cry to Newton for help was wasted breath—he had his back to the gate and a sword to his throat.

The captain pulled her hard against him; the steel links of his hauberk bruised her breast. "All right," he said. "Since you will have it thus, we'll take you in your husband's stead. I imagine Wardell will come fast enough once he knows we have his wife as hostage to his good faith."

"Good faith! You bastard!" Alyce shoved against him. Her move caught him by surprise, but he was too quick for her. His grip on her arm tightened. With his other hand he grabbed a hank of her hair and brutally twisted it as he half pulled, half dragged her toward his horse.

Alyce kept on fighting despite the pain and the uncertain footing, despite the dragging weight of her cloak with its mud-caked hem. Rage and panic drove her. Dimly she was aware of worried shouts from the gate, the scrape of the bar being lifted, the angry cries for help, but it wasn't until her captor stopped short in the street that she caught the muted *screek-screek* of cart wheels and the sound of horses' hooves coming toward them through the swirling fog.

"Robert!" The scream ripped from her throat.

The knight who held her laughed.

And then it was all a blur—a cry from the dark, the sudden, pounding hoofbeats of a galloping horse, the gate swinging wide to the cries of boys eager for their first real fight, and the shush of a dozen swords sliding free of leather scabbards.

Robert burst out of the mist like an angry demon, sword up, eyes dark holes of fury. He pulled his mount to a plunging, snorting halt at the far edge of the light, his gaze sweeping the crowd before his gate.

"Robert!" It was a cry of joy as well as of warning.

He'd come! Mist-blinded, outnumbered, not knowing what hazards he might find, he'd come to her.

For a moment, for one precious moment, his eyes fixed on her, then his lips pulled back in a snarl and he drove his mount toward her, heedless of the soldiers in his way.

Alyce's captor crowed in triumph and shoved her into the arms of one of his men, then drew his sword and advanced to meet this new challenge.

The man who held her, a great, burly brute who stank of ale, sweat, and horses, grunted at his new task and dragged her to the side. Alyce squirmed and kicked and bucked against his hold, to no avail. The brute held her fast as a shoat for the slaughter, safely out of the way where she couldn't so much as put a foot in anyone's path. The only course left her was to watch . . . and pray.

There was no hiding from it. The sound of fighting filled the air, heavy as the mist, of sword on sword, of sword on wood or flesh, of snorting horses and swearing, shouting, angry, frightened men. She could hear it all, see it all. At the first sign of a fight, the soldiers had tossed their torches away. Some of them had sputtered and died in the mud, but some burned still, reflecting off the shifting mist, casting the scene in an orange-red glow.

Robert and his guards were mounted and armed, but they had no armor and they were outnumbered almost three to one, their opponents trained and battle-hardened soldiers, not the poorly armed thieves for which their weapons had been intended.

The men and boys from the house fared even worse. Untrained and hopelessly disadvantaged against mounted men, they stumbled and went down or fell back, their useless weapons lost, their heads streaming blood from the soldiers' brutal blows.

Alyce watched it all in horror. The residents of nearby houses must surely have been roused from their beds by now, but no one so much as poked his nose out of the doors to watch, let alone to render assistance.

The melee didn't last long. The soldiers hadn't come for stable boys and aged gardeners, nor even for a merchant's guards. They'd come for Robert.

"Alive! I want him alive!" the captain roared.

A raised sword was turned, and the hilt crashed down on Robert's head. He crumpled and would have toppled off his horse except someone shoved him back to sag over his mount's neck like a rag doll tossed aside by a careless child. His sword slipped from his nerveless hands.

"To the Tower!" The captain kicked the sword aside. One of the his men led his horse up.

The bear who had hold of Alyce laughed and shoved her away. She stumbled and landed with a sucking plop in the churned-up mud of the street, her nose not six inches from the end of Newton's short sword.

She blinked. A clump of sodden hair covered one eye. She dragged it aside and blinked again, then raised her head to see Newton groggily forcing his way to his knees, one muddy hand plastered over a wicked-looking slice across his scalp.

With a cry of triumph, Alyce snatched up the sword and sprang to her feet. The fight was almost over, the defenders weaponless and too battered to keep on. One fierce lad lunged after Robert's horse but was kicked aside by a soldier, who laughed when he went sprawling face first in the mud. They paid her no heed as the captain trotted past, the soldier who led Robert's horse right behind him.

She'd darted in front of them before they realized what she was about. The soldier tried to turn out of her way, but she grabbed his mount's bridle and pulled him to a halt. At his shout of surprise, the captain turned back, cursing.

"I'll kill the beast, then kill the man if you don't return my husband," she said, pressing the point of the sword to the vulnerable juncture of the horse's jaw and throat. The horse snorted and tried to shy away, but fear and fury had given Alyce a strength she hadn't known she possessed. The sword point never wavered.

The captain laughed and swung his own mount closer. "Fiery words for a merchant's wife. I swear Wardell armed the wrong men."

Then he leaned out of his saddle and with his mailed fist gave her a vicious backhand blow to her temple.

The world went black.

THE WORLD WAS a small and painful place.

Alyce could hear the hollow echo of hoofbeats on a wooden bridge, the scrape of steel against stone, men's voices fading in and out. An unpleasant pressure on her belly made it hard for her to breathe.

Memory, faint and filled with frightening gaps, crept slowly back. This was London Tower. King Henry's fortress, now Earl Simon's.

With memory came a dull awareness: she'd been flung facedown over the withers of a horse; her head felt like an overripe melon that was about to burst, her body ached, and her belly churned. She turned her head and opened her eyes, then quickly squeezed them shut, blinded by the bright flare of torches. Nausea gripped her.

Robert. The thought wormed its way through her misery. *Where was Robert?*

More voices, an argument. She fought past the pain and the nausea, struggling to make out the words.

"The earl's abed, for all I know," a rough voice said. "That or closeted with the messengers who came in earlier. You'll have to wait."

Someone cursed. The captain, Alyce thought dully. Her head was too heavy to lift to make sure.

"I was told to bring in Robert Wardell."

"Were you, now?" Slow, arrogant footsteps. "Wardell I can see plain enough, but what's this baggage?"

Someone grabbed her hair and yanked her head up for a better look. Alyce didn't have any trouble keeping her eyes shut—the abrupt motion hurt so much she was afraid she'd pass out again.

"That's Wardell's wife."

The brute laughed and let go of her hair. Her neck snapped painfully as her head fell back.

"Weren't enough you had to drag her out of bed, so you dragged her through the mud too?"

The captain was not amused. "She's a damned interfering merchant's whore, for all she's a lady bred. We had no choice but to bring her."

"Well, take the pair of 'em through that passage there. There's a room beyond with a good stout door and a lock. You can leave 'em there till they're wanted."

As if from a distance, Alyce caught more voices, the creak of saddles as men dismounted, footsteps on stone coming toward her. Then a disrespectful hand landed square on her rump, grabbed a handful of her cloak and shift, and dragged her off the horse.

Stars burst behind her eyelids an instant before the blackness claimed her.

HIS HEAD HURT. He was vaguely conscious of other injuries—a burning across his shoulder felt very like a knife cut he'd received some years ago—but his head *really* hurt.

Robert groaned and forced his eyes open. A wretched hag was bent over him, her hair a Medusa's nest of mud-caked snakes. No, two hags, one superimposed on the other and just a couple of inches to the side.

He jerked upright with a startled cry. His head

exploded in pain, but not before he got a better look at the crone. He rocked forward, clutching his head.

"Ah, Mother of God! It's you!"

Alyce sat back on her heels and eyed him with disfavor. "Had I known you were going to be this pleased to see me, I'd have let Montfort's men carry you off and been done with it."

He started to shake his head, and immediately thought better of it. "I thought you were— That is—" He groaned, squinting against the candlelight, trying to make the blurry edges of her features come clearer. Even squinting, he'd swear there were two of her. "Your hair. What's wrong with your hair?"

"I—I landed in the mud."

He knew there was something important about her hesitation, but he couldn't think what it was. He couldn't think, period.

"What happened?" He probed at his aching head, wincing as his fingers encountered torn flesh and blood-matted hair. "A fight. Must have been a fight. And I—"

He stopped, looking at her. "I remember! You screamed. I thought you screamed. The mist . . . And there were Montfort's men—"

She brushed his hand away from his head and gently pressed a cold, wet cloth to the wound.

He sucked in his breath.

"Sorry," she said. "They brought me water and a cloth for your head, but with only one candle, it's hard to see."

"Especially when there's two of you."

"What?"

He grimaced, squinting harder. The two faces slowly resolved into one, and that one had an ugly, bloodied scrape at the temple. "What the hell . . . ?"

He grabbed her jaw and turned her face to the side.

She flinched, pulling away. "The captain hit me when I tried to stop them from taking you. I'm all right."

Anger shot through him, driving out the pain. "What captain? Why were you out in the street in the first place? Why didn't someone stop him? *Where the hell were my men?*"

Her chin came up. "In the mud, unhorsed, disarmed, backed up against the gate. They didn't have a chance against a dozen armed and mounted men."

Rage made Robert's head spin. Rage and guilt. He should have foreseen . . . should have guessed . . . should have *known*.

Alyce didn't offer any sympathy. "As far as I could tell, no one was hurt. Not seriously, anyway. You're probably in the worst shape of any of them, and you can't be too bad if you're already yelling at me."

She tossed the cloth into the basin and climbed stiffly to her feet. Robert tried to follow her. Even that small effort was too much for his battered head. He sank back with a groan.

Alyce ignored him and crossed to the single door. She pressed her ear against it and listened, then sighed and straightened. "Nothing. Not a sound."

"The door's locked?"

She nodded. "And barred."

He studied the room around them. "Where are we? The Tower?"

Again she nodded, but this time he caught a hint of uncertainty in it. "Montfort summoned you."

He sighed and leaned back against the cold stone, careful not to jar his head. "He has a rather rough notion of what constitutes a summons."

"It was the captain. He started it." She scowled at the unyielding door. "Aren't you going to do anything? Try to get us out of here?"

He couldn't tell if her scowl was meant for the captain, Montfort, or him. "No."

Her head snapped around at that.

"Only fools waste time trying to break out of a locked and barred room in the Tower." Even talking made his head ache. If he tried to stand up, he'd probably keel right over. "I'd rather get some sleep in the hope my head will clear."

She shrugged, then shivered and tugged her mud-crusted cloak more closely around her.

"Come here."

She frowned at the peremptory tone.

"Throw that damned dirty cloak away and come here." He extended his arm, opening the folds of his own dry cloak. "At least the captain was considerate enough not to drag me through the mud with you. I'm dry and my cloak is large enough for both of us."

She looped a dirty lock of hair behind her ear, clearly uncertain. "I—I've only my shift, and that's muddy too."

He smiled up at her, despite the pounding in his head. "We'll manage."

Reluctantly, she tossed her cloak aside. Her shift, sleeves and hem blotched with mud, revealed nothing of her slender frame, yet still she wrapped her arms protectively around her middle.

Robert gave a mirthless chuckle, and immediately wished he hadn't. He closed his eyes against the throbbing. "I'm not bent on rape, milady, I assure you."

He didn't hear her cross to him, but he knew when she stopped in front of him. He opened one eye and looked up at her, and once more spread his cloak in invitation.

Sighing, she settled beside him, then cautiously laid her head on his breast. He shoved her tangled hair aside and pulled his cloak around them, enfolding them in its warmth.

"You'd make a sorry knight, Wardell," she informed him, snuggling closer. "All this whimpering, and for naught but a sore head."

"Indeed?" he said, staring down at the top of her

head. She fit so easily against his body, felt so right. "Then I'm grateful that I'm no more than a merchant, milady, for this head of mine is like to split from the aching."

He'd missed her, he thought muzzily. Missed her warmth and laughter and the fire in her that flared to the fire in him.

What was it they had quarreled about, anyway?

He drew her closer still, then tilted his head back against the wall and closed his eyes against the throbbing pain.

IN THE NARROW band of morning sunlight streaming through an arrow slit, Alyce cleaned the dried and crusted blood from Robert's head. The wound oozed a bit, and he winced, once, as she worked, but he would survive.

She refused his offer of assistance with her own toilet and washed her face as best she could with the dirty, bloodstained water that was left. She could do nothing with her hair but comb it out with her fingers and shove it back. The muddied strands were stiff and clumped together, their bright red color dulled to a faded brown. Never had she wished for her veil and wimple more, and never had they been farther out of reach.

At least Robert had given her his cloak, flinging it around her shoulders in a sweeping arc, then stepping back, away from her, his face inscrutable.

She settled it more comfortably about her, adjusting its folds so that her muddied shift was hidden, her dirty, shoeless feet invisible. When she looked up, he was watching her.

For an instant their gazes met, locked. Then he turned away, jaw muscles bunching, to stare out at the strip of morning that was visible through the arrow slit.

Alyce's fingers curled over the edges of the cloak. In his dark gaze she'd seen no recognition of the night just past, no hint that he remembered her warmth as she remembered his.

If it weren't for the gulf that lay between them, she could go to him, just as she had last night. She could touch his arm, his shoulder, his beard-stubbled cheek. She could—

The sound of footsteps in the passage shattered her self-absorption. Montfort's men come to take them to the earl.

Alyce straightened, thrust her shoulders proudly back. God knew what she looked like. An unwashed waif from the gutter perhaps, a commoner, a whore, but not, she feared, a lady born.

Her grip on Robert's cloak tightened. Oh, most certainly not a lady born.

IT WAS HIS fault she bore those bruises on her face, his fault her hair was dulled and dirty, her shift soiled past redemption, her feet unshod and bloodied.

Robert stared blindly out at the soft blue sky, unable to face Alyce or his guilt for what they'd done to her. Shame twisted in his gut, a sharp-toothed, living thing.

He should have warned her, armed her, left her more men for her defense. He should have planned for such a summons, yet he had not, and he'd left her vulnerable because of it. *He should have, should have, should have—*

The sound of Montfort's men in the passageway was welcome distraction from his bitter self-reproach. He turned as the door was flung open and two glowering guards stomped in, bristling with threat and self-importance.

Robert put aside his guilt and shame. There was no room for any of that now. Not now that Montfort had summoned him and Edward was too far away to help.

"It's about time," he snapped, arrogantly stepping forward. "What kept you?"

• • •

WITH ROBERT AN angry, coolly distant presence at her side, Alyce followed their escort out into the bailey, squinting at the sudden assault of light. Despite her pounding heart and the hard stones beneath her feet, she kept her head high and her tread firm. She might look a muddy wreck, but she would give no one the chance to call her coward.

It wasn't easy to hide her fear. The central White Tower gleamed in the morning sun as if grateful to have shed the night's heavy mists, but the high walls and towers that formed the outer limits of the great fortress loomed gray and forbidding against the pale blue sky, grim reminders of the power wielded by whoever controlled their heights.

To her surprise, their destination was not the public rooms in the White Tower, as she had supposed, but a high-roofed stable that had been built against an inner wall. Instead of the usual smells of a stable, the sharp stench of urine and rotted meat assaulted her nostrils, and beneath that . . .

Nose wrinkling in distaste, Alyce sniffed the air, trying to identify the dark scent that underlaid it all. A ferocious roar unlike anything she had ever heard came from inside. She faltered, but Robert urged her forward.

"It's only the king's wild beasts," he said, "and his lion and bears are caged. They can't hurt you."

She stopped so abruptly that he was half a dozen paces beyond her before he realized she was no longer beside him. He turned and came back to her. Their guards scowled as if they intended to drag her forward by force.

She ignored them. "A lion? A *real* lion?"

Robert blinked at her sudden enthusiasm, then grinned and thumped the end of her nose with the tip of his finger. "A *real* lion. A leopard too, and I mistake me not. The beast of the changeable spots."

This time, Alyce led the way, the guards and Mont-fort's summons forgotten.

After the sunlit bailey, the barn was dark, the air heavy with an unholy animal stench that made her eyes burn and her nose twitch. None of it mattered. Right in front of her, regally sprawled on the floor of its iron-barred oak cage, was the animal of legend, the great beast she had seen on battle flags and banners, on shields and coats of arms and seals and rings and, oh! a hundred other things. Rumor had not lied. King Henry did indeed keep a lion in his great Tower.

In a cage beside it, a leopard paced. It was smaller than the lion, leaner, yet what it lacked in size and power it more than made up for in deadly grace. As if sensing her regard, it stopped and turned its head to stare at her with its ferocious amber gaze. Alyce stared back, enthralled.

"Impressive beasts, are they not?"

She looked up, startled, to find a handsome, gimlet-eyed man of fifty or so watching her in amused interest. His powerful build and practical garb proclaimed him a warrior, but he leaned on a wooden staff, one hip cocked to take his weight off his leg, which seemed to pain him. A handful of men stood behind him and on the ground at his feet sat a basin, heaped high with massive chunks of raw meat.

Alyce had never met the man, but there was no mis-taking Simon de Montfort, Earl of Leicester.

"My lord." She sank into a stiff curtsy, blushing fiercely at being caught gawking like an ignorant peasant.

"Madame." His sharp gaze took in her muddied hair and dirty face, slid down over the too-large cloak to fix on her feet.

Alyce followed his gaze downward. Her right foot peeked out from beneath her borrowed cloak. The great toe was bloodied where she'd stubbed it the night before. Her blush deepened as she twitched the hem of the cloak around to cover it.

Montfort looked away, his expression bland. "And you, I trust, are Robert Wardell?"

Robert nodded. His eyes sparked with anger, but his voice was coldly restrained when he spoke. "I am."

Montfort eyed the ugly lump at the side of Robert's head. "I am told my men were rather . . . forceful at inducing you to come. Far more forceful than I'd intended. For that, I am sorry."

Robert's gaze hardened. "Your men might as easily have taken my gardener for all the courtesies they expended on introductions."

"I wanted to talk to you."

"That's scarcely justification for your men attacking my house and people, insulting and injuring my wife, and damn near killing me."

Montfort's eyes narrowed. He seemed to be debating whether to apologize or have Robert thrown into chains on the spot.

"It was a mistake, Wardell," he said at last. "A mistake for which I am heartily sorry."

Alyce's stomach churned at the angry exchange. The two men were as intimidating as the caged beasts at her back, and just as hazardous. Two proud men with every reason to distrust the other. The difference was, Montfort had power, wealth, privilege, and armed men behind him. Robert had only his wits and anger. It was a dangerously uneven match.

She put her hand on Robert's arm in warning. Outwardly, he seemed in control of himself and his fury, but his muscles jumped beneath her hand as if he fought the urge to strike the earl.

"Though I would have preferred a more mannerly

invitation to the Tower, my lord," she said, "I must have come sooner or late. No one else has been able to give me news of my father and brother."

"Your father and brother?" Montfort frowned, studying her face. "Ah, I remember. You're Fitzwarren's daughter, are you not?"

She nodded. Her chest constricted painfully, as if her ribs had suddenly grown too tight. "Do you know of his fate, my lord? His and my brother's, Sir Hubert's?"

"They yet live, milady, that is all I know. Edward handed his noble prisoners over to his Marcher Lords for safekeeping. I do not know who holds Sir Fulk or your brother." He shrugged. "Not that it matters greatly, for Edward refuses ransom. He'll not let them go till this is ended."

They lived! Relief made her ribs expand. She sucked in air, fighting dizziness. They might be wounded, hungry, held in a cramped prison cell—it did not matter so long as they were alive.

Montfort frowned. "I had thought you must have had word of them long since. Surely—"

He stopped as his gaze swung to Robert. Whatever he'd meant to say died unspoken.

Alyce's grip on the edge of her cloak tightened. No need for him to explain. She hadn't had word because her husband was Edward's supporter, not Montfort's.

Robert met the earl's gaze squarely. "I trust you summoned me for something other than the pleasure of a night spent sleeping on cold stone, milord. I've not yet broken my fast and I find it difficult to be civil on an empty belly."

Montfort's eyes narrowed. "They said you were a proud man and not inclined to give your betters their due."

"I always give my betters their due, milord. Unfortunately, I am little practiced in the art for I've not met many of them."

Alyce tensed, but Montfort laughed. "You're a haughty bastard, Wardell."

"And one who knows his own worth. An earl you may be, milord, and an honest man, but while I might forget the injuries done to me, I will not forget nor easily forgive the harm that was done my wife."

The earl glanced back at her, his gaze sweeping from muddied hair to bloodied feet in one great arc. "I would kill the man who had treated my wife thus."

Robert smiled. Alyce had seen wolves with sweeter smiles. "I have thought of it, milord, believe me."

Montfort eyed him pensively, then bent and picked up a chunk of raw meat from the basin at his feet. He tossed it through the bars of the lion's cage. The beast roared a challenge, then snatched up the piece and retreated to the far side of the cage. Alyce would hear the rending sound as it ripped the meat from the bone.

The smell of fresh meat roused the leopard, who roared out its hunger. It slipped a paw through the bars, futilely swiping at the meal that lay just out of reach. Its claws gleamed white and deadly.

"The lion is King Henry's beast." Montfort stared at the feeding cat, which kept a wary eye on the humans who stood just beyond its reach. "It can gut a man with one blow. It's more powerful than I am. Stronger, faster, more deadly. Yet it is caged. Without someone to toss it meat, it would starve."

Robert's gaze was fixed on the earl. "And with the help of others to set it free, it would destroy you." Robert wasn't talking about the lion any more than Montfort was.

The earl raised his head to meet Robert's stare. "Or destroy those who set it free. It has no loyalty. Certainly not to any lesser being, not even to other creatures who are its equal. It is as like to turn against the man who helps it as it is to turn against me."

"But it is you the creature eyes, milord, and if it is free

to hunt, rumor says it will share its prize with those who
aided it."

"A man would be wise to mistrust such tales."

"I do," Robert said. "But I know that few beasts hunt
alone, milord. They have need of their followers, and well
they know it."

Montfort shifted his grip on the staff he held. His fingers curled around the polished wood like the talons of a
hawk around its perch. The men behind him stirred restlessly, but he waved them into stillness.

"You have rather more fire in you than do others of
your ilk, Wardell," Montfort said at last. "But you are a
London merchant still, and it is I, not Henry or Edward,
who control London."

Robert shrugged. "True. But I do not think you will
control it forever, milord."

He bent and picked a bloody shoulder joint from
the basin, hefting the meat like a housewife judging its
value, then tossed it to the leopard. The beast shrank
back, snarling. The lion roared a challenge. The leopard
growled back, then dug its claws into the meat and pulled
it to him.

"They say a leopard can change its spots," Montfort
said with the air of a man sharing an interesting tale.

Robert pulled a handkerchief out of the purse at his
belt and carefully cleaned the blood from his fingers. "So
they say. But I've had no experience of it, milord. Were I
you, I would not place too much faith in such reports."

The earl's face darkened. "Enough of this word play,
Wardell. I know that you are the leader of those in London
who oppose me. I would not care for that, for I do not concern myself with the business of merchants, but I do not
like to leave dangerous men at my back unwatched. Especially not when they provide so much of the gold and silver that Edward uses to war against me."

"Since you will have it with the hair on, then, milord."

Robert tossed the bloodstained handkerchief aside. "I agree with much of what you and your followers fight for, but Henry is the king and the Lord Edward is his son. So long as our leaders are chosen by birth, not ability, we must make do with what God sends us. Henry has been a weak king—and, no, I do not forget that he is your brother-in-law—but Edward will make a strong, shrewd one. And he understands the value of trade as his father does not. If I can help end this warring among you by helping finance Edward's forces, then I will do it, and no one save God Himself can prevent me."

To Alyce, it felt as if the very ground beneath her feet had grown dangerously soft and treacherous. Robert risked everything with his defiance. There was nothing to stop Montfort from confiscating his property and casting him into the darkest cell in the Tower—nothing except her family connections, and there was no guarantee the earl would respect even that.

Montfort seemed to have forgotten her existence.

"I do not concern myself with trade, Wardell, but with England," he snapped. His grip tightened on his staff, until Alyce wondered if he would break it.

"England *is* its trade, my lord," Robert shot back. "It is trade, not great men in fine castles, that keeps England alive. A shepherd may tend his sheep, but he will die of cold without the weaver to turn his wool into cloth. Nobles like you control the land, but without the men to work your fields and build your castles and make your armor, you would live naked in the forest, scrounging for food. Without markets for the produce of your manors you would have no gold to pay the soldiers who march at your call and die at your feet. And without the soldiers, you would have no means to hold the land you gain with their blood."

"You have a damnably high opinion of yourself, it seems."

"I do." He leaned closer to Montfort, jaw thrust

forward. "A merchant could survive without men such as you, milord, but you could not survive without us. Nay, we would flourish if we were not taxed to finance your power nor troubled by your quarreling and your wars."

Alyce gasped and shut her eyes against the inevitable slaughter. An eternity passed, then Montfort broke into laughter. Her eyelids snapped up as her mouth dropped open.

Montfort gave Robert a friendly clap on the shoulder. "By God, they had the right of it when they told me you had balls, Wardell!"

Robert eyed him suspiciously.

"I ought to have you flayed for your presumption," Montfort went on, "but I like a man who speaks his mind and isn't likely to change his colors at the first threat of trouble."

He turned and gestured to one of his men. "Run tell them in the kitchens that I want ale and meat and good bread set out for Master Wardell and his lady wife. And have their horses saddled and an escort prepared to accompany them when they're ready to leave."

"So we're free?" Robert asked, still suspicious. "Just like that?"

"Oh, not just like that. I'll have you watched, Wardell, be sure of it. No doubt I should have had you watched ere now. But don't forget that I control most of the Cinque Ports"—Montfort smiled with dry amusement—"*and* the port warehouses where your goods are stored, waiting for you to carry them to London. That should be sufficient surety for your good behavior."

Robert grunted dismissively, but Alyce sensed that Montfort's threat hit far harder than her husband would care to admit.

"There are limits," Montfort added significantly, "even to the debts I owe your wife's father. I would advise you not to forget it."

"I trust you don't expect me to say I'm grateful for this little . . . interview, milord."

The leopard behind him snarled in perfect counterpoint to his defiance. Montfort's lips twitched as turned his attention to Alyce.

"What think you of the king's playthings, milady?" he asked.

"I'd heard tales of them, my lord," she said, grateful for the change of subject, "but I'd thought the half of them nothing more than myth."

"And the tale bearers drunk, or mad, or both?"

She nodded, remembering other incredible tales she'd heard, and peered into the shadowed depths of the building. "I've heard it said there is a . . . an effelunt? A great beast, taller than a house and with a nose like a snake." She wasn't sure if she sounded more like a credulous villein or a prying fool.

"Indeed there was. It died a few years back. Seemingly the creature couldn't bear our clime, though there are those who say it died of a broken heart at being chained here, alone of all its kind." His tone was sardonic, as if he were amused by so strange a notion.

Alyce didn't find the idea so strange. She knew what it was to be apart from her own kind, and never more so than now when she seemed trapped between two worlds, and alien to both. She could sense Robert's gaze upon her, but she kept her attention on the caged beasts, which had finished the first chunks of meat and were hungrily eyeing the pieces that remained in the basin.

"Be that as it may," the earl continued, "the animal was just as you describe, milady. Taller than a house, and wide, and with a nose that could pick an apple off the ground and bring it to its mouth."

"My lord?" said Alyce doubtfully. She did not care to call the earl a liar, but a nose that could pick up apples?

There was reason in all things, and that tale did not sound at all reasonable to her.

"On my honor, lady! There was also a great white bear that came from a land that is snow and ice all year round."

Alyce stiffened, wondering if she was being played for a fool.

"I saw the beast myself, milady," he assured her. "It was wont to swim in the Tower's moat and catch fish for its meal."

Alyce snorted. "The bear I can believe, for I've seen other animals, even humans, born without color to their skin. But snow and ice all year round, my lord? Surely God would order things more sensibly than that."

Montfort smiled. "I confess, I've not seen it myself, but I have met men who swear that such a place exists. And the bear was no normal beast sapped of color, but truly white." He shrugged. "There are some things a man must take on faith, milady. I would as soon believe there's such a place as I would believe that elephants copulate back to back."

Alyce couldn't help but laugh. "They *could* not! Could they?"

"Without a female, it was impossible to tell. But the beast's keeper swore it was so, that he had seen it with his own eyes."

"Eyes can deceive, my lord," Robert said harshly, breaking in. "As can everything—and *everyone*—else."

Alyce looked up, startled by the sudden vehemence in his voice.

Alan of Hensford stood in the doorway, eyeing Robert with the unhappy air of a man who'd just been presented with a lively pig when he'd hoped for a well-roasted joint.

HOME AGAIN, HOME AGAIN

HIS HEAD THROBBED, his empty belly squeezed unpleasantly against his backbone, and his muscles still ached from a night spent sleeping on cold, hard stone, yet Robert Wardell was a happy man.

Now that Alyce knew her father and brother still lived and that Edward would not release them until the war was over, she'd have to admit that he had not lied, that there was nothing he could have done to help them. She would have to let him back into her bed. Into *his* bed, by God!

He'd refused Montfort's offer of food and ale, but accepted the loan of a horse for Alyce and an escort home. He hadn't cared to linger to taste the earl's belated hospitality because he wanted bread from his own kitchens and ale from his own cup. He wanted a bath, a shave, and clean clothes.

Most of all, he wanted his wife.

He glanced at her. Her head was up, her gaze fixed on the street in front of her, but she had the vacant look of a woman who had withdrawn into her own thoughts and forgotten the world around her. Forgotten him.

So long as she forgave him for not protecting her, he didn't mind, for he could make her remember him quick enough, make her remember his touch and the way she felt when he was lodged deep inside her. He would make sure she remembered, for right now he needed to have her safe and warm against him so he could forget what his lack of foresight had cost her.

Somehow he would make it all up to her. He swore it. He just hoped she'd believe him when he did.

A scruffy beggar darted into his path, hand outstretched for alms. Robert fished in his purse for a penny, but one of Montfort's men had already swung his horse into the fellow's path, mailed fist raised to strike. The beggar shrank back, cursing, then snatched a clot of mud and dung off the street and flung it after them.

The man's aim was off. The dirt sailed harmlessly past them to splat against a peddler's wheelbarrow on the opposite side of the street. The guard laughed, the peddler swore, and the beggar retreated into an alleyway and disappeared.

Perhaps it was just hunger, but as Robert watched him go, his empty belly turned over in protest.

So much for good intentions.

ALYCE FOLLOWED THE escort Montfort had provided through the streets of London, but she was blind and deaf to the sights and sounds around her. Her nose was still filled with the scent of rotted meat and dangerous beasts, her ears with the words of dangerous men. It was Robert's face she saw before her, not the jostling strangers who shoved in front of them. Robert's mouth drawn into a forbidding line, his eyes hard and expressionless as he listened to Montfort's veiled threats and Hensford's swaggering taunts.

She felt a fool for having prated about wild beasts after Montfort had smiled and threatened Robert with destruction. She was, in truth, doubly a fool. Just because her husband had not taken up arms, she'd thought him safe from this war that ripped at England's heart. Last night's en-counter had taught her different. Small wonder that the relief she'd felt when Montfort had laughed and let Robert go had loosed both her tongue and wits.

Her tongue had stilled quick enough when Hensford appeared. Sneering, arrogant, and sly, he'd made his bow to Montfort, smirked over her bruised and muddied state, then casually talked of his recent visit to the Cinque Ports, a trip he'd taken at Montfort's behest.

"There are rumors of looting in some of the ware-houses," he'd said, his expressions cruelly gloating. "I saw no proof of it, but it would not be surprising if there weren't some losses here and there. Wouldn't you agree, Wardell?"

Robert had feigned indifference, but Alyce had seen the angry tension beneath the mask. He held several ship-ments in warehouses at the ports, foreign cloth he hadn't been able to bring into London and could ill afford to lose. For the moment, Montfort's forces controlled most of the ports and the land between them and the city. Not a good time for a known supporter of Edward to risk hauling a rich load of cloth along the roads, not even with armed guards, and Hensford knew it.

Montfort had watched the exchange between the two men. Alyce was certain the quarrels of merchants mat-tered little to him when he made war against a king and a prince, but merchants were a useful source of money, and money was often in short supply during war. Support the merchants who financed him and he strengthened the forces at his command. Destroy the merchants who fi-nanced the king and prince and he struck a blow against them as if he'd raised his sword in battle.

The earl might respect Robert and dislike Hensford, but that wouldn't stop him from supporting one and bringing down the other. He'd scarcely notice if he tram-pled both of them beneath his feet. War destroyed too much for the fates of two London merchants to weigh much in the balance.

A clot of mud sailing past her horse's nose made the beast start and jig to one side, rousing Alyce from her dark thoughts. One of the guards escorting them had raised his mailed fist at a beggar, but the man darted into an alley and out of reach before threat could be transformed into action.

She hunched deeper into her borrowed cloak, chilled by the thought of how easily her world could fall into pieces at her feet. Unlike the beggar, neither she nor Robert could slip into a convenient alley to avoid the blows that were aimed at them. Monfort's men had proven that last night, and Hensford had reinforced the lesson not an hour since.

She glanced at Robert, seeking reassurance, but he didn't notice. He was far too intent on his own thoughts to heed her or her worries.

WARDELL HOUSE HAD shut its face against the world. The gate was barred, the shutters closed. One of their escort dismounted to pound on the gate. "Ho, there! Open up!"

The wicket slammed open and a face appeared in the grilled opening. At sight of Montfort's colors, the face twisted into a ferocious snarl.

"To the devil with you. You'll not come in, not if Earl Simon hisself was to ask it!"

"But if I command it?" Robert moved his mount to the front so Newton could see him more clearly.

"Master Wardell!"

"Open the gate."

Newton slammed the wicket shut. They heard a muffled shout, a clatter as the heavy oak bar was lifted, then the gate swung open. Newton held it for them. Blood-stained bandages swathed his head. He bore a heavy club in his hands and he eyed Montfort's men like the lion in Henry's tower had eyed the meat in Montfort's basin—as if he would happily devour them in a single gulp if they came within his reach.

With Alyce right behind him, Robert rode through the gate and into a milling confusion of people and horses. It took him a moment to realize that not all the people and the horses were his.

"My lady! Alyce!" A stout woman he recognized as one of Alyce's women from Colmaine broke free of the crowd and charged toward her, arms outstretched.

"Maida!" Alyce was out of the saddle before anyone could take her horse.

"Oh, milady!"

"And Hilde!" she cried as a dried-up wisp of a woman darted forward in the wake of the fat one.

"Your head!" the first one shrieked. "Who struck you? Where's the beast? I'll soon show *him* a thing or two."

"No, no. I'm fine." Alyce hastened to soothe her. "It's not so bad. More mud than anything and—" The rest was lost in the clamorous din as his people and Alyce's crowded about, jabbering and asking questions until not one could be heard above the uproar.

Robert watched Alyce's tearful, laughing reunion and felt his heart sink. She hadn't spoken a word to him since they'd ridden away from the Tower, and now that she had her people from Colmaine, she seemed to have forgotten him entirely. Or perhaps she meant to punish him for what she'd suffered, for what he'd let them do to her.

Piers abruptly appeared to take his mount. "Milady's people come from Colmaine, master," he said by way of explanation. "Knocked on the gate not half an hour since, wanting in."

Robert dismounted. "I recognized the serving women. Milady seems pleased enough to see them." He wondered if his voice sounded as flat and lifeless to Piers as it did to him.

"When they heard that my lady had been dragged away by Montfort's men"—Piers cocked his head to indicate the women who'd rushed to Alyce—"the wailing they set up must have roused folk for five blocks in all directions."

"You'll not come in!" Newton's angry roar carried clearly, even over the din in the yard. "Not an inch past this gate, I say. You want your master's horse, you wait in the street where you belong until we see fit to give it to you."

"Master Wardell!" Erwyna, chin outthrust and elbows at the ready, descended the steps from the hall and headed toward him. One officious fellow from Colmaine made the mistake of trying to detain her.

"Out of my way, fool," she snapped, shoving him aside. "The master's back and *he's* the one will say what's what, not you!"

"She's been like that ever since the fat one from Colmaine shrieked at her for letting milady be taken away," Piers said with relish, clearly enjoying the commotion.

"Here," Robert said, thrusting the reins into the boy's hands. He squeezed his eyes shut against the throbbing in his head. "Take the horse, then do what you can to settle all this. I want a cup of wine before I hear any more. A very large cup of wine."

DESPITE THE CONFUSION and the shock of finding her two old friends waiting for her, Alyce knew when Robert brushed aside half a dozen clamoring retainers and made his way into the hall. His face looked carved of stone and he moved as though a thick oak board had taken the place of his spine.

Headache, she told herself. That's all it was. Headache and the weariness that comes of spending a night sleeping on cold stone. Besides, he didn't need her. There was nothing she could do for him that someone else couldn't do just as well. Bathe and bandage his head, bring him a cup of ale, a bit of meat and bread.

He certainly didn't seem concerned about her. He hadn't so much as glanced her way since they'd ridden in the gate. No doubt he was glad to leave her in the care of her women so he could deal with the other, more important matters.

Alyce set her jaw, forced her mouth into a smile, and resolutely turned to settling the confusion that reigned around her. It didn't take much to sort things out. A boy sent to the kitchen with a message that there would be another dozen for supper. Orders to Newton to return Earl Simon's horse to his men so they would go away and leave them in peace; to Joshua to stable as many of the horses from Colmaine as he could and find accommodations in a public stable for the rest; to a hostile Erwyna to have ale brought for the guests, a meal prepared, and water heated for a bath for her. The familiar habit of command relieved her of the effort of thinking and feeling. If she was busy with ordering others about, she would not have time to worry about Robert.

"Come," she said at last to Maida and Hilde. "We'll go upstairs to my bedchamber, have Githa light a fire and bring you some wine to drink. I know you must be tired."

"Aye, but it's you is most in need of wine," Maida scolded. Dark circles ringed her eyes and her face sagged almost as much as her shoulders, but she took refuge from her weariness by ordering her lady about.

"If I didn't know better," Hilde added, "I'd think Earl Simon's men had dragged you through the mud." Her joints would be aching from the hard journey, Alyce knew, but there was a stout heart in that scrawny little body and Hilde wasn't any more willing to give in than Maida.

"Shameful, that's what it is. Shameful, to treat a lady so. And her a daughter of one of Earl Simon's own men!"

Alyce smiled, grateful that *someone* worried about her even if Robert did not. "Come, then. We'll leave the others to take care of the details."

They willingly followed her into the hall.

"A little small," said Maida. "You'll not seat more than a hundred here, and then only if you pack them like salt cod in a barrel."

"Two fireplaces?" said Hilde. "A great waste of firewood *that* must be."

Maida surreptitiously stirred the rushes with her toes. All fresh, and not a dog bone in sight. Alyce thought of the packed rushes of Colmaine's hall, and smiled. All the way up the stairs they poked and peered like curious cats, clearly impressed in spite of themselves.

"Stained glass?" Maida exclaimed. "In a *solar*? I've only ever seen it in a church."

"And two beds?" she added. Colmaine's solar had boasted of no more than a wooden platform with a pallet thrown on top.

But it was the fireplace in Alyce's bedchamber that made both their eyes go wide.

"Town ways," said Hilde, nodding wisely. "I've heard tales of how soft the living is."

Maida gaped, struck dumb by the luxury of a curtained bed and fine silk bed coverings. "Stained glass here as well," she murmured. "And painted wall hangings. And one, two, *three* wax candles. No, four!"

Alyce couldn't stop a small, wry smile, remembering her own astonishment. The room was a far cry from the cold, narrow chamber with its lumpy bed and patched and mended covers that the three of them had shared for so many years. How quickly she'd forgotten!

"But what's this?" Hilde demanded suspiciously.

Alyce's smile widened, despite her aching head. "Carpets from Castile. Just like the ones the Lady Eleanor brought with her when she wed the Lord Edward."

The two women plopped onto the stools, awed and overwhelmed by the unexpected luxuries. Alyce took the chair. She felt very tired suddenly, and older than her years. "You know about Father? And Hubert?"

Maida broke off her inspection of the fireplace and nodded. "We'd word they were taken at Northampton, but nothing since then."

"There's trouble come to Colmaine, milady," Hilde added. "That's why we're here. With all the men-at-arms gone off with your father and no castellan and only Thomas Gibbons to steward . . ." She shook her head, her wrinkled face screwed up with worry.

"The king's men know your father supported Montfort and there's fear they'll take advantage now your father's prisoner of the king," Maida said bluntly. "Taken all in all, Thomas decided Colmaine could do without its bailiff for a few weeks, so he's sent Richard to you to ask for help. We made him let us come along."

She hesitated and her round face grew rosy under its cover of dust from five days' travel. "We've missed you, milady," she continued, almost apologetically. "Everyone's missed you, but Hilde and me, we've missed you most of all. We had to come, make sure you were all right."

Hilde nodded vigorously. "We couldn't decide between us which was to come, so we both of us packed up our things and told Richard we were coming with him."

"He didn't argue overmuch," Maida added. "Fair strange it's seemed without you at Colmaine, milady. Without a word from you—"

"Without a word?" Alyce latched on to the one thing in this spate of words for which she had an answer. "But I sent word to my father. More than once! And there was always a message for you. Had you none of them?"

"Not one!" Hilde said. "But, then, what did you

expect with your lord father packing you off like that, married to a merchant. And look what's become of it. What's become of you!"

Two pairs of eyes raked over her, cataloging each mud-caked strand of hair, every bruise and scrape and cut. Even a curtained bed and four wax candles couldn't make up for her abused and disreputable state.

Alyce flushed under the women's disapproving inspection. Their tally, she knew, would add nothing to Robert's standing in their eyes. They would think he should have protected her, that he should somehow have kept her safe from harm. They wouldn't understand how it had been, and she didn't have the energy to explain.

She shook her head. "Master Wardell has been good to me. More generous than Father ever was and—and kind."

She didn't dare put any more into words, didn't dare admit that she loved him. He had forgotten her, too wrapped up in the concerns of his business to think of her. Perhaps she'd earned his indifference. She'd blamed him for refusing to help her father and brother, barred him from her bed, denied him so much as a pleasant word—all in punishment for having told the truth, that he could not help them no matter how impassioned her pleas on their behalf.

With stern resolve, Alyce set aside her doubts. However glad she was to see these old friends, they had not journeyed all the way from Colmaine just to inquire after her health. She propped her elbows on the chair arms and leaned toward them.

"Tell me about Colmaine," she said. "Tell me everything you know."

A CUP OF wine, two strong draughts of ale, some meat and bread—it wasn't much, but it was enough to pick his belly off his backbone and reduce the pounding in his head to a dull ache. With a quick, cold wash, a shave, and a patch on his battered head, Robert felt more human than he had since he'd awakened as Montfort's guest in the Tower.

Resolutely, he put aside all thought of Alyce. She would be too busy with her women to have time to listen to his awkward explanations and even more awkward apologies. Her bailiff—her father's bailiff, rather—had sought an interview, but Robert had brushed him off for now.

He could guess what had brought them all this way. Colmaine was without its lord and lady. Robert himself had taken the one and the other languished in some dank castle on the Welsh Marches, leaving Colmaine to exist like a dragon without its head—blind, deaf, and dumb. In times of peace it might not have been so great a concern, for castles and manors were often left in the hands of their castellans and stewards. But with war set loose upon England, the dragon needed at least one eye and ear, someone capable of defending it, especially since much of the countryside around Colmaine was held by the king's supporters, not Montfort's.

He knew all this, but there was nothing he could do to help. What did he owe Colmaine or its master, after all? Absolutely nothing! He had taken the daughter to wife and gotten a far better bargain than he had ever hoped for, but there was an end of it. He'd met his end of the agreement; he owed them nothing more. Surely Alyce would not expect it of him.

In the meantime, he had work to do. William and the others needed to know what had happened, needed to know about Montfort's threat and Hensford's innuendo. The report of troubles in the ports wasn't unexpected, but it was thoroughly unwelcome.

Little though he liked the risk, he might have to retrieve his goods himself—his and the others'. If they moved quickly, they might evade the armies swirling across England and the outlaws and scavengers that inevitably followed in an army's wake.

Of course, there was always the chance that the king and Edward would regain control of those crucial ports and all the countryside between them and London. Either that or win the war outright, which would be the best solution altogether. For him and the king, at any rate. He hated to think what penalty the king might exact from the men who'd warred against him . . . or what Alyce would expect him to do if those exactions fell on her father and brother.

Robert shoved the thought aside. He had business to attend to, urgent business, and the sooner he got to it, the better for all concerned.

Yet still he lingered in the hall while his people scurried about setting up trestle tables and benches to accommodate the extra mouths at the meal. His gaze was fixed on the stairs that led to the solar and to Alyce.

She would be busy with her women, perhaps in her bath. Either possibility meant an interruption would be unwelcome, an apology impossible. Did he dare interrupt, regardless?

He took a last gulp of ale and set the tankard aside. His foot was on the first step to the solar when she appeared above him.

"Master Wardell!"

"Milady." He stepped back so she could descend. "I came to see how you fared. I—I wished to beg your pardon for . . . everything. I should have known—should have expected . . ."

The words caught in his throat and tangled on his tongue. There was so much he had to say, so much he *ought* to say, and none of it came out right. The servants in the hall were forgotten.

"Oh." she hovered on the steps, clearly taken aback. "You could not know——"

"But I could have recognized the risk, provided against the unexpected."

She came down five steps so that her head was level with his. This close he could see that dark circles under her eyes, the unhealthy pallor of her skin brought on by weariness and pain. He reached to touch her, but stayed his hand, then let it fall.

"I though perhaps you were in your bath. You ought to be in your bed." He frowned. "Promise me you won't trouble yourself with household concerns until you've rested."

"Githa is helping Maida and Hilde to bathe. I'll have my bath after." She gave a wry little laugh. "As much dirt as I'm wearing, I ought to bathe in the garden like one of Joshua's turnips fresh out of the ground."

He winced. He didn't find the thought amusing.

"Master Wardell?"

His head came up. He would do anything for her to atone for what they'd done to her. "Yes?"

"They came . . . Colmaine. That is, do you——"

Almost anything. He shook his head. "I know why they came, milady. There is nothing I can do to help."

She drew in her breath. "Nothing?"

"No." Then, "I'm sorry."

She didn't say anything, just stood and stared at him, her eyes hollow and dark.

He couldn't bear to see it. "I have business, milady. Urgent business. Perhaps later . . . ?"

"Of course." Her head bobbed up and down as if she were nodding agreement.

The ale in his stomach churned unpleasantly.

"You'll take care?" she said. "Take one of the men with you as escort?"

"Of course. I won't be gone long. A few hours . . ." The words died away. He could not say them. He could not take her in his arms either, or kiss away the doubts he read so plainly in her face.

Instead, he snatched up her hand, holding it against her startled effort to pull free. Her skin was cool against his lips and dry, her fingers roughened instead of soft as a lady's ought to be. He kissed the tips of her fingers, then pressed her hand again and let her go.

"Madame," he said, and bowed. "Forgive me." Then he turned and strode from the hall without a backward glance.

A HOSTILE ERWYNA cornered Alyce in the hall before she had a chance to escape.

"Master Wardell?" Alyce answered her distractedly. "He . . . he's gone out. On business."

"So soon? And after all—?" Erwyna bit off the rest of what she'd meant to say, opened and then closed her mouth. It was the first time Alyce had seen her bereft of words. "Well," she said at last. "Hmmm. Who'd have thought . . . ?"

"Yes. Well, then." Alyce struggled for something to say herself. She still had responsibilities to attend to, tired and hungry people to be fed. "Have supper served as soon as it's ready. There's no telling when he'll return, and I've no doubt our visitors are as hungry as I am."

Erwyna glowered, clearly displeased that the household routine had been disrupted for something so unimportant as a handful of her mistress's people. "Yes, milady. He had a bite to eat, in any case," she added grudgingly. "Some meat and bread and ale."

Of course he had, thought Alyce. He had work to do, after all. He couldn't be expected to do it on an empty belly. "That's good."

Erwyna nodded, but her mind was clearly elsewhere. "The . . . the women who came. Your ladies." She hesitated.

"Yes?"

"We heard, Margaret and me, that they were . . . that is—" The older woman drew in a deep breath as if she were gathering courage to go on. "We heard they were cook and keeper for you at Colmaine and we wondered . . ."

Suddenly, Alyce understood. Erwyna didn't want to put her fears into words in case it made them come true.

"That's true. They raised me from a babe and ran Colmaine while they did it, but they're too old to start over when they know nothing of town ways and even less of a merchant's household. Thank heavens we have you and Margaret to see to things."

She frowned, feigning anxiety. "You're not thinking of leaving us, are you? I couldn't bear to let you go. I don't know where I'd be without you."

No doubt she'd have to allay Githa's fears as well, she realized. Tomorrow, perhaps. She didn't have the energy for it now.

Erwyna swelled with relief, though she tried to make it look like indignation. "Of course not, milady. As if I'd even think of it!"

"I know you'll see everything properly settled," said Alyce. "You'll know best how to maintain Master Wardell's honor with guests from a nobleman's household."

Erwyna's eyebrows arched and her mouth dropped open in a little O. Clearly, she hadn't seen matters in quite that light before. When it came to defending her reputation and the honor of Master Wardell's house, she would spare no effort to see that things were properly arranged.

She bobbed a little curtsy. "Of course, milady. You may depend on me. I'll see to everything."

Alyce smiled weakly and laid her hand on the older woman's arm. "Thank you." She lacked the energy to say more.

"You're tired," Erwyna said, suddenly solicitous. "And I've no doubt your head's about to fall off your shoulders from the aching. Well, get you to your bath, milady. Githa will be waiting. I'll have them brew a posset in the kitchen for you and bring it up myself once I've set all in train."

"That sounds . . . nice."

"Off with you, then," Erwyna said gruffly. "I've work to do and you're in the way."

Alyce turned to leave, then stopped as another thought struck her. "Oh, and Erwyna?"

"Yes?"

"You need not make a special bed for Maida and Hilde. They will be sleeping with me."

UNWILLING
TRUCE

"A LENGTH OF plunket at . . . mmm . . . forty ells the length." Piers looped the cloth from elbow to wrist with the neat efficiency of long practice, then as neatly rolled it up again and returned it to the leather chest that stood open at his feet. He straightened, groaned, and dug his knuckles into the small of his back. "This is the fourteenth chest we've inventoried this morning. How many do you plan to tally?"

Robert frowned at the account roll spread out on the table in front of him, then marked one of the tally sticks on the string he held. "All of them."

Piers stared at the chests stacked behind him. "*All* of them?"

Robert glanced up, face pinched with disapproval. "You had other plans for the morning?"

Piers hesitated, then shook his head. "Not if you didn't."

"Good." Robert turned his attention back to the account roll. "What's the next cloth, then?"

"Another length of plunket." The apprentice dragged the fabric off the mound on the dropcloth. He unrolled it with a snap and rapidly measured it. "Forty-one, no, forty-two ells."

_London, May 1264

"There's no cloth of that length listed on the accounts. Nor one of forty-one ells either. Measure it again."

Piers unhappily measured it again, more carefully this time. "Forty ells, then, just like the last."

Robert made another mark on the notched tally sticks. "And the next?"

Piers picked up another bolt and unrolled it, but cursed and threw it down again before he measured the first ell. "I'll not! It's too much. Too much! One task after another until my head aches and my back's stiff and every bone and muscle in me protests. I might as well be apprenticed to Master Milton for all the joy I get from the work these days. And I'm not the only one!"

With exquisite care, Robert set down his pen, then met his apprentice's angry gaze with an icy one of his own. "If you find the work not to your liking, feel free to seek another master."

"For God's sake, Master Wardell! You've always been fair and just, but these days there's nothing of fairness or justice in anything. You drive us like cattle, glare at us as if we were weevils in the flour, and say scarce one word that's not sharp as a knife and just as cutting."

Robert's jaw hardened. "There's no one kept here against his will."

"No, nor any that wouldn't follow you till Hell froze over, but we're all of us damnably anxious to see you well bedded again before you snap all our heads off and there's no one left to serve you."

"What?"

Piers straightened as if bracing for a blow. "It's not the goods stored in Dover and Rye that are worrying you, nor any of the other things that have the rest of London's merchants in a sweat. You're angry because you no longer share my lady's bed, and you're taking it out on us."

Robert opened his mouth to protest, then just as

quickly closed it. The boy was right, though the Holy Apostles would take up residence in Hell before he would admit it. "Perhaps I have been a little . . . harsh of late."

Piers snorted to show what he thought of that admission.

"It's difficult times—"

"And made more so by the frost that lies between you and my lady. For God's sake, master," he burst out, "have done with it. I have no doubt her ladies would be more than happy to make room for you—"

It was Robert's turn to snort.

"—and feed you oysters to see the job well done! Just last night old Maida was complaining of my lady's temper. Said she'd never seen her so betwattled—"

"Betwattled?"

"That's what she said. You'll have to ask her what it means, though there's none here can't make a guess!"

"I—" Robert bit off his words and threw up his hands instead.

Before Piers could press the issue, calls from outside drew him to the window. He leaned out to get a better look, then turned back, laughing. "It's Master Rareton come home mounted on the greatest slug I've ever seen. He must have walked ten miles just kicking the beast out of a crawl."

A moment later he was out the door without so much as a by-your-leave, leaving Robert to cap his inkhorn and roll up his accounts.

Piers was right, he thought. He had been distempered and sharp-tongued, but he was damned if he'd jump into Alyce's bed just because his apprentice said so.

At least Rareton was back, and none too soon. Robert was heartily sick of doing two men's work to distract himself from his other troubles.

He followed Piers into the yard, arriving in time to

see his steward dismount from the broadest-beamed horse he'd ever seen. A man's legs would ache from the stretch if he had to spend much time atop it.

"Decided to become a knight, have you, Master Rareton?" Piers asked laughingly. "I've seen war-horses smaller than that beast."

"Fit for nothing but a plow, and at that a man would have a hard time seeing the furrow with that fat rump in front of him." Rareton glowered at the beast, which sighed, lifted its tail, and farted. The stable boy giggled and took the reins.

Rareton turned his back on the creature in disgust. "It will be cheaper to send the price of the beast to the Lord Edward than pay a man to ride him back. I'd have been back three days earlier if I could have gotten that— that *thing* out of a flat-footed shamble."

Robert grinned. "Sell him and pocket the coins yourself. I doubt any save Edward's plowman will miss the beast."

"Take care he doesn't step on your foot," Rareton called after the stable boy, "else you'll be crippled for a week."

"I take it this has not been the best of journeys," Robert said.

Rareton glanced at him and as quickly looked away.

Like a man caught in some questionable dealings, Robert thought, then dismissed the idea. "Aside from the horse, you had no troubles?"

"None such as you mean." Before Robert could ask him what he meant by that, he squared his shoulders and added, "We have to talk. I promise you, you're not going to like what I have to say, nor will the Lady Alyce."

ALYCE WAS PICKING at her embroidery when Githa brought her word of Robert's summons. She didn't know whether to be glad he still remembered she existed, or irritated that he hadn't carried his message in person.

She settled for a curt acknowledgment and sent Githa to inform him she would be down directly. Her temper these days was none too sweet and she had to remember that it wasn't anyone's fault she was unhappy expect hers. Hers and Robert's.

The embroidery fell from her hands unheeded. She wanted him back in her bed. She wanted the coldness between them ended, the distance between them wiped away, but she wasn't certain how to manage it without making a fool of herself in the process. What was she to do? Plead with him like some lovesick maid or blatantly try to seduce him like a she-cat in heat? Her pride would permit neither, and she had too little experience to know any other way save stripping naked and throwing herself in his bed.

His bed. She sighed. *She* slept in his bed these days, and either Maida or Hilde slept with her, sometimes both. She'd shared a bed with the two women since she was a small child, but she now found their presence irksome and longed for nothing more than to boot them out and drag Robert back to her, whether he wanted to come or no.

She suspected he didn't. He'd been cross as a bear for days and so engrossed with business that he seemed to have forgotten her entirely. She couldn't even count on his presence at mealtimes when she might at least have shared a cup of wine with him, or had a chance to tell him of her day and listen to his tales of his.

Ah, well. If wishes were fishes, then beggars would dine like kings. If she didn't want to keep him waiting she'd do well to bestir herself.

From a chest beside the bed she retrieved the mirror he had given her. A short inspection revealed her nose was clean, her wimple sparkling white, and not one lock of hair worked free.

Alyce frowned, studying her image in the reflective glass.

He'd said once he loved her eyes. She knew he loved her hair for he had often brushed it for her, delighting in undoing her heavy braids and combing out the tangled curls until they sparked and glowed like fire.

With sudden decision, she set the mirror down, ripped off her veil and wimple, and dug in the chest for one of the silken hair nets he'd given her and she'd never worn. It was the work of a moment to refasten her braids, then bind them in the net; a little longer to adjust the linen band that went under her chin and the fillet that went around her brow. Perhaps with more practice . . .

She picked up the mirror and studied the effect, then sighed. She'd never be a beauty. Not like his first wife had been if Erwyna was to be believed. But if he liked her hair and eyes . . .

What about her nose? She tilted the mirror and turned her head. Her nose wasn't too bad either, if she ignored the freckles that stained its crest. And her mouth? She pursed her lips, tried a smile, a feminine pout, then sighed again and set the mirror down. There wasn't a drop of hope for her mouth or her freckle-spotted complexion or her too-long neck.

Her tunic and kirtle were clean, donned fresh that morning. No dirt showed beneath her nails, no mud splotched her shoes. A last check to be sure the hair net was in place and she was as ready as she'd ever be.

Alyce smoothed her damp palms over her skirts, then went to see what Robert wanted.

He was where Githa had said he would be, with John Rareton in his workroom. The grim expressions on their faces made her own heart sink. She locked her fingers together to keep them from trembling. "Master Wardell? You summoned me?"

"Madame, I did." He stood and offered her his chair. "John has brought word of your father and brother. I thought you would want to hear it."

He saw her seated, then turned away and crossed to the window that overlooked the yard. Bracing his hands on the timbers at either side, he looked out at the lengthening afternoon shadows.

Alyce stared after him, shaken by the violence she sensed within him. Of a sudden, air seemed scarce and what there was of it burned her throat and refused to move into her lungs. She turned her frightened gaze on Rareton, unable to speak.

"No, no, milday. It's not what you think," he hastened to assure her. "In fact, Sir Fulk emerged from the fighting unscathed. Your brother has a slight wound in his left shoulder, but is expected to heal. Is healed already if what my source told me is true."

She closed her eyes and sucked in air, then slowly let it out again. Montfort had not lied.

Then thought returned, and with it came more doubts. "That's not all you learned."

He shook his head, clearly reluctant to share his secrets with her. There was a brittleness about the man that frightened her, as if he walked, talked, and breathed by force of will alone.

"The rest is not so cheering, I'm afraid," he said. "They are both prisoners of Roger Mortimer and likely to remain so for some time to come. Edward has allowed no ransom. He prefers to keep Montfort's fighting men safely under lock and key so long as this war drags on."

Precisely as Robert had said he would. "And is it likely to drag on long?"

Rareton shrugged. "I cannot say, milady, nor can any man. It's a brutal war they fight and likely to be more brutal before it's done."

Her fingers laced together tighter, the nails digging into the skin on the back of her hands. "That's not all, is it?" she asked when Rareton kept silent.

The man drew back, uncertain.

Robert turned from the window. "Tell her, John. Tell her everything." The words seemed ripped from between his teeth.

Rareton swallowed, then nervously dragged one hand across his beard-stubbled cheek. Alyce could hear the rasp of it in the silence. He deliberately looked away, unable to face her. A muscle beneath his right eye twitched uncontrollably.

"*Tell* her."

Instinct drove her to reach across the table and lay her hand upon his arm. It was the only comfort she could offer, perhaps the only comfort he could offer her, to let her touch him. "For your sake, Master Rareton, perhaps as much as mine."

For a moment he stared at nothing. Then, like a millstone slowly grinding to a halt, his jaw hardened.

"They've taken Colmaine, my lady."

"What? Colmaine? Surely . . ." Her hand fell away.

"Roger Lincoln and his men. They've taken Colmaine. They sapped a corner of the curtain wall. When the wall fell, they took the keep and everyone in it."

"Sir Roger took Colmaine?"

What corner of the curtain wall had he sapped? she wondered. The entire structure was crumbing, the victim of time and Sir Fulk's years of niggardly management. It couldn't have been much of a job to tunnel under the stone and bring a portion of the wall crashing down. Why hadn't he just stormed the gate? No one had been left at Colmaine who could have defended it for long. Surely that would have been easier.

Her brain spun, latching onto useless details. Then it stopped spinning and settled on the one question whose answer she did not want to hear. "The people— *My* people. Are they— Surely they didn't try to resist?" With each word her voice grew higher, shriller, closing on the edge of panic. "They had no weapons. They were just old men and boys and women. Not soldiers. None of them were soldiers."

Once more she grabbed hold of his sleeve, but this time it was to compel an answer, not to comfort. "*Tell* me they did not fight!"

John Rareton shook his head. "No, milady. They did not fight. But—" He stopped, choking on the words.

"But?"

"But Sir Roger was one of the men who took Northampton." For the first time he faced her squarely. She could see tears glistening in his eyes. The last of his defenses were down, letting the ugly truth pour out. "My niece was at Northampton. She wasn't supposed to be, but she'd taken a cow to the market there. Once she was within the city walls, she was refused permission to leave."

"Your niece," said Alyce, dreading where the tale might go, yet needing to know, regardless.

"My only sister's daughter." His mouth twisted horribly. A tear spilled down his cheek. "They killed her, milady. The Lord Edward's men, they killed her along with all the others when they sacked the city. They took her and they raped her, and then they slit her throat and left her lying in her own blood with her skirts hiked up around her waist as though she counted for nothing at all to anyone."

His jaw worked. "Those are the men who hold Colmaine, milady. Edward's men. Edward's *murderers*."

"Oh, God." The words came out as a whisper. She couldn't get anything else past the constriction in her throat. "Oh, my God."

"God had very little to do with it, milady." Robert's voice cut through the burning silence like a sword through silk.

She turned to face him but found no comfort there. His face was hewn of granite, expressionless save for the dangerous glitter of his eyes. Her hands lifted as if of their own accord, pleading for what she already knew he could not give her. "Surely there is something—"

He shook his head.

Her hands dropped back into her lap. "No, of course not. There is nothing anyone can do, is there?"

"There's something *I* can do." Rareton shoved to his feet. His face had frozen into the same hard lines as Robert's. A tear glinted on his cheek, caught in the stubble of his beard.

Suddenly, like a man gone mad, he kicked aside his stool. With an icy violence that was more frightening than any red-eyed rage she'd ever seen, he bent and with one great heave swept pens, inkhorn, and account rolls off the table and onto the floor. The inkhorn shattered, splattering ink over parchment, paper, and floor.

"John!"

Rareton stood panting over the wreckage, eyes wild, mouth pulled back in terrifying mockery of a grin. "I'll join Montfort's army, by God. I'll show those murdering bastards. I'll show them!"

"Don't be a fool!" In three steps Robert was by his side. He grabbed his shoulders, pulling him around. "It's madness, John. War is for men who are bred to it, not men like you and me. You can't bring your niece back to life by throwing away your own!"

Rareton wrenched free of Robert's grip and stumbled back. "I never agreed with you, Wardell. I told you that. Didn't I tell you that? It's Montfort you should have supported, not Edward. *Not Edward.*"

He swiped his sleeve across his mouth, wiping away the spittle. "You can't stop me. I'm not bound to you."

Robert drew a ragged breath of his own. His hands worked, opening and closing as he fought for calm. "No, you're not bound to me. But it's madness, even so."

Rareton eyed him, then Alyce. And then he laughed.

Alyce shuddered. That was how the damned in hell might laugh, loud and long and bitterly.

"You did want to know, my lady," he said. "You told me you did want to know."

An instant later he was gone. The sound of his boots on the stairs echoed hollowly, then the door screeched open and slammed shut, leaving Alyce to stare at Robert in the sudden silence.

A THOUSAND EXPLANATIONS chased one another through his brain, a hundred thousand words. Robert found he could not grab hold of one of them.

Instead, he stood admidst the wreckage John Rareton had left behind him, gazing at his wife.

She'd gone pale, so pale that every freckle stood out clearly on her skin. Her eyes were wide and frightened as she stared back, a thousand questions lurking in their depths. No more than he, could she give voice to everything that remained unsaid between them. He hadn't the courage for it. He doubted she had the strength.

His loans had financed Edward and his men, his money had paid for weapons and horses and men. His.

That there were others who had given far more did not matter. Nor did it matter that Edward would have found the money elsewhere if Robert had not provided it, or that Montfort's men were just as capable of rape and murder as Edward's, nor even that Sir Fulk would as gladly have taken Sir Roger's lands as Sir Roger had taken his. What mattered was that *he* had raised the money, made the loans, backed Edward.

Like Roger Lincoln, he'd sapped the foundations of Fitzwarren family power and brought everything

Alyce valued crashing down so that it lay in dusty rubble at her feet.

With a groan, Robert turned back to the window and stared blindly out at the sun, whose waning light shone yellow over the roof of his great hall.

What had he done? Sweet Mother of God, what had he *done*?

TWO DAYS HAD passed since John Rareton had returned with the news of Colmaine's fate—two dawns, two dusks, two nights of sleepless misery, and now another dawn.

Alyce stared out her bedchamber window at the bright blue sky of a perfect morning and thought how strange it was that everything looked so . . . normal. The world should have been off kilter somehow, the days too short or long, the sun rising in the west and setting in the east—*something* except this too-familiar ebb and flow of hours. Her world lay in shambles on the ground. Why, then, did everything else go on as if nothing had changed nor ever would?

Alyce dropped her gaze to the silver infant's rattle in her hand. Thoughtfully, she twirled it between her fingers, watching the play of light across its polished surface. Mary Townsend had given birth to a lusty man child the night before. Judging by the message bidding them to the christening that morning, William was as pleased as if it were his first son and not his fifth.

His *fifth*.

Her belly ached with a cramping envy. She shook the

rattle. The pebbles sealed inside it made the silver ring—
ping-ping. Ping-ping-ping-ping.

Some changes were worth having after all. A babe,
that's what she wanted. Five fine sons and just as many
daughters, no matter the difficulties of finding dowries for
them all. She would have a dozen babies if she could, yet
her womb was as empty as if she were unwed and virgin
still. And empty it would remain if she continued to exile
Robert from her bed.

She shook the rattle again, savoring the sound. Robert
had ordered it made weeks ago. The silver had been hammered thin, then worked with exquisite care, a *T* engraved
on the side and the braided silver handle looped in a
teardrop shape so a small child could hold it. She had
knotted the silken ribbons around the base, but it was
Robert's gift, not hers.

He needn't have spent half so much since he wasn't
standing godfather to the child, but William was his
friend as well as business partner. He hadn't stopped to
calculate the cost of doing what he felt was right.

Ping-ping-ping.

Alyce sighed and set the rattle aside. If only doing
right were always so simple and straightforward!

Her husband's support for Edward had been carefully
thought through, she knew, weighed and measured and
cut with a mercer's eye for cost versus benefit. Her marriage had been part of that measuring too. He'd put the
cost of marrying her on one side of the scales, then added
and subtracted benefits and disadvantages on the other
side until he'd been sure the venture was worth the price
of wedding her.

Had he ever, even once, calculated the same careful
balance on her behalf? Weighed what she might gain
against what she'd lose? Thought of the price she'd pay for
the new life she'd be given?

She doubted it. What man ever did except a father,

and her father wouldn't have bothered. He'd weighed the silver that would line his pocket against the cost to family pride of wedding a daughter to a merchant. The silver had more weight than pride. She had never entered into Sir Fulk's calculations at all.

So why was she so unwilling to forgive Robert for his choices when her father had been far less inclined to favor her in his? Why not admit that she was the one who had gained the most, and that she could no more have held Sir Fulk and Hubert back from this mad fray than she could have defended Colmaine against Sir Roger's sappers? She was a fool to think that Robert could have changed matters by one whit if he'd kept his money in his coffers instead of putting it in the Lord Edward's hands. And yet . . .

She pressed her forehead against the window glass and stared at the street below.

What *did* she want? What had she expected? Nothing that had come between them had stopped her loving him, and yet—

"Milady?"

Her head came up at Robert's voice, calling from the hall stairs. He'd been waiting for her and no doubt was wondering why she was so tardy in descending.

He reached her chamber door before she did. "Alyce? Is there aught amiss? We've been waiting—"

"I'm sorry. I set the rattle down, then couldn't find it." She held it up and shook it, forcing a careless smile.

He paid no heed. His gaze was fixed on her face, his expression unreadable. "We shouldn't linger. With London in such turmoil we may be delayed in the streets. I don't care to miss the christening because of it."

"Yes, of course."

She'd forgotten. The news had roared through London yesterday—King Henry's forces had regained control of the Cinque Ports and all the land between the coast and

London. The first of the city's troops were already preparing to march to Montfort's aid.

"I'll just get my cloak—"

"I have it." He held it up. "We shouldn't tarry longer."

"No." This close to him she felt clumsy and half-witted. "No, of course not. I'm sorry. I—"

"No matter." He swept the cloak around her shoulders.

Was it her imagination, or did his hand linger on her shoulder longer than was necessary? She looked up at him. He glanced away, a muscle along his jaw flexing as though he were grinding unspoken words into silence.

"Robert—"

"We shouldn't tarry longer, madame. They will be waiting."

"Yes," she said, and felt her shoulders sag. "Yes, of course. You're right."

He gestured for her to precede him, then followed her down the stairs and out into the yard like a shadow, silent and accusing.

THE CHRISTENING WAS brief, the guest of honor thoroughly displeased with his role in the ceremonies. Young David Townsend fussed through the exorcism on the church's step, cried at the taste of salt on his lips, then squalled in protest and urinated on the priest when his blankets were stripped away and he was immersed in the chill water of the baptismal font. Even the comforting warmth of his christening gown was not enough to calm him. His screams made the church rafters ring with his displeasure.

The guests laughed, and David's proud and rather bleary-eyed father boasted of how lusty all his boys were and how greedy they had been at the tit and how quickly they had grown.

Robert listened, conscious of a gnawing envy deep in his vitals. Someday, he told himself. Someday he would have a son of his own. A son and a red-haired, green-eyed daughter. Eventually Alyce would accept what was and would invite him back into her bed. And when she did . . .

He squelched the thought. It roused far more than daydreams, and lustful thoughts were frowned upon in church even if they were of one's own wife.

Leaving their servants to follow after with the horses, the christening party walked from the church back to the Townsends' house. William eagerly led the way, his whimpering son tucked into the curve of one arm like an ill-wrapped bolt of cloth. Alyce was swallowed up among the other merchants' wives. She never once glanced his way, yet she hadn't seemed either cold or distant earlier, only . . . troubled. Troubled and wary.

He hadn't time to dwell on it for the two blocks between the church and the Townsends' house were covered quickly despite the confusion reigning in the streets. London was rousing to war, but William's guests were more than happy to ignore it for the nonce and concentrate on celebration.

"Welcome, friends, and come in," William said, flinging his front door wide.

Young Master David roundly echoed the invitation. Accompanied by wailing loud enough to drown their clatter and with much laughter and not a few jests at William's expense, the christening party went inside.

They found Mary Townsend ensconced in her husband's great chair, her feet up and her eldest son crouched on a stool beside her. Her round cheeks were a trifle paler than usual, but other than the abrupt shrinking of her belly, there was nothing to indicate she'd given birth only hours before. At the sound of her youngest son's cries, she started to rise.

William was at her side in an instant. "Here. It's you he wants, not me."

"I told you to let nurse go with you," she scolded, taking the bundle William was so eager to be rid of. "There, my pet, my love," she crooned. "There, there."

William stepped back, clearly relieved at being freed of his responsibility. "No harm done! There's naught amiss with him that a full belly won't cure. And his lungs are working fine. He was as loud as young James here at *his* christening," he added proudly, ruffling his older son's hair.

The boy grinned, craning to get a better look at his new brother.

"Peed on the priest too. That's three out of the five have done it. We'll have to find a new church the next time round. One where they've never heard of the Townsend reputation for bad manners and bigger mouths."

"Hah!" Mary hastily unlaced the front of her kirtle with one hand while she juggled her irate infant with the other. "I intend to sleep on my belly every night for the next year, William Townsend, so if you want another child, it's you who'll be doing the getting and the bearing of it, not I."

She bared one milk-swollen breast and shifted her squalling bundle to a more strategic position. An instant later, peace descended. "Ah, that's better, then, is it not, Master David? Run fetch me a pot of ale, James, will you? Both Davey and I will sleep the easier for it. And tell Agatha to start carving the roast. Your father's so distracted, he's as like to slice his finger as the meat, then serve the bone and throw the choice cuts to the dogs." James laughed and ran to do her bidding.

While her servants scurried about with final preparations for the meal and her husband dispensed wine and ale with a liberal hand, Mary received her guests and the gifts they brought with dignified aplomb. Alyce presented the silver rattle, then retreated to a far corner with two other wives who, if Robert had understood aright, wanted to share secrets for the proper pickling of eels.

For himself, he found a strange reluctance to talk of newborn babes. It was too close a reminder of what went into the making of them. He was the last to pay his respects. Forcing a smile onto his face, he made his bow to Mary.

"I should have known you'd be mistress at the feast when lesser ladies would be still abed, and grateful for it."

"Someone has to keep an eye on William," she replied. "Babies unman him." Mary deftly pried her son's mouth off her nipple and shifted him to her other breast. "Proud as a bishop when it comes to his sons, my William is, but let them spit up or fuss or dirty their clouts and he's as eager to be rid of them as a dog of fleas."

Robert laughed. "And here was Mistress Manson talking of hiring him as nurse for her two youngest."

Mary settled the babe more comfortable, adjusted her gown, and favored him with a disconcertingly sharp glance. "Don't think you can get round *me*, Robert Wardell."

"Madame?" Robert said, taken aback.

She glanced around to make sure no one was listening, then lowered her voice anyway. "I know you and your good wife are at daggers drawn. And no, she hasn't said a word"—this in response to his angry stare—"but I've eyes in my head and I can see that this foolishness is breaking her heart."

"Mistress Tow—"

"You're a man and a merchant, Wardell, which means you're pigheaded, stupid, and blind. But you're a good man for all that, and I care too much for Lady Alyce to let it go without saying something."

"You know nothing abou—"

"I know all I need to know—that you've supported Edward while her family and home have suffered at Edward's hands."

"The one is scarce the cause of the other," he said stiffly.

"Which doesn't stop her being troubled by it."

"No, but—" He didn't finish. She was right, after all. Not that it did him any good to admit it.

"What you need to do is bed her, Wardell."

"Force myself on my wife? Damned if I will!"

"And damned twice over if you don't. And since when is force necessary when a few soft words could accomplish the same thing? What do you want? To spend the rest of your life living as enemies under the same roof? Do you want sons or don't you? And, yes, I know all about your Jocelyn," she added, eyes shrewdly narrowed.

"Madame Townsend . . . *Mary*—" Anger and a creeping horror knotted his tongue, stilling his protest.

"You don't think such things are common talk? I swear half London knew or guessed that she'd kept you from her bed for months. Nay, years! Nobody blamed you when you claimed your rights at last. Your precious bride was a spoiled child with no more sense than a kitten, and less than half as much use. If she'd wanted to keep to her prayers, she should have joined a convent."

"Jocelyn—"

"Was a fool. But Alyce is not. She's a flesh-and-blood woman who wants a husband and babes just like any other woman. But she was born and bred to be a nobleman's wife, Wardell, not a merchant's."

"It's kind of you to tell me. I'd not have known else."

"Don't sneer. I'm trying to help, however little you may like it."

"What do you suggest I do? Buy a love potion to add to my wife's wine? Or a ram's dried penis to dangle down my braies in hope of aiding my flagging manhood?"

She waved the suggestions aside. "Bah! Rank superstition, all of it. I've no patience with such folly. A vial of holy water and a little courage are all you need."

He didn't try to argue. Courage and holy water weren't near enough to bring Alyce around.

Mary eyed him doubtfully, then slumped back in her chair. "Trust me, Wardell. Alyce wants her husband back, but she's as proud as you and far less experienced. If you keep your distance, she'll keep hers, and there's nothing like a husband and wife in different beds to set a household on its heels. Is that what you want for this fine marriage of yours?"

It was one thing to argue with a prince, quite another to cross swords with William's tart-tongued wife. Robert's gaze dropped.

Young David had fallen asleep, his small mouth protectively circling his mother's nipple. Mary pulled free, then wiped the drool from his chin and drew her kirtle closed.

He watched, but what he saw was Alyce's breast grown ripe and heavy, her rosy nipple darkened, tender with the suckling of her babe. *His* babe. His son, pink lips still parted, satiated and drifting into sleep.

The vision made him ache with longing for what he'd never had, for what might yet be if only Alyce would understand . . . and forgive. But he'd be damned if he'd bull his way into his wife's bed if she did not invite him first.

"You think I'm rude and meddling."

Mary's words jolted him from his reverie, brought his gaze up.

"William will scold and shout if ever he learns I've said aught to you," she admitted. "But when I saw your lady wife's face this morning, so pale and drawn as it is, I couldn't bear to keep my silence."

Her gaze locked on his, unwavering. "I warn you, Wardell, if you let her slip through your fingers, you'll be as great a fool as any man I've known and I've known a fair share."

Robert drew back. "I'm sure you have, mistress. I'm sure you have. But no matter what you think, I'm not one of them."

He said it boldly, irritated by her interference. Yet even as he spoke he couldn't help wondering if she might be right.

"WE'LL USE PACKHORSES, mules. Our own mounts, if necessary. No carts. They'd slow us down, be too easy a target."

"You're mad, Robert." William shook his head and set his ale pot down. "There's no telling how long Henry's forces will hold the ports or the roads twixt here and Dover. The goods are safer stored in a dozen warehouses in the port towns than risked in one great move to London. That way, there's far less chance we'll lose it all. Once things quiet down we can retrieve them easily enough. If Montfort's army or a band of thieves take them from you on the road, they're lost for good with no one to repay our losses."

"Curse it, William, you're not listening. I said we'd separate into a half-dozen smaller pack trains, return at different times by different routes. And the goods *aren't* safe in the warehouses. Hensford as good as told me he intended to claim them for himself. In Montfort's name, I'm sure, though we both know who'll end up the richer for them if he does."

Alyce listened to Robert's and William's low-voiced exchange and wondered how much longer she'd be required to sit there pretending to be interested in the food upon her plate or the wine in the cup she shared with Robert. The christening feast was near its end, the celebrants heavy-eyed and slow-witted with too much food and drink, and she was more than ready to go home.

Mary hadn't lingered for the meal. Exhausted but clearly pleased with the stir she'd made, she had taken her son and herself to bed once her conversation with Robert had ended. Alyce would dearly like to know what they'd said to each other. She'd watched the two of them from her corner of the room, wondering what made them look so grim. No doubt she'd find out eventually. Mary wasn't one for keeping secrets.

Certainly Robert had made no secret of his mad plan to recover the goods stored in warehouses in the Cinque Ports. He'd broached the idea over the roast mutton. A few of the merchants had seemed inclined to go along with him, at least at first, but in the long run, it was the timid souls who'd won out.

Robert wasn't giving up easily. "We have to get that cloth to London while we still can," he persisted. "If we don't, whatever Hensford doesn't steal, others will. You know that as well as I do, William."

William scratched his nose with the tip of his thumb, considering possibilities. Too much wine and food on top of a sleepless night had made him thick-witted, but no less dogged in his objections.

"God rot it, Robert, you go too far. We've followed you thus far, but this——" He shook his head again. The slight motion seemed to cost him as much effort as the thinking did. "No, this is too dangerous. I've a new son to think of. And Mary, what of her? How can I leave them when London is in an uproar and half its able-bodied men off to fight at Montfort's side instead of staying home to tend their own affairs? What if Henry attacks the city? Or, God forbid, Edward?"

"We have Edward's protection——"

William snorted contemptuously. "Much good that will do us when his soldiers break down our doors to rape our wives and murder us as they did the people of Northampton. To them, one merchant will look much like another—fat plums ripe for the picking. They won't stop to ask whose side we're on!"

Alyce shuddered. There would have been supporters of the king and the Lord Edward at Northampton, just as there were in London. Had they gone unscathed while Edward's men pillaged and raped and burned? Or had they fallen victim to the soldiers' fury too?

Listen to him, Robert. Listen *to him!*

She didn't say a word. It was Robert's decision, not hers. But not his risk alone. Oh, most certainly not his risk alone!

NOT HIS RISK alone.

The words kept circling in Alyce's brain like crows over carrion, black and ugly and inescapable.

Someone in the solar muttered in his sleep. Someone else was snoring, a rumbling bass just at the edge of hearing. Most nights she ignored the familiar, muffled sounds. Tonight they grated on her ears like stone on stone.

She burrowed under the pillow to escape the noise. Instead of soft linen, her cheek rubbed against the coarse cloth of the mattress cover. She'd turned and tossed until the sheets were wadded beneath her or tangled around her legs instead of decently in their place.

The bed seemed vastly empty. Hilde had abandoned her long since, grumbling at Alyce's restlessness as she took her pillow and a blanket and went in search of more tranquil accommodations. Maida had followed, but only after informing Alyce that she would rather bed down in the street than endure one more sleepless night of abuse. Besides, she'd said, Alyce ought to be sleeping with her husband and not two old women who'd once wiped her snotty nose and scrubbed her dirty face, and if she didn't have the sense to see that, then perhaps *she* ought to consider sleeping in the hall, not they!

Alyce had sworn good riddance to them both, then felt sorry for herself and not a little lost.

With one great heave, she threw away the pillow and rolled onto her other side, dragging the covers with her.

She squeezed her eyes shut and willed herself to sleep. The darkness seemed to swallow her whole, but brought no oblivion with it.

His decision, but not his risk alone.

His decision.

Alyce threw the covers aside and sat up. *Was* it Robert's decision? Did he have the right to risk so much on this one mad plan? The laws of God and man said yes, but her fate was inextricably tied to his now. His success was hers, his failure—

Would he fail? Was he wrong and all the others right? Or did he see more clearly than they? He was bold, she knew that. Clever and quick-witted, a good strategist, superb tactician, strong-willed and determined. Was it enough? He would need such qualities and more if he was to succeed.

God help him, he would need luck as well. And, perhaps, another pair of hands.

With sudden resolution, she swung out of bed, fumbling in the dark for tunic and shoes and to light the candle that stood on the chest beside the bed. Githa, as always, had laid her pallet across the doorway, but Alyce waved her to silence when she roused at the opening of the door. The maid blinked at her a moment, then obediently rolled over and went back to sleep. No one else stirred as Alyce made her way across the solar and down the stairs to the buttery.

With only the single candle to light the dark, the heavy wine butts loomed large and threatening. Alyce ignored the shadows—it wasn't demons in dark corners that she feared. She carefully poured out a pitcher of wine, tucked a cup into the pocket of her tunic, then made her way across the hall. None of the slumbering shapes strewn around the sides of the room so much as muttered in their sleep as she passed.

Once outside, she breathed deep, grateful for the cool

night air. The rooftops of the buildings around her were sharp black lines and odd jumbles against the star-swept night, but the yard itself was a well of blackness. No light shone from the workroom where Robert had made his bed, but she could see a faint vertical stripe of gold just where the strong-room door must be. He was still awake, then. No one else would be there at this time of night.

That made things easier. She hadn't cared for the thought of rousing him from sleep.

Pitcher and candle in hand, she picked her way down the steps to his strong room and lightly tapped on the door. "Master Wardell?" No answer. She rapped harder. "Robert?"

The door swung open. He filled the doorway, staring down at her with eyes that glittered in the dark.

"What the devil are you doing here at this time of night? You ought to be in bed asleep." His voice grated harshly, as though he'd fallen out of the habit of using it.

I could not sleep without you. She didn't say it, but raised the pitcher instead. "I brought you wine."

Silence, then, "I've no cup."

"I have one, but it's in my pocket and I can't pull it out if you keep me standing in the doorway."

For a moment, for one long and aching moment, she was afraid he would refuse her. Instead, he drew in a deep breath, slowly let it out, and stepped back from the door.

"Come in, then, if you must."

She did, ducking her head as she walked past him, refusing to meet his eye. Robert had to fight against the urge to reach out and touch her as she passed. He closed the door behind her, shutting the darkness out.

"If you've come to talk me out of retrieving my property while I still can, you're wasting your time."

"I didn't come for that." She set the pitcher and candle on the table. "And you don't have to keep your back to the door like that."

Robert didn't budge. He liked the feel of the solid oak behind him.

Her attention caught on the swath of moss-green velvet he'd spread across the table. "What exquisite cloth!" She rubbed a corner between thumb and finger, delicately brushed her hand over the lustrous surface.

His tarse twitched. He remembered *exactly* how her hand had felt brushing across his skin.

"Is it Flemish?"

"What?" He dragged his gaze away from her hands. "What did you say?"

"I asked if it's Flemish."

"Venetian." He bit the word off, afraid to trust his tongue too much. Let her make what she liked of his curtness.

Her face fell, and guilt pricked him. "I bought it in Ypres the last time I was there," he added, less sharply. He'd been right. The velvet *was* the same color as her eyes. "I thought to give it as a gift to the queen."

She snatched her hand back. "Oh. I'm sorry. I didn't mean . . ." She wilted under his unwavering stare. "Even a queen would be pleased with such a gift, I'm sure."

The velvet would suit her better than the queen, he knew, yet Alyce would never ask for such a costly gift. He sucked in his breath at the thought of her gowned in the regal cloth, her unbound hair tumbling down her back in an erotic tangle of silken curls, her eyes—

"God rot it!" He stormed across to the table. Wadding up the velvet, he crammed it into the nearest chest, then slammed the lid shut. "You didn't come here to discuss the fine points of cloth."

Her chin lifted. "No."

"What then?"

"I'm going with you."

Not "May I go?" but "I am going." He didn't need to ask, "going where?" "No you're not."

"Yes I am." As though that settled it, she calmly pulled a cup from her pocket and filled it from the pitcher, then extended it to him. "Here."

He frowned, irritated by her certainty. "I don't want wine."

She shrugged and took a sip. Robert watched her throat work as she swallowed. When she flicked her tongue out to catch a drop on her upper lip, his groin tightened.

"It's good wine." Again she offered him the cup.

He could see the dark spot at the rim where her lips had pressed. "You're *not* going."

She didn't even blink. "And if Montfort's men regain control in the meantime?"

"They won't."

"But if they do?"

"Then I'll deal with it. But you're *not* going."

It wasn't easy getting the words out. He could take her, right there on the table. It would be so easy. Toss the wine cup aside, pull up her skirts, and make wild, hard, passionate love to her and to hell with everything else.

The worst of it was, he suspected she was thinking the same thing. She kept licking her lips and flicking glances at the table as if measuring possibilities. That didn't stop her from pressing her arguments, however.

"If you won't take me with you, then I'll follow on my own."

"Milady—"

Her eyes flashed green fire. "No! I'm not 'milady.' Not any more. I am 'Alyce' or 'Mistress Wardell' or 'wife,' but I am *not* the Lady Alyce!"

She slammed the wine cup on the table. "This is my home now, not Colmaine. *This* is my life"—she threw one arm wide as if to encompass all of London in its sweep— "and if you think you can shove me into a chest and slam the lid on me as though I were no more than a piece of cloth, then you, sir, are mistaken. I will not be put aside or ignored or treated as if I'm incapable of understanding anything except the proper arrangement of wine cups on a banquet table!"

Robert had the feeling she was trying to convince herself as much as him, but that didn't slow her down. "This plan of yours is mad. Mad! But if you go in spite of all, then I go with you. I am your wife, Wardell. Not your maid or your mistress, but your *wife*—"

"Milady—"

"—and what you do affects me and my future as much as it affects you and yours. We are bound to each other now no matter how little it pleases you—"

"Alyce!" He reached to grab her but she dodged back. Her chin came up to a haughtily height. "*Or* me!"

And then, before he could stop her, she whirled about, dragged open the heavy door, and vanished into the night.

Robert didn't try to follow. For what seemed an age he simply stood there staring at the open door, his thoughts tumbling round in his head like pebbles in a storm-tossed stream.

A sudden draft of cold night air roused him at last. He shut the door, then wearily slumped into his chair. The wine Alyce had left in the cup slid down his throat in one quick gulp. He poured out more, but made no effort to drink, just stared at the flame of the candle his wife had left behind.

In one blinding moment of insight, all his carefully laid plans of how this marriage would be had been knocked askew like a feather-cock in the wind.

Without intending it, without ever considering the possibility, he had done what he'd sworn he never would do again—he had fallen in love. He had fallen in love with Alyce.

WHEN ROBERT RODE out of the gates of
Wardell House two days later, Alyce rode with him, a
small bundle of her clothes tied onto her saddle and a dagger in the sheath at her belt. Behind her were a dozen
packhorses and mules with empty panniers, a half-dozen
hired guards, and every able-bodied man in Robert's employ who wasn't needed in London.

It was a grim-faced cavalcade, especially compared to
the eager folk they encountered in the streets. London was
in a martial mood and confident of victory. The men who
had not already gone to fight in Montfort's army were as-
sembling under the leadership of the lord mayor himself,
and all London seemed intent on bidding them farewell.

Like water, the people flowed toward London Bridge,
the rivulets and streams of alleys and side streets dumping their burden of humanity into the more crowded
thoroughfares, which in turn poured down to the great
stone bridge that spanned the Thames and led to Southwark and the coast.

The human current swept them through the streets
and flung them onto the bridge like bits of bark, then
swirled past, oblivious to their existence. Alyce fought to
keep close to Robert's stirrup, unwilling to lose him in the

crowd. The others, hampered by the animals they led, weren't so quick. When she craned round in her saddle she could see his men, singly or in twos and threes, caught in the crowds and cursing the confusion.

Robert ignored them, too intent on moving forward to worry about what happened behind him. His men knew the way, after all, and would catch up when and where they could.

Alyce looked about her, curious and a little nervous. She'd never set foot on London Bridge before. It had withstood countless storms and floods while carrying half of England on its broad back, but she couldn't quite suppress the thought that she was suspended in air with only a few feet of mortared stone between her and the cold gray waters beneath.

Yet nothing could have been more mundane than the face the great bridge presented to the world that passed over it. Narrow, multistoried timbered buildings crowded shoulder to shoulder on either side, their backs to the river, their work-a-day fronts as familiar as those in any shopkeepers' lane in London. Vendors hawked meat pies and trinkets and ale. Children darted through the crowd. Horses snorted and neighed, their iron-shod feet clattering on stone. Carts creaked, oxen bellowed, and half of the people seemed to be yelling. Still, nothing blocked out the muted roar of the river as it raced between the great stone piers that held the bridge and all of its humanity aloft.

Alyce kneed Graciella closer to Robert's mount. She couldn't bring herself to ask him to move closer to the center of the bridge, but she managed—barely—not to grab for his sleeve. She was grown and wed, she chided herself, too old for the childish comfort of clinging to someone else.

A broad gap between the houses provided her first clear view of the river and the Southwark shore with its huddle of warehouses, taverns, and stews. The river was louder here, its voice unmuffled. A flock of boys perched on the low stone wall that marked the bridge's edge, clearly determined to get a good look at London's army as it marched past and oblivious to the risk of falling. Alyce shuddered, remembering Piers's blithe description of his passage beneath the bridge and the gruesome tales of those caught in the river's embrace.

The sound of horns shattered her grim thoughts. The noise of the crowd swelled as those behind pushed forward, forced to give way for the lord mayor and the army of Londoners who followed him, pennons flying.

Thomas Fitz Thomas rode at the head of his motley force, a proud figure in fine clothes with a suitably stern expression on his face. Behind him were more mounted men, merchants mostly, with here and there a knight who hadn't yet been drawn into the fray. Judging from the looks of the men in armor, Alyce suspected they were landless knights who had waited to see who would pay the most for their services before committing to the fight.

Behind them came the lesser merchants and laborers and common folk of London, some mounted, most afoot. Some wore mail or old-fashioned metal helms. Others wore armor fashioned of leather, boiled and shaped, then dried to an inflexible hardness. Not as good as steel, but better than the padded vests and worn-out wool-stuffed gambesons that others possessed. Most had no protection at all. At least there were a goodly number of archers, since London's laws required its male citizens to train with bow and arrow. They would be at the back of the army, shooting over the heads of their own forces and thus protected by distance, if not by mail. But those not so fortunate or so skilled would face mounted steel-clad knights with nothing but a woolen tunic to guard against the arrows, swords, and spears of their enemy.

Among the hundreds going past, Alyce spotted some

hard, grim-faced men who obviously knew what lay ahead, battle-scarred veterans who had given up soldiering and settled to life as shopkeepers or butchers or blacksmiths until this latest war had thrown them back into the fray. Others were solemn, no doubt frightened, but determined to fight, regardless. But some—

Alyce felt bile rise in her throat. Some were only boys, bright-eyed and eager, alight with visions of glory and far too young and foolish to know what lay ahead.

The women they left behind had few illusions, however. Pale, wide-eyed, trying to be brave, they clung to the edges of the army, shouting to husbands and sons and lovers to keep their heads covered against the rain and their feet dry and to come home safe again, soon! Some carried babes or held the hands of small children who, confused by the crowds and noise, teetered on tiptoe, staggering and stumbling as they struggled to keep up. Older children shouted with excitement or ran sobbing, wailing against what they could not understand. Old men hobbled after them, proud to see their sons and grandsons off and boasting of their prowess as if the boasts alone were sufficient wards against the risks of war.

Alyce's blood turned cold as she watched London's ragtag army pass by. Robert had been right. Montfort might well win this war of his, but his London followers would be slaughtered if they ventured into the fighting. The men of London marched not to battle, but to a bloodbath.

ROBERT STARED BLINDLY at the people going past, furious at the madness of it all. Let Fitz Thomas and the others sneer at what they termed his cowardice—they should have left the fighting to the ones who'd been bred for it.

How many of the men marching past would not come

home? A tenth? Half? More? Too many, whatever their number. So many that in the end the dead would be buried in mass graves, nameless and forgotten, the survivors anxious only to get the bodies below ground before they started to swell and stink. And who then would care for the wives and children and aged parents that had been left behind? An ungrateful city that would rather see an orphan starve in the gutter than find the coin to feed him?

An eager cry from Alyce dragged him from his dark thoughts. It took a moment for him to spot the man who had broken away from the ranks of would-be soldiers and was forcing a path through the crowds toward him. Robert urged his mount forward. "John! Good God, man, I didn't think to see you."

Rareton reined to a halt in front of him. "Nor I you, Robert. Milady." He gave a curt half-bow to Alyce, clearly uncomfortable at meeting her again. "Did you come to see me off?"

Robert shook his head, loath to admit that he'd been so caught up in his own troubles that he'd had little time to devote to thinking of his steward's. His former steward's. "No." Then, because his denial sounded too harsh, "I'm headed to the coast to retrieve my goods. And the others', if I can."

"I see." If the admission stung, Rareton gave no sign of it.

Robert's hand closed around his reins in a futile fist. "Give up this madness, John! You're a merchant, not a warrior. You've no more taste for battle than I do. Not even so much as a just-whelped pup."

Rareton nodded. "True. But better this than to be fighting Edward's men in the streets of London."

"He won't—"

"No?" Rareton shrugged. "Perhaps not. But ask the good folk of Northampton if they thought to face him. Or the people of Colmaine."

Alyce gave a stifled murmur of protest and brought her mare closer to Rareton's mount, leaning from the saddle to lay her hand upon his arm. "One man more or less in my lord mayor's army makes no difference, Master Rareton. You are needed here. Montfort will never know the difference."

"No, milady, he won't." He gently plucked her hand from his sleeve. "But I will."

Gathering up his reins, he turned away.

"John, wait!" Ignoring the bystanders in his way, Robert spurred his horse after him. Rareton reluctantly pulled up.

"Be sure and come back to us, John. Your place will be waiting for you when you return."

The only acknowledgment Rareton made was a noncommittal tilt of his head. "Be careful of your lady, Robert," he said at last. "The roads between here and the coast will not be safe no matter whose men control them." He hesitated, glanced back at Alyce, then added, "You're a fool to take her with you."

And then he was gone, swallowed up in the crowd that flowed across London Bridge, headed to whatever lay beyond.

ALYCE STARED AT the cringing old man who stood before them and tried not to swear.

She had expected a hard journey. She had expected to be wet and tired and hungry, to go days without clean linen, to sleep in uncomfortable, musty beds and dine on whatever a tavern or roadside inn might have to offer. But she had not expected to be angry, so angry that she would gladly have snatched the old man bald if time and nature had not already done it for her.

"What do you mean, they're gone?" she demanded. "How could all of Master Wardell's goods be *gone*?"

Gudolf, the bald warehouseman who'd had the responsibility of guarding the stored goods, grimaced ingratiatingly. "They just is, mistress. That's all. A week ago, it were, or thereabouts. I'd jus' took a little walk t' the alehouse for a bite and a drop, ye see, an' when I comes back . . ."

He shrugged, throwing both hands wide, palms up, the picture of aggrieved and toothless innocence. "The door were broken open an' ever bit o'cloth an' sack o' wool an' barrel o' salt was gone. *Pffft!* Jus' like that."

"Just like that." Alyce had never heard Robert's voice sound flatter.

Gudolf nodded. "Aye. Jus' like that."

Alyce shut her eyes, unable to bear the sight of that greasy, grizzled face. Robert had been right to insist on this mad expedition. They had found the goods in Dover undisturbed, but they'd recovered less than half of what should have been stored in Romney, the cloth in Rye had been damaged by mice and damp, and they had arrived in Winchelsea only to find that the warehouse had been stripped bare—whether by common thieves or Montfort's representatives, Gudolf could not, or would not, say. In either case, the results were the same—the goods were gone, no one knew where.

Alyce forced her eyes open, but when she turned from Gudolf, the only thing she saw was the empty space where the linen-wrapped torsels of Robert's precious velvets ought to be. Robert simply cursed and walked away.

"Honest, mistress," Gudolf whined. " 'Tweren't nothin' I could do onct things was gone. Master Rupert, him what owns t'place, he'll be that put out—"

"As will you once he's informed of it," Alyce snapped. "Out in the street. But only after a good thrashing, which is a great deal less than you deserve."

She would have administered the thrashing herself if she could, but something in the man's sly look told her he would be neither thrashed nor dismissed. She had no doubt that Master Rupert whatever-his-name-was knew far more of the disappearance of the goods entrusted to his care than he would ever be brought to admit.

"Y'see, mistress——" Gudolf began.

With an exclamation of disgust, she spun on her heel and followed after Robert. When she emerged, his men were busy retying the oiled leather coverings over the woefully slight loads on the packhorses. The morning's drizzling rain showed little sign of lifting and it would be foolish to risk damage to what goods they had been able to retrieve.

If Robert was disappointed or enraged or frustrated, he gave no sign of it. Instead, his expression impassive, he stood at Graciella's head, patiently waiting to help her mount.

Alyce stopped short, frowning. "Surely you're not leaving? Not like this? Isn't there something you can do to——"

"There's nothing I can do. Not now." His expression became cold and hard. "A merchant must expect losses from time to time."

The warehouseman bobbed up at Alyce's side. "There now, sir. I seed you was a sharp'un as 'ud understand——"

"Be quiet, fool!" Alyce snarled, so viciously he ducked and retreated to a safe distance. She turned back to Robert. "But that was *your* cloth, Robert! Yours and Master Townsend's and——"

"And half a dozen others', madame. And all of it is lost. We have no time to waste trying to find what will not be found. Henry and Montfort are closing on Lewes, or so report has it. If they meet . . ." He shrugged.

"Better to take this loss now," he continued, "than dally here and risk losing all on the road. Come." He beckoned like an adult summoning a recalcitrant child. "There is nothing to be done here and I do not care to linger."

Alyce's chin came up. "My father would not walk away."

She hadn't meant to say it; the words were out before she realized she'd even thought them. Dimly she was aware of Robert's men, some gaping at her like befuddled fish, the rest pretending such intentness on their tasks, they had to have heard the insult in her challenge.

Robert was the only one unaffected. He simply took her stirrup and held it as if he expected her to put her foot there any moment.

She sighed, ashamed and angry and so frustrated that she could scarce keep from cursing. Forcing her shoulders to relax, she crossed to him and let him help her mount. She should apologize, she knew, offer some explanation, but pride kept her silent.

The trip had worn on them all, fraying tempers and turning even the most good-natured of them surly. Spring rains and mud and the constant threat of war, on top of the discouraging losses, had kept them all on edge until even the slightest irritation provoked curses and occasional scuffles between the men. Through it all, Robert had been a cool and distant presence, so focused on the task he'd set himself that everything else seemed to pale to insignificance. Sometimes, she suspected he even forgot she was with him, his merchant's brain too engrossed with the problems that faced him to concern itself with such a mundane detail as a wife.

Not that he ignored her, however. He was always courteous and attentive of her comfort to the extent the road and cramped accommodations permitted, but he spoke not one word he didn't have to, never touched her if he could help it, and never once revealed what he was thinking. They might as well have stayed in London, for nothing had changed between them. Nothing.

Alyce glanced down. All she could see was the top of his dark head as he bent to check her girth. Raindrops glistened in his hair. It needed trimming. She remembered the last time she had trimmed it for him—how long ago was it? Weeks? A month? More? Before the rift opened between them, certainly.

She remembered it clearly. Laughing and teasing, she'd dragged him from his work and upstairs to their chamber. She'd made him sit on a stool before the cold hearth while she plied her embroidery shears, clipping and shaping the unruly dark locks until they lay in orderly curves against his head. Like a sheep, she'd said. He'd laughed, feigning insult, and sworn he was no sheep, but a lusty ram, and more than ready to prove it if she doubted him. It had ended, as such things so often ended then, with them making love on the soft red carpet from Castile.

Without thinking, she bent and brushed her fingers over the shaggy curls, scattering the raindrops. He glanced up, startled, then pulled away.

"I just noticed— It's past time your hair was trimmed, Master Wardell," she said, forcing a light note into her voice.

"Indeed?" Even under the week's rough growth of beard she could see a flush mount in his cheeks. For an instant his gaze held her, choking in its intensity, then the dark lashes lowered.

"I am in need of many things, madame," he said, so softly she almost didn't catch the words. "And they will all of them have to wait."

Without another word, without a backward glance, he turned away, flung himself on his horse, and set off at a quick trot, heedless of whether his wife and men followed after him or not.

THE MORNING'S MIST cleared only to bring wind, the wind brought fat, dark clouds, and the clouds dumped a chilling rain that turned the road to a treacherous mire. Conversation became impossible. Half the time, Alyce wasn't even sure who was riding at her side. Features blurred with the wet. Even colors dulled, transformed to varying shades of gray and scarcely distinguishable from the sheeting rain itself.

It didn't help her mood that Robert was proving as bullheaded as any male bent on having his way. Thrice they'd passed small villages, but he'd refused to stop to ask directions to any nearby manor house where they might have found lodging, preferring to stick to his original plans regardless of the weather or the growing weariness of their horses and themselves.

They encountered a few straggling bands of armed men along the way. Though each group warily eyed the other as they passed, no one was in the mood to start a fight. The main armies were moving farther west, toward Lewes, and no one cared to issue a challenge to a merchant and his sodden band.

Throughout, Alyce kept her mouth shut, but it wasn't easy. Her gloom of the morning had turned to irritation, then to a distempered conviction that Robert's refusal to halt for the day was due at least in part to his wanting to prove something to her. More than once she considered shoving him off his horse and into the mud, but he never got close enough for her to try. By the time they rode in the gate of the small monastery dedicated to Saint Pancras that was their destination, her temper was the only thing keeping her warm.

Summoned by the guard at the gate, the hospitaler splashed across the stone-paved yard toward them, head bent against the rain.

"I fear there are others before you, Master Wardell," he said, nose twitching like a wet rat's as he unhappily surveyed the quantity of men and horses that would have to be housed and fed. "There is some space yet in the hall, but not enough to accommodate you all. Your men will have to sleep in the stables. Really, I don't know how . . ."

His worries trailed off in a sigh as he scuttled away to oversee the work of receiving them. One of the monastery servants, as eager as they were to be out of the wet, herded Alyce toward the small wood-and-stone guest house while another led Robert and the rest of their retinue to the stable.

Light and a smoky, welcome warmth greeted her. Alyce had the impression of a low-ceilinged room with a fireplace at one end and narrow, shuttered windows at intervals along its length, but her attention was fixed on the dozen or more faces that turned her way, eyes wide with interest at this latest addition to their numbers.

A family with two small children and a swaddled babe huddled against the far wall. A peddler sat cradling a mug of ale at one side of the fire, back propped against his shabby, lumpy pack. His eyes gleamed like polished coals in the darkness, wary as a rat's. Bundled lumps along the walls were cloak-shrouded wayfarers who had chosen sleep in favor of conversation with strangers. At the sound of new arrivals, they roused one by one, some to sit up against the wall, sleepily regarding the room, others to roll back over, tugging their cloaks and blankets about their ears and muttering curses against whoever had let in the cold and damp.

The group that held her attention was the knot of men seated in a circle at the far side of the broad hearth, cross-legged on the rush-strewn floor. Judging by the speed with which they tucked hands in pockets or scrabbled something under the rushes, they'd been playing at cards—an activity their hosts might not approve of. One man, his face cast in shadow by the fire at his back, stood behind them, his foot on a stool, elbows negligently propped on his knee as he leaned forward to watch the play.

With a warning scowl at the card players, the monastery's servant muttered something about his duties and slipped back into the rain, leaving Alyce to fend for herself. There was no question of what came first. With a weary sigh, she moved toward the crackling fire.

The man who'd been observing the game of cards straightened, then kicked aside the stool and deliberately turned to face her. In the light of the fire he looked like a half-starved hunting hound, eyes aglint at the prospect of quarry.

Alyce stopped short. Her eyes grew wide and a sick feeling formed at the pit of her stomach.

Alan of Hensford.

THE STABLE WAS dry and clean, pungent with the aroma of sun-dried grass and the sharper, earthier smell of animals and their dung. Robert gave his palfrey's reins to one of his men, but led Alyce's mare into a stall himself. The beast followed willingly, ears pricking at the hay that filled the manger. He slipped the bridle off, but left the rope halter beneath, then looped the reins and hung the bridle on a peg above the manger. The mare bobbed her head and worked her mouth as if glad to be free of the bit, and eagerly plunged her nose into the hay.

Robert grabbed a handful of straw to scrub away the worst of the mud that caked her belly, undid the knots on the girth, and slid the saddle off. Relieved of the last of her burden, the mare sighed, then gave herself a shake, flinging mud and water in all directions. Grimacing, Robert tossed the saddle over the wooden bar of the manger and set to work brushing down the mare with a handful of fresh straw.

My father would not walk away.

The words had burned themselves into his brain, so often had he turned them over and over and over.

What would Sir Fulk do? he'd wanted to ask her. *Beat the man's brains out? Run him through with a sword?* That sort of violent, unthinking act was the only thing Fulk Fitzwarren was capable of, but it wouldn't accomplish anything except ridding the world of a venial, lying fool.

What *was* there to do, for God's sake, save accept the loss and return to London? Theft had always been a possibility. He'd known it from the moment the first ship had been turned away from the London docks. The damage from rain and mice was just as likely, especially when he could not ensure the stoutness of the warehouse where his goods would be stored.

None of that made the loss any easier to swallow . . . or less damaging to his finances. Certainly not now, when everything was stretched across the sharp edge of a prince's sword.

Teeth clenched against his anger, Robert scrubbed at the mud that caked the mare's belly, grateful even for this small act as relief for his frustration. Graciella was not so pleased. She stomped her foot to protest the rough handling, then, when he persisted, gave a halfhearted sideways kick. He glared at the mare. She turned her head and glared right back. Satisfied she'd made her point, she snorted dismissively and plunged her nose back into the hay.

Robert laughed ruefully and tossed the muddied straw aside. "You're right. But do you think she realizes that I had no choice?" Graciella blew into her hay, then grabbed another mouthful.

Sighing, Robert crossed his arms over his chest and slumped against the wooden poles that divided the stalls. "Perhaps you're right about that too. God knows I don't seem to be able to explain myself."

Graciella's ear twitched.

"I haven't the courage, for one thing. And I wouldn't know what to say, for the other."

He knew what he wanted to *do*. The back of his neck still tingled from the thrill that had shot down his spine when she'd brushed her fingers through his hair. Had she remembered the sweet fury of their lovemaking that time she'd trimmed his hair? What would she have done if he'd dragged her from her horse and into the empty warehouse, thrown her down on the bare dirt floor, and made love to her there like any rutting, lust-crazed beast? He'd thought of it.

Graciella sighed, then resumed chewing on the great mouthful of hay she'd dragged out of the manger. The sound of her teeth grinding, crunching, grinding, made a comforting counterpoint to the drumming of the rain on the thatch overhead.

"It might not be so hard if I didn't know that she's aflame as well, that she wants me as much as I want her," Robert continued, oddly grateful to have someone to talk to, even if that someone was a dumb beast.

"I can tell, you know," he added. "I can see it in her eyes. They go soft and unfocused, and her lips part, and her breath comes fast and shallow. She can't seem to help it any more than I can. More fool the both of us!" he added roughly, shoving himself erect.

"Master?" Henley's ugly face appeared over the top of Graciella's rump. "Did you say somethin'?"

Robert shook his head. "No, nothing. I was talking to myself, that's all."

"Oh," said Henley, nodding sagely. "I see," he added, though it was clear he didn't see at all. His forehead creased in a troubled frown. "Hadn't you best be gettin' back to milady, then? We'll take care of the beasts, never fear."

Robert sighed again and dusted off his hands. "Yes, I suppose I ought to join her. I suppose I really ought."

· · ·

HENSFORD'S HOT GAZE fixed on Alyce. "My lady! Such a pleasant surprise. I'd scarce expected to find you in such a place as this. Certainly not on such a night and at such a troubled time."

"Nor I you, Master Hensford," Alyce said calmly.

"I trust your good husband is with you?"

"In the stables," she said, more sharply than she'd intended. "Tending to the horses."

"Of course." He made it sound like something disreputable. "But come, where are my manners? You need to rid yourself of that damp cloak and come stand before the fire, where you'll be warm."

She would rather have huddled in a dark corner of the hall, forgotten and alone, than exchange pleasantries with her husband's enemy, but there was no avoiding it. Murmuring some polite inanity, she lifted her sodden skirts above the rushes and picked her way toward the fire. Her rain-soaked shoes made rude sucking sounds with every step she took, which only rubbed her temper rawer.

Hensford prodded one of the card players with his toe. "Move, you flea-bitten lump. Make way for the Lady Alyce."

The man grumbled, but made room for her to pass.

"Thank you," said Alyce, swinging her skirts to the side as she edged around him. "Pardon."

Both thanks and apologies were wasted. She could feel the men watching her, eyes narrowed in speculation. Had she been any place other than a monastery's guest hall, she'd have loosed her dagger in its sheath, just in case.

The fire, at least, was welcoming, its warmth a relief after so many hours in the saddle. Let the men quarrel and snap, she decided grumpily. She'd take her comfort where she might and be grateful for it. She dropped her cape on the hearthstones and stretched her hands to the blaze, careful to keep her head down and her gaze on the flames.

Hensford's men reluctantly moved away from the

fire—no doubt seeking a spot where their card playing was less likely to be noticed. Only Hensford remained where he was, one shoulder arrogantly propped against the edge of the fireplace, arms laced over his chest. Alyce could *feel* him watching her.

"I'd scarce have expected to find you dragging through the wet and mud like this, milady."

The tone was biting. She looked up to find him staring at her with insolent directness. She stared back, equally direct, and shrugged. "The weather has never been known to pay much heed to a man's rank, Master Hensford. Or a lady's."

The corner of his mouth lifted in a sardonic grin. "But Wardell usually does." He cocked his head. "Am I to take it, then, that you and he are leaving London for the nonce? Or leaving England? A . . . business trip, perhaps?"

There was no mistaking the implied insult, that Robert was fleeing London for fear of retribution for his support of Edward.

The muscles in her shoulders tensed. She shook her head. "No. Quite the other way around, in fact. We are just returned form the coast. Robert had . . . business there. Only the weather has kept us so long on the road."

His jaw hardened as though he were biting down on curses he dared not utter. She would swear the color drained from his face.

Slowly, very slowly, he shoved away from the wall, straightening until he loomed over her. She could see the hot red flames of the fire reflected in his eyes.

Before he could say a word, the hall door burst open and Robert blew in with the driving rain. He slammed the door shut behind him, then swept off his cloak, showering the stones around him.

"It's damnably cold out there, and the rain's heavier than ev—" He froze. His gaze locked on Hensford; his eyes turned cold and hard as obsidian shards.

As though from a distance, Alyce heard the snapping of pitch in the fire and the faint rustle as someone shifted nervously, stirring the rushes at his feet.

Robert shook out his cloak with the offhand ease of a man in his own home.

"Hensford," he said, and smiled. It wasn't a pleasant smile. "What thievery brings you here?"

The firelight glinted on the jewel in the hilt of his sword as he walked toward the hearth.

Damn the ill luck that had driven Hensford and him beneath the same roof! Robert thought as he took Alyce's hand in his. Her fingers were like ice.

"Milady. Forgive the delay. Even the stables are filled tonight . . . though I fear not all the beasts hereabouts are under its roof."

Hensford stiffened at the insult.

Good! It was a small barb to catch in the man's flesh, but a barb nonetheless. Robert bent to press a kiss to Alyce's hand, then smiled up at her. She stared unblinkingly back. No fool, his Lady Alyce, but no coward either, and all too well accustomed to the hatred that could flame between men.

Something deep in his chest twisted tight, tighter. "I'm sorry to have left you to strangers' crude courtesies for so long," he continued smoothly, ignoring the pain. "I trust someone has seen to your comfort?"

Hensford answered, not Alyce. "Sadly, your lady has to tend to her own comforts . . . such as they are." His mocking gaze raked her from top to toe. "Were I wed to a baron's daughter, I should not allow her to go unattended. It is not . . . seemly."

Robert felt Alyce's hand twitch in his, but she made no effort to pull away. His grip on her tightened.

"It is most kind of you to trouble yourself for me, Master Hensford," she said before he could speak. "But my affairs are none of your concern, after all."

"True, true. But surely no man can be expected to remain silent when so beautiful a women as you is forced to go about in waterlogged shoes and with mud caking the hem of her skirts?"

Robert's hand snapped to his sword, but Alyce covered his hand with her own before he had a chance to loose the blade. Her gaze, however, was fixed on Hensford, not on him.

Slowly and with effort, he forced his hand to relax. Alyce's tongue and wits were both sharp enough for her defense. She had no need of crude methods.

"Your concern is unnecessary, Master Hensford. My . . . beauty"—she almost spat the word—"will survive a little drenching, I think."

It was Hensford's turn to blink at that steady, unflinching gaze. Whatever mocking comment he'd been about to make died unspoken. His eyes narrowed, grew thoughtful. Robert could tell the instant his malice seeped back.

"Perhaps that's as well," he said at last. "One would like to say that a lady might always enjoy the comfort of her home and hearth, but that, I fear, is beyond any man's power to guarantee."

"I never look for guarantees, Master Hensford," Alyce said.

She pulled her hand away from Robert's and turned back to the fire, crossing her arms over her chest. The gesture, however, made her feel like a spoiled child in a fit of temper, and she stretched her hands to the flames instead.

Behind her she could hear Hensford move away.

Robert remained where he was, his back to the fire and only a foot from her. She could easily touch his arm, if she wanted. If she dared.

She didn't move, but every sense she possessed was coming alive with the sharp awareness of just how near he was. Beneath the tang of burning oak and alder she could smell the scent of man and horse, and the clean, wet scent of steaming wool that rose from his rapidly drying clothes.

He rocked on his feet, rolling back on his heels, then onto the balls of his feet, and back again. A pebble grated under one of his feet—she could hear it scratching against the hearthstone as he rocked. He'd clasped his hands behind him as if to warm them, but she could see his fingers twitching—just the way young Erik's did whenever he was contemplating the theft of a tart.

She smiled at the thought, and felt the tight muscles of her back and shoulders relax. Despite the presence of Hensford and his men, Robert was as intensely aware of her as she was of him, and just as uncertain how to act. The knowledge cheered her.

He cleared his throat. "I am sorry for the—the unpleasantness of the past few hours, milady," he said, and frowned at the far end of the hall.

Alyce abandoned her pretense of concentrating on the fire. "It *was* unpleasant, though not the first time I've spent half a day swimming in my own saddle."

He scuffed his toe in the rushes at the edge of the hearth. *Just* like Erik, she thought.

"Not only that," he admitted, a little gruffly, as though he disliked even mentioning it. "I meant Hensford. If I'd known he'd be here—"

"But you couldn't have known."

"No." He shifted his weight and with the opposite foot dragged a sliver of wood toward him across the hearth. He poked at it for a moment with his toe, then kicked it backward into the fire. "If I'd stopped at that village to ask directions to a manor, as you suggested, we wouldn't have run into him in the first place."

"But you didn't stop." Alyce shrugged. "There's no use crying over spilled ale. And it's only for one night, anyway."

"Yes," said Robert. It didn't sound as if he found it much consolation.

"At least now I understand why you don't mind paying a shilling four pence for the privilege of annoying him," she added by way of a peace offering.

The corner of Robert's mouth twitched. Imagine her remembering the guild fine he paid each time he and Hensford quarreled. "That's something gained, at any rate."

He shifted round so that he was facing the fire too. The rest of the hall and its occupants might have disappeared, for all the heed either of them paid to them.

Robert's respect for his wife had risen another notch. She was tired, cold, hungry, and cast among strangers, yet she carried herself with a dignity that was all the more impressive for being so unobtrusive.

That didn't mean she was happy—with him or the situation he'd put her in. The dangerous glitter he glimpsed in her eyes warned him he'd best tread with care.

To his relief, the monastery servants soon arrived bearing ale, bread, and cheese, and one of his men appeared with the straw-filled sack he'd ordered them to prepare as a bed for Alyce. It was all the excuse he needed to drag her away from the fire . . . and from Hensford's malicious pretense of goodwill.

It wasn't enough to ease the tension that crackled between him and Hensford, however, or to prevent the rest of the hall's occupants suffering from it.

Hensford's men and those few in Robert's employ who had been fortunate enough to be allowed into the hall rather than relegated to the stable had drawn into two groups at opposite sides of the room. Both groups pretended to be engrossed in their own affairs, but every once in a while one or another would cast a wary glance at the opposite side of the hall, as if wondering when the trouble might come. They obviously knew from *where* it would come.

The peddler had already forsaken the precious warmth near the fire and taken his pack to the farthest corner of the hall, as safely distant from whatever trouble was brewing as he could get without going out into the storm. Most of the would-be sleepers had settled for sitting huddled under their cloaks, each with one eye warily cocked for the first hint of fighting. The father of the small family had drawn his two children closer to him and was trying to hush them into sleep while his wife tended to their swaddled child.

It was the babe that made sure the brewing conflict never came to boil. No doubt sensing its mother's anxieties, it began a mewling protest that soon turned to a shrill wail that no amount of soothing could silence. The more the mother tried to shush her babe, the louder the child wailed, until its screams echoed among the smoky rafters of the hall.

Hensford was the first to snap. He sprang from the stool were he'd been sitting, fists clenched in frustrated fury.

"By God, woman! Can you not quiet that filthy brat? As well let a pack of howling infidels loose in here as listen to its shrieks!"

The woman shrank back against her husband, hugging the child even more tightly against her breast. The child's screams rose to a screech that made Robert flinch.

"I beg pardon, sir," the mother said. "It's just, he won't have none of me and I'm past knowing what to do to make him shush."

"It's but a babe, good sir," the father said anxiously.

"And babes do wail and carry on, and nothing there is will stop 'em once they've well begun."

"*I'll* show you how to stop it!" Hensford advanced on the frightened family like a mounted knight on defenseless foot soldiers.

Alyce didn't wait to see what he intended. She'd been sitting on the straw pallet Robert had laid for her bed, picking at the bread and sipping the bitter ale the priory servants had given them, but she tossed both into the rushes and jumped to her feet.

"Stop it!" She stepped into Hensford's path, forcing him to a halt. "It's your fault the babe complains, you and every other man here who would make this place a battleground for your quarrels. You've frightened this good dame so she'll never get her babe to sleep, and that means *we'll* be treated to its wailing for God knows how long!"

She glared at Hensford, then at the gape-mouthed men behind him. "And if you've never had to listen to a child screech for hours on end, all I have to say is, you'll soon regret that ever you thought to quarrel!"

The babe didn't wail for hours . . . it just seemed like it.

Several of the travelers gathered up their belongings, threw their cloaks about their shoulders, and stamped off to the stables. One of them muttered something about the presence of asses, but Robert wasn't sure whether he meant the stable's residents, or the guest house's.

At Alyce's command, the family was granted the choice spots near the hearth. Alyce gave up her straw-filled pallet to provide the babe and the children a soft bed, and ordered several of the men about her—she didn't seem to care whether they were Hensford's men or Robert's, just grabbed whoever was nearest—to help the family move their bundled possessions.

When even those measures proved insufficient, she strode across the hall to where Robert stood talking to

Henley, who had gained a spot in the hall by right of se-
niority. Robert watched her approach with the wariness of
a sinner fearing to be called to judgment.

"Have you a wineskin with you?" she demanded
without preamble.

"A wineskin?" Robert gaped, startled by the unexpected request. "Surely there must be one about. Let me
but find it and fetch you a cup—"

"And a clean kerchief."

"A kerchief?"

"For the babe."

"Of course," he said blankly.

"There's a wineskin or two amongst the saddlebags we
brought in with us, milady. I'll fetch what you want,"
Henley told her with the air of a man granted reprieve from
the gallows. He bustled off. She would have followed him,
but Robert laid his hand on her arm, holding her back.

"I'm sorry for this. I want you to know that."

She met his troubled gaze. "You're not the cause."

"I didn't mean that. I meant—"

"I know what you meant, Master Wardell, and I—"

"Robert." His hand tightened around her arm, then
eased its hold and slid upward in a fleeting caress. "Call
me Robert."

Alyce drew in her breath, then gave a quick nod.
"Robert."

"We have to talk."

She nodded again. "Yes. But not here. Not with so
many curious ears to hear us."

"Here you are then, milady," Henley said as he returned. "Wine *and* a cup *and* a clean kerchief. 'Twas the
kerchief gave me the greatest pains. Scarce a clean one to
be had amongst all this snot-nosed band."

Alyce laughed, but there was a mad note to it. "One is
all I need, I thank you. Give me the kerchief first."

The guard obediently handed it over, frowning as she twisted one corner of the linen square into a tail.

"Now pour some wine onto the knotted cloth," she ordered.

"Milady?" He blinked at her, eyes wide as an owl's.

"Just do as I say. Unless you'd prefer to listen to those wails for yet another hour."

Henley almost dropped the wineskin and the cup in his haste to comply.

"Now fill the cup. That's it."

Robert watched her, a quizzical half-smile on his lips. A slow heat was working its way through his blood that had nothing to do with the fire or the meager meal.

"But what's the kerchief for, milady?" a puzzled Henley asked, restoppering the wineskin. "Why would you—"

"It's for the babe to suck on," Alyce said. "To calm him. The cup of wine is for his mother, for half his wailing is because of her upset."

"A body'd think you'd had babes of your own," Henley said admiringly.

The half-smile disappeared from Robert's face as if wiped away in one sweep of a cloth. "You'd best tend to the child before we all go mad from its screeching."

Alyce did as he bid, but he didn't find it so easy to tear his attention from her, not even with half the crowded hall between them.

WITH THE WINE-SOAKED cloth to suck on, the babe eventually quieted, just as Alyce had predicted. Robert wished there were something so simple to calm his own troubled thoughts.

The occupants of the hall were gradually surrendering to sleep, though it was noticeable how many of them slept with their daggers unsheathed beside them. The family's removal to the hearth left the corner they'd occupied untenanted. Without asking, and while Alyce had slipped out to the latrine, his men picked up the blankets that had originally been laid on the straw-filled pallet and spread them out on the rushes, instead. That done, they retreated to as great a distance as they could manage, given the limited space, and rolled up in their own cloaks.

It wasn't much, but it was as close to privacy as he and Alyce would get.

Robert hesitated, then doubled the blankets until they made one bed. Unbelting his sword, he laid it beside the blankets, close to hand where no one save himself could reach it in the night. No doubt she would prefer he made his bed with his men, but he had no intention of letting her sleep alone that night. Not with Hensford and his men about.

A gust of cold air swirled through the door when she eventually slipped back in. She stopped before the fire to warm herself, then bent to murmur a word to the mother of the now-sleeping infant. Robert sat cross-legged at the edge of the makeshift bed, trying not to stare, yet unable to keep from watching her.

Even wearied by the day's hard ride, she moved with a simple, unassuming grace. As if, he thought, she were accustomed to picking her way through difficult places and over the obstructions that others put in her way. He grimaced at the rushes on the floor, then poked at them with his toe. In the few months they'd been wed, she'd had more than her fair share of troubles, and she'd have more before it was all over.

He bent to unbuckle his shoes, then thought better of it, and instead tugged on a corner of the top blanket, pulling it straight and flat. He should have heaped up some of the rushes to form a makeshift pillow for her. Too late! She was already coming toward him, treading carefully so as not to disturb anyone.

Robert got to his feet. "Come, lady," he said softly, gesturing to the blankets. "My men have made a bed for you. We've an early departure on the morrow and you've as much need of your rest as that wailing babe."

Her chin came up. "I thank you, sir, but I am not so weak as that."

He couldn't help but smile. "You've no need to tell me that. But if you'll have no thought for yourself, I beg you'll think of my old bones and take pity on them."

"You're not old!"

Two men nearby lifted their heads, blearily curious as to the cause of such sharp words.

She lowered her voice and leaned closer. "You're *not* old."

"No," he said. Slipping the damp cloak from her shoulders, he gently pushed her down until she was sitting on the edge of the bed.

She looked up at him, suddenly uncertain. "It's not necessary— I don't— That is—" Her protests came to a stumbling halt as he knelt to unbuckle her shoes.

The stout leather was soaked through, but the buckles worked easily enough. He tugged the first shoe free and set it aside, then moved to pull off the second. Only then did he realize her hose were as clammily damp as her shoes.

Her foot was narrow and high-arched, her ankle slender. He slid his hand under her skirts and up her calf, feeling the smooth swell of muscle, noting in some distant part of his mind how the knitted wool went from sodden, to cool, to dry and warm the higher up he went.

"You'll be more comfortable without such cold, wet hose. I never thought to bring in dry ones."

More than thought, his senses ruled. He was achingly aware of the nubbly surface of the woolen hose against his palm. The almost imperceptible scrape of fabric as her skirt slid aside. The shape and line and heat of her. As his hand cupped the inner curve of her knee, she jumped and tried to pull free.

"Master Wardell—Robert—I can do that. Really!" Her protest was a shrill gasp of panic.

He froze. Fool! He'd meant it as a gesture of concern, an act of contrition. At least, that's how it had begun.

He reluctantly pulled away. "You'll sleep more easily if your feet are warm and dry. I will sleep with my shoes on, should aught arise during the night, but you—"

He rocked back on his heels and pointed to the sword. "I think it best to be prepared, but there's no reason for you to suffer such discomfort."

"Oh," she said, very faintly. Her glance flicked to the sword, then back to him, then down to the rushes. "Of course."

A sudden heat rushed up his neck and face that had nothing to do with the fire behind him. With exaggerated casualness, he stretched out, pulling his cape up as cover. The stone floor was damnably hard, but he'd slept under far worse conditions. Any other time, he would have thought nothing of it, but tonight . . .

He crossed his hands under his head and shifted so that his back was pressed flat against the floor. There was a disturbing ache and swell in his groin, but it would ease. Eventually.

"Good night, my . . . lady," he whispered to the fire-lit rafters. He had almost said "my love."

"Good night . . . Robert."

Beside him, Alyce was a dark shadow limned in dull red light. Her veil and heavy tunic hid the lines of her body, but there was no mistaking the way she bent and swayed and straightened, nor the soft rustle of her clothes. Lady Alyce was removing her stockings.

The ache and swell in his groin grew.

In all the years of his manhood, how many nights had

he spent with a woman? Why had he never realized until now how tantalizing the sound of her undressing could be?

Freed of the sodden hose, Alyce swung her feet up, tucking them under the folds of her gown, then raised her hands to fumble at her veil and wimple, finally discarding them. Another few pins and the two heavy braids that she'd coiled around her head tumbled free.

The firelight softened the sharp lines of her face and turned the curls that had worked their way free of her braids into a red-gold nimbus about her head. Like a painted saint with her gold-leaf halo . . . only Alyce was not a painted figure, and most certainly not a saint.

Unbidden, a memory stirred, of her hair spilling over his skin as she writhed beneath him, arching into him while her breath came quick and shallow and hot.

He stifled a groan and hastily turned on his side.

Definitely not a saint. Thank God.

As soon as he dared, he would forbid her to wear a veil and wimple ever again.

He stared at the firelight reflected on the far wall, and the dancing shadow of his wife as she loosened her braided hair.

On second thought, perhaps the veil and wimple were a good idea, after all. A wise man never revealed his treasures to the world if he could help it.

There were far too many thieves waiting to take it from him, if they could.

ALYCE CAME UP out of a troubled half-sleep, uncertain of what had wakened her, yet with every sense on the alert.

The hall was silent save for the snorts and snores and rumbles of weary men. Beside her, Robert lay on his side facing her. There was just enough light from the dying fire for her to make out his features, the hard edges softer than when he was awake. His mouth worked, as though he were talking to someone in his sleep, but no sound escaped him. His hand was curved around the sword that lay between them.

She rolled over, unwilling to stare into his unconscious face when so many unanswered questions were plaguing her. The motion pulled her blanket down, letting cold air hit the back of her neck. She shivered and drew the blanket tighter about her, trying to will herself back into sleep, eyes squeezed shut against the glow of the fire.

A faint scrape of leather shoes against stone tightened her every muscle. Her eyes snapped open.

Alan of Hensford stood before the fire, head bent, one hand braced on the stone of the overhanging chimney. The flames limned his face with a dull red light, sharpening the line of brow and nose and chin and casting impenetrable shadows in the hollow of his cheek and his deep-sunk eyes.

Something about the angle of his body or the wary tension that seemed to hold him, even in this room of sleepers, warned her to keep silent and feign sleep even as she watched.

He stirred the fire and added another log, then turned his head and looked right at her, his eyes like live coals.

And he smiled.

It was a very long while before Alyce fell back into sleep.

THE BELLS OF
LONDON

THE SKY WAS a dull and rain-washed gray early the next morning when Hensford and his men filed out the monastery's gate. Robert watched them go, his face carefully expressionless.

Alyce found him still standing there a few minutes later, staring down the road that they had taken. "Hensford's gone?"

He nodded. "Yes."

"To Winchelsea, I suppose?"

He nodded again, and frowned. "Yes."

"Ahh," said Alyce, looking wise. "And how many of those pack animals will he need to carry your missing cloth, do you think?"

His head snapped around at that. She met his questioning gaze with a look of guileless innocence. "I have no proof," he said at last. "It's bad business to slander another merchant without it."

"Is it slander if it's the truth?"

He eyed her warily. "You're in exceeding good humor this morning, madame."

She didn't miss the cautious, questioning note in his voice. A faint blush stained her cheeks as she held up the pot of ale and half loaf of bread she carried. "The good monks' morning offering to their guests. I brought you your share. Your men have already had theirs."

He hesitated, uncertain how to respond to her small peace offering. His belly answered for him by growling.

She grinned. He flushed red. A moment later their joined laughter spilled like honey, temporarily sealing the rift between them.

Taking care to find a dry spot, they settled on the stone wall surrounding the stable's well where Robert could keep an eye on the work of loading the packhorses while he ate. It was a casual, comfortable arrangement, and Alyce, evidently reassured by the laughter and the company of others, dropped her wariness and pestered him with questions about the road ahead and when they might expect to reach London.

Robert tried to make the simple meal last. The bread was flavorful and freshly baked that morning, but the ale was bitter. It required no great skill at acting to make his portion last longer than it would have otherwise. Even it came to its end however. There was work to be done, he reminded himself, and a good thirty miles or so to be covered between here and London.

He squeezed his shoulder blades together, trying to work out the morning's remaining stiffness, then picked up his cup, took one last sip of the monastery's bitter brew, and grimaced. "I'll be glad to be home where I can get good ale and sleep in my own bed again."

The words slipped out before he realized what he'd said. Alyce abruptly stiffened and drew in her breath. He glanced up, surprised. "What—"

The shuttered expression on her face was all the answer he needed.

She rose, brushing imaginary crumbs from the skirt of her tunic, head bent so her veil fell forward to partially cover her face. "I'd best check the guest hall. Make sure

I've left nothing behind." She was gone before he could gather his wits to explain.

The devil of it all, he thought as he watched her pick her way across the muddy stable yard, was that he'd spoken nothing less than God's honest truth. He wanted to be home. He wanted his good ale and better wine instead of this foul stuff. He wanted to sleep in his own bed, and he wanted—God! how he wanted!—his wife there with him when he did.

TO EVERYONE'S RELIEF, the storm that had made the previous day's travel a penance had missed London and the surrounding countryside, leaving the roads dry. They reached London Bridge at dusk. Candlelight gleamed from a window here and there. Out on the river, Alyce could see a few boats with lanterns hung in their prows to illuminate any of the floating debris that could so easily foul an unwary waterman and his craft.

The great bridge seemed strangely empty. The crowds of a week ago had vanished, leaving grim-faced wraiths who slipped past, heads down, intent on their errands. Except for the ringing of its church bells, the city itself had fallen silent, a hulking beast crouched on its riverbank, anxiously awaiting news.

Robert stopped to inquire at the bridge's gate. The guards had heard nothing more recent than the scraps they themselves had gleaned along the road. The armies had met at Lewes, Montfort with the Londoners in his train, Henry and Edward with their separate forces.

Only God knew their fate, a burly guard said, crossing himself and looking grim. The people of London did not.

When they rode into the yard of Wardell House, everyone who'd been left behind came running to greet them. The relief on their faces betrayed the strain of waiting.

Hilde and Maida scolded and fussed as Alyce wearily dismounted, and even shy Githa fretted as she scurried to bring Alyce a cup of wine and to have water heated for a bath.

Robert waited only long enough to see her into the hands of her women before turning to oversee the unloading of the horses and mules. Alyce paused on the hall steps, torn between going after him and her own intense need for solitude in which to think.

All day she had waged a silent battle with herself, caught between her pride and her hopeless love for her husband. Had his words, spoken so carelessly in the easy, unexpected intimacy of that shared morning meal, really been intended for her? An indirect warning that he intended to share her bed whether she would or no, and without a word of explanation or reconciliation between them? Or, as was far more likely, was his comment simply the casual words of a man with a full belly and a morning's work before him?

It wasn't that she didn't want him in her bed again. But if not that, what? She did not expect him to love her—that would be to ask God for the sun and moon as well as the stars—but she wanted . . . *something*. Something more than what she already had.

Alyce's shoulders drooped as she watched him disappear into the gathering darkness. What could he possibly give her that he hadn't already given her . . . except love?

ONCE THEY'D UNLOADED the horses and mules and stacked the bundled goods in a storeroom, Robert freed his men to a late supper. Tomorrow would be soon enough to sort things out, add his cloth to his inventories, and turn the rest over to their proper owners.

Rather than wait for water to be heated, he washed by the garden well, naked and with only a small tin lantern to stave off the dark. Timeo, the stable boy, willingly pulled up bucket after bucket of cold water, then watched in awe as Robert first scrubbed off the mud and grime of a week's hard travel, then rinsed through the simple expedient of emptying the contents of a couple of buckets over his head. The combination of water and cool night air shriveled his privates and turned his hide to gooseflesh, but Robert was glad to be rid of his dirt—and even more grateful to pull on a clean linen shirt and warm wool tunic afterward.

When he realized Robert had no intention of dining in the hall, or even of entering the main house, Piers brought a pitcher of wine and the simple meal Margaret Preston had prepared for him out to the workroom. Sweeping aside a bolt of second-rate Lincoln green, the boy cleared the worktable for him, then spread out the food and wine.

"A mad week it's been," he said, chattering as he worked. "The town's on edge, waiting to hear, and everyone trying to calculate the gain of Montfort's winning because they can't bear to think of him failing. A hundred rumors a day we've had, and I've no doubt there were a hundred more we never heard. Master Townsend's come 'most every day, asking if we'd had word of you. The others as well. They're nervous, every one of them, and more inclined to squawk and run around in circles than stay at home and work. Like hens when there's a fox about and no one to drive the beast away. What could I tell them? If it hadn't been—"

"Enough!"

Piers froze, mouth gaping, at the sharpness in Robert's voice. Robert wearily waved him away. "Tomorrow. You can tell me tomorrow," he said, and poured out a cup of wine.

He took a sip, closing his eyes and savoring the rich, smooth flavor, so superior to the usually horrid stuff he'd had to choke down for the past week. When he opened his eyes a moment later, Piers hadn't moved an inch.

Robert let one eyebrow arch upward in reproving query. "Well?"

"Excuse me! I didn't think— That is— Er . . . good night!"

The boy was halfway to the door when he remembered the basket in which Margaret had packed Robert's meal. He retraced his steps, snatched up the basket, and with a last puzzled glance behind him, bolted through the door and down the stairs.

Cup in hand, Robert crossed to the window. The yard was swathed in blackness, but here and there a light gleamed at window. Only his bedchamber had no window on the yard—all of them faced outward onto the street.

It was not so great a distance to cover if he wanted to find out if Alyce was still awake. Down the stairs and out the door, across the yard and into the hall, up more stairs, across the solar—

Robert sipped his wine, tracing each step in his mind, over and over again. The path was always the same, but the ending varied. She was asleep. She was awake but weary and unwilling to see him. Half-asleep before the fire, dreaming of him. Awake and eager and warm, laughing at the foolishness that had separated them, pulling him into the room, then shutting the door and leading him to her bed. *Their* bed. And then she was asleep again.

He turned away from the window at last, but went no farther than the table where Piers had laid out his meal. With deliberate precision, he refilled his empty wine cup, pulled up a chair, and sat down to eat.

THEY WERE HALFWAY through sorting the goods they'd stored with such haste the night before when William Townsend appeared.

Alyce welcomed him with what she hoped wasn't too-obvious relief. In John Rareton's absence, she had volunteered her services as clerk, writing down the information on the lengths, and kinds, and condition of the cloths they'd retrieved. But Robert was in a fine, foul mood and Piers was on edge, clearly puzzled by his employer's ill-humor. Between the two of them, what should have been a simple, straightforward task had turned into a war of nerves and tight-lipped courtesy.

That she herself had gotten little sleep helped matters not at all. At first, she'd sat beside the fire, combing out her hair and listening to every footstep in the solar, straining to catch the sound of Robert's. The fire had died to flickering embers before she finally gave up and went to bed, only to lie there staring into the dark, too conscious of the vast and empty bed to claim the rest her body craved. She'd awakened heavy-eyed and aching, and even two stout pots of ale had done little to sweeten her temper.

Impossible to ignore William's bluff energy, however. "I trust you robbed one of our friends' warehouses for this wealth," he said, appreciatively eyeing the sizable stack of his own goods that they'd retrieved. "Beaumann's now, or Fitz Allen's. He owes me money. Or Hensford's, maybe, in payment for his threats."

"I might have taken Hensford's stores if I'd known where they were," Robert said dryly.

He told William about the empty warehouse and their encounter with Hensford and his men at Saint Pancras's monastery. The only thing he left out were his suspicions about who might have had a hand in the theft. He didn't have to add that because William did it for him.

"I wouldn't be surprised if that yellow-livered dog didn't arrange for the goods' disappearance himself," William said, disgusted. "He talked enough about claiming them for Montfort."

Piers's ears were pricked to catch every word. Alyce

was debating how to turn the conversation when Richard Tennys, another of Robert's supporters, showed up. Then Walter Gournay came in, shortly followed by John Byngham. The word of Robert's return had gotten round.

Only William feigned good humor. Everyone else was closemouthed and tense, though no one cared to bring up the question that most concerned them. What had happened at Lewes? Was the battle over, and if so, who had emerged the victor? The questions hung in the air like smoke, choking and impossible to brush away.

The cloth was handed over to its proper owners with much muttering all around for the goods that had disappeared in Winchelsea. Pilferage and damage were one of the risks of storing goods, but outright theft roused angry blood.

The conversation was turning to the more immediate concern of how best to move the goods from Robert's storeroom to their own when the bells of a nearby church began ringing furiously. Robert was on the point of sending Piers out to discover what was toward when one by one the other churches joined in the clamor.

Alyce's hands started to shake. Everyone around her went quiet. Either a serious fire had broken out in the city, or there was news of the battle at Lewes.

"May God and the saints protect us," someone murmured.

Bolts of cloth were flung or kicked aside in the sudden rush for the door. For a moment, Alyce stood rooted. Waiting for word had been hell, but learning the truth might be worse by far.

She didn't even notice Robert until he touched her arm. "Come," he said softly. "Nothing will change by being afraid to face it."

The street was crowded, the nearest church filled to overflowing, but Robert kept her close, forcing a way through the crowd for her. The priest was already at the altar, calling for quiet. Alyce craned on tiptoe, trying to see. Robert's gaze was fixed on the brightly painted image of Saint George that occupied a niche at the side of the altar. The saint, oblivious to the folk in front of him, seemed to be staring at something far beyond the confines of the little church. A sweet smile graced his boyish face, an expression at odds with the raised sword and blood-stained lance he held, and the dying dragon beneath his armored foot.

"My children," the priest began, his voice raised to carry over the anxious murmuring of the crowd. "Word has come from Lewes. By the grace of God, the forces of London and Earl Simon have emerged triumphant."

The murmuring rose to a roar of relief and jubilation. To Alyce, it seemed as if the very walls rocked under the blow. She tightened her hold on Robert's arm, but he didn't take his gaze from the smiling Saint George. A muscle along his jaw flexed like a drawn bowstring.

"The king?" someone called from the crowd. "What about the king?"

"And my husband?" a thin woman beside Alyce cried. Her pale face was pinched with fear. The boy at her side was stoically silent. Her pleas was lost in the tumult. It might be days before anyone had an answer for her.

Again the priest gestured for silence. "The king and the Lord Edward live, but they are Earl Simon's prisoners. The battle—"

His voice cracked under the strain of the news he bore. He paused, fighting for mastery of himself. The crowd, more affected by his display of emotion than by the news itself, grew so quiet that Alyce could almost believe she heard their hearts beating.

The priest gulped, drew a deep breath, and continued raggedly. "The battle was hard fought. The priests and clerks who attended the dead and wounded say that of the more than six hundred that were killed, only a few were knights. The rest, God save us, were all soldiers and our good London men."

"IT'S NOT THE end, my lady. I swear it. This is a blow, but I am still on my feet and I intend to stay on my feet."

Alyce lifted her unseeing gaze from the inventory roll to find Robert standing before her, his eyes dark as night.

Of them all, he had seemed the least affected by the news that his gamble was lost, his loans to the Lord Edward scattered in the wreckage left on the battlefield at Lewes. Where the others had been dazed or angry or blustery, Robert had remained silent, his face an expressionless mask carved of stone.

In the wake of the priest's news, they had made their way back to Wardell House through the jubilant yet anxious crowds. Robert had invited his friends into the hall and offered them wine. Too stunned by the blow to face their families yet, they had eagerly accepted his offer. But the deeper their inroads on Robert's wine casks, the gloomier their words became.

"Edward is alive," Robert insisted in the face of their dire predictions. "And so long as he is alive, our plans are too."

The others mocked him or swore at him. All except William Townsend, who said only that time would tell. When he rose, saying he needed to tell his wife, the others reluctantly rose as well. They took away the goods that Robert had retrieved for them—every inch loaded on packhorses that he had loaned them—but they kept their gazes averted and didn't offer a word of thanks.

At Robert's orders, the outer gate was shut after them. Yet even that thick oak wasn't sufficient to keep out the shouted insults and taunts from passersby who knew that Robert had supported the fallen prince. Alyce listened to the shouting and calmly ordered Erwyna, once things quieted down, to send a couple of kitchen boys to scrub off the obscenities that would no doubt be scrawled on the outer wall.

Even that required an effort. All she could think about were the dead. More than six hundred the priest had said, and most of them from London. She tried to forget them by insisting to Robert that they finish the inventory begun just a few short hours before. But no matter how hard she concentrated on the roll of parchment in front of her, all she could see were the faces that had passed on the bridge a week ago—young and old, world-weary or youthfully eager, haunting in their remembered clarity. The women's faces rose before her too, eyes hollow with fear and grief, silently accusing. Alyce would swear she could hear the crying of the orphaned children, even now.

With an effort of will, she forced the memories away and tried to focus on Robert and what he was saying.

"I won't let you suffer because of this." He was pacing, back and forth and back again like Henry's great leopard, furious with the bars that others had built up around him. "I won't deny that it's a blow, nor that my coffers are not as well filled as they were wont to be, but I swear it won't touch you, milady. With Montfort's triumph, the chances that your father and brother will be freed are increased, and there's Colmaine, of course. You can demand its return, perhaps claim damages—"

She could bear no more. Alyce leaped to her feet, shaking with anger. "Is that what you think? That all that matters to me is the money in your coffers and the fine clothes it puts on my back?"

He gaped at her, startled by her fury.

"Damn your money, Wardell!" she shouted. Tears streamed down her face, blinding her. Her throat burned and felt so tight she feared she might choke on her own pain. "Damn your cloth and your trade and God-cursed loans to Edward. And damn you for thinking of such things at a time like this!"

His head came up. His eyes flashed fire. But at the heart of him, Alyce sensed a dangerous, unfathomable stillness.

"God damn me, milady? No doubt. Perhaps He already has." He spun about and swept from the room and down the stairs, away from her.

Alyce stood frozen, listening to the sound of his footsteps, the scraping of the latch as he opened the door below. With an anguished cry, she flung herself across the room after him.

"I am *not* a lady," she shouted down the stairs. "I am a merchant's wife. I am your *wife,* Robert Wardell!"

He didn't hear her, for he was already gone.

DETAILS TRICKLED INTO London in the days that followed—Montfort's demands, the king's promises, the prisoners held, the disposition of the wounded. The names of the dead.

John Rareton was among the latter, struck down with the rest of the ill-equipped townsmen who had sought to guard Earl Simon's left flank. His name had been listed in the priests' long rolls of dead, his body interred in a mass grave with his fellows. What few possessions he'd taken with him had been plundered on the battlefield, claimed by the human scavengers who had no qualms about robbing the dead.

Because his niece's death had left him without heirs, the Crown would normally have claimed his estate. In the confusion, however, it wasn't hard for Robert to set aside the bulk of it as an endowment to the small church that served Rareton's niece's village. His personal possessions were divided among his friends and the household servants, the valuable fur-lined mantle to Master Byngham's steward, his oldest pair of shoes to the stable lad who had cared for his horse, with Alyce overseeing the disposition of everything else.

Robert himself paid for masses to be said for Rareton's

soul each Sunday for a year, but it wasn't enough to ease the regret that festered within him. Nothing he had done or could have done would have changed the outcome, but knowing that couldn't fill the hollow at the pit of his stomach.

Risk had always been inherent in what he did. It was an inescapable part of life, set loose with all the other evils when man had been cast out of Eden. He had blunted its edge as much as he could, but it had not been enough.

For himself, he would regroup, rethink, rebuild. Edward was not dead, and even if he were, Montfort's supporters needed cloth as much as the prince's. He could refill his empty coffers and restock his depleted stores— eventually—but he was not sure he could ever heal the breach that divided him from Alyce. Not now.

She had damned him, enraged by what she had seen as his heartless concern for his business in the face of the dead at Lewes. A hundred times since he had tried, to no avail, to find the words to explain that it was not his business, but her future that most worried him.

He had wed her in all honor, but he had not expected to fall in love. He wouldn't have had the courage to marry if he'd thought he would ever be so vulnerable again. But he *had* fallen in love, and though he knew that Alyce was not the frail-hearted creature that Jocelyn had been, he could not help wanting to protect her, especially from the consequences of his own actions.

INVENTORIES AND ACCOUNT rolls made for dull reading, but it was better than inspecting linens or barrels of salted herring or having to settle another quarrel between Maida and Erwyna. Alyce squinted at the parchment in front of her, trying to make out the abominable scrawl that some Flemish merchant passed off as writing. That squiggle there *had* to be ells because she seriously doubted that Robert would have shipped that many eggs to England, no matter how productive the Flemish hens were. But if that was ells, then what in God's name could *that* squiggle be?

She sighed and set the sheet of parchment aside, then dug her fists into the small of her back and arched her spine, working out the stiffness that came with too many hours spent hunched over accounts. The day was far advanced. It was long past time she put these old accounts aside and attended to household matters.

Despite Robert's objections, she had spent the past few days acquainting herself with the documents that John Rareton had left behind. He'd been a meticulous record keeper so there was a lot for her to go over, but she was learning a great deal more about Robert's business than she might have otherwise.

The scope of his activities left her a little breathless. She had known of the journeys across England and as far away as Lucca and Venice and the Levant, but she'd never really appreciated the breadth and complexity of it all . . . until now.

But while her understanding of his affairs had advanced, relations between them had not. If she could, she would take back her damning words, but he was so coldly distant that she hadn't yet found the courage to broach the subject with him.

He had enough to concern him, in any case. She was determined not to make matters worse by pressing him when his grief for John Rareton was still so raw.

As for Montfort's victory, well, at least Robert had the protection of her family's name, for what little good that brought him. There were others who were not so fortunate or farseeing, though Montfort, thank God, was not a vengeful man. And Robert was right in any case—Edward was not dead. While he lived, so did their hopes for his eventual triumph. The prince's cunning and indomitable will might yet gain the final victory.

Her dark musings were interrupted by the sound of footsteps on the stairs. A moment later, William Townsend walked in.

Frowning, he glanced around the room. "Your pardon, mila—er, mistress. I thought to find Robert here."

"He's not—" The sound of more footsteps on the stairs cut her denial short. Robert might avoid her, but he had no similar aversion to his friend.

William didn't waste any time on courtesies. "Hensford's back. I'm told his packhorses were almost staggering under the weight of the cloth they bore. They unloaded it all in a dockside warehouse last night, but I'm also told," he added angrily, "that there's a ship conveniently moored nearby, waiting for a shipment he'd promised them even before he left London."

Robert's eyes narrowed. "We've no proof the goods are anyone's but his."

"Even you would not be carrying so much," William said, "and your business has always been greater than his."

Reluctantly, Robert shook his head. "He could be carrying the goods of other merchants, just as I did."

William threw up his hands in disgust. "Have you an answer for everything?"

Robert's lips curled in a dangerous smile. "No, but I'm sure that Hensford will have taken care to have one." He frowned. "Haven't you a relation who's an undersheriff?"

"Mary does. He's her cousin. But he's Montfort's man and he'll be little inclined to help us against a man who's in the earl's good graces." William scratched his chin, then shook his head. "I'm not averse to paying a little visit to Master Hensford, but we need proof the goods are stolen. Solid proof that even Mary's cousin could not deny."

"And that will be damnably hard to come by." Robert finished the thought for him.

Alyce listened with only half an ear. Something

nagged at her. Something important, but . . . what? Every time she thought she grasped it, it slid out of reach.

". . . see what's there before it vanishes altogether."

"He must be planning to ship it north, to Hull perhaps, or Scotland."

"Ships are hard to come by these days. How did he know one would be waiting?" The two men stared at each other, considering possibilities.

"One thing's sure," William said. "We're not likely to learn anything by standing here exercising our jawbones."

Alyce still hadn't latched hold of the thought that teased her by the time they rode out the gate of Wardell House with two of Robert's men at their heels.

PROOF! ALYCE BLINKED at the darned linen table-cloth she held. They *had* proof! Her thought spun as she tried to remember where.

"Mistress?" Erwyna's brows wrinkled in puzzlement. "Is there aught wrong with the darn? It was the kitchen maid who did it but I saw naught amiss and—"

"And I know where it is!" Alyce crowed, flinging the mended tablecloth aside. Without waiting to see where it fell, she darted out the door, calling back over her shoulder, "Have Graciella saddled and tell one of the men to be ready to accompany me. Immediately!"

It took her a few minutes of scrabbling through the bundles and rolls that Rareton had carefully stored away to find the documents she wanted. "This!" She snatched up the sheet of parchment she'd remembered. "And this!"

She scanned them quickly, making sure they were what she remembered, then folded them and tucked them in the leather purse at her belt. To her relief, Newton was waiting for her in the yard. His sour face had given her a comforting sense of security ever since the night Montfort's guardsmen had come calling. He didn't ask any questions, not even when she put Graciella to a fast trot despite the crowded street.

Night had fallen by the time they found their quarry—a cluster of angry men caught in the circle of light cast by a torch and the lantern that hung in the prow of the ship behind them. Hensford had been clever, passing over the warehouses and docks that the cloth merchants used for the docks farther west where coal and lumber were unloaded. His unexpected presence would draw attention, but coal vendors and lumbermen worked and lived in a different circle from that of mercers like Robert. By the time word had gotten back of Hensford's unusual dealings in this part of town, the goods would have been sold and his purse fattened with the profits.

Over Newton's protests, Alyce dismounted and looped Graciella's reins over the end of a cart drawn up near the warehouse door. He hastily did the same and, easing his sword in its sheath, followed her down the steps.

"It must be comforting to have an undersheriff running tame at your bidding, Wardell."

Alyce's hackles rose. There was no mistaking Hensford's sneering tones.

"I don't run at any man's bidding save my superior's," a man she didn't recognize responded. Mary's cousin the undersheriff without a doubt. That meant Robert and William had opted to bluff and hope for the best. The thought made Alyce smile as she unlaced the fastening on her purse.

"But there seems to be some question as to the rightful owner of the cloth, Master Hensford," the man continued. "It's my duty to investigate. And I must say," he added dryly, "that your hurry to ship that cloth rouses my curiosity. Most London merchants are not so quick, especially of late."

"You're wasting your time. All of you. Why would I

bother to steal another man's goods when I have more than enough of my own?"

"Because you're a greedy bastard?" Robert suggested. "Or is it because the troubles of the past months have caused more problems for you than you can handle, despite the favor you curried with Earl Simon?"

"You're bluffing, Wardell. Desperate."

"Am I, Hensford? Try me!" In the flaring torchlight, Robert's eyes gleamed like black diamonds.

"Show me your proof, then. Show *all* of us your proof!"

"*I* have your proof!" Pulling the sheets of folded parchment from her purse, Alyce boldly stepped into the ring of light.

"*What?*" Hensford's glare could have melted rock. Robert stared at her a moment, face blank with astonishment, before bursting into laughter.

"Letters of account, Master Hensford," she said, handing the sheets of parchment to the startled undersheriff. "The first is from a merchant in Ypres detailing the goods he was shipping at Master Wardell's orders."

"What the devil would that prove?" Hensford demanded. "There are any number of shipments—"

"The second is from the hand of one Captain Alexander Picot, master of the barque *Fair Weather,* who took charge of the goods at Ypres and who, because of his inability to deliver them in London, placed them in a warehouse in Winchelsea instead. A warehouse that was emptied less than a week before you so conveniently arrived there yourself. It should not be difficult," she added when he started to protest, "to obtain statements from the hospitaler and servants at Saint Pancras's monastery, testifying to your presence and your intention to travel on to Winchelsea. I'm sure we could find innkeeps and alewives who saw you in the town itself if we tried."

Hensford glared at her. She hadn't frightened him—yet—but the letters had shaken him. William was grinning, hugely amused. The undersheriff was dividing his energies between squinting at the letters of account and eyeing her with the air of a man who'd just been introduced to a dancing bear. And Robert—

Alyce rubbed her damp palms against her skirts. She didn't look at Robert.

"And who are you, madame?" the undersheriff asked.

"Master Wardell's wife," she said. "I keep his records for him." She did not mention her father.

"That's all well and good," Hensford said, recovering quickly, "but that proves nothing. The cloth is *mine*."

His eyes were mere slits, his forehead beaded with sweat. The sweat made Alyce smile. He wasn't nearly as calm as he was trying to make them believe.

"He's right, you know," the undersheriff said. He held up the letters of account. "This proves nothing."

"No, but if you check those torsels of cloth"—Alyce pointed at the linen-wrapped bundles stacked at one side of the quay—"I imagine you'll find that at least some of them have the mark of the Ypres merchant. The same mark that appears on his letter of account."

Robert, William, and Hensford already knew where she was headed. The undersheriff was just beginning to see. His eyes narrowed thoughtfully as he considered the implications of her words.

"Master Hensford would have had no reason to open those torsels before now," Alyce continued calmly, despite the pounding of her heart, "and he certainly would not have received the same lengths and types of cloth as those that were shipped to my husband. If you check the lengths of cloth in those torsels against the letter, I think you will find they match."

For a moment, the undersheriff merely stared at her. His gaze shifted to Hensford, then dropped to the goods piled on the quay. When he looked back up, his lips had thinned to a determined line.

"You!" he said, pointing at one of Hensford's men. "Bring that torch. We'll settle this right now."

They watched in silence as two more of Hensford's men, at his direction, sorted through the pile. When the first marked torsel was discovered, a collective gasp went up, but as more and more were set aside, the silence became a living, dangerous thing. Though Hensford was several feet to her left, Alyce could hear him breathe, quick, shallow breaths that were audible even over the sound of the river at their backs.

Robert stood on the opposite side of the pile from her. He was the only one who paid no attention to the undersheriff's search. His gaze was fixed on her. Despite the dim light, Alyce could swear he smiled.

"All right, then," the undersheriff said once eleven marked torsels had been pulled from among the rest. "We'll see what's inside them, shall we? You, William. You know cloth, I don't. Open that one on top and tell me what you find."

William pulled his knife from the sheath at his belt and sliced through one of the knotted cords that bound the torsel. He didn't get any further than that.

With a feral snarl, Hensford grabbed Alyce's arm and twisted it up behind her back. She cried out in pain. An instant later, his knife was at her throat and he was dragging her backward toward the river.

"Hensford!" The furious roar seemed to echo off the river. Pulling his sword, Robert vaulted onto the piled cloths, then leaped to the quay in front of Alyce.

Hensford tightened his grip, making her gasp. "Careful, Wardell!"

He backed up, pulling her with him. Forced on tiptoe and off balance, she stumbled, staggering against him. He yanked her arm, wrenching another sob of pain from her.

Robert growled. "Hurt her, Hensford, and there won't be enough left of you for the fish to feed on."

"One would almost think you loved her, Wardell," Hensford sneered.

Robert stopped, a shadow among the twisting shadows. "I do."

Alyce cried out. The knife pricked her throat, drawing blood. The cry turned to a gasp.

"Do you, indeed?" Hensford drawled, making every word an insult.

"I do," Robert said evenly, "and I will see you in Hell before I'll let you harm her. Let her go, Hensford. Your quarrel is with me, not her."

Alyce would swear she could feel Hensford's smile.

"Nooo," he said, just as if he were savoring the possibility that he might actually slit her throat. "I find it more . . . convenient this way. You never were known for your sweet temper."

"Nor you for your intelligence." Robert's voice was low and soft. Alyce didn't need to see his face clearly to know there was a world of menace in it. The others stood like statues behind him, hands frozen on swords and knives.

"You've lost, Wardell. There's nothing left you except, perhaps, a little shop in the cloth sellers' street." Hensford laughed. The laughter had the taint of madness in it. "Why, I might even offer to supply your cloth . . . for a price."

His grip on her tightened. Alyce had the sudden, horrifying sense that he was enjoying this, that he'd waited so long to fling his hatred in Robert's face that even murder would seem a small price to pay for the pleasure.

She didn't have a chance to follow that thought for he was moving again, dragging her back. Robert advanced, sword at the ready, but stopped when Hensford brandished his knife along her jaw in unmistakable warning.

The others were yelling orders, swearing, calling for help. She could hear shouts from the ship, but they were in its shadow now, the lantern's light no more that a dull glow at the edge of her vision. There was nothing behind them but the edge of the quay and the river.

Her heart thudded, pounding in her ears. Think. *Think!* Robert couldn't help her so long as Hensford kept her between them. She had to get free, had to—

"Let my wife go, Hensford." Robert's voice cut like honed steel. "You've as good as admitted your theft by grabbing her no matter what the letters of account proved. What can you gain by harming her? *Let her go.*"

"So you can kill me? Or see me hung for a thief?"

"If I bring no charges—"

"You'd like that, wouldn't you? To see me hang? To see me choke my life out at the end of a rope while you stand by and laugh?" Panic edged his voice. Panic and hatred. "I won't give you the satisfaction, Wardell. Stand back!" This as Robert tried to take advantage of the deeper shadows in the lee of the ship to slip closer. "I'll kill her if you move. I swear it."

"I'm not moving."

Hensford wavered, head turning from side to side as he tried to see a way free. Alyce sagged in his grip. It wasn't hard—her legs were trembling with fear and the strain of being kept off balance and on tiptoe. If she could force him to let her go . . .

Cursing, he jerked her upright. "Throw away your sword, Wardell. And your knife."

Robert hesitated.

"Now!"

The sword clattered, spinning across the quay. The knife followed.

"Back away."

Robert cautiously backed up. Alyce's heart fell. If they got close enough to the edge, perhaps she could shove backward, push him into the river. But how to keep from following him in?

She had a sudden vision of herself as a bloated, fish-nibbled corpse. He stomach churned. Her face and hands felt cold.

"Grab that rope." Hensford's harsh command banished the vision.

He eased his hold just enough for her to reach the rope he indicated, which was looped over an upright post at the edge of the quay. The instant she had it free, he grabbed it, then tossed it behind him. She could hear the dull *thunk* as it struck wood.

A boat! There must be a small boat drawn up beside the quay. And if there was one, there might well be more.

"Now that rope. *Keep your distance, Wardell!*"

The angry warning made her flinch. If Robert couldn't move closer—

"Jump!"

Hensford dragged her with him, jumping from the edge of the quay into a long, narrow boat. Her ankle twisted under her as she landed. She cried out, tried to rise, but pitched forward onto hands and knees as the boat dipped, then swung about, bobbing drunkenly. She could feel the instant the current grabbed them, pulling them away from shore.

Hensford leaned out and tugged at the other boat, forcing it into the grip of the river. Her heart sank. Now Robert would have to waste valuable time trying to find another craft while Hensford slipped away, invisible in the night.

And then what? Why would Hensford keep her when it would be so easy to throw her into the river? If he could get to the coast undetected, he could flee to France and be out of the reach of English justice forever.

Think! She had no weapon and she couldn't swim, didn't dare risk throwing herself into the river even this close to shore. She tried to rise, then bit back a moan as her injured ankle protested. Still on her knees, she craned to see behind her. She could make out black figures darting in and out of the torchlight, but she couldn't pick out Robert from among them.

By now they were well away from the quay. Cursing, Hensford fumbled in the bottom of the boat and pulled out two oars. As he struggled to fit the first into its oarlock, she considered the possibility of grabbing the other and using it as a spear. She leaned forward, stretching out her hand. Almost—

The water on the right side erupted as a dark shape exploded upward, grabbing for the side of the boat.

Alyce gasped and fell back. Hensford screamed in fury. He yanked the oar he held out of the oarlock, trying to drag it free of the water so he could swing at Robert. Robert grabbed the broader end, pulling it out of Hensford's hands. As Hensford fumbled for the second oar, Robert abandoned the first to the river and heaved himself over the side and into the boat.

The rest was a blur of curses, of grunts and flailing arms and fists striking the flesh. Robert and Hensford swayed, fell back, then closed again in the desperate, dangerous dance of two men fighting to destroy each other. Alyce crouched at the back of the boat, afraid to move for fear of getting in Robert's way and desperately clinging to the sides of the boat as it rocked and swung under them like a mad thing.

The river, racing with the outgoing pull of the tide, dragged them farther and farther from shore until the city seemed impossibly distant. The only light was that of the stars and the frail quarter moon just peeking over the horizon. Beneath their cold and distant whiteness, Robert and Hensford were nothing but black shadows, writhing like souls in Hell.

Like Hell laughing, the river roared, its voice growing

louder, deeper. The boat bobbed dangerously, throwing Alyce against the side. She twisted, fighting for balance, and realized that the vast black bulk ahead was not the horizon, but London's bridge; and the river's roaring was its protest as it was forced to part and race between the bridge's huge stone feet. Appalled, she could only stare as the bridge loomed larger and larger, the roar growing until it drowned out everything.

Everything except the scream of the man who rocked back, teetered precariously, then tumbled from the boat into the deeper shadows beneath the bridge. The roar of the river rose to a thundering triumph, swallowing all thought even as the blackness swallowed sight. She could *feel* the water towering over her.

Alyce crouched at the bottom of the boat, engulfed in sound, blind, deaf, half mad. *Who had fallen from the boat?*

And then they were free of the bridge, back out into the blessed light, and a dark shape was cautiously making its way back to her.

"Alyce? My love? Alyce? *Alyce!*"

With a strangled cry, Alyce threw herself into Robert's arms, laughing, sobbing, choking on fear and blessed relief and a swelling joy. His tunic was sodden, his skin was cold, and he dripped dank river water, but his mouth was warm, his arms strong and comforting around her, his chest a secure anchorage. She sobbed and laughed and gave him kiss for hungry kiss, and forgot all else in the soaring wonder that he loved her.

Eventually, despite her protest, he pulled back, laughing softly.

"I would hold and kiss thee until dawn, my love," he said softly, tipping her face up to the moonlight. "But if we're to come ashore anywhere within reach of London, I'd best see what's to be done. Is there another oar?"

There was, and somehow he brought them back to shore. "Just past the Tower, I think," he said, helping her to scramble up the bank. "It will be an unpleasant walk, no doubt, but better than huddling here until dawn. Unless," he added, "you'd rather see me catch an inflammation of the lungs as payment for having put you at such risk."

Her only answer was to wrap her arms around his neck and claim another kiss, and then another and another and another until even the stars spun in the heavens with her joy.

"I love you, my lady," he said. "More than my life, I swear."

"I'm not 'my lady.' I am—"

He laughed and gently pressed his finger to her lips, silencing her. His smile was golden in the dark.

"You *are* my lady. Mistress and wife, in truth, but my lady, still, and nothing can ever change that, as God is my witness."

And then his lips pressed where his finger had, silencing his lady's protests on the matter forever.

⌒ London, December 1265

"CHRIST'S BONES, MAN!" said William Townsend. "Sit down before you fall down. You'll do your wife no good by drinking yourself into a puking stupor, nor by keeling over from exhaustion at the end of it! The one will irritate Erwyna, and you'll likely break your neck in the fall with the other, and then where will you be, I'd like to know?"

Robert stopped his pacing of the solar to glare at his friend. Before he could collect his wits sufficiently to snap a reply, he was interrupted by a cry from behind the door of his bedchamber.

He groaned, a man tormented, and snatched up his empty cup and the pitcher of wine that stood on the table beside it. His hand shook so that he slopped wine over the sides of the cup, down the front of his sweat-and-wine-soaked tunic, and onto the floor, coloring the already wine-stained rushes at his feet a deeper purply-red. For a moment, he simply stared at the widening spill of wine, then he slammed the pitcher on the table, tossed whatever wine he'd gotten into the cup down his throat, and collapsed into the chair at William's side.

"How do you endure it?" he demanded, dragging his

hand through his uncombed hair. "Five children! I'll no
survive the birth of this first, I swear!"

"How?" William's mouth twisted in a wry grin as he
raised his own wine cup in mocking salute. "I drink myself into a puking stupor and pray I don't break my neck
when I keel over. But that doesn't mean you need be so
foolish, my friend." He shrugged as the grin turned downward. "It will do her no good, one way or the other."

Robert slumped forward, elbows on knees, his aching
head cradled in his hands, and scrubbed at his face and
stinging eyes. The scrape of his palms on his stubbly beard
sounded loud and harsh in the silence.

Silence. He froze, then shot upright, staring wide-
eyed at the door that barred him from his wife. He was
halfway on his feet, fearing the worst, when another cry
came. He slumped back in the chair, limp as a puppet
without its strings.

"The Lady Alyce is no frail Jocelyn, Robert," William said gently. "She's like my Mary—stout and strong,
for all she's nobly born. She'll do fine, but keep up that
drinking"—he cocked his head at the puddled wine on
the tabletop and the splattered rushes beneath it—"and
it's you they'll put to bed a wreck, not her!"

Robert grimaced. "I'd take the pain for her, if I
could. If only I could." His voice sounded rough and
rusted, even to his ears.

William laughed. "Fine words, but it's we men can't
bear the pain, you know, regardless of our brave show." He
rocked back on his stool, remembering. "When our first
was born, I vowed I'd turn monkish and forswear the bedding rather than put my Mary through it twice. But next
day she was up and scolding the cook for having burnt the
broth while I still sat before the fire, stubble-faced and
dirty and moaning of my head."

Robert stared wordlessly into his empty cup.

"Come, man!" William chided. "What have you to be so forlorn about? The babe will make its appearance when it decides to come and not one breath sooner. Arrogant and bullheaded as its sire, I have no doubt, and just as determined to have its way, regardless."

William leaned forward to clap Richard on the shoulder. "Trust me on this, my friend," he said more gently. "Any man who could see through the troubles of these past two years as clearly as you did ought to be able to wait out the birth of one small child."

Richard regarded him bleakly. "It could just as easily have gone wrong, you know. All of it. And then I'd have brought you all down with me."

"Instead of which, Montfort and his son are dead at Evesham these five months past while we sit here with plumper pockets than ever and the goodwill of a grateful king and prince, to boot. The rest of London will bleed for years to pay the fine the king's exacted for their defiance, and all the while we sit high in Henry's favor with trading rights and new customers amongst the king's men, who'd not have bothered, else."

William shook his head in wonder. "If it weren't for you, we'd have been ruined, Robert, and well you know it. I thought you'd run mad to risk so much, yet it was you who saw most clearly, after all."

"Arrogance and pride, my friend, that's all it was," Robert whispered. "I came near to losing all."

"But you didn't, did you? And nor will the Lady Alyce fail you now, for all your worrying."

Before Robert had a chance to replay, the bedchamber door swung open. He shot to his feet, then stood there, swaying slightly, unable to take a step forward for fear of what portended.

Mary Townsend stepped through, pulling the door closed behind her, and came across the solar to them. She stopped in front of Robert, plump hands fisted on her hips, and looked him up and down.

"As bad as William, thinking the worst and draining the wine cask dry while your good wife does all the work—and all because you took your pleasure nine months since!" She sniffed and rounded on her husband. "I've work for you, Master Townsend, if you think you can keep your feet long enough to help me."

William grinned at Robert and set his wine cup down, then rose to his feet and bowed to his wife. "You always were a meddlesome scold, but I'll come, good wife, docile as a dog at heel. Better that than endure your sharp tongue for a week after if I don't."

"Hah!" said Mary, but there was a glint in her eye that belied her belligerent stance. "And you," she added, poking Robert in the chest with one stubby finger, "sit you down before you trip over your own fat feet."

"I'll help," Robert said eagerly. "Anything. *Anything.* You've but to tell me and I'll do it."

"Hah!" said Mary again, snorting like an angry warhorse. "The state you're in, I'd not trust you with a bucket of slops. You're more like to fall down the stairs and break your neck than be of any use."

Robert scowled at her. She poked him again, pushing him backward into his chair. He sat with a plop. He opened his mouth, then closed it again, unable to force out the questions that burned at the back of his tongue.

"And stop your fretting," she added sternly. "Your Alyce is fine and the babe as well. First ones always take longer. That's just the way of things, and there's naught you can do about it. Were you the king himself, it would be the same!"

Satisfied that she'd cowed him sufficiently, Mary stumped off. To Robert's surprise, halfway to the door she

...urned and crossed the solar to throw open the lid of a tall, heavily carved chest that stood against the wall.

"Why'd you do that?"

She hesitated, her hand still on the open lid. "They do say it helps," she said, her plump cheeks reddening at being thus caught out. "That opening chests and doors and windows will help the babe come out."

"Indeed?" His fingers curled around the arm of his chair so tightly his nails dug into the wood. "I thought you didn't believe in superstitious nonsense. Isn't that what you told me once?"

"And if I did? What of it?" she demanded huffily. She slammed the lid down, anyway, and stumped off with William dutifully trailing behind.

Eyes shut, Robert listened to their footsteps dying away on the stairs. Better that than the small moans and hard panting he heard from beyond the bedchamber door.

And then there was silence. When the silence stretched, Robert rose to his feet and somewhat unsteadily crossed to the chest and raised the lid again.

HIS DAUGHTER MADE her appearance at eventide, coming into the world with a lusty squawl that brought a cheer from William and a choking laugh from Robert.

The midwife and Mary and Alyce's women kept him at bay for another hour, though, and might not have let him in even then if he hadn't been pounding on the door and threatening them all with mayhem if they did not let him in to see his wife.

He made a sorry show of it, he knew—haggard, red-eyed, and wearied as no hard journey had ever wearied him—but he could not endure it longer. He *had* to see Alyce, had to touch her, assure himself she truly lived.

When the door swung open, he staggered and almost

fell to his knees, startled at being thus deprived of his support.

Vaguely, as from a distance, he heard one of the women scolding. He had a dim sense that there were others in the room as well, but nothing mattered except the radiant creature who lay propped up in bed with fat pillows behind her back and a fine white coverlet spread over her.

He crossed the room and dropped to his knees beside the bed. Collapsed, more like, for his knees were unsteady and his legs shaky with relief.

"Ah, sir!" Alyce said, laughing at him. "You reek of strong drink. What have you done these hours past? Gone swimming in a wine barrel?"

He dug his fingers into the coverlet to keep himself from pulling her into his arms. "Not swimming, lady. Spilling it on my clothes and on the floor like a man gone mad, and not the half of it down my throat, I swear!"

He wasn't certain whether the tears in his eyes and the knot in his throat were closer to laughter or to sobs. Both, perhaps. It did not matter which so long as his lady lived.

"I was so afraid," he faltered, and felt the tears sting his eyes. "I heard your cries. I tried to pray but there were no words, only you and—"

She brushed the tip of his nose to stop the painful spate of words. "You should have trusted me more than that, sir. I've no intention of abandoning you. Or our child."

Robert blinked, gaped like a fool. "Our child?"

"Our daughter, sir." The candles set on the table beside the bed seemed to burn in her eyes. Her face might have lit the morning with its glow.

"A beautiful girl. As fair a child as ever I've seen," little Hilde said happily, laying a swaddled bundle in Alyce's welcoming arms.

Robert's gaze flicked from the bundle, to Alyce, then back again. He sucked in a burning breath and hesitantly poked at the edge of the blanket. A tiny *chuf!* as though of disgust emerged from within the folds. He snatched his hand away.

"Now isn't that just like a man!" Maida scolded. "Good at the begetting but as useless at the back end of it as a bowl of twice-cooked mush."

Alyce laughed. Robert didn't care. With trembling fingers he pulled back one edge of the swaddling clothes to find a wrinkled red face topped with a thick thatch of bright red hair. The face blinked. The perfect pink mouth opened to reveal a perfect little pink tongue.

"There. There! Did you see that?" Robert demanded, awed. "She smiled at me!"

"More like yawned," said one of the women.

"Gas," said another.

"Of course she smiled at you," said Alyce. "You're her father and the handsomest man she's ever seen."

"The *only* man she's ever seen," said Mary. "But she's a knowing one already. Look at the way she's screwing up her face and squirming."

Their laughter made the babe grow still as though she were straining to catch their every word. Robert gently stroked his fingertip across her silken cheek. His daughter turned toward his touch, eyes wide with wonder.

"It *is* a marvelous world out there, my love," he whispered, leaning close. "But of all the marvels in it, I swear it is your lady mother that amazes me the most."

Alyce laughed. The sound of it washed over him like a blessing.

"'Tis true," he said, lifting his gaze to meet his wife's. His lips softened in a smile that acknowledged the same wonder his newborn daughter saw.

Tears glistened in Alyce's eyes as she stretched out her hand to him. He claimed it and drew it to him.

"I swear 'tis true, my lady." His voice dropped, grew soft with the wonder of it. "My love," he said, then, softer still, "My life."

"Oh, Robert!" Her tears spilled over, liquid diamonds to match the golden radiance of her smile.

"Ohhhh!" said Hilde, sniffling.

"Humpf!" Maida and Mary chorused.

Unimpressed, his daughter smiled, then yawned, then shut her eyes and quietly went to sleep.

Dear Reader,

Bartered Bride is carefully wrapped around the bones of history.

During the Barons' Rebellion, which was led by Earl Simon de Montfort against King Henry III and Henry's son, the Lord Edward, London merchants were faced with potentially disastrous upheaval in their business. Although London supported Earl Simon in his quarrels with the king and served as one of his chief strongholds, several wealthy and influential London merchants chose to side with the Crown, instead. They did so despite the fact that Henry and his son, who was to become King Edward I, generally favored Italian bankers and merchants at the expense of their English counterparts—primarily because the Italians had greater access to money that the Crown could borrow in time of need. (A London-based cloth merchant of Lucca who provided Henry with many of his most expensive acquisitions was named the "king's merchant" on Edward's accession to the throne, for example.)

Edward's brutal conquest of Northampton is often considered the beginning of the war. Montfort's victory at Lewes—a battle in which the ill-prepared Londoners were slaughtered under Edward's ruthless pursuit—left both King Henry and the Lord Edward as his prisoners, but brought only temporary calm. Edward escaped the following year to lead his followers against Montfort in the decisive victory at Evesham, a battle that cost Earl Simon his life.

Fearing attack by a vengeful king and prince, London quickly capitulated to the king, then spent the next thirty-five years struggling to pay off the enormous fine of 20,000 marks which was levied on it. Montfort's supporters were deprived of their wealth and their holdings, only to see them given to those who had supported King Henry and the Lord Edward.

On a lighter note, Edward's wife, Eleanor of Castile, roused a great deal of interested commentary when she first arrived in England with her costly carpets. Although some of the wealthiest and most fashionable English households soon followed her new fashion, more sober-minded folk viewed the matter with skepticism. Rushes, after all, were cheaper, and could be thrown out come spring.

The Tower of London did serve as home to King Henry's exotic collection of beasts, a collection that at various times included an elephant, lions, tigers, and a polar bear, which often went fishing in the Tower moat.

And, yes, there were schools for merchants' children, and while their rude graffiti, scrawled in chalk, has not survived, there are too many examples of other graffiti—rude, trivial, or otherwise—carved into the stone of churches and castles, to doubt that it would have existed.

ABOUT THE AUTHOR

ANNE HOLMBERG was born in Colorado and graduated from the University of Colorado after having studied engineering and finance. She became the first woman to work as an outside plant engineering technician for Mountain States Telephone and Telegraph. After several years in engineering and a year as a commercial forecaster, Anne joined the United States diplomatic service. She served as Budget and Fiscal Officer at the U.S. Embassy in Cyprus, then served as Assistant Cultural Affairs Officer at the Embassy in Venezuela and Cultural Affairs Officer at the Embassy in Ecuador. She also worked in press and public affairs in Barbados and later in Grenada. After leaving the diplomatic service, Anne spent two more years in Ecuador as a free-lance journalist. Back in Colorado, she became Director of Company and Community relations for Current, Inc. Anne now writes full time.